CW01638186

'In the follow on from the Skiathos Scandals, the author continues to evolve the characters and storyline, with excellent plot twists, bringing it all to a pulse-racing conclusion. A must read and difficult to put down.'

Lesley Clayton

'Having read the first book, I waited for the sequel and what a ride!
Many times it was on the edge of your seat stuff.'

R.Rogers

'What I loved about this novel is the enlightenment offered which was gladly taken, thank you. It really makes you think about the big questions in life and a thrilling story providing a wonderful attempt to answer some of them.'

Anne Freyer

This is the sequel to 'The Skiathos Scandals'.

It is a work of fiction.
All names, characters and incidents are fictional and any resemblance to actual persons, living or dead, is entirely coincidental.

Most places are real. Those that are not, are fictitious and any resemblance to actual places in these cases is coincidental.

All the real places used, I treat with the utmost respect and realism as far as I know them, especially to the beautiful Greek island of Skiathos.

ISBN 978-1-9998595-3-4

Beyond Skiathos

Peter Neal

Prologue

10.35 am Sunday February 18th 2018
The Island of Skiathos, Greece

Silenos Drivas could not sit still on the bench.
He was restless and had good reason, well several actually.
His cheeks glistened with tears.

Silenos, Mayor of Skiathos, sat on the hillside overlooking Small Banana Beach, a nudist beach, one of his favourite places. Today its distractions had no effect.
In the past he had mused as to why the bay next door wasn't more suitable.
It was called Large Banana Beach.

He grabbed a tissue from his pocket and wiped his face. Looking round and far back to the car park, his car was still the only one there.

Thinking 'Where the hell was Irving? He's what? ......thirty minutes late!'

Irving Dekker had talked down Silenos' fears last night and the fact that they had been rumbled. Their life long businesses of cigarette smuggling and the legitimate manufacture of reproduction Greek artefacts had hidden the real covert trade.

This was the secret salvaging over many years, of an ancient underwater wreck.

The sunken flagship of the Persian king Xerxes, disappearing beneath the waves two thousand five hundred years ago.
480 B.C. to be precise.
The secret diving had revealed almost priceless artefacts, vases, bowls, jewellery, gold coins and many other items. Most of these

had been sent under cover to very rich foreign clients, some via Edward Durgas in the UK.
This illegal trade had made Silenos and Irving very wealthy.

Irving Dekker lived in Skiathos town. The smooth talking American shipping agent jealously guarded his illegal activities. Silenos frowned and struggled with his thoughts, 'My life long friend Irving has changed over the years. The man was... possessed by a drive these days to explore macabre subjects... he talked about...what was it? Yes some sort of immortal life for those prepared to *make the rites of sacrifice.*'

All was not right.
For some years Silenos had suspicions, first was that Irving had not 'declared' all his finds to Silenos.
The second, that tied Silenos's stomach into a knot, was over the years his wife had been unusually friendly towards Irving. Dealings perhaps, had been hidden from him Silenos, his own wife up to something. Weren't her souvenir shops providing enough income to keep her happy on top of everything he gave her?
Sarra had some separate bank accounts which she was very secretive about.
She dismissed any questions with, "Oh those, that is my small change Silenos, you know that. So that I can purchase trinkets and clothes, without keep bothering you for money, dear."

Silenos, had everything to lose, his status as Mayor, his expensive Greek life style and now his wife. An investigation was being mounted.
'Oh God' he thought, chucking away his smouldering third cigarette. What's more he had started smoking again last night, after giving up nearly twenty years ago.

Wearing a fraying straw hat and sunglasses, he was avoiding any recognition today.

Fat chance with most of Skiathos knowing him through his many charitable events.

His mind wandered to the fierce argument with his wife Sarra late last night.
She had heard about the government investigation through one of her girlfriends.
He thought 'The bloody woman demanded a divorce right there! Wanting out with her share, to make as much distance between us as she could.'

'Something is not right; in fact everything is falling apart.'

A hand on his shoulder.
Silenos jumped, his hat fell off, and he turned around quickly.
"Pa, Pa ! It's ok, it's Angelo."
"Angelo, my son! ah god you startled me !"
Silenos unconsciously wiping his cheeks again.

"Pa, it's Ma-ma, she has had a heart attack, and I've just come from the hospital."
"Oh my dear Lord. Oh Angelo, Sarra! SARRA! How.... how is she?"

"Not good Pa, she's in intensive care." Angelo stifled a sob.

Silenos Drivas stood up, bent down, picked his hat up and grabbed his son's arm.
"We must go there at once. Now.....Ah!"
He tripped but Angelo, a wiry forty something, grabbed his Pa and hauled him up to his feet.

Silenos cursed a thought 'Irving Dekker can wait; well he had made me wait.'
Then he screwed his face up in anger, 'What's more that bastard has scarpered.'

They walked briskly back along the hill top path to the tree lined car park.
The rising sun even now was hot on their faces.
Silenos uttered, "How did you know where to find me?"
Angelo said "I remember you saying you sometimes come here Pa."

They had almost reached the cars, when a police car swung into the car park and quickly came over to where they stood. Heavy braking made the tyres skid on the dry sandy gravel, pushing up little clouds of dust.
Quickly men got out.
One approached Silenos, his hand on his holstered gun.
"Silenos Drivas?"
Silenos was perspiring, water trickling down his face. "Yes, I am Silenos, Mayor of Skiathos, what is the problem officer?"
Angelo knew, he froze looking at the cops then his Pa.
"Silenos Drivas, I am arresting you on the charge of misappropriating and an accessory to stealing national treasures."

"What? WHAT ARE YOU SAYING? This is ridiculous!" stammered Silenos.

Angelo started to protest, pushing between them "You cannot do this, do you know who my father is?"
The policeman gently moved Angelo to the side, saying "Son if you want to be arrested too, we will gladly oblige."
Silenos grew angry "My wife is seriously ill in hospital, I must see her."

"In due course you will."
With that Silenos was handcuffed and pushed into the rear of the police car.
Silenos shouted to Angelo, "Angelo, call my lawyer, tell him to come immediately to the station!"

Angelo glared, cursing silently at the police car, and then said "I'll do that Pa, don't worry. We'll get you out."
He reached for his smart phone, and called a number.
"Stanton."
"Hi, this is Silenos's son Angelo; we urgently need your services sir."
"Explain."
"He has been wrongfully arrested, something about national treasures. They have taken him to the police station. My mother has suffered a heart attack and Pa needs to see her now."
The lawyer spoke slowly, articulating his words, "Go home to your father's place immediately, and do not let anyone in, not even the police. If they say they have a search warrant, say your father's lawyer requires seeing it first and will be there shortly. Then ring me."
"I will after I have seen my Ma-ma, Mr Stanton. She is very ill, you understand?"
Stanton curtly said "I am sorry to hear about your Ma-Ma. I, myself will go directly to the station. Obviously say nothing. Reference me as your counsel as necessary."

Click, he was gone.

Angelo watched the police BMW disappear down the road.
His mind was in a mess.
He punched another number, it went straight to answer phone.
The thick drawl of Irving Dekker was heard "I cannot take your call right now, please leave your message and I'll get back to you."
Angelo bit his lip, punched another number.
"Yeah…"
"Franco, it's Angelo…I… I need a favour."
"What's up? you sound stressed man."
"My Pa's just been arrested, can you do something for me urgently? Usual recompense arrangement, plus a bonus."

The conversation was short and criminal.
After a few minutes Angelo sheathed his phone and got into his pickup, driving off in a cloud of dust.

The small hospital was quiet, the day was approaching noon. Olive green shrubs surrounded the faded building. A duskier row of shrubs channelled up the drive and walkways. Further out, dry reddish earth surrounded the place and then spread along either side of the road and far into the island's hills. Water was a precious commodity on Skiathos, nearly all of it piped from the mainland…when the pumps worked.

Angelo sat by his mother's bedside. His brother Philippe, sisters Anthousa and Doris had gone to the cafeteria for coffee.
Sarra was calm, her heart back on some sort of normal rhythm. It was as much as could be expected. The monitor close by, flicked along a series of blue pulses on the screen..
"Oh Ma-ma." Angelo eyes glistened with water.
"Angelo, do not worry son, they have said I am lucky and that surgery is possible."
Angelo took a deep breath as though to say something but he didn't.
Sarra looked at him with her deep brown eyes. She had retained her attractive looks even into her seventies.

"Angelo, while your brother and sisters are gone, I must tell you something.
It is very important. It is about your father."
Angelo already knew. "Ma-ma I think I know what you are going to say."
Sarra's face contorted a little as though she might cry.
"Angelo, my dearest Angelo. Please forgive me, I should have told you long ago."
"Ma-ma, I… you should rest, get your strength up"
She took his hand and held it in both of hers.
"Sil….Silenos is not your real father. It is an Englishman, his name is Edward."

Angelo cut in, "Edward Durgas. I have known for some time. It's ok."
Sarra sighed "Ah……I suspected you might have. Well there is more, I am so sorry my son to tell you…"
She faltered, put her hand across her mouth and started to weep.
She stammered "You will never have a chance to meet him because of my stubbornness."
Angelo his eyes wide exclaimed "Why…. oh please Ma-ma, he's not? …."
Sarra "Yes, I'm afraid he died very recently and I don't think he knew about you."
She continued to cry, the tears running down her cheeks.
Angelo squeezed his Ma's hand tight. "It's ok Ma-ma, maybe we were never destined to meet."

Inside he was tearing apart.

Sarra stifled a sob and said, "Son he was quite wealthy and you will be entitled to some of his estate. He also has a daughter, Karen."
Angelo turned slightly and gazed out the window. The view was of a slope tracking through clumps of scrubby trees up the side of a small grey rocky mountain. A scattering of little pale green shrubs near the bottom of the slope, threw squat shadows from the near midday sun.
He turned back, couldn't find any words.

His sisters returned with long worried faces.
Philippe had gone on to the police station.
Angelo's father, yes the life-long father that he knew and loved, was in the station jail and he would free him no matter what it took.

That slippery double crosser Irving Dekker will pay…….maybe with his life.

Chapter 1

10.25 am Sunday 5th March
Waikiki, Hawaii

Ming let out a cry as the water crashed over them.
Spray dripped off her helmet and wetsuit.

The jet ski had ploughed into a big wave, making Akoni hang on to the rear seat strap.
A surging ocean swell in Mamala Bay had caught them some two miles out.

Time passing was wonderful; he had slowly recovered and put on a few pounds.
More important was that Ming's presence seemed to accelerate his recovery.
She was so happy.
With that the hospital had discharged Akoni on Friday.

Ming eased off the throttle and turned around anxiously to look at him.
He grinned and put an arm around her waist.

She shouted, "You ok?   Shall I stop and return?"
"Do your worst!" he cried back with a bigger grin.
Ming laughed, "Let's stop for a breather."

She shut the throttle off and they coasted to a stop, gently going up and down in the dipping ocean swell.
Further in towards the shore were a few surfers.
Many had not braved the seas since January's ugly tsunami.
She looked around at the deep dark blue ocean, her childhood lake accident put to the back of her mind. It seemed minor now, compared to recent traumas.
A good thing.

Akoni said out loud through the wind noise, "That was great Ming, my arms and back are aching a little, but my strength is slowly coming back."
She smiled and felt warm, so warm. Not that the wetsuits had anything to do with that.
Cosy and close to the man that mattered, the man that had come back to life in Queen's hospital. It was on the very day she was to return to duty with the US Air Force, her leave finished.
With a lot of pleading, her boss Colonel Arrack Mondone had given her a couple more days leave.
A wonderful time, seeing Akoni gradually improve, his amnesia starting to fade.

Large gaps remained in his memory, but thank god he had retained their Diamond Head picnic high up in that extinct volcano. Afterwards remembering nothing about his desperate rescue of Lekika, his Ma, nor the floating tree that knocked him from her roof and into the swirling mass of the raging tsunami torrent.

Ming turned to Akoni, said "Shall we head back and get some lunch?"
Akoni nodded and put his thumb up. She thought 'God, he must be quite exhausted even though he doesn't say. My gentleman.'
Akoni was still convalescing from his severe trauma. Waikiki Tour Coaches would have to wait a little bit longer for one of their drivers to return.

She was about to press the starter, when something odd caught her eye.
Gushes of bubbles in the sea surface appeared just to the side of them.

Then gently, ever so gently, a huge grey shape surfaced within five metres of them.
Another surfaced just beyond the first, snorting then blowing water and air, high into the sky.

Two beautiful hump back whales. Their mottled backs glistening in the sunshine.
As the nearer one rolled slightly, Ming saw the great eye looking at her.
She felt in awe, just hypnotised by the magnificence of these huge beasts.
They circled the Jet Ski then dived, their massive dark tails rising up and plunging majestically into the water.
The whales then turned in front of them and crossed over under water, making the Jet Ski bob and rock in the creatures' wake.
Ming started the engine and gently eased the throttle to slowly move forward.
The whales stayed just in front, crossing again just under the surface.

With a final spouting of water, the marine mammals plunged again, their tails disappearing into the dark blue heading off into the open sea.
If you could attach a colour to this ocean, it would be deep and rich, yes Prussian Blue from the watercolour palette.

Ming shouted "Did you see that Akoni? The pattern the whales showed us?"
"Sort of, what does it mean?"
"Wait till we're back on land, I'll explain."
She turned for the shore.

They moored the Jet Ski and walked up the wooden pontoon. She held Akoni, in fact she had to support him. Not easy, he was still a big man. 'Damn' she thought, I've overdone it, he is exhausted.'

"Ming, thank you that was wonderful. You made me feel alive again."
"So glad you are on the mend, I feel though that maybe I should have cut short our trip today. You're worn out."
Finding a table in the Miranda Café, they plonked themselves down and ordered.

Ming looked out of the window spotting storm clouds on the horizon.
"Huh just in time, think the weather is changing."
Akoni smiled at her, his forehead scar was not so prominent now and the hospital had shaved off his moustache. Much better thought Ming.
She continued "I like you clean shaven; I think it knocks a few years off."
He laughed "Ha! You think so? Well Ming you are one smooth talker. Better keep it this way, you think?"

She just glowed, said "I'm happy Akoni and you know I missed you a lot, not just the worry of a lost friend who might have been dead, but a responsibility I guess to properly finish our picnic day." She laughed. He caught her mood and reaching over to squeeze her hand, he replied "Thank you Ming, I was on life's edge. I was conscious a couple of times when you were there, but I couldn't even open my eyes nor say anything. You hung on for me."
He looked at her in his calm knowing way.
Ming's eyes filled up, "Oh Akoni, I want to be with….."

"HERE YA GO…"
Abruptly the waitress arrived.
Clam chowder, chorizo salad and hot bread.

Ming distracted from what she nearly said, "Mmmm that looks lovely."
Akoni dived in with a voracious appetite.

Ming smiled, so nice to see him slowly becoming his old self.
He looked up, "So what was that about the whales?"
She paused then replied "Well I may be mistaken, but they swam and crossed to make a figure of eight, twice."

Akoni, his soup and bread nearly finished, said "That's unusual, certainly haven't heard or seen them do that. What do you think they wanted to convey?"

Ming hungrily ate her food; an appetising sea air had done its bit. Then she glanced up at the counter eyeing the pastries. Turning to Akoni. "You know in Chinese the figure eight is very lucky? Maybe they know something we don't? "

Akoni sat back and watched Ming, he said "Lucky? Yes we sure are."
He broke into a beautiful smile.
His eyes held something, a gleam, a knowing warmth, a yearning, a keeping what they saw.
Ming's countenance took on a slightly puzzled look, "Maybe it is to give us good luck for the future. In times of challenge?"

Akoni laughed "Ha! You are the ultimate analyst Ming. Perhaps we just take this sign as a wish from our mammal friends. Take each day as it comes."

Ming had a far away look, she said "You know my sister Lei spent some time in China, she studied their hieroglyphs, ancient cultures and languages. She is a natural at breaking down dialects, deciphering old texts."
Akoni replied "Wow, fascinating. Sounds a very useful skill to have, especially as the Chinese language is so complex."

They finished with hot coffee.

Ming said, "How do you feel now?"
Akoni looked up "Much better, that meal has made all the difference."
"Let's go outside, I need a smoke."

He winced a little, "Ok, your indulgence."

They sat outside on one of the café benches.
Ming drew on her cigarette, carefully exhaling in the opposite direction.
She said "How is your mum?"
Akoni "Yeah, she moved back into her place a few days ago. The insurance company paid to fix a lot of stuff that got water damaged. Also drying and sealing her ground floor walls. She was so adamant to get back into her home."

"Your mum is made of tough stuff."
"You're right, although she does get badly upset; she has lost some of her close neighbours she had known for years.
You see many of them have completely disappeared with the tsunami."

He continued "Her house was the lucky one, others around got completely washed away, gardens wiped out, just covered in crud. It will take a long time to re-establish any sort of community there again."

Ming sighed "Oh dear, sometimes I just want to leave this place." She looked pensively at Akoni. Then he said something, so quiet she didn't catch it.
"Akoni I didn't hear, say again…."

"Ming, if you left. I couldn't…."
He was unable to finish the sentence; his eyes were tired yet yearning.
"Couldn't what? Akoni I was going to say, to be with ….."

He grabbed her hand and looked into her eyes "Ming, I want to thank you for being here right now. You make me feel so alive."
Akoni slowly smiled looking into her eyes.
She felt warm, a rising hypnotic enthusiasm, "Oh Akoni…"

Something large and soft hit her cheek; she glanced up at the sky. A water droplet trickled off.

The late afternoon blue had been replaced by a darkening grey cloud mass.
The storm was on them.
A few spots flicked down, followed instantly by heavy rain which started to lash the waterfront and their exposed bench.
Ming got up "Ooh …Quick let's head for the car."

Slamming the doors they breathlessly slumped into the car seats.
Akoni was done in.
Ming looked across as she started the car. "Come on let's get you home."
He had a fourth floor apartment towards the west of Honolulu where the rents were lower. They used the lift, forget the stairs.

Akoni sat down heavily on the single couch with a sigh.
Ming "I'll just go into the kitchen. Fancy coffee, tea ….or something else?" she smiled at him.
He grinned and said "Mmm something else …" letting it linger just a moment,
"Tea I think, thank you."
She laughed and vanished into the kitchen.

Bringing out the tea, she sat down on the large couch, it was bamboo framed like the other chairs in the room. She glanced at the pictures, Hawaiian scenes, some family photos and a painting depicting a group of grinning natives with the letters ALOHA in a curve underneath.
She turned to a gentle snoring on the sofa. Akoni was fast asleep.

Later after ploughing through some lifestyle magazines, a few Hawaiian ones and the local newspaper, she glanced at the clock. "God, 10 pm where did the time go?" she thought.

A car backfired outside.
Akoni woke and slowly came to.
Ming "Welcome back sleepy head. Fancy some hot chocolate?"

"Yeah, that'll be good, thanks. Needed that nap. Sheesh… I'm tired."
She replied "Damn right, you need all the sleep you can get, not that coma stuff."
Ming ferreted in his cupboards for some biscuits, bringing them and the drinks in on a small carved wood tray. It had little human native figures for handles.

Akoni got up and moved to the end of the couch where Ming was and took the drink as she passed it across.
"Ming, what a day, the sea, the whales and you! ….mmm ….Good chocolate."
She smiled, said "Yeah I like this, it is such a good nightcap."
His eyebrows rose as he looked over the cup towards her.
Ming quickly said "Well what I meant was that it's a warming drink at the end of the day! ..And …" she hesitated, looking at him.
His smile was hypnotizing.
She thought 'this feels so right….'
Letting the meaning drift, she glanced at his mouth, and then their eyes locked.

Akoni murmured "Yes perfect. What I started to say just before the rain came was I think you are really special. Hard for me as there is our age difference."
He left it hanging, his yearning impeded by this dilemma.
Ming frowned "What do you mean? In what way?"
He smiled, accentuating his crows feet wrinkles.
Ming just melted, she moved slightly closer to him.
He said "You know I am quite a bit older than you and I have feelings that I want to share, but to keep our friendship means much more to me Ming."
Ming "Well you don't look it, you look after yourself. For some women it is the man inside that counts."
"Thank you."

Silence took over, each sipping their drink, trying not to stare, but to fleetingly look.
Akoni drained his cup and put it on the table leaning towards Ming.
He whispered "Ming, I know you had some sort of bad relationship, probably still feel the effects of that?"
She replied, "I'm over that now, was very bitter at the time. It was a shit period in my life."
A minute or two went by. Ming stared into her cup, then at Akoni shyly.

Akoni looked into her face, "You know you have the prettiest eyes?"
Ming broke into a beautiful smile, "Thank you Akoni, you're not a bad looker yourself." she winked.

'It was now or never' he thought '…here goes.'

"Um….. It's just that… that I am falling for you."
He gently took her hand and kissed it.

She closed her eyes, savouring the precious moment.
Slowly opening them, she angled her head, she was ready, "Akoni, I feel things are right you know, fate has a hand, I feel the same. …..you know honey let's…….."

She didn't finish, Akoni took her other hand and gently pulled her close to him.

He softly kissed her lips, a brief pass, just a touch.
"Ooh Akoni … more… please…." she grabbed him close and they entwined on the couch, passionately kissing. Then they parted with a popping sound.

Ming laughed out "Ha ha, god so nice…. again?"
He was already there.

They held each other tightly, she said “I want you Akoni, want you so much.”
Their canvas shoes and socks had come off an hour ago. He rubbed the inside of his foot along hers. The old tingle came back.

Bedroom and nakedness were achieved very quickly.
Ming straddled Akoni as he lay on his back and pressed her hands against his chest. She panted and moaned, “Uummm….Gonna build you up again, get those muscles firmer.”

His rapid movement sent her into heaven, she moaned. “uh mmm.. Akoni …. Some muscles are pretty good already!”

Time to love, slowly, finding each other’s ways.

It was a gentle surging, a demanding and intimate passion without any hesitation.
A massive union of warmth and love.

The night had just begun.

Monday morning

Breakfast was a slow affair.
After a night of sparkling passion, the morning had a special glow, everything around shone brilliantly and sparkled in the shafts of window sunlight.
Colours stood out brightly.
The thin and broad leaf plants caught the bright beams. Strong colours, greens and yellows shone out along the window sill. Even a mix of cacti seemed alive, some with vivid red flowers.

“Akoni hun ?”
“Yes Ming.”
“I’m departing for the Jet Propulsion Lab on the mainland, tomorrow morning back on duty you know.”

Akoni looked at her seriously "Yes you said. How long do you think? that you'll be away?"
She looked at him, a little pain in her eyes, "I don't know, my next leave spell is some weeks away. Things are becoming very busy as the year goes on."

Akoni looked away; he had a distant look, then said "Not easy with my job being here in Hawaii. Maybe I can get a job in California and be closer to you?"
Ming opened her mouth to speak but Akoni continued, "It won't work though, thing is Ming, you could get posted anywhere."

He sensed her tension and said,
"Maybe tell me a little about what you're involved with. Remember, I was in the marines for a short spell, so I also am bound by National Security."

"That's true." she murmured. "Well I can tell some, want to tell you the whole lot really! The secrecy is driving me mad."
Akoni laughed "Ha yeah, you give me the feeling that you are bottling up stuff.
You know with the responsibility of your job? Perhaps tell me what you can."

Ming took a deep breath, slowly exhaling she spoke very quietly "It is indeed true; I and Colonel Mondone have been involved with some high security stuff that is starting to bother me."
Before Akoni could speak, she whispered "Come on let's go for a walk."

Down on the almost white sands they strolled halfway to the water's edge, kicking up fine puffs of the stuff.
Back up from the beach, the white luxury hotels towered above them, every room facing this side had a balcony. Top price these, each offering a magnificent view of the bay.

The sky blue sea sparkled with trillions of dancing lights from the rising sun.
Laughter rippled across from a bunch of youngsters in the water, a beach ball bouncing and flipping in the air.

Ming turned to Akoni, she held his hand firmly. “I didn’t want to tell you back there as the apartment might be bugged.”
“What!” he replied “My place?”
“Yes it’s possible; I just didn’t want to risk it. There are some strange things going on and the CIA, FBI or maybe foreign agents could be involved. Probably all three….”

Akoni took her down towards the waters edge where the green-blue sea came in, the waves gently crashing and rolling back. He sat down a few metres from the edge on the warm sand, pulling Ming to do the same. She sat close to him as he held her waist with one arm and her hand with his free one.
She looked into his eyes.
“To be honest Akoni I am very apprehensive at the moment.”
He looked worried “In what way?”
Ming continued and smiled “No, nothing to do with us, we are just fine you lovely man, we have something special.” She squeezed his hand. “It is to do with my work and some discoveries.”
“I’m all ears” he nonchalantly looked around checking if anybody was taking an interest in them. His gaze returned to Ming.

She said “I guess you have seen the news reports about the object in space, beyond our moon?” He nodded. She hesitated, and then said “Well we have discovered it may be a portal to another time and space, maybe another dimension or universe. Nobody has approached it, only the Chinese with an unmanned probe and that just disappeared.”

Akoni “Yes I read about it, the scientists have been speculating as to what it might be. There are many other groups, some religious, some crazy people who are sort of claiming it as a sign. So what are NASA or the military up to? Can you tell me?”

Ming looked at him sternly, "Akoni, this stuff is ultra top secret, if I tell you it cannot go any further, no one must know."
"Sure Ming, to share what's stressing you is a good thing. It is utterly safe with me. Knowing what you're struggling with can allow me to understand, to help you, you know? Maybe a second opinion for what it's worth?"
"Ok" She glanced briefly toward the towering hotels, her eyes sweeping the balconies.

She continued "In summary, this is what we know. The British with their new gravity array detectors can see a shape and entrance to this portal. They have shared technology and we are building our own detector array like theirs, as I speak.
Next year in January the portal which the British have called Crackwell...." she chuckled, Akoni smirked, puzzled. "God Akoni, what a name and I'm sure it's linked to Bill Craswell, a senior physicist there.... He seems to sort of...well own it I think, a weird pride I guess.. ha!"
Ming became more serious, she said "Next year we launch a number of vehicles into space to rendezvous with Crackwell, some now will be manned. One is a military device that I don't as yet know anything about."

Akoni was following with intense interest. "Go on."
Ming paused; she looked out to sea, to the horizon shading her eyes against the sun.
"What is really scary is something I discovered on the moon, at the vicinity of the Chinese moon base. You see Colonel Mondone and I reworked the telescope images and discovered something incredible, some cloaked objects. That is they were disguised like chameleons, practically invisible. One might be a large spaceship. Yet they are not there anymore, and we are certain they cannot be Chinese nor from any of the space capable nations here."

"Aumakua! Can you be sure?"

"I wish to God I had been mistaken, you know false shadows from tiny asteroids or rocks circling the moon. But no, we checked and rechecked and these objects were definitely there. Also we discovered an ion trail from the portal to the moon. It could be a propulsion engine signature."

Akoni said nothing, his eyes had widened, very white. "Serious stuff Ming..."
Ming sighed loudly "To top it all, a so called meteor strike very close to the Chinese moon base, badly punctured the main habitation dome and all the astronauts died before they could don space suits."

"Oh hell."
Ming looked into his eyes, "So you see things are getting out of hand. Our intelligence is very good. The Chinese are very agitated and have had several meetings with our politicians saying the meteor hit was in fact a deliberate strike by a western missile."

Akoni puzzled said "Why would anybody want to launch a missile at the Chinese moon base?"
"Exactly Akoni, why? Well I found out that it wasn't a meteor, nor a missile or any deliberately launched projectile."
He frowned "So what was it Ming?"

"During our visit to the UK I had a chance to talk to Bill Craswell. He was so nervous, not only about our awful time at the Wales Gravity Array, with some people killed, and poor Karen on death's door. The Colonel was badly wounded and the others too, but Bill had something else on his mind."
"Oh... did he say what Ming?"
"I told him some details of our moon base investigations, but not the cloaked objects, only the very close meteor impact. We had found out that this was why the astronauts had perished. At this poor Bill went deadly pale and he almost fainted, I had to grab his arm. He sat down and I asked what was up. He then told me something in confidence and I was blown away. Apparently they

had a disastrous lab explosion which generated a brief but powerful gravity wave. It was focussed upwards from their laboratory. This happened over a year ago and produced a very dense yet tiny high velocity particle which rode out on that gravity pulse. It had enough energy to leave Earth's orbit and fly across to the moon. It is the culprit. The cause of those astronauts' deaths.
Bill said that they were experimenting with explosive compression forces on a matrix of exotic materials, of which some were fissionable. Nuclear that is."

"Ming, that is amazing, what will happen now?"
She gave a look of almost help me, get me out of here, her stomach was not comfortable. She said "The Chinese sent a manned mission to find out what happened at their moon base. I spoke with my sister Lei, she knows some of these things I have told you and I swore her to secrecy. We have a mutual understanding. She told me stuff that is dynamite."
Akoni now intensely interested "Dynamite?"

Ming paused, she watched a surfer skip under a curling wave, a rare big one.
Her eyes flicked to the horizon, where not so long ago she saw the foaming tsunami wall of water rushing in.
Akoni placed his hand on her arm, looking intently at her.
She continued "Yes. Lei said that in her researches of ancient Chinese culture and more, apparently the placing of their moon base is not an accident. By that I don't mean they located the spot because of frozen water or mineral resources, but because of something else. You see my sister and I are very close, we think in a very similar fashion, methodically, meticulously. Get it from our Pa I guess, he flew Air Force fighter jets in the Vietnam War. Military discipline you know, getting things right, checking and rechecking stuff."

Ming hesitated, trying not to believe, not to accept what she now knew.

"Lei said there is something under the moon's surface, where their base is. What is more it may be very deep, as the Chinese have been drilling but have found nothing so far."
Akoni frowned, said "How do you know that? I mean anything like this would be highly secret?"
Ming smiled, "Lei and her boyfriend Steven Crowley have the skill and equipment to break some of the top encrypted messages. Crowley used to work for the British Communications Security organisation based at GCHQ in England. He is a genius at this stuff. It's a wonder they let him go, although I think he rubbed up a few people the wrong way and they got rid of him."
"Yeah, but Ming, they have to sign up to the Security Act or whatever they call it, surely he wouldn't be able to carry on?"
Ming laughed and shrugged her shoulders, "From what my sister said, Crowley seems a weird secretive guy, he is part of some clandestine group with religious undertones.
Akoni still puzzled said, "You seem to know a lot Ming, your sister must really trust you." her eyebrows hiked, he said "No I mean despite being close, there are some things that people just don't share?"
"Well we do. We trust and love each other. And I am telling you this stuff Akoni because I trust you too."
She left the other emotion for him to read…

"That's about all I know. What is interesting is that whatever came out of the portal Crackwell, went straight to the Chinese moon base. The particle impact, whatever is buried there and this spacecraft presence are just too coincidental. These events appear to be linked. Seems quite spooky Akoni….."

He gaped but said nothing, then slowly closed his mouth, pressing his lips hard together. Akoni was deep in thought. He squeezed Ming's hand, then he looked up and casually back towards the sand, where it met the sidewalk.
Quite a few strollers were about, nobody taking any interest in them.

Well he thought, any covert observation will be pretty much hidden anyway.

Ming got up "Right enough of that, fancy a strong coffee at the café over there?"
Akoni "Yep, good idea."

They walked slowly hand in hand, two lovers just out for a stroll on the sand.

The coffee was welcome, strong and creamy. Akoni was demolishing a large jam donut. After a while Ming said, "I shall be at my parents place this Easter, they live in Little Venice in Los Angeles. Would you like to come?"

Akoni turned to her, "That would be lovely, thank you. I'll check the coach rosters."
Ming continued "My sister Lei will be there as well, Ma and Pop are so pleased."
She wrinkled her forehead said," I wonder….. Probably not."
He spoke "What …. What are you thinking?"
She replied "Oh it's her boyfriend Steven Crowley, I was wondering whether we will see him at Ma's. That would make for some lively discussion."

Abruptly their conversation stopped as Ming's phone rang.
"Ming Zhao?"
"Yes, that you Colonel?"

She noticed the military encryption app had kicked in on her phone.

"Yes, Mondone. Hello Ming. I know you're back on duty tomorrow, but there are a couple of items I need you to research?"
Ming looked across at Akoni , giving him an apologetic glance.
"Yes sir, what do you want?"

"Ming, I know you have some leave during Easter which you said was important and I think we can still save that, but the situation is changing."
"Oh should I be worried Sir? like some sort of danger ?"

Akoni looked up, his concerned face remembering her description of the Wales one sided fire fight, the Chinese soldiers opening fire with machine guns. The disintegration of their robot android Benji, as he tried to protect them.

"Ming, remember that Chinese guy you mentioned? The CEO of Arragon Systems. The oddities with their website and your concern over them being the new supplier for the rocket vehicle fuel control modules?"
"Yes Colonel, so what's up?"
"We're going to meet him and some other Chinese folks in France."
"France?"
"Yes the French with their close business and military liaisons with the Chinese, are facilitating a meeting. Apparently the Chinese want to talk about gravity arrays and what we know."
Ming's eyes opened wide, she looked at Akoni as he took her hand.

"Sir, that could be so useful."
"Yes it's a turn around. We shan't give much away, but it will be interesting to see what they can bring to the table. I need you to find out as much as possible about Arragon and all the board members. Also have a look at the company history, financial status and any murky links. Use our commercial department."

"Ok sir, I'll get on it today."
Mondone continued, "Now with regard to the mysterious disappearance of our video moon data, Ming?"
She replied "Yes sir, very strange indeed."
She thought back to when she discovered the cloaked objects near the Chinese moon base. Then not long afterwards, the information

had disappeared. The videos still had the moon base coverage, but no cloaked objects. Someone or something had removed all traces.
Mondone paused; he was carefully choosing his words.
"You know Ming, when I had my top guys investigate these recordings; they said the videos were perfect, too perfect. Apart from our missing objects the recordings had no blemishes at all."
She cut in "Blemishes?"
Mondone replied "It seems the recordings were just that little bit too good. You see normally there are video abrasions, tiny imperfections in the detail. Tiny, tiny specks on the orbital telescope lens, that sort of thing. But it was all clear as a bell."
"I think I see where you're going Sir."

Mondone said "The evidence is in the perfect absence."

"God yes Sir. What the devil is going on?"
"Whatever or whoever was there, is doing their utmost to eradicate the evidence.
It seems it is because they don't want us to know. The reasons for this I want to discuss with you back at base."

Ming drew a deep breath, looked briefly and painfully at Akoni. He acknowledged her concern. Went to speak....
"Sir, I feel we need to get a handle on this quickly."

"Too right Ming. So I have some new footage of the moon taken recently by the James Webb telescope team. I want you to examine it in a similar way when you looked at the moon base, but it will be a wider area. The details are included with the video files. Also there is a radar scan done by one of our satellites and there is something else Ming."
"Sir?"
"I have included some wide sky shots where the anomaly Crackwell is. As you know it is now many millions of miles behind Earth and we won't come close again until next January.

However, our cosmologists have identified a field of space that appears distorted."
"What, what do think it is sir?"
Mondone continued "Ming, they have no idea. I want you to do your stuff again, use your special skills and analyse it to see if you can identify more than the telescope guys?"
"Ok, I'll give it my best shot Sir."

"See you tomorrow, Ming."

"Yes sir, goodbye."

She turned to Akoni, "Did you get some of that?"
He replied "The bit about France, yes. Sounds like a nice trip?"

She laughed, "Ha! Trouble is it will be all duty and business, not much time to visit the sights." then she became a little sad, "Oh Akoni, hold on to what we have. I'll be back before you know it." She felt torn inside, life's demands suppressing life's wants.
Her hands reached out to him.

He took her arms, slid his hands down to her wrists and held her hands, then moved his around her waist pulling her close. He said, "When duty calls, you gotta go. I won't be far. Thank God for modern technology with live video across the net."
She smiled "Yes it's good we can do that. Can't wait for the day when you can have an electronic hug from thousands of miles away, as though that would be the same."
He laughed.

Then her mind drifted to the new work on a piece of 'distorted space'.

'What the devil could that be?….'

Chapter 2

Some days earlier….

7.30 pm Thursday 1st March 2018
Bird in Hand public house, Lovedean, UK

Gavin Deerwood had just dropped a pint of beer he was carrying. With a crash it smashed on the floor.

"Bugger!...sorry."

His other hand firmly held onto Jane's half pint.
Glass and liquid splattered on the floor and under tables. A man and a woman leapt quickly out of the lager's flight path.
"Oh crap! …Sorry." said Gavin again, knowing the outside of the glass had been wet to hold onto.
He was a bit rattled though; the coppers had really put the frights up him.

Jane frowned at Gavin as he gingerly came back with a second pint.
A barmaid was busily clearing up the mess.

"What's up Gavin, you seem a bit shaky tonight?"
He sat down wearily thinking 'She's very irritable lately. How to tell her?'

Gavin took a deep gulp of ice cold lager, almost half the pint.
The freezing liquid put tears in his eyes.
In his heart she was the girl of his dreams, he had said he loved her, but a certain amount of murky water had now flowed under the bridge.
Swallowing, breathing, wiping his mouth with the back of his hand, then taking a slow breath he said "The cops visited me today. Christ knows why. Kept asking about my relationship with Roger, you know Luke's Dad."

"What!" Jane eyes locked on him, she stared.
"Well I told them I just owed Roger about eight grand and he was getting a bit heavy about it."
"Yes Gavin and those questions you kept asking me, they come from Roger?
You know the questions about our instruments where I work and the sky object?"

He dug deep trying to save the situation, no…. their relationship.

Jane swallowed hard, the penny dropped.
Roger had been blackmailing Gavin.

Gavin's eyes were flitting about, first the pub customers, then the windows, over to the entrance door, he said "I…. I was sort of interested in your work, especially after you told me about the supernova."
He squirmed trying to think, realising too late that Roger had set him up and now driving a wedge between him and Jane, his clever scientist girlfriend.
Jane fired back at him "I don't think that for a moment Gavin. I think Roger is up to no good, a spy or something. That submarine which kidnapped us, the awful killings in Wales, how did they know where we were? HOW GAVIN? "

An awkward moment of silence enveloped them.
Gavin was trying to talk, he felt clammy, couldn't speak. His face was turning red.
Then Jane came over very cold, the thought suddenly engulfed her.
Her fault, whatever she had said to Gavin had been passed to Roger.
The Chinese soldiers opening fire, the death of her friend Amit, and Roger Stoneham their bodyguard. Karen almost fatally wounded. Colone Mondone shot.
She came to an awful realisation, thinking 'I'm guilty; their deaths are on my head…omg!'

Gavin gulped, looked at her, he took the plunge, "Yes they say... HE IS A SPY!
So I stopped. Have nothing to do with him now. The police arrested him this morning."
"Good God Gavin! .....I feel so awful."
She realised the larger scenario, her own exposure.
"You are a fool, my career, hell I could be arrested under the Official Secrets Act or worse, just by association."
Gavin frowned "By assoshan..... ? What's that mean Jane?"
"Treason Gavin, it is the one crime in this country that the death penalty is still in force for."
"Oh hell, oh holy shit Jane, I didn't know...."
She continued "and what's more, that business with Crowley, him trying to get to me by offering to pay your debts."
Gavin stuttered, thinking, trying to save the situation, "Ye...yeah he was out of order. You were good there giving him some stick."

Jane took a deep breath, paused looked around the pub. Lucky it was quiet where they sat. "Well I did give him a piece of my mind. We talked on his yacht after he rescued all of us and I got the impression that his loyalties seemed to be in the right place."
"You mean Steven Crowley's not a spy?"
"I think not, he has some other agenda, saving our world sort of crap."

Steven Crowley the self styled evangelist, a crazy stuntman, vanishing under water in front of the whole of GunWharf Quays. Then later machine gunning the stricken Chinese submarine from his yacht and rescuing them in the nick of time.
Crowley and Lei his girlfriend, had plucked Jane, Ming, Arrack, John and Brad from the sinking submarine.
Torpedoed, courtesy of a British Navy hunter-killer helicopter.

Finally he and Lei dumping thousands of contraband Greek cigarettes overboard as the British warship approached.

'My God what is happening' screeched Jane's thoughts.

Gavin became silent.
He was in pain, she could see Gavin was falling apart, but what a hole he had dug them into.
Jane carried on "What I did realise is that Steven Crowley is part of some sort of secret organisation. He mentioned 'we' a few times and I think accidently.
Not meaning him and Ming's sister Lei, but a powerful group of people, again with some crazy idea about saving the planet..... hmm... maybe not so crazy....."
Her dialogue tailed off.
Jane said quietly, "What a bloody mess....."
She realised there were so many pieces of the jigsaw missing, people trying to manipulate her. Suddenly she felt a chill, shivery. Need to do something.
Jane eyed Gavin coldly.

Gavin spluttered "What shall we do?"
"WE! ...God, Gavin it's a case of what I NEED TO DO!"
Gavin looked at her like a spaniel that had been scolded, ears drooping down, sorrowful eyes, mouth open, eager to make amends.
Jane finally said, "I think WE need a break Gavin. I think WE need some time apart.
I cannot risk my job and my life through your short sightedness."

Jane Horsham got up there and then, scraping her chair back and very quickly left.
Gavin downed a huge gulp of beer; well he had just bought them......
Outside she got in her car and started it.
He came running out as she drove through the pub car park.
"Jane please, please don't do this. I can change, make good you know."

She rapidly left the car park, flooring the accelerator and the car snaked on the dusty gravel, then shot up the road.

Previous day – Wednesday February 28th 2018
Verbena Close, Cowplain, UK

Karen Durgas was convalescing at home.

She was due to return to work in a week, back to her physics job at ESS (European Science Services), based in East Meon.
Tomorrow Thursday, she would pop in for a short spell, say hello to everybody and spend a little time on a special project, with her lover and work colleague John Creeson.
The near fatal bullet wound in her chest had healed fast.
She wondered on that, her mum used to heal quickly too.
Karen glanced at the photo of them on the mantelpiece, thinking 'Didn't stop your cancer though Mum ….. Love you Mum… miss you so much.'

She cast her mind back over the last couple of months.
Enough action, scares, deaths and other frightening things happening, to last a year. No…. a lifetime.
The discovery of that strange object in the sky, now away on it's orbit parallel to our sun. A portal maybe, made of energy, created by enormous forces, yet not physical.

Karen thought, 'At least we won't see that thing again for ten months or so, need some time to think and plan…. what to plan ?'
At home she now had a remote computer link into the lab at work. Access to her files, the databases and powerful visualisation tools. On her large screen television she could display the 3D map of outer space surrounding the object, Crackwell its name.
Yesterday she briefly logged on to work from home and used the systems, sorted some email, particularly one from Jane Horsham, the bright maths graduate hired at the same time as she joined.
As a result she had run some analysis programs on the trail behind Crackwell, using Jane's specific spectrographic requirements to try and identify gases, and trace elements in this trail, almost certainly the portal corridor. The direction pointed to the vastly

distant and ancient Omega Centauri dense star cluster back towards the centre of our galaxy.
A cluster of millions of very old stars.

Karen had not tried again to use her ancient Heart of Grace cross to spiritually travel, and consciously peer inside Crackwell, now rapidly moving away from near our moon.
She was too scared.
Her spiritual strength was remarkable but she was petrified and sensed that if she travelled mentally and entered what appeared to be the Crackwell portal, something hugely evil might trap her forever.

The point of no return, where her mind could be trapped in some grotesque world, never to return, while her body slowly died on Earth.

Along the mantelpiece were candles, a small gold framed clock and a shiny porcelain statue of the Virgin Mary holding the Christ child, a gift from her parents.
Karen walked over and picked up the purple coloured statue and slowly rotated it.
She wondered about Christianity, the religion's faith and strength, 'where does it fit in my life? How does it fit? Because it is there and I know it's real. As real as my own spiritual path.'

She replaced the statue, turned and picked up a letter from the coffee table.
It was to confirm her permanent status at ESS, with a salary increase, very nice too.
Signed by her boss Richard Armitage.

'That happened much quicker than I thought. Guess they badly need to keep me.'

Then she reflected and smiled thinking about the teaching job that she had left so abruptly.

Genuine love from the school kids and wishing her the best in her new role.
Sometimes she wished all this hadn't happened, the school job was secure, predictable, good regular money.
No nagging worries, only misbehaving teenagers.
The worst moments being a bit of shouting and detention at times. Piles of marking work now seemed par for the course. Aggravation can be relative.

Karen thought 'Now, I find myself in an environment that one could read in a fiction thriller. Danger, scary, unknown entities, spies, senior politicians ducking and diving and then we are friggin kidnapped by the gun wielding Chinese navy.
People dying violently.
To top it all, the machine gun mad preacher, Steven Crowley on his yacht, rescues all of us in the nick of time. '

"Oh hell…" she sighed.

Then there was the corroded ancient sword found by her now deceased Dad, Edward Durgas, in the remains of the Druid oak tree groves, on the Island of Anglesey.
John Creeson, her boyfriend, being pursued by unknown henchmen and their dogs. He had risked his life to retrieve the sword from the stone ruins of that Iron Age village of Din Llugwy, where Edward had buried it.
Soon after that, her poor Dad had succumbed to pneumonia and quickly perished.

Dad and Mum gone.

She felt lonely, yet she knew her spiritual destiny meant she would meet them again one day. Recently she had come close in Wales to realising that very event.
She had nearly bled to death.

Karen shivered.

She thought about the tiny blue light beam and the mystical but seemingly useless power that the cross and sword seemed to invoke when they were brought close together. Strange and yet no real answers, no guidance as to what they are or how and why they might be used.
Too many questions.

Karen frowned hard, thinking 'We need answers, badly and pretty soon.'
She sat on the sofa staring at some research printouts, idly flicking and leafing through graphs, projections, insanely large numbers……..

Her reverie was suddenly broken by the phone ringing.
"Yes, hello."
"Is that you Karen? Anne here."
"Ah hello Anne, nice to hear your voice."
Anne replied "Thanks. Karen, Sabrina wants to see us together."
"Oh ? what's up Anne, does Sabrina know about your hypnotherapy ?"
Anne sort of laughed "Well funny you should mention that, over the phone she said she sensed something about me that disturbed her."

Karen smiled as her minded drifted into fantasy, she was thinking about the myriad of spiritual paths people take.
Worlds beyond the physical universe.

"Karen, Karen? you there?"

"Sorry, yes…umm… so when do you think Sabrina will get us together?"
Anne quickly said "Tonight, at her place, 7pm if that's ok with you?"
Karen "Oh? yes ok , meet there ?"
Anne "Good Karen, we shall see what's cooking."
She ended the call with a little laugh.

Anne Whitfield had confided to Karen, of her spiritual soul life and her belief of her soul's human paths in the past. Back then they had met for a momentous evening, when Anne had revealed her faith with a vibrancy and jubilation that was hard to deny.
Karen at the time was spellbound and fascinated by a very believable woman.
She was considering this path of Anne's to see what comes.
However, her own intensely gripping spiritual experiences were so dominant that she couldn't think about other roads at the moment.

This was all prior to the catastrophic Wales episode that put Karen and John in hospital.

That evening.

It was just the three of them in the large house in Catherington.
They sat in Sabrina's smaller lounge, not the spacious one used for the group's dreaming meditation sessions. Soft drinks were on the table.
Sabrina had suggested that alcohol and caffeine based drinks were not recommended, being inhibitors to true dreaming.

She spoke first.
"Karen, Anne, it's good to see you, thank you for coming over. Things are shall we say coming to a head."

Karen puzzlingly looked at Anne, thinking 'Maybe we will be asked to leave the circle.'
Anne replied querulously, "What is on your mind Sabrina? you mentioned you are sensing something unusual ?"

Sabrina, the normally calm, collected shamanic teacher, paused and looked at each of them in turn. Her face showed a little sign of strain.
She quietly said "I know."
They both frowned.

Karen began to speak, “Know what? …I…”
Sabrina put the palm of her hand towards them, fingers splayed. “It’s ok. Tonight is not about individualism, following other paths, nor my focussed methods that may not suit every dreamer. There are much more powerful forces to be concerned with.
Our strengths are in the perception of what may come.”

She was acknowledging their talents.

Both Karen and Anne remained silent, their attention now absolute.
Sabrina continued, “I have many connections to other groups around the world who follow the shamanic principles. As you know not only western based circles like ours, but also some indigenous native peoples too.”
She paused, took a long breath, and then said “I have also participated in a circle of Elders that has been recently convened.”

Anne then said, “So why are we here Sabrina, just the three of us?”
Sabrina smiled, a warm almost motherly glow, “You see it is because you Anne have the ability to be strongly perceptive and I believe your hypnotherapy is strengthening your soul connection. Correct me if I am wrong but is this how you feel?”
“Yes you are right. It is the true path for me, to learn about one’s past and one’s current destiny I believe. What is missing and this may be from the fact that I am a relative newcomer, is that I still want to learn to dream and to really integrate into the spiritual world. Your teachings Sabrina are so important?”
It was veiled as a question.
Sabrina’s eyes seemed to widen with ancient wisdom. “Time is the key, yes to spend much time to learn the dreaming is paramount, many years as we know. Which we may not have……” she paused then said “….now Karen”
She looking deeply into Karen’s eyes. “Karen, you are, how shall I put it?’ succumbing to, no… more like being dominated by your exceptionally active spiritual soul.”

Karen stared at Sabrina "You think so? Well I have had some powerful experiences lately, even frightening."
Sabrina replied, "Yes, I know. What's more I think that pendant you are wearing is central to them."
Karen realised just how aware Sabrina was. She continued "Karen, Anne, let me get to the point. After the Elder's meeting, we acknowledged that a serious problem is manifesting itself. A most perilous challenge."

Sabrina continued "The consensus has been reinforced by other such circles across the globe."
Anne squeezed her eyes almost shut, but continued to look at Sabrina, then said,
"Serious? Is there something that is worrying? I have never seen you look so strained Sabrina? How can that be? You are on the path for all that is and know that the afterlife is all that is."

Sabrina looked very solemn, "Yes the afterlife. Our ancestors, our guides, our loved ones. There is a monumental threat. The perception of it has been raised by the ancestors. As you know it is very difficult for them as spiritual beings, to physically interact in this human world, so they ask us to do their bidding. Always for the good, for the betterment of human kind."

Karen quickly spoke, "What is this threat Sabrina? Let me ask, is it from the object in the sky that has been discovered ?"
Sabrina slowly spoke, her voice dropped an octave. "We believe it is, though not directly."
Anne felt cold, goose bumps on her arms. She pulled her cardigan sleeves down, and then said, "How can we help? What more do you know about this,…this threat?"
Sabrina replied "Just to know for now is enough. Soon, in a few weeks I shall convene a special meeting to which I would like both of you to come. It will include our circle and many more. In the meantime I will talk to others in our groups, much the same as we are doing now."
Karen exclaimed, "Sabrina, you are obviously very concerned

about this. Do you know that the powers that be are going to launch space vehicles early next year, with a plan to intercept this object?"
"No, I was not aware of that."
Karen continued "Well, some of this is confidential, but I can say that some very powerful military weapons may be onboard, together with some already in orbit.
It is likely that they are nuclear."

Sabrina sighed "If they are to try and counter this threat, these weapons will be of little use."

Anne's eyes went wide. Softly she said "Oh my dear lord….."

The meeting broke up soon after that.

Chapter 3

10.25 pm Thursday 1st March 2018
Horndean, Hampshire UK

Bill Craswell looked at the clock.
'Where is my wife? She said she would be back around 8 pm.'

The two of them led almost separate lives.
July was spending much time away, as a senior executive at the cosmetics giant RealRouge.
Bill too, his job based in ESS, a Ministry laboratory in East Meon, meant he spent long hours on the new projects there.

He thought 'Making love tonight would be lovely, guess she will be tired though.'
He had showered, had a clean shave and then casually dressed, picking a shirt that covered his bulging tummy, then plastered on rather too much Armani aftershave.

The scent was so strong that the wallpaper was almost curling off the wall.
Propped up on the hall table were a bunch of roses and a box of her favourite chocolates.
July had been away for almost a week, some promotion or other with several key clients she said.

Then the front door flew open and banged against the wall.
July staggered in with her suitcase and small travel bag.
"Thanks for coming out and helping me!"
Sarcasm hit him.
"July sorry, didn't hear your car pull up. Guess you got caught in the traffic?"

She looked at him briefly, dumped her bags and went upstairs saying "So hot and sticky, I'm straight in the shower."

Bill was halfway to her, a hug and a kiss so badly wanted.
But she was gone.
He stood open mouthed watching her back as she disappeared up the stairs.
Bill shouted up "Want a cuppa, or something stronger? Perhaps a glass of vino to relax and blow away the work blues?" He smiled as she halted and briefly turned to face him. "Thanks Bill, but I'm straight to bed after the shower, totally shattered."
She carried on up.
He swore under his breath.
Bill couldn't hide his disappointment. 'Where has the warmth in our life gone?'
He pondered, grimaced then had an idea.
He carried her bags from the hall into the lounge.
The shower was going, steam drifting out into the upstairs hallway.

Quickly he opened her shoulder bag. Full up, woman's things, everything except the kitchen sink he thought. There, there it was. Her zip up bag containing receipts.

He glanced out the doorway, shower still going.
Bill fumbled through the receipts, and then found what he was looking for.
He stared beyond the receipts back into the bag, what is that? Pulling back the stack of receipts and paper, he saw some condoms tucked into the back of the bag. 'What the hell?' he thought. His face screwed up. 'July is on the pill, what the devil are these for?' his thoughts churned, 'unless she has come off it now…'
Bill's thoughts twisted and turned 'She did say she might, was worried about the long term medical effects of the pill. But the condoms, she never said?...I knew nothing about these……'

His stomach knotted, denying the growing evidence.
Then he looked at the Hotel bill.

Hotel Galstone, Milton Keynes.

Invoice	*£*
Four nights – double room	*360*
Room Breakfast x 8	*64*
Dinner 2 places x 4	*210*
Papers	*5*
Room service various	*35*
Minibar	*15*

…………..

His thoughts cursed,
'Room breakfast times eight for four nights, oh god, oh July you shit.'

"Bill, BILL ! can you get me the hair shampoo out of my suitcase?"

"What? Oh yes……. Hang on a minute."

Quickly replacing the hotel bill, he unzipped her suitcase and found the shampoo.
Running upstairs he paused momentarily at the bathroom door then opened it.
Steam poured out.
"Here you are my love." She grabbed the bottle and closed the shower door quickly.

Bill was now becoming really pissed off.
The reality of his suspicions welling up inside him.

Long after his wife went to bed, Bill had curled up with a bottle of Famous Grouse whisky on the sofa.
The television quietly mumbling through a political documentary.

He slowly sipped the amber liquid, letting its mellow warming magic slide down his throat. 'Aah....so good.'
Before he knew it, his glass was empty ....lovely stuff he thought as he refilled.

The News came on, he turned up the volume and idly watched.

'...and we have a major incident on the M1 motorway just north of junction 14.
A multiple vehicle accident has closed the northbound carriageway. We believe at least sixty vehicles are involved.......'

"Lord..... Sixty?" uttered Bill quietly. "Why are people so impatient....."
He half smiled at his own impatience.
Trying to get things moving at work, pushing for real progress, that sort of thing.
Then he stared open mouthed at the next News piece,

'.......what is extraordinary is that some fighting has broken out at the crash scene. We have just received reports of several dozen people including women, struggling and punching each other. This is occurring on the road and the hard shoulder. The police and medical services have arrived and are attempting to restore order.......'

Bill mouthed "What..... hell, what is our country coming too?"

Even the broadcaster looked strained.
Bill changed channel and stopped on the ITV news. After some items on the current Middle East crisis, with the usual politicians steadfastly maintaining their positions and criticising the other side, the newsreader picked up a new item.
Bill became alert and watched intensely.

'......scientists are working on various theories as to what the object in our sky is.

This little area was lit up by the supernova of the exploding star Betelgeuse. Originally about a million miles away from the Earth, this object is now far behind us on its own orbit. The scientists say we will not come close to it again until next January.
Our own resident expert, Professor Matteus Riverstein explains.'

The TV picture changed to a library setting, a grey bearded man of about fifty appeared, white shirt, brown patterned tie and dark tweed jacket.
The studious look was enhanced by rows of books behind him.

'Yes, our researches so far have shown that this object, this anomaly in our sky is not physical. That is not physical in the sense of matter like an asteroid, or large rock or even something solid, artificial. In fact it appears to be constructed of pure energy. It may be a portal, an entrance to another universe. The thing is invisible and very small. When the gamma rays from the supernova lit it up, we estimated its size to be maybe a couple of hundred metres in diameter.'

The professor paused and drew a breath, but quickly continued before the interviewer could interrupt. His eyes were red and tired.

'Many of the world's nations are extremely interested in this phenomenon. Already the Chinese have dispatched a probe from their manned spacecraft when it was on its way to their moon base. The Chinese have kept their findings close to their chest, although from another quarter we hear the probe may have disappeared. I believe the Americans will not be long in establishing contact with this object.'
Bill felt a knot in his stomach; he put his hand against it.

The interviewer interjected, *"But Professor, what do we make of this anomaly, this invisible object, could it be a threat?"*

The professor replied slowly, deliberately,

'Whatever it is, we must treat it with respect and caution. We must keep a completely open mind as to what may exit from it, or what we may find if we can enter it somehow. Certain nations may try and how shall I say, yes, they will want to illuminate this object to understand it more. However, huge energies are required to do this. Indeed very substantial, possibly destructive energies may be required in order to light up the energy fabric of this object. This could provoke an unknown and potentially dangerous response from it.'

The interviewer ended the discussion thanking the Professor. Then he picked up a related news item and started to read,

'A number of economists in the western world have already reported a slight panic in some quarters. Supermarkets have reported increased sales in long life food items, such as tinned meat, fish and vegetables, powdered milk, dried pasta and salt.... In addition, the world financial markets are generally down. Gold prices have crept up.'

Bill frowned, rubbed his face in disbelief, thinking 'Oh hell … it has begun. To think the world has enough problems without Crackwell appearing.'

He turned to another channel; an old black and white movie was playing.
Smiling, he warmed to the character George Bailey played by James Stewart.
Bill had seen the film 'It's a Wonderful Life' a long time ago.

In the film, George the good little banker, the budding entrepreneur, was trying to avert a financial crisis, and then becoming suicidal as he tried to fight the much larger but evil wealthy financier. Finally as George was about to throw himself off the town's river bridge, an angel in the form of a glowing middle aged man appeared, who showed him there's more to life than taking one's own.

‘Something about the ‘angel’ man, some significance, but what?’ Bill pondered, shivered, trying to retrieve a feeling he had, a thought from last week.
Then he leant over grabbing his glass for another glug of warming scotch.

6.40 am Friday 3rd March

“Bill, BILL! Why didn’t you come to bed?”

Bill jumped, opened then closed his eyes as the streaming morning daylight hit them. July had pulled the curtains back. “Gaaah! Oh ah….”
He muttered holding his head.
“July… I must have fallen asleep here.”

The sofa was not forgiving, he ached all over.
She gave him a sharp look, and then snapped “Blame the whisky Bill.”
July stomped into the kitchen, rattling cups and plates.

Bill staggered into the hallway cloakroom and splashed cold water on his face.
He grabbed a towel and stared at the mirror. ‘What an ugly sight’ he thought.
In the hallway, the roses, his card and chocolates were still there, untouched.

July had laid the breakfast table. Toast and soft boiled eggs, tea and jams.
Bill returned and sat down saying “You must have been dead beat last night, not even a kiss goodnight.” he half smiled.
July said nothing, just battered the shell off the top of her egg and spread some butter on her toast.
She sort of tutted.

“You look like shit Bill.”

Bill frowned, thinking when to confront her, when to mention the hotel receipt.
She would probably initially retaliate by saying what was he doing rummaging in her paperwork.
'Then maybe, maybe she had a female colleague with whom she had shared a large room. Yes that's it, of course.'

He slowly spread Marmite on his toast and bit a large piece off, vigorously munching it and watched July.
She avoided eye contact.
The Marmite worked instantly, his taste buds reviving, the enzymes eagerly grabbed by his body to replenish those destroyed by the alcohol.

His vision seemed to blur just a little, July was not quite in focus,

She quickly finished her breakfast. Already dressed and made up. July stood and said, "I'm off to work, early meeting today."
She made to leave the table and Bill said "July there is something wrong. We don't seem to be together much these days. I know our careers make things difficult, but I miss you .....I "

He didn't get to finish.

July shouted "You drink too much Bill and your job owns you, all me, me, me. Look at how important I am, Bill fucking Craswell !.......Nobel Laureate.. ha ! NOT."
Bill was flustered; she was thrusting the sword in.
He thought 'Well that's it, no option but to say it.'
"Tell me about the hotel July, room service breakfasts for two?"
"WHAT? have you been going through my stuff ?"

He started to fluster, "Well July, I....I accidentally came across it when you asked me for the shampoo. Sorry, course ..um...you had a friend, a girlfriend colleague I guess, sharing? "

He was offering her a lifeline.

Instead July screwed her eyes into needles, "The shampoo was in my suitcase, the receipts in my hand luggage."
Bill tried to hold his gaze on July. There was something odd about her; a sort of thin dark hazy edge appeared around her upper torso. He closed his eyes hard and thought 'Flaming whisky, need to give it up.'
Wincing from the onset of a bone sharp headache, he slowly opened his eyes again.
July's dark halo, if you could call it that, was more pronounced now, almost like a black shadow tight in behind her, bloody weird. Bill pinched the bridge of his nose, and said "I accidentally looked in your hand luggage first, that's why? God, July are you ok?"

July's face became thunderous. Her complexion became very odd, like the speckled surface of a pale grey moon.

"Now you know. Well, I have met someone and I want a divorce Bill."

"Oh July..." Bill whispered. His soul knew deep down, he fought hard not to acknowledge the tearing nagging pain.
But now she had confirmed it.

His heart became stone, his stomach churned. He just sat at the table speechless and stared at her retreating back, her check blouse softly flickering like a faded chess board.
Something wispy, like faint dark smoke trailed slightly behind her.
Bill frowned, uttered "What the …?"
Then she was gone, the front door slamming hard.
Amazingly the glass panel in it didn't break.

Bill was open mouthed, thought 'What the hell was that, she looked flippin strange.'
He glanced across at the empty whisky bottle on the carpet next to the sofa and let out a soft groan.

The shower was long and hot, steam had blotted out all the glass windows and drenched just about everything in the bathroom.
Finally a rather red Bill emerged and towelled dry.
Feeling more human, he quickly jogged down the stairs.
Grabbing a hot coffee and cramming some buttered toast in his mouth, for a moment he stopped and pondered the morning's events.

Then the door slammed a second time.
He drove to work in a daze, narrowly missing a wobbling cyclist on the country lane near ESS (European Space Systems, East Meon).

Bill Craswell, Exotic Projects Director, was having some terrible thoughts.
His mind was in turmoil, yet numb.
His adulterous wife at the forefront.
Then the project's gravity array which highlighted the anomaly Crackwell. A mysterious object, possibly a portal to God knows where.
Squinting through the very bright sunlight, he glanced up at the sky to see if a faint moon was around. The portal had been near to it.

His boss Richard Armitage meddling and micromanaging instead of delegating stuff.
Bill's mind was fuzzy, painful… he frowned his face into a mass of wrinkles.

Something that Karen had mentioned at work, sounding him out.
He pooh-poohed it at the time, said what a lot of spiritual mumbo jumbo.
Bill remembered his words clearly "What we need is hard evidence….empirical data, tangible proven facts. Not ephemeral gazing……"
And yet he felt the addition of something, a presence maybe, and intangible, yet there….

‘Perhaps low air pressure caused by the current weather? that can get you down.’
He nodded to himself.

Unlocking his office, Bill slowly flopped down in his chair with a big sigh, and powered up his computer.
He flipped through a few papers and letters that Constance had left in his in-tray, and then he got up and wandered down to the gravity laboratory.

Jane was already in.
She rattled away on her keyboard, occasionally glancing up at the battery of displays surrounding her.
“Hi Jane” he sighed, and then he followed quickly with “Morning” brightening up with a smile.
She had tied her red hair back in a pony tail.
Today saw pale yellow top and black trousers.
He thought ‘slim and pretty, but very young. Probably a generation between us.’
Jane looked up and smiled “Good morning Bill. How are we?…. gees… Bill you look a bit pale, are you not well?”

Bill sat down on a chair across the other side of Jane’s desk.
“You know Jane, I think today is the first day of the rest of my life.”
The melancholy oozed out of him.
Jane frowned “What do you mean Bill?”

He looked at her in a father like way. “We live and learn life’s experience and all that. Funny how one day you think everything is going pretty well, nothing to really worry about…. Then POW you’re knocked flat to the floor by something that you didn’t see coming.”
Jane replied “So what’s up Bill, can you talk about it?”

“July’s leaving me, wants a divorce.”

"Oh god Bill, I'm so sorry....and you wondering why you didn't see much of her...ah..mmm... she say why ?"
Bill grimaced, looked even rougher, and said "Yeah...she's been seeing someone. Probably one of those shiny plastic executives where she works."

"Oh Bill." Jane got up and walked around to Bill, she touched his shoulder.
He let out the biggest sigh, and then tightened his demeanour, "But if she thinks she's getting half, HA! She's in for a big surprise. The house is nearly all mortgage loans."

Jane wandered over to the wall screens and leaned her back against one.
"You been married long? Any children?"
"God yeah quite some time now Jane, must be ..um..twelve years, I'd say.
No, no children.... We didn't want any in the beginning, although I did hope that later maybe we might....Then both our careers took over and children seemed to be forgotten."

He stopped, his eyes looked a bit watery.

"Oh Bill, I am so sorry. Well I think you're better off without her, fresh start you know, look forwards not backwards."
"Goddam you are so right Jane." He perked up and thought about the mortgage loans he had topped up using the house as collateral. Loans for his little covert project that was outside ESS.
July knew nothing about these.

Jane felt the urge to empathise, she murmured, "Well, you..... you aren't alone."
Bill looked across at her "Yes I know, I guess the divorce rate is pretty high these days."
"No Bill, what I meant was that I am in the same predicament, only there are no other players, just Gavin and me. You see we parted company last night, my doing actually."

"Oh Jane, why?" Bill was instantly thinking she was 'available', then quickly dashing it out of his head. 'Stupid rash thing to think, I really don't need any complications right now. God what am I thinking! she's far too young.'

Sixteen years between them, she twenty five and he forty one.

He deftly looked away, just in case she caught a flash of his thoughts.

She replied "Well Gavin and me are two different people really, not a lot in common. Although he says he loves me. Things have been a bit sticky lately and do you know Roger, Luke's dad, got arrested for spying?"
Bill looked up "Yes I did, after your amazing escape from the submarine, apparently Special Forces here tracked Roger down. It was through a foreign agent that they were keeping tabs on."

Bill's mind absently wandered to things sticky.
Jane continued "Well Gavin owes Roger a lot of money and was asking me stuff about my work. Naturally I was careful and thought why Gavin is asking me some quite particular technical questions. You see Gavin couldn't even begin to comprehend these areas. So I was suspicious."

Bill threw the question "and Roger was leaning on Gavin to get to you?"
"Yes and then the police interviewed Gavin. Surprisingly what with the Wales incident nothing came of it, but I had to make a decision about Gavin and me. There's no way I am going to jeopardise my career or safety for Gavin.
He seemed insensitive to my feelings and position. So it wasn't hard and I think I had already made the decision in my mind. I have been feeling really uneasy lately."
Her mind wandered to the Wales calamity.
Guilt flooded in.
Bill pondered, he looked at her strangely, 'Shall I…'

Jane looked quizzically at Bill, "You are about to tell me something?"

Bill paused; he tapped the side of the desk with his hand.
"You know Jane, I am troubled by something I saw this morning."
"What?"
"Crazy and I want to blame it on a bit of a hangover I have. You see as July and I were arguing, just before she stormed out, I saw a strange freaky thing..."
His voice faded away.
Jane became intensely interested, "Like what Bill?"
He felt awkward, unusual admissions can backfire and he was her boss.

"Nah, I guess it's nothing.... must be tiredness, a hallucination I had there, eyes not focussing properly. No worries, another coffee will shrug this off. Join me in the cafeteria?" he false smiled.
Jane shook her head. "No thanks Bill. Got some stuff I need to finish. Catch you later." Bill got up, said "That's ok." and walked slowly out.

He struggled to make sense of the day, thinking 'what the hell is bugging me....really?
I'm normally in control, positive direction, and maximum drive, everything that makes Bill Craswell tick..... And yet I feel anxious and it's not July, well mostly not......'
He pulled his gargoyle face, turned and walked to the exit.
The double doors swung shut and he was gone.

At lunchtime Bill had to get out, a walk in the countryside, some fresh air, anywhere except remain in ESS.
He strolled down the country road then turned into a dirt lane that the local farmer used. Bill stepped in and out of the tractor ruts trying to avoid the puddles and mud. Drawing in great lung full's of the cold wintry air, his head was clearing.
Spring was slow in coming.
Nature knew when the real frosts had gone.

He needed to get away from people, space to think.

After about two hundred yards the track widened so that a grassed area to the right came into view. The hedgerow was alive with bird song and the track was lined with thin spindly leafless trees that swayed slightly in the breeze. He was coming up on the large old oak tree with its great rough angular branches. It grew out of the opposite bank. The tree was a stark craggy giant, no leaves yet, matching the rest of the bare woodland. It could have been standing there for all time, generating a huge flush of acorns every autumn.

The day was dry, chilly, but quite bright, the sun halfway up in the sky. A few cumulus clouds scudded along. Bit windy but with his thick woollen coat he felt quite warm. As he neared the oak tree on the other side, there it was just in front of him.
The battered bench, with the back broken at one end.
He sat down on it, put his lidded coffee on the side and looked around. Behind the right rear of the bench were the remains of a flint wall some farmer or labourer had built probably a couple of centuries ago.

Bill closed his eyes and thought about his wayward wife.
'Oh July, July...........July why oh why....."
His head felt as though it was being squeezed.

A twig close by cracked.
Bill opened his eyes and looked in the direction of the sound.
Nothing, just swaying grasses.

The sun was too bright to look at, even momentarily.
Bill squinted then looked away.
Something caught his eye, a sort of reflection. He turned slightly to see one of the shiny flints in the wall was dazzling, must be just at that angle with the sun.
Then what the hell?

Down near his feet there were a few loose pebbles. A broken flint stone, about the size of an egg was, well it was catching the reflection on the flat chipped side. Flickering blue light shone straight up at Bill.
He shaded his eyes and went to pick up the stone.

Just before that time, back in the office:

Sitting in the ESS Pascal laboratory, John Creeson suddenly spoke.
"You know Karen; we are taking a risk testing this stuff here."

Karen Durgas looked up from the test bench "I know John, we could have some tricky explaining to do, but all the rest of the kit is here. We can't do this stuff elsewhere.
We're ok, the door warning light is currently on."

Outside, the illuminated sign above the door displayed 'Do Not Enter – Testing in Progress – Dangers of Laser Light'

"True" he said. "Also these are our, well, *your* property and we are investigating physics phenomena."
Previously they had discovered that a very faint blue light emanated from both objects and when brought closely in line, the light intensified and locked both the cross and sword in place. John the engineer and physics buff, could not explain it.

Karen spoke "John, You know with the scans you did of the stones, the fact that they seem opaque to magnetic and x-ray techniques, what do you imagine they are?"
He paused, said "Strangest thing, I would hazard a guess that the stones' outer shell is a material unknown to man. It may hide a very sophisticated miniature machine."

They had set up Karen's Heart of Grace cross in a jig on the bench. At the other end of the bench was the ancient sword mounted on

a swivel, so that it could be rotated to line up with the cross, with the lapis lazuli stones in the old artefacts facing each other.
Several jigs in the middle held reflective prisms, glass blocks and various sensor blocks. A battery of monitoring equipment had been wheeled across to the bench.
Wires and cables went everywhere.
John spoke into the recorder, describing the test details. He then initiated cameras that would see right across the electromagnetic spectrum far into the infrared and ultraviolet bands.
Areas that the human eye cannot see.

"Ok here we go."
They both donned protective shaded glasses.
John gently swung the sword around to line up with the cross, then he slid it forward on the little guide rails. Suddenly the blue beams appeared out of the lapis lazuli stones mounted in the cross and the sword.
Both objects froze in position.
Subsequently Karen operated the remote for a motor to move the prism. It slid along a guide rail set at ninety degrees to the parallel blue beam. It came between the cross and the sword, intercepting the intense blue shaft of light.
Apprehension mixed with the unknown.
They needed to measure the properties of the blue beam.

John exclaimed "Look at that, ah yes some of the blue light is split out.....but at a strange angle?" he glanced at the direction. "It's going straight out the window."
The blue beam stabbed right out through the second floor window and out into the countryside, vanishing in a distant clump of trees.

"And yet see most of the blue light continues to go right through the silvered reflector and onto the cross. How can that be? Energies we have yet to discover. Well I'll be damned."

Their clothes seemed to brighten, especially Karen's white blouse.

Karen said "That light split is unusual, it seems to flicker, it's rippling a number of colours......"
Suddenly she shouted "oh JOHN! LOOK OUT!"
The prism suddenly twisted and shot out of the holder, flying very fast upwards, to embed itself in the soft lab ceiling with a loud thwack.
They quickly pulled the sword out of alignment stopping the experiment.
John sat down opposite the large display and keyed in some commands, Karen quickly joined him. She said "Hell that was close...."
They ran the spectral analysis programs, then pulled up and started playing the videos of the last couple of minutes, in slow motion.
Nothing appeared over and above what they saw.
Karen said, "Let's have a look at the spectrums that are invisible to the human eye, infra red first."
John acknowledged. The infrared display showed a slight glow around the prism just before it twisted itself out of the mount. A little heat generated.
He panned around the bench using the entire camera's footage.
Nothing else.
"Ok let's have a look at ultraviolet."

As the display proceeded something extraordinary appeared.
John exclaimed "Look at that, a sort of halo, no a bubble maybe?"
A large faint ultra violet spherical ball shape seemed to envelop the entire bench, upwards to the ceiling and downwards to the floor. Karen halted the video replay.
She gasped "This is amazing. Wait. WAIT look at that over there, can you magnify the area towards the window?"
John "Ok."
A black dot appeared in the display screen. Karen said "John, wind the video back and rerun very slowly."

"Good god, it's a... yes it's a fly and look what happened to it."
Karen stared utterly mesmerised.

Sure enough, though a little hazy, a large bluebottle fly had come in through the open window right at that moment. It carried on until it met the ultraviolet 'bubble'. It violently bounced off and then it disappeared into thin air…….

John uttered "My life, see that. We were standing outside of that bubble, but the fly has been repelled. Must be a shield of sorts."
Karen startled said "Yes, but see the fly has gone?" She looked around the room walking towards the window, looking at the floor, no fly anywhere.
John then ran the gravity wave analyser.
"I'll check for any gravity disturbance, unlikely though……… wait … look at that."

In the fine 3D superimposed grid, framed over the bench, was a tiny, tiny little buckle, a slight distortion. He magnified it. Then John commented "Wow, even that blip needs a huge amount of energy, where the hell has that come from?"
Karen's eyes grew wide, she stuttered, "Goodness, the more we look the more questions arise."

John looked at her speechless; he felt a shiver this time.

Then the door opened and Richard Armitage breezed in.
"Hello I see you guys are beavering away as usual."

He stopped and observed the bench and the mounted artefacts.
"What the?....."
Karen quickly took hold of the situation, "Richard glad you popped by, let me show you our dating techniques for gravitonic materials."
Richard cocked his head, "Ah yes, yes tell me."

John Creeson looked a little worryingly at Karen and then at Richard, thinking this is not good. Richard could theoretically confiscate the cross and sword, or least impound them here if he wanted to be really awkward.

Karen had the situation in hand, a 'sod anybody, let's do this' type of attitude.

She continued, "As you know we have already measured some side effects of gravitational flexing in materials such as granite. Here we can show residue in very old objects such as these artefacts of mine. Mere old rocks can have residue, but it is much harder to detect compared with worked items like these ancient artefacts of mine, where we have finite dates to start from."
Richard nodded in the right places trying to keep up. He was looking intently at the cross then the sword. He hadn't spotted the prism still embedded in the ceiling.
She then turned to the computer displays gesturing Richard to look and brought up some of the equations, plus their derivatives and carried on talking.
At this point Richard held up his hand, "I'm sorry but I'm afraid even with my knowledge, you are losing me Karen. Do continue, I must press on.
Hope you get some results with those old battered objects?" he had that querulous look.

Karen replied "Early days Richard. Hopefully our computer processing runs will extract the correlations." She gave a thin smile, with just a pinch of impatience, like they needed to get on with the job.

Armitage took the hint, said suddenly "Right, I must press on, good luck."
With that he left as swiftly as he had arrived.

John breathed a sigh of relief and said "Blimey Karen, you know I started to believe you myself."
Karen gave a little chuckle "My spiel was utter tosh, but it worked. Think we need to return these items to my place or somewhere safe."
She was a gem.

Outside the establishment.

Back up the country lane, Bill examined the stone.
The blue light had vanished.
Just an ordinary whitish flint with a darker, but shiny flinty area towards the centre.

Another twig cracked loudly just across the way.
Bill jerked his head up and then dropped the stone.
"Uh !.... what…." he said quietly.

A man was standing in front of the oak tree.
His feet seemed to vanish in the long grass.
Bill became quite rigid; he gripped the arm of the bench hard with his right hand.
His left hand with the two missing middle fingers, splayed out as he pressed it hard against the bench seat. His neck hairs prickled.

You see the man was not quite in focus, a sort of whitish haze enveloped him.
His simple clothing was that of a robe or gown. All glowing purplish white.

Bill exclaimed "Who the hell are you?"
The man appeared to say something, but no sound could be heard.
"That's it!" shouted Bill, "I've just about had enough of tricks today."

He closed his eyes hard, took a long deep breath and started counting.
Then he stopped, a voice was saying something in his mind.
Bill moaned "Oh for God's sake, I've had a few hangovers in my time, but this takes the biscuit."
He slowly opened his eyes.

The man was still there, he was mouthing some words.

Now Bill started to get up, he was frightened and said "Shit you must be real…"

"Bill Craswell, this is very important. Please stay where you are, no harm will come to you."

"WHO? …. Who are you? What do you want?"
Bill frantically looked up and down the lane, nobody around.
He turned back to the white man.
'If only somebody, anybody could walk up right now. Witness that I am not going mad.'

Nobody appeared.

Bill fiddled with his mobile phone in his pocket, get it ready to whip out and turn the camera on. Despite the chill, he was hot and shivery with perspiration running off his forehead.
He thought 'I've had some amazing happenings in my life, but this, THIS could be that one time event. Something beyond our comprehension, magical, enlightening.
I must keep my presence of mind to absorb everything about this.'
He hammered the thought hard again and again, keep control, and maintain his focus.
However, the pragmatic part of him was saying 'What magician's trick is this?'

The man continued, "*Bill, I have come from a very far away place. A colossal distance to your people. You need to know that your particle caused us a problem.*"

"Oh God…."
Bill immediately felt faint; he started to sway on the bench, his consciousness going.
The man raised an arm and curved his fingers towards Bill Craswell.
Bill suddenly felt fresh, alert as though he had just gulped strong coffee.

"We have now rectified the problem, but I must stress that you do not repeat your research. Albeit that the direction of the particle was extremely unfortunate."

Bill's mind was racing; their explosion particle had impacted very close to the Chinese moon base. Through Arrack Mondone's recent intelligence, it was discovered that the astronauts had died there trying to repair severe punctures to their base habitation dome. Highly confidential information.
He was fraught with guilt, had been struggling with his conscience for the last week. He thought 'I can't take much more, but who is this person, he seems so weird?'

Bill said shakily "There is … no chance of it happening again."

"Oh but there is, your gravity engine operating out of Earth's orbit, may prove embarrassing. So I will implement a change to ensure the danger is avoided."

Bill shrieked with pain "Aaaarh…..oh dear god….aaaaarh !" he clutched his head.

He fell off the bench and into a pile of dead leaves.

The sun had moved across the sky, a stray dog finishing its pickings in the farmyard had wandered down the lane.
It came across Bill's prone form. Sniffing his face and then nudging his ear with its wet nose.
"Aah…uuummm…what the fff….."
Bill Craswell woke up with a start, rubbing his head. The dog scampered off.

The first thing he did was sit up too quickly looking around for the white man.
"Oarhh….my poor head."
No sign of anyone.

Then he screwed his face up, thinking, trying to remember. What on earth was that all about? had he been dreaming? dozing there on the bench?

Bill brushed some wet leaves and grass off his clothes and walked unsteadily back down the lane. He glanced at his watch, 'Damn, it's nearly 2.30pm'

Halfway back to ESS his head cleared somewhat and he suddenly stopped, looking up, around, drawing in a deep breath of the chill air.
Clear in his mind was a modification to the gravity engine, 'of course that is so obvious, we need to stream the fuel feed into three separated stages, to avoid a runaway explosion.'
He stood up straight and marched determinedly back to work.

Then a second thought had struck him to the bone.
The particle was neither an element nor a compound, well nothing that could be measured properly or identified. Its massive density was the result of a huge compressed mass.

It was able to pierce the thick steel roof beam in the laboratory at high velocity and travel at colossal speed across to the moon. He stopped abruptly and exclaimed, "no…NO! oh God … surely not?"

Bill muttered all the way back. "Holy crap….. oh my god… it can't be, but it must be …..oh dear lord what have we…. I done?............what to do?"

His headache came back.

Chapter 4

7pm Sunday 4th March
Bill & July's House

Bill Craswell had just endured probably the worst weekend of his life.
He had been delving through books, online references and remotely from home, the project databases at ESS.

And he was distracted frequently by thoughts of adulterous July.
He had tried to call her a couple of times, but her mobile was off.
Probably disappearing to her sister's place.
As though there was any hope for the salvation of their marriage now.

He still could not fathom out the 'dream' he had Friday lunchtime in that country lane.
'Asleep yes he was; well some of the time….
If it was real, then who the hell was that man by the oak tree?'

He had pulled up Amit Pachar's files on the second explosion.
The event was almost a year ago now, the one that cost Conrad Thursule his life.
Bill had tried to forget the five weeks he himself was in hospital.
Therapy and more therapy.
But it worked and they eventually got Bill walking again after a serious fracture to his left tibia.
He was not the perfect patient, by far.
Then the fleeting thought came of poor Amit being gunned down and killed in Wales.

He analysed Amit's observations.

"Explosion of March 9th 2017
Investigation notes:

1. *Analysis of the steel strut hole, generated by the explosion particle.*
   It has carbonised sides, some deposits of silica, iron and various oxides.
2. *All residual chemicals are from the steel beam and not the particle fragmenting. No traces relative to the sphere fuel elements were detected.*
   Particle speed deduced to be close to light speed. This measurement has been derived from the gravity sensor array data and the atmospheric distortions in the immediate vicinity.
3. *With regard to the steel strut penetration, first pass calculations indicate a particle speed of 261 million metres per second.*
   This is slightly below that of light at 279 million metres per second."

Bill had started to pale, he read on.

"Using the calculations as per the Appendix Section 2, the particle has a very small profile, possibly not much larger than a piece of grit. Moreover the particle was not inhibited by the density of air. The conclusion is that to achieve the huge speed with such a small particle would suggest it is an extremely dense object, with a huge compressed mass of unknown composition."

Then it came, Bill had grabbed the side of his table. He started to shake his head saying very quietly "I knew it……oh my gawd." Suddenly he felt very cold and a bad taste filled his mouth.

"It is possible that the particle is in fact a micro miniature black hole.
The consequences of creation and the passage of this object into the moon, create the distinct possibility that if this particle is indeed a black hole, then it is buried deep under the lunar surface. Secondly just after impact, it would have started to absorb matter in its immediate locality.

Just postulating this possibility is incredibly depressing, an unscientific term I admit, but one that I pray has not occurred. My calculations below are a rough estimate of how long it would take for the particle black hole to devour the entire moon."

Bill stared at the screen, he couldn't stop trembling.

10 am Monday 5th March
ESS, East Meon, UK

Getting up and going to work this Monday morning for Bill was the hardest thing ever.

"BILL !, Bill !...ah there you are " exclaimed John Creeson as he came through the doors of the lab. He stopped abruptly "You ok?"

Bill slowly turned from his slumped over the desk position, and greeted John.
"Oh morning John, yes I'm ok, just very tired."

John stopped for a moment, stared at Bill. He held a coffee in his hand. "You want a coffee Bill? Blow the cobwebs away? I don't mind going back and getting you a real one, not the machine stuff."
Bill leaned back, he was unshaven and wearing what looked like one of last week's shirts. "No thanks, I've just put one out."
John sat down in a nearby chair, he looked at Bill sympathetically "I heard from Jane, you know about July, so sorry to hear and I can't believe it."

Bill grimaced.
"Yeah, divorce on the cards. July's seeing some shit at RealRouge. You know John, I never really suspected. Deep down I wondered why she spent so much time away, but my subconscious seemed to give her the benefit of the doubt. "

John nodded, said “It’s a bastard; I’ve been there as you know. Didn’t spot it.”

Bill sighed “I think I was in denial, hoping what she said about her working away was true, like work demands and so on. Thursday night after she came home in a funny mood and went to bed, I decided to make love to a bottle of scotch.”
John laughed, caught his mirth and said “Can seem attractive at the time.”

“Well I had one awful hangover Friday morning and she told me of her affair over breakfast then stormed off to work. Strangest thing ever was some sort of greyish black mist following her.”

John frowned “Mist?”
Bill screwed his face in a puzzled look “It was the damndest thing John, despite my head, I’m sure I saw it.”
John hesitated, became a little detached, then said “Bill, maybe you should take a few days off, have a break. Then go and see a marital solicitor, get things moving you know.”

Bill looked at John, then stood up and said loudly, “John, I must confide in someone. You know me I stand no nonsense. I am a pragmatic guy, and yet I am coming across events and stuff that are very worrying….”
He paused, holding the back of the chair. He turned, looking out the lab window at the cloudy sky. Rain lashed and rattled on the glass, streaming down in rivulets.
“Maybe I do need a break, time to think, you know.”

John spoke “Divorces can be pretty stressful… ..”
Bill interrupted “John there is more. On Friday lunchtime I went for a walk up the old lane, get some fresh air, blow away the cobwebs, clear my mind. I think I fell asleep on the bench there. You see I had a dream and this guy dressed in some sort of white robe mentioned that the particle had caused *them* bother and that

it was a micro black hole! ……and I thought who the hell are '*them*'?"

John tried to interrupt again, "Well Bill, I…"

Bill raised his hand "So over the weekend I worked through Amit's notes on the particle and he raised the possibility that *it is a black hole* and as we know the damn thing is buried in the moon."
John said "I know."
Bill's voice increased in crescendo, said "and what's more naturally, the thing is slowly consuming the moon, oh my God John. What did you say ….you know?"

"Yes I know. I have been through Amit's notes myself. I revisited his calculations and there are flaws. Bill, the energy produced by our disastrous explosion was way short of anything needed to create a singularity. Even a tiny black hole."
Bill gathered himself, looked straight at John with an incredulous look "Really John? Then why am I getting bad feelings about this?"

"Bill, calm down. Even if it is a tiny black hole, it would take tens of thousands of years for it to consume the moon."
"Oh bloody hell; well that's some relief! …..I think not."

Jane had already come through the door.
"I heard the shouting, what on earth is going on?"

Bill looked at Jane, "Oh Jane, this is confidential."

She pointedly looked at John and said "Confidential? The moon is going to disappear, well I think people ought to know don't you think? and if you both hadn't followed the process through, after the moon is devoured by this black hole, it will be quite a bit bigger and the proximity of Earth makes it next in line……."

John pushed his hands down in the air shouting, “Whoa, whoa! Let’s talk facts here! Are we scientists or comedians! ”

Jane stepped backwards; she had never seen John lose his rag. John turned quickly on Bill, “What we discuss here, and this includes you Jane, does NOT, repeat NOT go beyond these four walls. Guesswork, dreams, tenuous links, ifs and maybes have no room here. Can you imagine the sheer panic if this hypothesis got out?”

Bill “Sorry John, totally with you. You are right, time to get a grip.”
Bill even with his seniority had backed into the mouse’s corner.
Jane was wide eyed, she said quietly straight at John “So there is no black hole buried in the moon?”
John curtly replied, “Until it has been proven and we acquire conclusive evidence, then yes, there is no black hole.”

Nothing further was said. The deathly silence could have been shattered by a pin drop.

In his office, Richard Armitage turned away from the monitor app on his screen and keyed a command to store the recording from the camera.

He took his pipe and feverishly pushed tobacco in as hard as he could.
It made his finger sore.
Going to the window he lit up, rapidly drawing and puffing out dense clouds of smoke.
He broke into a spasm of coughing and with his eyes streaming from the smoke he stared up at the faint white lunar crescent in the pale blue sky.

Noon that same Monday
Chez Nous, Denmead

Karen Durgass had gone over to her Mum and Dad's house. Need to concentrate.

Hard because her mind kept going back to the weird experiment they did on Friday. She touched the cross under her jumper. Munching the cheese and pickle sandwich, she then gulped down the last of her tea.
As the Executor of her Dad's Will, she needed to go through his papers.

She sighed "Oh Dad. Where to start?"

Her Dad's study was a mess, piles of books on the floor. Two large dishevelled bookcases, their contents in turmoil. Stacks of periodicals rested alongside similar ones of old newspapers and teetering towers of dusty bulging brown folders.
Dust was everywhere.
She had cleared his desk to make the only empty flat space in the room.

It was difficult to make out what part of the mess was caused by the burglary and what was her Dad's own untidiness. She glanced across at the forced glass cabinet in the corner. The door hung slightly open. Inside the shelves were bare, the old Greek vases and other objects had been stolen. The police had combed the place for fingerprints and other clues. Apparently the silver ware, a desk with money in and her mother's jewellery had been left untouched.
Nothing, only her Dad's fingerprints, a few of hers plus some from her long deceased Mum were found.
Obviously a gloves job.

Karen turned back to the desk and picked up the large brown envelope, marked

‘The Last Will and Testament of Edward A. Durgas’

She sat down and opened it.

“Dearest Karen

If you are reading this then I have departed this world for the next life.
I know you are grieving, but please find comfort in that I am now with your dear Mother.”

Karen welled up, “Oh dear, dear Dad…….”

“Firstly I leave all my estate to you, this includes this house and all its contents……………
………………………
Further more if you look at the included bank deposit statement I have left some money to you………”

She glanced at the bank slip, the balance was fifteen thousand pounds.

Then it read, *“There was more but we spent it on our Blue Sky holidays.”*
Karen frowned, ‘What’s he on about, Blue Sky? They went on a few cruises with Saga, but ….’
She paused seeing the edge of a blue envelope peeking out of the one containing the Will. Pulling it out she saw the words ‘Blue Sky’, she tore the small envelope open, pulling out a letter.
Her countenance wrinkled.

“Karen, once you have read this, either hide it somewhere very safe, or destroy it now.”

She flipped through some papers in the blue envelope and pulled out the bank statement, her eyes quickly scanned down to the balance at the bottom of the sheet.

She gasped and put her hand to her mouth.

"Oh Dad, where did you get all this money?"
The bottom line read just over one million pounds. The date was some years ago.

"Over time I have withdrawn this cash and hidden it for you. This is to counter any suspicion and also inheritance tax which I hate. Go to the Castle in Colchester and about half way along the east wall at the base, you will see some brownish stones. Look for one with tiny orange flecks. It looks cemented in, but cement was not used. With a sharp blade the brick will come loose. In the package there are some puzzles and only you will be able to solve them in order to determine the whereabouts of this money.
The significance of the castle is that its foundations are those of the Roman temple that Queen Boudica sacked and burnt back in 61 AD.
There are spiritual links.
To repeat, please destroy this blue envelope and all its contents as soon as possible."

'Oh Dad, you crafty devil. ' thought Karen.

Continuing with the Blue Sky envelope, she read,

"Dear daughter, what I must tell you now is of paramount importance.
As of the time of making this will I am about to embark on a mission to the Island of Anglesey. I have determined through much research that an ancient relic owned by the Druids is buried there. This artefact is a sword and belonged to Queen Boudica's father. As you may know, Queen Boudica was the leader of the Iceni tribe in Norfolk.
This sword has a very special significance and it is possible that her father was a custodian without knowing of its powers. Yes powers. In conjunction with your Heart of Grace cross, it gives

enormous protection to the holder. I sincerely hope that I have found it by the time you read this.
There are factions that are also searching for this sword and indeed your cross.
If I manage to get the sword to you, take great care my daughter as I have discovered that there are people that will kill for either of these objects."

'Yes I have found that out dear father." thought Karen, as she cast her mind back to John's perilous mission to the ancient Iron Age village near Moefre in Anglesey.
Discovering the sword, then his narrow escape from the snarling dog and those men. She shivered at the thought.

"The contents of this Blue Sky envelope must be kept secret, burn if necessary, memorising as much as possible. In my desk behind a false back, there are research papers and maps of extreme importance.

During this research I have uncovered the following.
I know there is at least one more artefact, possibly two. The first is an ancient helmet that will 'power up' in the vicinity of your cross and the sword, although it may have independent powers of its own. The helmet is almost certainly in the wreck of King Xerxes flagship, which lies off the coast of Skiathos. This wreck over the years has been salvaged secretly by Irving Dekker. He may well have discovered this helmet, I just don't know. The second artefact if it exists, may be some sort of wrist bracelet. The old scriptures and markings I have investigated are very vague.

Now most important of all.
I will try to convey what I know about the mystical powers of these objects, an issue that must torment you……"

The doorbell rang.

Karen jumped, she looked up quickly, who could that be?
She replaced the papers back into the envelope and walked into the front lounge and peered through the lace curtains. A person's shadow could be seen coming from the front doorstep. She couldn't quite see as the front door had a deep porch.

Tentatively she put the door chain on and then opened the door a fraction.
"Yes, who is it?"
"Your postman."

Karen laughed inwardly and slid back the chain, opening the door. He handed her a bunch of mail with a parcel.

Her pulse had quickened a tad.
She was naturally jumpy these days.
Maybe talk to Anne Whitfield again, her close friend and spiritual confidant.

Her mind wandered to John her boyfriend. Thank god for John, difficult to imagine coping with all of life's demands without him. Events seem to be accelerating.
After their reunion in Queen Alexandra hospital, John and Karen had agreed never to spend another night without each other.
Not always easy when you live in different houses. Giving up your independence doesn't happen overnight.

They had forged a bond, a beautiful relationship. As work colleagues it was tricky to hide all emotion, but being together sustained them. She paused, thinking, 'yes he was starting to warm to my spiritual abilities and perceptions.'

Yet so much was in the realm of the unknown. She knew her particular situation with her spiritual talents and her astrophysics skills, gave a unique insight into the physical and spiritual worlds. Again she dwelt on the fact that within reach was an enlightenment, the scope of which may be beyond what she could handle.

The known spiritual worlds a tiny, tiny fraction of what could really be out there.

If only John could come onboard.
John the sceptic, wanting scientific explanations for everything.
She recalled his frustration at not knowing how the blue light had been generated from their artefacts.
She thought 'Was the light of a spiritual origin, or perhaps some very advanced technology?'

She had a far away look, glancing through the window up at the sky.
'Protection? Against what?'

All of a sudden Karen felt alone and awfully vulnerable.
She felt chilly.

Walking back to the study, she took out her father's Blue Sky instructions again.

"...mystical powers of these objects……… I have made some inroads into a staggering hypothesis that if true is extraordinary. The Chinese have established a base on the moon in a particular location. Ancient Chinese mythology indicates that this particular place holds 'safety for mankind'. This is the best interpretation I have been able to make in my crude translations. The cross and sword artefacts are extraordinary items and my increasing suspicions are that they are not man made.
If true, this information in itself is incredulous.

Also I have made observations of a curious phenomenon. It is connected with many religious buildings such as churches, mosques and temples around the world.

All my notes on this are with my colleague Quentin Huxley, who I first worked with at the university. You know him. He has been retired for many years now and lives in Southwick.
I haven't been in touch with Quentin for probably six months and although he has become somewhat of a recluse he would make you very welcome. Be very careful as this information is dynamite.

Dearest daughter this is an incredible burden for you to bear, but the decision is yours. You may decide not to become involved, forget all this and bury the artefacts deep in some far way location and have no more to do with them.
That is perfectly ok and I would understand why.
All I can ask of you is to be aware of events that are bigger than mankind, use your spirituality to interpret the meanings of these. Most important of all is to pre-empt a possible threat that is almost beyond comprehension.

All my love always, Dad x."

Karen frowned hard 'threat almost beyond comprehension' ....what the hell do you mean Dad?' Then she thought about Sabrina's meeting and her mentioning of a threat too. 'Same one?'

For some reason Karen's mind drifted back to the hundreds of strange hair like shafts of light arising around the Earth, that she had discovered back in January. They had been highlighted by the arriving gravity waves from the supernova.
Yet it was no ordinary light, it was not within the known spectrum and thus invisible. Even Jane with her spectroscopy skills couldn't explain these tiny light shafts.
Karen puzzled on what they could be. The gravity waves would magnify any object that distorted space and time. 'What the devil are they?'

A profound thought hit her.
'Oh my… it is because it is light… *but not of our space and time.*'

Then it slowly dawned on her.
'No can't be? Surely not?.. Am I the first to see this?'

Her mind flitted to her conversation with Anne Whitfield that chilly night in the Denmead Queen pub. 'We are made of light, our souls are part of this light.'
Karen denied what she had deduced.
Meticulous analysis was needed, but the thought excited her. If true this revelation was both incredible and beautiful.

These tiny faint spikes of light were the individual transferences of souls into the spiritual world after a human death.

'My God...............' Her pulse thumped hard.

After a long pause, she gathered her thoughts and refilled the Will pocket.
Then she shuffled through the mail that had just arrived.
'Hmmm mostly junk mail, the inevitable pizza flyer, and a few periodical wraps'

The parcel was a bundle of books returned from a colleague friend of her Dad's.
Then she looked closer at one letter.
It had a Greek postmark on a Greek stamp.
It was a pretty stamp depicting a brightly coloured harbour, the blue sea intense and many yachts moored there. The little bay was surrounded by a mixture of whitewashed and pastel coloured houses.
All with ochre terra cotta roofs scattered amongst scraggy trees and down below people swimming just off the beach.
She casually opened it and withdrew the letter inside.

"Hello Edward
I writing to you as I have been unable to get to talk on phone.
I apologise. My English is little.

My name is Angelo Drivas and I live in Skiathos, Greece with Ma and Pa.
They are Sarra and Silenos Drivas. Pa is Mayor of Skiathos.
Why I write this?"

It is because I know you are my real father..."

Karen's hand went to her mouth.
"Oh my God!"

The letter slipped out of her hands and onto the floor.
"What.... WHAT? oh Dad .... no.... it must be some sort of begging letter."

She snatched it up and continued reading,

"............you see I have the same red birthmark as you. It is on my ankle and Irving Dekker said that you have the same mark on your ankle. He saw from photograph.
It is shape of serpent. This is not new for me. Long time I have felt, that my brothers and sisters are different."

Karen gasped. She stood up holding the letter with one hand and turned to look at the beach photo of her Mum and Dad on the mantlepiece. She already knew, but there it was that wiggly red line on his ankle. She glanced at her own leg reminding herself of her own human tattoo, the faint port wine stain.

"So Edward, if you had no idea I am sorry to do this. But I need to see you.
Please phone me.

Love from Angelo."

Karen looked at the bottom, a telephone number had been scribbled under an email address.

Then she felt the implication sink in, her half brother. No longer was she the only child.

She puffed, sucked through her teeth.
Out loud she exclaimed "God, things just keep happening, well I never…. a brother."

Her eyes filled up and a little tear trickled down her cheek.

Chapter 5

7.30 pm Wednesday 14th March
Karen Durgas's House, Cowplain

Karen was grinning, feeling a number of emotions and it wasn't wholly the large glass of wine she had just put away.
They had booked a last minute holiday, wonderful.

She looked across at John. He stood holding and staring at the newspaper.
Despite the authorities trying to hush things up, their escapade in north Wales, then their kidnapping by the Chinese submarine had made headline news.

"God, look at that Karen, now the whole flippin world knows about us, even our gravity wave discoveries."
"Yes, fame… Isn't it fabulous John? 'Top physicists in narrow escape' ha!"
She laughed, "Well it's out now and to be honest John, I am a little relieved, all that secrecy, all that pressure on us."
John Creeson was a serious man, a bit too serious at times.
The fact was he tended to look serious even when he wasn't.

He pulled a face "But Karen, now we have a different pressure, the bloody media."
She got up, grabbed his hand and pulled him back on the sofa, then picked up his untouched wine and handed it to him.

"Come on John, loosen up, and relax. It's not our problem; let the likes of Richard Armitage and his bosses at Whitehall worry about it now."
John took a gulp, then smiled, the red wine on his teeth giving them a weird violet stain.
Karen burst out laughing, "Ha ha …. if you stay serious with those teeth, I think Count Dracula could have competition." John

gave her a strange glaring look and then guffawed loudly. Karen jumped, screwing her eyes at him. "John!"

After a pause, he said "You're right Karen and do you know what, there is no mention of Bill. You see he actually spotted the anomaly first when we saw the supernova data. Poor Bill so desperate for real fame. His day will come I'm sure."
Karen frowned and quickly replied "Yes, by blowing us all up with his new gravity engine…."
John "Not if I can help it and there are many people keeping an eye on him and his group to ensure that any live testing doesn't happen. As we know this thing can only be tested safely in outer space, far out of Earth's orbit."

Karen pondered "Bill seems very anxious these days, you know, more than usual.
I guess what with July divorcing him, that's added to his stress levels, but I'm….I'm not sure…. he seems distracted."
John looked puzzled said "Yes he is a trifle disturbed, do you know what he thinks he has uncovered?"
Karen stared at John, "Well, there have been rumours. Jane was angry about something, said it was to do with the explosion in the laboratory, but she wouldn't say what it was."
John took a deep breath, sighed, and said "Well you ought to know. Bill through some sort of premonition believes the explosion particle that impacted close to the Chinese moon base, is in fact a miniature black hole."
He waited, watching Karen's face.
Quickly her colour drained, he could see she was working through the implications.
"Oh my God John, my God….. And is this particle or black hole still in the moon or has it passed out the other side?"
"I checked Amit and Jane's work and there were no trails showing a possible exit position from the moon. So yes the particle is still under the lunar surface. I did…."
Karen interrupted him, her voice growing louder, "Oh goodness, that means if it is a black hole, our moon will eventually disappear.

The thought is unbearable John, because we, the Earth would be next!"
"Yes I agree a very scary prospect, but I did some checks on the calculations and there are errors, it is extremely unlikely that it is a black hole Karen."

"How can you be sure? Bill and Conrad's *planned explosion*, compressed all those rare elements, some fissionable into a horrendous explosion, powerful enough to create a thumping big gravity wave that hurled that particle at the moon. The uranium was completely consumed John, yet a nuclear explosion didn't happen, or did it?
Or maybe a malfunctioning fusion reaction?"

"Karen, I know we have yet to fully understand what happened. I am still doing analytical work, computer modelling to try and understand what happened. As I said to Bill, the energies released were too small to create a black hole, even a tiny one. Until we complete our analysis, this is absolutely top secret.
We cannot afford for it to become public."

Karen wide eyed, put the side of her hand in her mouth and subconsciously started to bite. "Oh John.........what can we do?"
"I think the Americans know more. Bill confided in them about our particle and where it went. Ming Zhao and Colonel Arrack Mondone have shown unusual interest. It seems they have been conducting their own investigations into the moon base. We need to meet them again and work through this, sharing our technologies."

She replied "I'll drink to that." and downed her wine.

He topped up her glass, then his.
"Come on Karen let's eat before the wine goes to our heads."

She thought 'there's not enough wine in England to numb tonight's revelations.'

Mid morning Saturday 17th March
On the M25 motorway to Gatwick Airport, UK

John gripped the steering wheel and sighed; he turned to Karen, and then grinned.
"At last….. we're off, holiday here we come."
Karen smiled and squeezed his leg, said "Brilliant John, we so need this break, pity it's only a week but it will be enough. Escape, freedom and peace for a little while."

"Yeah, Armitage wants us back on the project as soon as."
John frowned as he turned back to the windscreen. "He has something up his sleeve you know. Said it could wait until we get back, left me dangling, wondering."

Karen became serious, "He can wait too. We hold all the cards, he is just a manager, and he can be replaced. Not like us almost indispensable."
They laughed together.

She continued, "You know John there are many things swinging our way."
He glanced across, said "I feel it Karen and your spirituality is becoming something that I can understand now. I get um… I guess a sort of joining sense with you."

Karen felt momentarily warm, comfortable, starting to know her destiny, but a cold knot grew inside her stomach, as she tried to play out the future.
A destiny that seemed dark, far away, yet perilous.

The motorway was heaving with traffic, the inside full of large lorries, tankers and slow cars sandwiched in between. After a while, the M23 turning for Gatwick Airport came up. Then the airport was on them. Dropping the hire car at the rental office, they heaved their luggage onto the convenience bus and numbed the ride to the terminal.

Finally post check-in, Karen sat heavily into the nearest of the seats with her coffee.
John followed with a tea.
"Ouch god that's hot !" she cursed "These insulated polystyrene cups are good, but it takes ages for your drink to cool. Burnt my tongue."
John looked at her, pulled a sympathetic face and bit into a cereal bar.

Crunching away, he looked at the tickets, two to the island of La Palma, Canary Islands, way out in the Atlantic Ocean.
"Weather should be ok; we could see twenty degrees or more. Make a change from our chilly weather." He smiled, swallowed, then leant across and kissed Karen, their eyes locked dreamily. She held him for a moment, they kissed again slowly.
She wanted to taste the oat and honey again.

The island of La Palma was at the western edge of the Canary Islands, an almost forgotten little Spanish paradise. Whilst Tenerife, Lanzarote and Gran Canaria had their individual charms, La Palma was quieter, no club 18-30 and no lager louts.

The forest covered island loomed in the window, a huge dark green, almost extinct volcano greeted them. As their plane approached at low level, the crinkly mountain rose high straight out of the sea.

"Oh John, look at that!"
He peered over Karen's shoulder past her window seat.
"Wow, so green and lush, nothing like I expected. Gina at the travel agent said we would love it."

The island filled their vision. Large, steep rutted mountainous sides covered in pine forests, then ragged deep gorges running and forking into the sea.
Going up three thousand metres, the steep rising, forested volcano walls, stood stark against the clear sky. There down at almost sea

level, was the airport, clinging to the edge of the island, practically hanging out over the sea.
The runway looked tiny.

Their plane banked sharply and rapidly landed.

"Oh err, God that was a trick landing." exclaimed John "For a moment I thought we would overshoot into the water!"

After picking up their Nissan 4x4 and arriving in Los Cancajos, John said "Come on let's dump our bags in the chalet and get some sea air."

The sun was still high in the crystal clear sky.
Quiet, just the waves crashing lullaby greeted them as they joined a few couples hand in hand strolling along the meandering coastal path.

"I love this John."
She held his hand tight. Karen pondered to herself, 'To be with, to stroll with, to chat and laugh with that person who is yours, is so nice'.

John looked at her then out to the sea's misty horizon, then up into the brilliant blue sky. "Karen, it is so good to get away. Just the two of us, a bit of time together without any distractions."
He winked at her.

Then he continued, "… and yet that thing is still there, ok millions of miles behind us now, but still there….."

Karen sighed "John, we need to forget work."
John "It is difficult Karen. My mind churns you know. What with your cross and the sword, just what are they? What is their function? Are their makers long gone, dead even?"
"Come on let's get a drink."
She tried to ignore his questions, just for now.

Back towards the main road, they strolled past a small stone walled field.
"Hey look!" exclaimed Karen "All those banana trees."
There over the wall the field was full of the stubby palm like trees.
They had large leaves, the lower ones brownish and dishevelled, hanging towards the dusty ground.
She pointed "There see, bunches of green bananas."
John "Crikey yes, now you wouldn't think it would be warm enough in the Canaries to grow bananas?"

Later that day.

Karen looked all around.

The bar, lined with tasty tapas samples, was cosy, dimly lit and welcome.
Across the ceiling were draped various dried sprigs of unknown shrubbery, possibly hops.
Dominating the restaurant corners were tall large leaved green shrubs in terracotta pots.

Outside, darkness had descended quickly.
Fresh flowers and bright candles adorned the tables.
Behind the bar some Spanish music quietly drifted across and the attentive barman made sure they got refills quickly.

Several beers later, tongues started to loosen.
John had become a little red faced.
He had cracked a couple of extremely funny jokes.
Karen was almost wetting herself, "Ha…hahahah .. God … hmmm."
She carried on laughing "Ha ha… look at you, glowing like a beacon!"
John just grinned.
Karen said "Come on let's have a look at the menu, get something to eat."

Over the meal she paused, looked at John, he seemed fairly lucid despite the bottle of wine they had now cracked open.
"John?" He looked up, she had that serious look, "John, I have a feeling, almost a premonition."
"Well let's hear it."
She pulled an impatient face, "You need to believe in me John. I am having and receiving some sort of enlightenment. It is part of me, do you sense it?"
"I think so, I want to understand and believe the stuff you say Karen, it's just that….."

She put a hand on his and said "You just need to trust me. Can I explain?"
"Sure I'm all ears Karen."

"Ok where to begin? Well I had a chat with Anne Whitfield. It was before our awful time in Wales. You see she explained her recent journeys through life."

The restaurant was nearly empty; an elderly couple were eating across the room.
A solitary grey haired guy had finished his meal and was engrossed in a newspaper.

Karen continued quietly "I have had some experiences through my Shamanic circle, but Anne has been down the hypnotherapy path. I've done some reading on the subject."
She looked at John and waited.
He said "Ok, tell me more."

"Hypnotherapy John is not always hypnosis based. It can allow you to very deeply relax and connect with your inner soul. The therapist guides you on your journey, but it is not suggestive. Anne has experienced several sessions and has regressed back into her past. A past period that involved many of her human lives."

John's eyes widened, he picked up his glass and gulped, then started to say, "Well that's all very well, re-incarnation is not really my……"
Karen cut him short "Stay with me John, there is more. I need to follow this path to provide light on my past and possibly my future. As you know I have had these dreams using my cross to see down Crackwell, our anomaly, the portal we think."
John sighed inwardly, gulped more wine and said "Dreams yes. If only we could perceive your visions with our equipment, you know to examine any corridor which you say exists, but using our technology."

She had started talking about work……

Karen stopped and then she looked out through the restaurant window.
She paused, took a breath, said "I'm thinking of doing the same, you know via hypnotherapy. I want to understand where I come from."

John reflected, sat back in his chair and said something unusual for him.
"Maybe I should join you? I need to broaden my view, perhaps to the edge of my comfort zones."
He was serious.

Karen looked into his eyes; she leaned towards him across the small table.
"You should, but you will need to prepare yourself beforehand. Meditation is a good start, probably a few weeks of that to begin with."
He replied "I see, ok maybe you can help me or I can join a group?"
Karen smiled "Yes, both I think."
John said "I want to believe you and maybe the only way is for me to experience what you do. Trouble is, you have a spiritual gift Karen, a head start. So I may fail anyway."

She continued "Failure doesn't come into it. If you approach this openly then there is a way for everyone. If you allow your mind to relax and connect to your soul, you will make progress. I wish and hope you can, this is a huge burden for me alone. If I could include say Anne Whitfield into our technical confidence, it will provide relief for me." Karen paused, " She has the way, John."

"How Karen? we are bound by the Official Secrets Act, ESS secrecy and security and all that."

She looked away, remembering the day at Langstone harbour with her mum Jenny.
The cancer had taken Jenny from her five months ago.
"Well if my mum were still alive I would have no hesitancy in sharing with her right now."
John was thinking hard. He said "If you really trust Anne and she is able to convince me of her reliability, then perhaps we can give her limited information about Crackwell and see what the two of you can reveal."

Karen took John's hand in hers, she knew he needed reassurance badly, something extra, anything extra….. To yes, help humanity. Deep down her shamanic feelings gave rise to obscure worries… distant warning bells.

"John, if there is danger with Crackwell, and if Anne and I can illuminate or discover more about it now, say through a dreaming session. Then we may be able to prepare mankind early…. early enough to understand and do what is necessary…. I guess before the spacecrafts that launch early next year as it might just be too late then."
"Too late?"
Karen sighed "I know this spiritual stuff doesn't have a scientific basis, but I can bridge both given time, I know it or I could die trying."
He gasped, "Karen, what are you saying?"

She replied “I seem to have a destiny. A feeling I have is strongly willing me to engage spiritual people like myself in some important global mission. So important, that my life is inconsequential.”

“Hell Karen don’t say that….”
He paused, and then said, “But you are right we should pursue this. Any additional information we can glean would be very useful.
Just need to work out how to ‘officialise this’. The greatest obstacle is probably convincing the authorities about what you discover.”
She nodded, paused looked at him strangely and said, “Maybe they don’t need to know for now. Our revelations might give us the direction we need. What I mean is that we need to divulge to the right people. People that really matter and can do the right thing.”
John repeated “Yes, do the right thing.”
Thinking ‘Whatever the hell that might be.’

Finishing the last of the wine, John then took care of the bill.

Walking back to their apartment, He looked up at the sky.
“My God look at that! So black, absolutely full of stars. Stunning! There see? Above Orion’s belt, see the star Betelgeuse, it has changed colour; the red is now a whitish pink I believe. Also notice a tiny haze around what’s left of the star, that’s probably its nebula, all the gases and material spreading out from the supernova explosion.”

Back in January, the distant giant red star Betelgeuse had exploded.
Cosmologists called it a supernova event. The explosion had generated a gravity wave which on its arrival at Earth, caused an underwater earthquake, followed by a tsunami in Hawaii.
Also the gravity wave and then the gamma waves illuminated the tiny portal in space, not far from our moon. They had dubbed it Crackwell.

She stopped and stared, said "That supernova has driven everything that has happened lately........."
Karen trailed off; she reached up with her hand as though to grab a piece of outer space. She grasped and then pulled her hand back. "Need to take hold, to grapple, absorb and just be..."
John wobbled a bit, he checked his balance touching Karen's arm. Very good wine that.

"Carry on Karen, I'm with you."
"Come here, hold onto me John. I need you to be my rock, to weave our way safely through whatever may come....."
John faltered and looked at her wide eyed, exclaimed, "Karen, I shall draw my sword and brace my shield and go into yonder battle!..." he stumbled on the path "ooh aarh.... I think the wine has gone to our heads!"
She laughed, holding him, as they wobbled onwards.

Karen thought 'When I get back I will talk to Sabrina and Anne again, we need to combine our feelings and plans. Also I need to seriously think about giving up alcohol. My dreaming destiny requires an uncluttered and clear mind.'

Locking the door, they started to undress, the same thing on their minds.
A night of passion.
The effects of the beer and wine tumbled them into bed, clothes strewn all over the floor.

Frantic, fumbling, love making. They caressed clinging together.

Karen shuddered as she approached ecstasy again and again.
"Oooh... mmm...aaahhh.... John come here and kiss me..."

All too soon it was over, mega tired, a lot of alcohol and the long day of travel had taken their toll.
The night of passion was actually about twenty minutes.

Entwined they quickly entered the land of Nod, falling into the deepest of slumbers.

The next morning

It was 10am before they left the apartment and strolled down to the coast.
A few high clouds scudded across the deepest blue backdrop.
Walking along the snaking path, they followed its careering track around the charcoal coloured lava foreshore. Dark ragged outcrops of hard sharp rock were everywhere, contrasting with small clumps of bright green trees.
Even the sand was pounded lava rock, a sort of fine grey black gravel.

The sea came in great big rollers, crashing and trying to scour the solidified lava.
Above the foaming restless waters, rose the forested volcano walls soaring steeply into a high misty top.
A brooding mountain, stark and still.

Further on they saw a solitary middle aged guy, sitting down. He was painting the bay that stretched across to Santa Cruz de la Palma, the capital city of the island.
The man wore a panama hat, paint palette in his left hand, brush in his teeth, as he searched for something in his paint box.

As they drew close, Karen gave a little gasp. “I think I know him.”
John turned to her “Oh really?”
“Yes I’m sure……….Hello there, ooh nice painting…. Are you from England?”
“Hello… yes, I am.”
He pushed back his hat over long silver hair. His tanned face broke into a brilliant smile. She continued, “Do you know Langstone harbour, the Royal Oak pub. I think you took a photo of my Mum and me there?”

He scratched his chin, and then said "Why yes I do remember now, bit of a while ago. How is your Mum?"
Karen pensively said, "I'm afraid she was very ill and passed away not long after you took that picture. I treasure it."
"Oh, I'm so sorry to hear. Guess she is in a better place now? By the way I'm Phil." His vanishing smile reappeared.
Both Karen and John shook his hand.
"Karen. This is my partner John." John shook hands. "Have you painted much here?"

"Oh a few landscapes, the scenery is breathtaking. I seem to have quite a few unfinished you know. I take some photos then complete them when I get back home."
He grinned.
A shapely, blonde woman approached. She wore a brightly coloured wrap over her beach suit contrasting her deep suntan. Her long hair and wrap fluttered in the breeze.
"Hello" she smiled, white teeth flashing in the sunlight. Phil turned, then said to Karen and John, "Ah let me introduce Brianna, she mixes my paints you know……." He gave a wicked chuckle.

They laughed and walked on, waving a goodbye. Phil and Brianna returned the gesture, and then he turned back to his painting and grabbed two tubes of paint.
Then part merging their dark and medium colours in the palette with the merest of water. Grabbing a great glob of paint on the brush, he pulled a freckled, crinkly, dark lava crag across the rough white paper.

Karen breathed deeply, taking in the fresh salty sea air, so nice, such an escape.
They stopped further on at a little beach café.

John looked over his teacup and was about to say something when his phone chimed.

He pulled it out and squinted at the screen. Bright sunshine was streaming in beams through the café window frame. They created alternate white patches and contrasting dark shadows inside.
Karen said "Not work is it?"
John "Ah, let me see. Hmmm… text from Armitage, says he has sent an email that cannot wait."
Karen pulled a face and muttered "Bugger him. We're on holiday."
John read on, then he looked up, his face pained, "Don't think this can wait Karen, something has happened to the anomaly, Crackwell."
Karen suddenly grew serious, she said quietly, "What? …like what John?"

"They think it has grown enormous.
Ok it's behind us now, going on in its own orbit. From telescope and satellite observations, a large area of space has become visibly distorted."
Karen wide eyed said, "What the devil? ….."
John continued "Well, the distortion is slight but everything behind, stars, planets, galaxies and so on, are just slightly out of focus. The anomaly itself is still invisible. Armitage says to await further instructions."

"Does he now? It must be changing its fabric………how big John?"

"Rough estimates are around…oh Jesus……. they reckon thousands of miles in diameter……possibly around eight thousand…"

Karen turned pale, "That's… oh my… …..nearly the size of the Earth."

Chapter 6

Late afternoon. Saturday 17th March
On board the yacht Nemain.
Dell Quay Estuary, Sussex, UK

"Xiu, have we received the updated meeting agenda?"

In Steven Crowley's yacht, she looked up from the computer desk.
"Nothing yet, Steven."

Steven frowned, replied "Ok, keep an eye out for it."
He inhaled deeply on the Greek cigarette and blew out a column of blue smoke.
"So why does Ming call you Lei?"
Xiu pensively turned around, said "Xiu is my middle name, sometimes I prefer it."
Steven took another drag and slowly exhaled, "So what do you prefer between us?"
She got up, walked over and kissed him, "Call me Lei. Saves the confusion my love."
He pulled her close kissing her again, jewel blue eyes looking into hers, his massive tall frame almost engulfing her petite form.
"Lei it is then."
He smiled.

She stared into his shining eyes; he had a charm, a mystical hypnotic look.
"Steven, you heard back from the British police about the artefacts they seem to have confiscated?"
"No, and my solicitor is trying to get them back. There is a lot of money tied up there. Strange now as Edward Durgas is dead and he cannot pay me the shipping cost.
Irving Dekker was naturally very agitated when I told him about our incident in the Irish Sea. So I reckon those old vases and particularly that emerald necklace could be worth a fortune."

"The police must sense their value. They said our shipping documents were invalid?"
Steven had a sombre look. "They may say that. Technically when they boarded the Nemain we were still in international waters, so they cannot automatically confiscate them. Taking our weapons was out of order too."

The yacht bobbed gently in the swell, high tide an hour away.
He climbed the few stairs to the cockpit, stood on the deck and reconnoitred the opposite bank.
The Crown and Anchor pub was busy, a few people braving the chilly outside patio. Wooden benches were dotted with couples and a couple of families eating a late lunch.
"Tea I think….." He went down below to the galley.

As they sat drinking the brown stuff, Steven waded through the digestive biscuits.
Lei sidled closer to him, grabbed his arm and said "Steven, we've known each other what? … Must be two years now."
He nodded and inquiringly cocked his head at her.
"Your meetings with these secret Druid people, can you not tell me more?"
"Yes Lei I'm glad you asked. As you know, they are a very special group of people, and we have a mission that is crucial."
She looked at him, said "Well it's time Steven."
He was about to talk when the radio burst into life.
"Purple Rain to Easy Rider… come in."
It repeated several times.
Crowey got up and took the mic. "Easy Rider to Purple Rain. I read you, when will you arrive? And have you the destination."

"We believe early this evening, about 7pm, repeat 7pm. Target is the Orange Grove. Do you copy?"
"Yes we copy both, see you then."
Messages continued coming in, with various codenames spoken. Steven acknowledged them all.

He had assigned codenames to all, even with encrypted radio links.

Lei repeated her question, "Steven?"
He looked at her, his long hair held back by a purple bandana around his forehead. Pausing he tapped a fresh cigarette endways on the table and rubbed his beard.
"Lei, if I tell you, there comes with it a huge responsibility. There are quarters that will torture you for this information?"

A question, a testing of her strength and loyalty.

"Tell me Steven. After all my work, I need to see the bigger picture."

"Yes I know, you have a right and your researches have been key to our mission.
We are in this together. Which means it remains our secret. The identities of these people *must, I repeat must,* be kept secret."

She nodded to concur, and then reflected, 'This life makes me happy, my research, our Mediterranean travels are fun. Steven my lover.'
Her thoughts paused, she looked slightly away and through one of the yacht's portholes, 'But I do I love him?..... I don't know.'

"You know I am careful Steven."

"Yes, I do Lei. Well I can tell you so much. I dare say your Chinese researches will help us out again. There are twelve members including myself. Your skills and knowledge are becoming critical to our organisation.
Your contact with the US operation through your sister is extremely useful."
She gave him a stern reminding look.
He took her hand.

"Of course, her identity will remain hidden and I always recognise the trust you place in me, Lei."
She relaxed, smiled and moved close to him.
"As you know, we are the Druid Circle for the United Peoples Church."
Continuing he said "Some you will not know, some you will. Like Irving Dekker our Greek contact. July Craswell is a member; she is an executive at RealRouge Cosmetics and the wife of Bill Craswell. As you know he works at the European Space Systems centre. She is a very useful information source.

Lei thought again of Dekker, their contact man for the Greek stuff, artefacts and cigarettes. A slippery American if she ever saw one.
Steven went on, "A guy from South Africa, Horst Van De Groot, is a member. He has many connections globally."
Lei remained quiet, her face non-descript. "Must be hard to stay in touch with all these far flung people?" she exclaimed.
Steven smiled "Can be tricky at times."
He carried on, "…and then there is Maxwell Blackwood, the Scientologist. You may know that he is married to Christine who happens to be John Creeson's sister."
Lei spoke, "Ah yes, Christine. She belongs to Karen Durgas's shamanic group."

The feelers of Steven Crowley had penetrated far.

Steven continued "Yeah. As we know Karen is a gifted physicist and Dekker has been asking questions. Too many we think about John and Karen. I suspect the man is up to something."

Lei's eyes opened, she said "…and the others?"
Steven replied "They are …. Elaine Murphy, she is an Irish politician, Nadir Patel a billionaire who runs many commercial enterprises, Valentin Goryunov, ex-KGB who now lives in the west.
Nigel Humble a close friend of mine, he works in the UK security industry and Craig Akerman, a NASA engineer. Finally our IT

systems expert, Bruce Jones is unable to make it. He is based in Australia."

He frowned for just a second. Steven Crowley was shrewd and particularly clandestine in his work.

"Wow, some collection Steven! … how did you select them?"
He smiled, his face momentarily showing great wisdom, almost beyond his years.

"Yes, the mix can make for our meetings to get very fiery at times, which is a good thing. We get to see many valuable view points. Also behind each of us are many individuals, even entire organisations and companies that work for this group. I have taken years to find and include these people in our circle."

Lei pondered at the revealing of so many names.
Names that could be her undoing.

He continued, "Also persuading some of them to join what can appear to be a strange circle was not easy. My mission is to include certain characters who will be of great value, but also so I can monitor them."
She followed his every word.
Steven, "There was another, making us thirteen back then, but he died in an unfortunate car crash. His name is irrelevant now."

He walked across to the computer, said "Ah here it is." He tapped the keyboard and the printer burst into life.
Then Steven looked at his watch "Need to go soon, our venue is on Hayling Island. Smart dress I think is the order tonight."
He had changed into a dark grey suit, blue shirt and tied his hair back in a pony tail.
Lei wore a charcoal trouser suit and a light red blouse to match her lipstick.
Steven nodded his approval.
'He seems extra particular tonight' she thought.

"Ok let's go." He said grabbing a large holdall.

They took the dinghy ashore, tied up and then up to Steven's blue Mondeo.
Starting up and driving down the lane, he reached under the steering wheel and pressed the hidden switch twice. The number plates electronically changed to display a different registration.
A valid one for the car model and colour, ……but a registration belonging to some company fleet car.

They parked in the Hayling Billy pub car park.
A sad scene to behold, the once bustling railway pub had its doors and windows boarded up.
At the entrance, on a now bare mound of earth once stood one of the little steam train engines. A beautiful reminder of the steam railway that ran from Havant, going almost all the way southwards along the coastal edge of Hayling Island to deliver happy holidaymakers to the sandy beaches.
Steven mentioned that he remembered his parents talking about railway trips for their summer holidays to Hayling beach.

Lei had a puzzled look, she said "Orange Grove, what does that mean? A code name perhaps?"
Steven smiled and looked at her as they walked southerly down the street.
He pointed to a small row of shops opposite with a little parking lay-by, "See those two shops, the cycle shop and the charity store?"
She nodded.
"Well they were once one long café with an entrance where the charity shop is.
My Dad used to ride his motorcycle here. It had a large orange frontage with the words 'The Orange Grove' "
"Ah that's cool."

Steven chuckled, "What's more he told me a story. One dark night the café was empty except for him and his two biker mates.

They jokingly said to Pete the café owner who they knew quite well, 'do you get any trouble here?' "
Lei said "And? …"
"Well Pete whipped out this huge machete knife from underneath the counter saying not often and grinned."
Lei laughed.
"And what's more on that dark night, Dad said he looked through the café window back up the main road and he saw all these lights approaching, thinking that's not car lights.
Sure enough just about the whole chapter of the DeadForEver Hell's Angels roared in on their motorcycles. He said must have been about thirty of them."
"What happened then?"

Steven continued "Well Dad said he shit himself. They were sitting right at the back of the café and would have to pass all these Hell's Angels to get out.
He said it was the days before wearing crash helmets became law and none of the Angels wore them.
The grubby bikers all arrived with long dirty, scraggy, wind blown hair and their red eyes streaming water down their cheeks from the wind. They wore crusty, unwashed, jeans blackened with engine oil, complimenting tatty leather jackets worn over their waistcoat colours."
Lei her eyes aglow uttered, "Hell! Yes HELL ha ha, must have been a scary sight?"

"Yeah, Dad said they lived up to their name!"
Steven went on, "Dad was waiting for Pete to get his machete out at the first sign of trouble. You see, these guys had a fearsome reputation, you know criminal activities, heavy drinkers, drugs and possibly guns……
But do you know what? Dad said the DeadForEver were all as meek as kittens, queuing quietly for hot coffee!
And sometime later Dad and his mates, casually as they could, squeezed past all these rough bikers, nodding at the right moments

to the Hell's Angels and saying 'Alright mate' … and left the cafe unscathed. What a laugh."

Lei grinned.

They turned down an alley and Steven unlocked the front door to a small terraced house.

After forty minutes, a bell rang. Steven watched through the outside monitor then operated the remote electronic lock to the front door.
The bell went many more times.
Eventually everybody was sitting around the large table in the lounge, curtains drawn and helping themselves to coffee and tea from the large flasks, or wine.
Sandwiches and cakes were piled on plates.
Some table lamps offered subdued lighting, plus a large number of candles flickered in ornate holders around the room.
Nobody seemed surprised at the presence of Lei.
She felt quite uncomfortable.

Steven stood up, bowed and welcomed them all.
"Member Druids, thank you for coming. We have some important issues to discuss."
Each made a slight bow towards him.

Then he said "As per our discussion and vote last time, Lei here has joined us as an associate member."
He turned to an open mouthed Lei and continued before she could speak, "I hope sooner rather than later, Lei's contribution will ensure her elevation to full Druid, just like us. She has already made significant inroads into the Chinese conundrum."
They stood, gazed at Lei, each doing a little bow, then clapping in unison.

Her mind churned 'It was already agreed by them, a done deed and I knew nothing about it…….'

Steven motioned for everybody to be seated. He remained standing, towering at six and a half feet tall.
He spoke, "Ladies and Gentlemen, we last met in December and although we have remained in communication, this meeting is essential. Much has happened."
He continued, briefly mentioning the supernova, the Hawaiian earthquake and the anomaly object in the sky. He then talked about public utterances by several religious leaders and the world in puzzlement as to what the anomaly could be.

Lei casually looked around the table.
Horst Van de Groot, his eyes locked on Steven, never blinking.
He was a stocky man of Dutch descent, probably in his mid fifties, with combed back black hair and a light green suit. Then a casually dressed Maxwell Blackwood, blonde in his thirties, slim build, piercing green eyes.
Next to Maxwell sat Irving Dekker wearing a white suit.
In his seventies now, fat and bald with a deep Mediterranean tan.
He gave Lei a nod of recognition, she smiled back. Something about his demeanour was odd, she couldn't identify it.
Then the Russian, Valentin in a red shirt and tan slacks, probably late forties, dark hair and a pale face sculptured out of granite.
His clothing was tight over his gym body.

She gazed back at Steven Crowley, "……and I believe we need an update from each of us in turn, in respect of operations and the current turn of events."

Lei casually continued her inspection.
Next to the Russian was Nigel Humble, Steven's security friend whatever he did. Guess he is in his late twenties, brown hair with lovely reflective brown eyes, slim build, chisel jaw and wearing a green roll top pullover plus blue jeans.
She thought, "He's nice." and then blushed a little as her caught her eye and did a hint of a wink.

Then July Craswell.
Lei stopped, almost froze, but kept her composure. She quickly glanced away, returning her eyes to Steven.

Lei had inherited the sharp eyes of her pilot father just like her sister Ming. They both knew they had vision that was exceptional, able to see slightly beyond the average human spectrum and also see pin sharp detail.

July Craswell had something odd about her, almost a slight halo, but showed as a dark blurry edge of sorts. Lei couldn't be sure without looking back, which would give away her perception. She thought 'the others must be able to see the same? …but no, nobody else was looking at July. Then perhaps only I can see it?'

Lei felt her skin crawl.

She fleetingly looked at Craig Akerman, typical American space mission material.
A would be astronaut with very short hair and a rugged face. He wore a light blue jacket over a white shirt. Dark blue trousers to compliment.

Horst spoke first,
"As you know we have a unique contact into the Chinese space program. Suffice to say that the South African government with our mineral resources have formed strong links with the Chinese authorities. Now we know that their moon base suffered a meteorite strike which killed the astronauts inside. Also what is more public is the launch of their manned space vehicle which discovered this tragedy. The launch had a secondary mission, which was to send a probe to the anomaly."
All eyes were glued on Horst.
He continued "Using radar, then lasers, and finally firing several very small needle craft at it, the probe was able to find an entrance to this object. I would say it was rather fortunate, as most of the sensor techniques failed to expand on what this object is. A short

data transmission was received just after the probe disappeared. I am not privy as to what this data transmission revealed.
Now with regard to our fuel control modules, which are being manufactured for the American missions next year."

He glanced at Steven, seeking something. Lei caught the hesitancy, maybe authorisation from Steven?

Steven nodded, said "What you have, can be disclosed to all here, everybody is sworn to secrecy. We have our oath."
Horst took a deep breath, "We believe the Americans are going to use a military weapon to illuminate the anomaly and so in their eyes understand it better.

They plan to use the Nuclear X Ray laser, a device designed during Ronald Reegan's Star Wars initiative back in the eighties. This weapon uses a specially focussed nuclear explosion to create, for a brief period, a narrow energy beam made up of extremely powerful X-Rays. Back then to knock out the electronics in enemy missiles.
What will happen when this strikes the anomaly is completely unknown, but it is likely to be seriously counter-productive in the sense that whatever has created the anomaly will detect this as an aggressive action.
To prevent the deployment of such a destructive device and with this group's approval, we recommend that their launch be sabotaged."

Lei stifled a gasp.

The Russian Valentin immediately stood up, "Yes I totally agree, they must be stopped."
Steven spoke, "I understand the gravity of this. We all do. Whatever or whoever has built this portal may see this as an attack and respond. If they are able to create a stable energy vortex across a great distance of space, and possibly travel through it, they will be very highly advanced. We must tread carefully."

He looked around the table, stopping at several of the attendees, and then he continued,
"Our mission as we know and for Lei's further enlightenment, is to develop processes and systems to protect mankind from a malevolent alien force. Lei, we believe this will come from deep space and we have no knowledge as to when. What we do know is that the anomaly has probably been created by another group of beings."

Lei was open mouthed, her eyes wide. She thought, 'Heavens above, they are talking about aliens ! ALIENS !!.... what on earth is going on here?'

Her astonishment was not shared by anybody else.

Steve Crowley looked at Lei and smiled, said "I know Lei, up until now I have protected you from this knowledge, but your valuable Chinese researches and the moon base location may have given you some clues?"

Lei felt out of her depth with the present company.
Slowly she spoke, "Yes, it is a revelation for me and thank you for allowing my participation here. With the possibility of a very large object buried under the moon, I had started to wonder about its nature and if artificial, how it got there. You know Steven, your questions about it prompted me to research further, but I was too unsure to speak my mind.
I did consider that an extra terrestrial intelligence may have been responsible."

She paused, "However, it is only conjecture on my part. We know the media have done the subject of ET stuff to death. People are exposed to so much false information on UFOs and the like, that they have become numb."

Steven replied "I think we need to start talking about them seriously….."

Lei interjected, "The whole world talks about them Steven. UFOs, Area 51 and so on, but nothing, no real solid proof has been extracted or revealed to the general public, ever. Unless our esteemed attendees here can produce that proof……. "

At that point Irving Dekker opened up in his New Yorker accent, his voice had a strange tiny echo.
"Sure there are. You don't think mankind is the only intelligent life in the universe?"
Lei cocked her eyes at him, she said sharply, "I happen to agree. Most educated people believe that anyway. I'm sorry but just what is happening here? How can this small group stop this evil… you say? Do you mean an… Alien invasion?"

For a small woman she could pack a verbal punch, even Steven raised his eyebrows.
Steven said "Please Lei, as matters proceed, hopefully you will have a clearer picture. Horst please continue."
She pursed her lips.

The Dutchman stood and spoke, "As I said we need to stop this horrific weapon from being used. The Americans have never tested it on a large scale. Military pressure may have crystallised this plan, with the carrot that it is just the device needed to understand the composition of the anomaly. But what the Americans will gain is a flag waving exercise to say look at our new weapon and its capability. What we must endeavour to do is to make the sabotage look like an accident."

He looked around, all the faces were sombre.
Horst then looked straight at Nadir Patel, the Indian armaments mogul.
A man so rich, he has an airliner readied in ten different countries solely for his personal use. Rumour had it that he had built up a secret army, based on an isolated pacific island.

Nadir stood, exclaimed loudly, "No, I believe the situation may become grave. You are right to suggest disabling this weapon. What we are unsure of, according to my latest intelligence, is just which vehicle it will be carried in."
He glanced around the room, the whites of his brown eyes a diluted red. Yellow nicotine stains were tattooed into his forefinger and middle finger.

Nigel Humble, the British intelligence expert, scratched his chin, spoke up.

"To be honest I believe the Nuclear X-Ray Laser will be carried in an unmanned NASA vehicle. Reason being is that it needs to be deployed far away from the manned craft that will be monitoring the anomaly. There is another third vehicle, the details of which are sketchy at this time. The USAF has been developing a jet engine technology that is extremely fast. They are building a large rocket. At this stage we could assume an orbit escape engine will be mounted above the jet engine."
He glanced at Craig Akerman.
"Maybe NASA can comment on this?"

Akerman stood and replied. His voice rang out strongly.
"Yes. This is highly classified."
He paused, looking around the members and especially at Lei.
"I can disclose that an Orion launch with the large boosters will carry this nuclear device into orbit. A second manned vehicle which is this rocket jet, will control and monitor the X-ray deployment. What has become recent speculation, but difficult to confirm at this point, is that a new British gravity engine is to be used for the orbit escape propulsion. In addition a second unmanned heavy lifter rocket is being prepared. This may carry another nuclear device. It would seem a somewhat perilous mission."

Lei felt uncomfortable. She just didn't know enough about these people or their agendas. It seemed that they were meddling in dangerous matters, in fact it smacked of terrorist activity.

Steven raised his hand.
"So….. Horst, the Chinese involvement using the Arragon Corporation and the fuel control modules they have subcontracted to your company. Can we access the fuel control modules and adjust their software, to cause a malfunction?"

Horst replied, "Yes, we can incorporate hidden software routines that can be called when certain conditions, like altitude, speed and position are met. These programs can be triggered as passive and waiting, by remote control. We have inserts in their telemetry equipment that can issue our covert control codes. It is not difficult to do, as we have full manufacturing control of these items. It can be done under the covers so to speak."

Steven then said, "Ok, proceed on a sabotage basis. We may not use it, but we need to have this option available. Thank you Horst."
He then turned to July Craswell,
"July, firstly what status do you have on the chemicals spin off project?"

She stood up and spoke in a tone that had a slight sound like castanets in the background. Steven stared at her intently as did some of the others.

Lei was riveted to her chair, the hairs on the back of her neck rigid.
She thought 'oh my god, there is something extremely strange about that woman…..'

July began "I have continued to divert some of our waste production away from the usual companies that manage this process. As we know it is stored in your hangar facility in

Cheshire, Steven. We now estimate after reprocessing, there are three kilograms of palladium."

She paused frowning, sniffing the air, "A strange smell in here."

Steven spoke up, "Ah that would be the aromatic candles, to give a relaxed informal atmosphere. I do hope they are convivial to tonight's discussion."
He looked around the table, still smiling.
Horst returned the smile, refilling his glass with the Chateau Neuf de Pape on offer.

Steven said "Good news, excellent work July."
She looked slowly around, her head a little jerky. "Because it is in very minute quantities in two of our cosmetic manufacturing processes, it has taken three years to get this far."
July seemed disturbed; she looked straight at Steven, "Our metal gathering operations are covert. I am dealing through third parties who are sworn to commercial secrecy. However, some questions are being asked. Therefore I propose a scale down or even a stoppage for a while, in case an investigation is mounted."

Steven pondered looking briefly around the attendees; he tapped his fingers lightly on the table.
Then returning to July, "As you wish. We must not risk our exposure."

Lei puzzled, piped up "What do you, I mean we, need this metal for?" she quickly looked around the table for someone to enlighten her.
Horst spoke up, "Palladium is just one of many rare elements that we are gathering in quantity. It is believed that mankind will face a threat sometime in the future.
This threat will try and extract the more valuable resources from our planet, such as rare elements. It is wise to have secret stockpiles that will assist man to retaliate. The metals and chemicals we have identified, are key to mankind's weapons technologies."

Lei nodded in acknowledgement, she gratingly thought 'this is the stuff of science fiction, yet I am here now, part of an extreme group that utterly believes its mission…..'

Steven continued, "and Craswell what has he been doing with his gravity work?"
July smiled, her face was hard, and again she spoke with the castanets whispering.
"The last update I can probably give is that he said that he, John Creeson and Karen Durgas were working with the Americans to share gravity technologies. I'm afraid Bill and I are divorcing, so it is unlikely that my access to this source will continue."

She nodded, smiled for the first time and sat down.
Lei thought 'what a phrase…. *access to this source*… dammit he is or was your husband. '

Steven was checking through some notes, he looked up, "Thank you July. Now Maxwell, the Church of Scientology, what updates can you give us on the anomaly and its creators?"

Maxwell Blackwood remained sitting, the fingers of his hands interlocked on the table. He had a serene look, calm, almost far away.
At length he spoke,
"We have undertaken some analysis and it is believed that the object is indeed a portal. In addition, a very useful leak from the British Gravity Array project has provided confirmation about what we already know."

Lei's face was growing paler, 'Christ what don't they know…..'

Blackwood paused; he seemed to be reluctant to say more.
Steven gently pushed him, "So please share Maxwell."
Blackwood slowly breathed in and out; he said "The origin of the anomaly appears to come from the globular cluster Omega Centauri. It is about seventeen thousand light years from us."

Dekker laughed out loud, "Hell, that's a long road! Take a while to travel that route."
Blackwood glared momentarily at Dekker, "For us yes, it would be impossible, but for the beings that live there, the distance is irrelevant."
At this the whole table burst into a confused babble, arms gesticulating, heads shaking.

Steven Crowley watched with a profound wisdom

He cracked the tabletop with the flat of his hand; they all stopped and looked at him. "Please, please we must discuss these issues in a procedural manner. Ok, what Maxwell has said cannot be proved at the moment, unless these beings make themselves known, right Maxwell?" he dropped to a whisper "Or do your people *have special access?*" he was slightly sarcastic. A deliberate ploy to try and glean every facet, every nuance of how and what information Maxwell might have.

Maxwell stayed cool, he quietly said, "We *do have special access* as you put it.
It is in our nature, especially for our more advanced members."

He continued "These beings represent a very old species. They were certainly at an advanced technological stage, maybe a hundred million years ago. They are able to do things today beyond our imagination. All I can say at this meeting is that we believe that these beings oversee humanity's welfare. Not the day to day suffering, or disease or the myriad of conflicts about our planet, but instead a long term concern as to our destiny."

Lei gasped making the others turn round to see.
She said "This is incredible! If you are correct then surely many more people would know about these 'beings'. Like leaders of countries, top scientists, the key people in the world's religions?"

Elaine Murphy the Irish politician spoke for the first time,
"We do, or rather we suspect. To clarify Lei, I work with our Minister for Science in Ireland. Our intelligence in terms of data collation and observation has ratified an energy path that does indeed lead a little distance from the anomaly towards the Omega Centauri system. We see the existence of what is a complex object or corridor composed of an unknown energy in the sky. This naturally begs the question of how a coherent extremely powerful force can and possibly at a huge distance, configure and hold this object in a precise orbit. We believe this cannot be by accident. It is likely the work of a very advanced civilisation, whose power may be almost unimaginable."

She paused, took a deep breath then said,
"I have to acknowledge an alternative, scientifically implausible but a remote possibility. This would be that the object has happened purely by accident, perhaps an energy cortex linked to a colossal plasma or X-ray jet ejecting from the black hole, the one in the centre of our galaxy."

The room was quiet, many minds working the possibilities.

"Thank you Elaine." Steven beamed at them all. "As we see, it is time to plan for our next event. Something of a much larger magnitude than my little escapade at GunWharf."

He restrained a chuckle.

Lei reflected back to the day and thought 'Yes and you almost froze to death.'
She was remembering his stunt at GunWharf back in late January.

The electronic valves opening to flood the little boat as he stood on its cabin in a white robe, his long brown hair fluttering in the breeze, his feet locked into some low metal rails on the roof.
He did look a sort of bearded 'Messiah'.

Then Steven's disappearance below the waves as the underwater electric winch pulled the little cabin cruiser and him under the waves. A dozen metres underwater, she in full dry suit and scuba gear, desperately peeling off Steven's clothes and getting him into the thermal wet suit, before he froze.
He, at the same time clutching and breathing heavily through the oxygen scuba mask.
The water had been deathly cold.
She smiled inwardly, crazy, lovely man.

Lei looked up as someone spoke.

Nadir took over, "Yes and we are almost ready Steven. To clarify to everybody here, the next event is in fact planned to be a world wide broadcast happening simultaneously to as many of the peoples of this planet as possible. The objective is to open the eyes and hopefully the minds of everyone. We must overcome religious barriers."
Everybody watched him earnestly. He continued, "Personally I am not sure that this is sufficient?" his hands were held high and wide. "We need a cataclysm to shake people, to drive fear into their souls……to galvanise the masses in one spiritual direction."
He paused and then slowly said, "To fight a menace that is beyond our comprehension."
Steven replied, "You are well informed Nadir and I do have more plans in place. They will be revealed soon."

Lei was vexed, she thought, 'What is he on about ? The objectives if there are any, seem vague? what did this circle really want to achieve ? What exactly is this menace?'
Questions, so many questions. She was about to give vent, when suddenly she felt giddy.

Instantly her mind was invaded, by something that knew, a reading of her thoughts.
'Ugh …what the hell is going on…' She felt a mental tug from, yes the direction was over towards Irving Dekker.

Lei glanced at him.
He seemed to be overheating, perspiring, and uncomfortable. His jacket had already come off. A napkin was clasped to his forehead. He turned to stare at her with beady red eyes. The real oddity was slightly behind him, a shadow…. no a tiny wavering black outline.
In a flash it was gone.

Lei then felt a second mental touch, she switched her gaze to July, the same thing, a tiny black outline flickered, and then disappeared.
For some reason Lei thought of slithering snakes, creeping, sliding through cracks in the floor and holes in the walls.

At this she felt awful, her stomach was so tight, her skin became cold, her neck crawled. She glanced at her left hand, as it was trembling she discreetly grabbed it with her other hand. Adrenalin was rising.

Her body had automatically started to prepare for survival.

Lei suddenly, desperately thought, she needed to get out of here bloody quick.

July seemed paler and looked at her with eyes that seemed to penetrate back into Lei's skull.
Lei stuttered "Uh… ah… sorry I feel a little sick, it's a bit warm in here.
Please excuse me; I need the bathroom and some aspirin."

With that she left the room, went to the bathroom and drank a full glass of water.
She then splashed her face with cold water and said looking into the mirror. "Oh Jesus…..those people….so weird."
At any moment she expected to see another reflection in the mirror, a gargoyle or some monster.
Lei started to shake.

She thought ‘Holy shit, this lot scares me witless. What on earth is Steven doing?
How have I not known? well perhaps I suspected something, but not THIS.’

The bathroom door abruptly opened and July Craswell glided in.

Lei turned to look at July.
All she could see was the gorgon’s head.

Lei cried so softly, a moan left her mouth as she fainted, part grabbing the wash hand basin, as she hit the floor.

Chapter 7

Same night – 'Orange Grove' meet house, Hayling Island.

The sponge was cold on her forehead.
Lei slowly opened her eyes.

Blurred images, a kaleidoscope of colour fragments.
She gasped, tried to get up "Oh god, oh please, I need ……"

A voice "It's ok… Lei, relax….. You've had a nasty blow to your head."

Steven Crowley bent over her as she lay on the couch.
"Oh Steven, I'm so sorry, forgive me."
She fully opened her eyes and sat up a little, looking around, then back at him.
He was alone, perched on the edge of the couch.

She shakily said, "Whe…Where's July?"
Steven had a sombre look.
He said "Everybody has gone. You have been out for about an hour."
Lei shook her head and touched the bump just above her left ear.
"Ouch, ooh that is sore."
Steven lightly touched her head, smoothing the skin around the graze.

"Yes, July went to look for you, she was worried as you had gone quite pale.
She said as she entered the bathroom, you turned and slipped on the wet floor and went down banging your head on the wash basin. I have been very worried."
"Steven, I want to tell you …. I fainted."
He interrupted, "Easy Lei. You're going to be ok, your pulse and temperature are normal, the bump is more of a graze. How do you feel?"

"Yes a bit shakey, but ok. Steven, I saw and felt some strange things at the meeting."
Steven eyed her carefully.
He took a deep breath and said, "Like what?"
Lei suddenly felt very vulnerable, almost an intruder. She thought 'What to say and what to hide? Maybe say nothing.'

The need to get away engulfed her again.

Steven sat back, said "It's ok you know, I'm no villain. I guess the meeting was a little too, what shall I say? Too revealing and too science fiction maybe?"

As her consciousness slowly returned she struggled to a sitting position.
He said, "Like a drink? Coffee, tea?"

Lei sternly replied "I think a large bloody Mary........ Steven... thank you."
Instantly he disappeared, returning minutes later with two full glasses, ice clinking in the red liquid.
Lei took a serious gulp, swallowed, breathed hard and put the glass on the table with a thud.
She paused for a while, and then said.
"Hell, that's better."

They sat for some minutes, silent.
She found herself in a backroom, and then Lei looked through the window which overlooked a small unkempt rear garden. It had tall uncut grass, a few overgrown shrubs and circular paving stones weaving down the middle, all of them patterned in green moss.

Steven was the first to speak.
"Lei, you mean the world to me and I think it is time for me to explain."

The big man dwarfed his love, the petite Chinese-American woman.
She looked at him and said, "I'm not sure I want to know anymore Steven. I've seen and heard far too much today already. It is so hard to comprehend."
She reached for her glass and downed the remainder.
"And I'm scared shitless by what I saw……"

Steven slowly spoke, "You need to know Lei. I could be in a very awkward position. Your new knowledge of these people and events means that you must remain in the group. Secrecy and security of what we are doing and our aims are paramount."
He looked at her, almost pleading, but an element of extreme glinted in his eyes.
She replied, "I know the gravity of all this, there is no way I would break your code. It's just that…… just…oh god Steven what is really happening? What danger is the world in? And …..I saw something tonight……" her voice petered out.

Steven topped up her glass, adding ice that splashed into the numbing liquid.

The alcohol was giving her guts, confidence, and a devil-may-care attitude.
She took another gulp, swallowed, and said, "For fucks sake Steven! I saw some scary stuff tonight. Didn't you? Dekker and that July woman, did you not see how bloody strange they looked?"

Steven's blue eyes watered as he looked at her, he then did something very non-Steven. He knelt on the floor before Lei and took her hands in his.
"Oh bless you Lei, you are what I hoped, a talent beyond… beyond what I thought could possibly be."

Lei looked at him puzzlingly. He continued, "You see I have suspected and now you have confirmed my suspicions. Like your

sister that you described to me, you have a gift for seeing details that others cannot.
A gift you have, that extends slightly beyond the normal human visible light spectrum."
Lei nodded slowly, although she sensed he had a slightly condescending manner. "Yeah, but I wish sometimes I didn't have it."
Steven "But it is a fact and now I must explain."

He took a swig of the vodka, and then gently put the glass on the table. Taking out a pack of Greek cigarettes he flipped one into his mouth. He offered the open pack to Lei.
She shook her head vigorously, but continued to watch him.
He was an enigma.
He lit up and took a huge first drag, holding it momentarily then slowly exhaling a column of blue smoke upwards towards the ceiling. Steven then swivelled his eyes back to Lei.
At length he said, "Both Dekker and July have been acting strange lately. What did you actually see Lei?"
She looked at him pensively, a hesitancy. "You may not believe me Steven. I don't want to believe me…to believe what I saw."
"It's ok, please tell me what you saw, I will not question it."
Lei studied him, she was trying to make the leap now, to trust him……… again.

She drew a long breath, then slowly said,
"Irving Dekker seemed to be able to enter my mind, don't ask me how, I just knew. At that moment he had an aura of sorts around his upper body and head. A darkish wispy corona is the best way I can describe it. July had the same. It was only momentarily, perhaps ten or fifteen seconds at most."

At this Steven's eyes widened, he took on a look of enlightenment. "Yeah, those two are not what they seem."

Steven Crowley thought 'In time I will reveal a lot more. She is entitled to know.'

He then rolled his left shirt sleeve right up past his upper arm. Lei could see an arm bracelet.
It was rather plain, looked old with some engravings on the greenish bronze metal and a small stone embedded in the middle of the band.
Lei mumbled, "What is that, can't say I've seen you wearing it before?"
Steven explained, "No, I put it on especially for tonight. This bracelet came from our friend Irving Dekker a long time ago. It is very old and has a unique affinity to me.
I purchased it from him years ago for a tidy sum. I think he has also passed on some of the other shipwreck artefacts not realising their true intrinsic value, only what clients were prepared to pay for their historical value. For Irving Dekker back then, it was the monetary gain that drove him. Now he has changed and I think he has become a dangerous man."

He continued, "You see I have a very old friend who worked with Edward Durgas, Karen's dad. His name is Professor Quentin Huxley and he examined this bracelet and its properties."
Lei was putting away the vodka, but still on alert, her eyes occasionally darting around, to the window, then to the door.

Steven then said, "After his early life of university lecturing, Quentin moved to GCHQ, the communications security centre. He worked on chemical marking, tagging, sniffing out dangerous explosives stuff. That's where I met him. His real hobby is archaeology and ancient relics."
Lei spoke "So what did he say?"

Steven paused, he slowly exhaled more cigarette smoke, then said "What I am about to tell you now is why I have gone down this path. Bearing this mantle of preaching, and my destiny to try and save the world."
Lei watched him, with a suspicious look she could not conceal. She started to say, "How can one man, or a small group, possibly……."

Steven cut in, “But I can, we can. It is because I am utterly convinced that this world has to wake up from its domestic wars, squabbles and forever pointless dances of politics and see the real threat.
A threat so frightening that mankind could be obliterated or worse, incarcerated in a dark, suffering limbo existence. Quentin enlightened me. He has this calm, studious manner that completely convinced me, that he was telling the truth, which is that…. ”

He was interrupted.

A rattling noise was coming from the garden.
Tap, tappity tap. Then a sort of dragging, scraping sound.

Lei’s eyes went wide, she gasped at Steven.
He quickly rose and looked out of the window and with a little laugh came back.
“A magpie is trying to pick up an old shiny spoon, dragging it along the garden path.”

She sighed with relief squeezing his arm as he sat down, “Thank God…”

“As I was saying Quentin has done some serious research over his lifetime and there is stuff that he has uncovered which is, well frankly mind blowing.”
“Oh Steven…. if only this was science fiction……” her voice stopped.

“I wish it was Lei, but you know, Quentin had found out something staggering.
He is a frail old man now, living in a warden controlled retirement complex.
We must see him soon, very soon.
Lei, I need your help to carry on this work.
In the beginning I saw it as a calling, but now the monumental implications can only be guessed at.”

He seemed to diminish in stature as he sat there, slightly hunched, the weight of his burden pushing him down.
Before she could interject, he suddenly gathered energy and said "But we have strength you know, a way to combat the threat. A long time ago, Quentin did some very detailed research into ancient cultures and manuscripts. He told me the following."
Lei watched him. She took his hand, looking closely at the bracelet on the arm.

"Quentin had discovered that there are four such artefacts, a cross, a sword, a helmet and this bracelet. On their own they have diminished power. I say power, in that they seem to have a built-in capability.
Their origin is unknown. They appeared around the time of Christ, but I suspect they are many millennia earlier. We can only guess at how or who made them. Possibly by some very advanced craftsmanship or engineering that is unknown to man.

What is more, only recently has this energy manifestation become apparent.
How shall we say? 'Activated' ? all Quentin could confide in me is that when all of these are brought together by the right people, their 'activation' will be vastly more powerful and offer an enormous sphere of protection. He could not elaborate further than that."
"Right people?" queried Lei.
"Yes the right people. I think he meant spiritually gifted, that sort of thing."
"and are you spiritually gifted Steven ?"
"No, I am sure I am not……."

He watched her, making sure she understood it all.

As she leaned in toward him, his open neck shirt revealed a tiny silver chain.
Lei gently reached and lifted it out revealing a silver cross, a crucifix.

"Steven? I didn't know you were particularly religious?"

He looked at her with a smile that seemed timeless.
"Oh… I guess I am really. We must all believe in something."
She looked at him, her eyes searching his. There was more she felt, deep, deep within those blue pools. They kissed gently.

The talking had stopped. They both stared out the window, Lei anywhere, to try and blank out the craziness of it all.
Presently she stood and put her hands on his arm and then the bracelet, gently running her fingers over it, feeling the smooth surface, stopping at the dull centre stone.

He said "It may seem strange, but when danger is present, it makes my arm throb. Sometimes it is a tingle. The different feelings are a measure of nearby danger. I am still learning to comprehend the differences. When I say danger I mean of a kind that is non-human."

Lei stared at him, her eyes locked, unblinking. "Non-human. What? Animals? snakes? That sort of thing?"
"No, not any living species on Earth."
He paused, "More towards ethereal, but sinister, possibly physical AND spiritual."

She said "Spiritual! oh gosh." then she had a hunch, "This threat is to do with whatever is buried in the moon? Yes?"
Steven shook his head, denying that avenue, "No, not that, something from far away, a long distance from the Earth, huge distance. It is very malevolent."
Lei became impatient, "What the bloody hell is it then Steven, ghosts, poltergeists, evil spirits?"
"Probably all of those Lei. You see my arm bracelet throbbed at the same time in the meeting as you felt unwell. I too received some strange but intangible thoughts.
I could identify as you did, paths of energy, coming from Irving Dekker and July Craswell."

She looked again at his armband.
Lei "Oh hell, can we not just leave this place, get away from here Steven. I am so afraid."
He got up, said "Yeah let's go, there's no reason to stay now, the meeting ended an hour ago and the group are all well on their way back. However, if I am right, I am sure that Dekker and July may be involved with powers beyond that which we can comprehend. Our only protection right now is to feign ignorance, no rash actions that sort of thing. It is unlikely that they have been able to eavesdrop this conversation.
I have fitted jamming devices, not only radio frequency ones, but spiritual ones too."

Lei suddenly stared at him "Spiritual ones? What on earth?"
Steven's eyes warmed, he smiled "Burning candles, you notice there are several around the room and some in the meeting lounge?"
"Yes I see those, but how?"
"I performed a circular path passing them all with a smouldering smudge bowl of sage to drive out evil and negative spirits, and any unwanted psychic clutter. I did this ritual before they arrived and after the people had gone."
Lei said "I see. Sounds a bit spooky to me?"
Steven "Yes it is and I know I said I wasn't…you know spiritually inclined, but I believe I can try and find the path. I have learned some techniques, relaxing and focusing are key."

Suddenly Lei stood up, quickly looked through the window then back at Steven, her eyes wide.
"God, that's why Dekker was so uncomfortable, yes? No can't be, but then July looked strained too. Am I on the right track Steven?"

Steven hesitated, he knew far more than he had implied, "Yes, you are on the right track, your perception is sharp.
Now I realise that they must normally be in some sort of remote

contact with whatever is out there, but my efforts tonight temporarily thwarted them.
I feel sure they didn't suspect, just felt confused."
He continued in a worried voice, "Unfortunately they now have information from which we must stop the supply. It is becoming necessary that we should plan a way to trap and eliminate them, surely and efficiently."

Lei was trembling, "Oh god, you mean eject them from the group?"
He nodded and said, "At least that…"
She continued "This is becoming weird, so bloody weird. Now all I want is *my* crucifix which is back on the boat."

Steven took her hand and whispered "Probably kill them, if that's possible, before they do the same or *worse* to us. Let's go."
Lei just stammered quietly "Kill them? Oh god…."

With that, they tidied up and left, walking casually and slowly as if nothing had happened, back to the pub car park.

Holding hands, past where the Orange Grove biker café used to be.

10 am Sunday 18th March.
The Yacht Nemain, Dell Quay harbour

They both endured a disturbed night and at one point 3:30 am in the morning, they sat together on the chilly top deck, smoking and drinking. Lei had given up smoking a long time ago, but events had shaken her nerves badly.

The morning came with blinding sunbeams bursting out, like spokes of a wheel, through the murky dawn clouds.
They were enshrouded in the light from a brilliant orange sunrise.
It gave a body charging warmth.

Lei in her thick boat jacket sat on the deck, clasping her hot coffee with both hands.
Steam slowly swirled away from the cup.
Steven had already finished his drink, 'stomach of cast iron' she thought.
He was tough, afraid of little and strong minded.

She wondered if he was the one, Mr Right.
He said "Ok, I'm off down below now. Work to do."
She nodded, thinking of what they had and where they were going. 'Yes where were they going? The future seemed scary.'
She sighed, took a sip of coffee, let it fill and warm her.
Lei ran her hand over the bump graze on her head just by her ear.
The plaster had come off in the night. She frowned, took out her pocket mirror from her little string bag.
Looking at the scar she thought 'That's healing quickly. I must be in top health at the moment.'
The frown didn't leave her face.

From her pocket came the sound of her phone ringtone and without looking she answered.
"Hello…"
"Lei, that you?"
"Yes, oh hi Ming! lovely to hear your voice."
Her sister was a little curt, not relaxed.
"Lei, I have to talk to you but it must be secure. If you can right now, then switch in encryption."
Lei looked around; Steven was busy below, on the computer.
High tide nearly up.
A few people fifty yards away on the embankment were walking the estuary track with their dog.
"Yes I can, switching in now."

"Lei, I have done some analysis that I think you ought to know about. It is highly confidential, but I feel you may be in some sort of danger…. you know sister to sister
….it's a gut sensation."

"Oh Ming, you are so right. There is a danger here. It's sort of intangible, yet very real if you get my drift. Please tell me what you know."

"Lei, I'll be brief as even these encrypted links can be broken eventually. Basically the moon base cloaked objects are real, the cleaned up videos were too perfect. Thank god my memory is good. What has now been discovered is that somewhere near the anomaly which as you know is far behind the Earth, is a patch of distorted space."

Lei listened, all the while scanning the shore and around the boat for anything unusual. She said "Sounds creepy Ming?"
Ming continued "Well I used our best telescope data and processed it, magnifying, resolving near and far objects that sort of thing."
Lei quickly interjected "and what do think it is?"

Ming slowly spoke, "There is no doubt that an invisible object is there. Any normal means we have of detecting it fail. Radar doesn't reflect back, guess it just gets absorbed, bit like the material sheathing our Stealth fighters' use. Laser light again just seems to go through, no returns or secondary reflections. No heat emission in the infrared spectrum either. But I carefully analysed all the distorted constellation and individual star images, and managed to get an approximate outline of this thing."

Lei spoke "What is it Ming?"
Ming hesitated "I'm not sure, only that it is the size of the object that is unbelievable, gargantuan is the word."

Lei "Is it connected with that object we think could be buried in the moon?"
Ming replied "We don't know. There are some very high frequency transmissions, ultra wide bands, very low power, that seem to emanate around the moon. Undecipherable. More work is needed on those."

Lei nervously, "Oh Ming, I am terrified of what may happen, you see we had a meeting last night and there were two really odd characters there."

Ming "Just try and keep calm Lei, we need each other. This invisible object may be a giant spacecraft. We estimate its size to be hundreds of miles across."

Lei thought 'UFOs, aliens, invasion….. Shades of that film, what was it? …yes Independence Day.'
Ming ended "That's all I have, speak soon, gotta go."
Lei "Oh? Bye, take care Sis."
Ming "You too Lei, bye."

Steven appeared at the top rung of the yacht stairs. He looked keenly at Lei.
She said "That was Ming, she has some news."

He nodded took a long drag on his cigarette, exhaling blue smoke that dispersed rapidly in the breeze.

She followed him down below.

Chapter 8

The Previous Day
10 am Saturday 17th March
Somewhere deep in the Norfolk countryside, UK

They had slept in what was left of the derelict farmhouse.
The nearest habitation being over three miles away.

Bill Craswell was the first to wake, excited yet a little apprehensive. He wandered into the ramshackle kitchen and put the kettle on.

Sitting at the old battered wooden table and sipping his tea, Bill pondered on the day ahead.
He looked out of the cobwebbed window across the farmyard, to the large barn. Ninety five percent of him said they would get wondrous results today.
Five percent of him didn't want to know.
The barn housed what could be the pinnacle of his illustrious career, or the destruction of it and possibly his farm too.

He had purchased the farm and its land at a good price; mainly because the farmhouse really needed pulling down and rebuilding. Plus the farm itself was barren, previously having cattle and sheep. The surrounding hills and land too uneven and rocky for arable use, but very secluded, just the place.
Bill had remortgaged his house heavily to get this gem. He felt smug, but a little guilty, just for a moment.

The kitchen door squeaked open.
A sleepy dishevelled head peered round the door. It was Antony Cressada, the bright Italian physicist and engineer. "Good Morning Billy!"

"Bill, you know I prefer Bill! ……morning Tony."

Tony helped himself to green tea and pushed a couple of slices of toast into the electric toaster. He grabbed a pack of ham from the fridge.
"Today's the day, eh Signor Bill! All or nothing! No farm left!" He chuckled looking at Bill.
A retort was imminent when another head popped around the door.
"Morning Bill, sleep well?"
Gustav Huck, the German scientist and another of Bill's team, came in bright and breezy.

These two scientists had agreed in secrecy to Bill's little side project. The large up front payment and the dangling of a healthy bonus had been the persuading carrot.
Mostly out of Bill's own pocket.
Also it could guarantee their future careers, plus some serious fame next year.

Bill replied "Yeah not bad, although I was thinking through the procedures at about 4am. Hope you guys were warm enough? I got in extra duvets as the oil heating is knackered. Thank god for the large wood stove."
Gustav spoke first
"Yes, I was snug, how do you say, ah yes… snug as a bug in a rug." His deep voice broke into a laugh.
Tony commented "I was ok, is warm enough, be even warmer later in the barn!" he joked.
Bill snapped "Nothing will go wrong Tony, believe me! There are safeguards in place, as you know."

They were all a little edgy.
After breakfast, the peak of several weeks work was about to commence.
The huge barn beckoned.

Bill opened the large aluminium doors to reveal a spacious interior. He operated a switch and the area became floodlit. The

long barn was of modern construction, no wood, instead concrete stanchions supported a high steel roof and side walls.
It had been the only half decent building in the whole farm purchase.
At one end was a new large concrete wall two thirds the height of the barn.
It had sides that formed a C shaped enclosure.
The other end of the barn had a smaller concrete construction in the corner, a sort of bunker room, with a studded metal door.
Sandbags surrounded it to halfway height.
Cables snaked from the bunker to the centre of the barn, where a glistening canister shaped object was mounted lengthways five feet off the ground on a steel frame.

The gravity engine.

Clusters of cameras and instruments dangled from the ceiling. All round the engine frame, were mounted dozens of sensors. Additionally, in a larger circle around the engine, bar the exhaust, were various instrument boxes and other equipment hooked up to it.

Bill announced "Gentlemen, what you see is four weeks of hard graft here in the barn.
Prior to this, I had a huge amount of concrete delivered and a lot of men to construct the walls. They asked what it was. I fed them a story about implementing new farming technology, high pressure storage techniques for holding fertilizer and so on."
Tony laughed.
Gustav commented. "Aah…good ploy Bill."

Bill looked on with huge pride at the shiny engine. He had worked hard to build it quickly. It was the size of a very long giant dustbin, about a metre and a half in diameter, by four metres long.
The engine frame was bolted to the barn concrete floor.
All the parts had been shipped in a clandestine manner to the farm, supposedly as part of an upgrade to the Norfolk Gravity Array.

There it stood, the dark shiny cylinder, brooding, waiting for its ugly moment.
It was a miniature of the planned orbital beast.

"Yes I have been flat out assembling all our parts. I've done several, dry test runs.
All the systems checked out. Looks good."
Tony's mouth stayed open, now he could see the monster complete, he felt quite nervous.
"Bill, it's… it's magnificent. Safe, no?"

Bill had expected an adverse reaction; he firmly looked at both of them.
"This is it Gustav, Tony. The pinnacle of what I want to achieve. If we fail here today, your names are out of the book, nobody will know and our control bunker there is eighteen inches of solid armoured concrete.
Over where the blast of the engine thrust is to be contained, you will see in the centre of the concrete mass, a metre thick absorption panel. This is military soft armour designed to absorb the thrust and heat. I can tell you I had to pull a few levers to get some of this stuff."
He paused for breath.

Tony quickly spoke, "How long do you intend to run the engine Bill?"
Bill replied, "Long enough, just long enough to get our measurements. Probably five minutes."
"MINUTES! What about the radioactive fallout?"

Bill snapped, "Goddammit Tony, the prediction is that there will be none, or very little. The control program will instantly shut the engine down if radioactivity is detected. There are hardened sensors that will detect this in the soft armour facing the engine exhaust."

Gustav was scratching his beard, he said "Well we're here and I have confidence in you Bill, and in all of us. This test is essential, as you said any failure when the engine is in orbit and our project will be cancelled."
Bill smiled, "Dead right Gustav. With the new three stage fuel feed, I feel confident.
We shall start the test on minimum thrust, just enough to blow away the spiders' webs in here. Then we will repeat between any adjustments, slowly increasing the thrust to two thirds maximum."

Tony still had a worried look.
Bill walked over to him and put his hand on his shoulders.
He said "Tony, you have been paid extremely well and I thank you for all your sterling efforts. We must have this test. As you know it is pretty much automated, any malfunction will be detected and the systems will shut the engine down far quicker than we could. So there's no need to worry."
Tony frowned; he started to say, "I know that…but Bill…"
Bill almost lost his temper, "TONY believe in me, believe in this…you know the theory, your engineering skills are second to none. You will not regret it.
Think of the accolades when the orbital engine performs perfectly. Any malfunction that happens here, we can rectify before the big event."

Gustav put his hand on Tony's shoulder, "Tony, let's do this." His eyes said it.

Bill breathed out heavily, "Ok, let's get started. We have several test phases to run through before the big burn. Once that's completed and we have the data, hopefully no more runs will be needed. I'll get this lot dismantled and the barn returned back to its original state."

They spent several hours, running the engine fuel feeds, collecting the unspent exotic fuel pellets through temporary collectors. Then

separately firing the liquid injected, tiny, explosive charges in the engine containment chambers.
They had written sophisticated software programs to control the gravity engine.
Gustav applied some minor changes. Tony was outside inspecting every facet of the engine as though his life depended on it.
The truth had never been closer.

The three of them pored over the screens in the bunker, checking and analysing masses of test data.

Finally they replaced all the engine covers, and then heaped sandbags up to the full height of the bunker and across its roof.

It was now late afternoon.
They quickly ate a hot ready made chilli that Bill had brought with him, finishing with strong coffee.

The stress had been mounting all day.

Now, finally the real testing will begin.
They huddled in the bunker with hardly any room to spit, with a battery of display screens in front of them.
With a clang, Bill shut and locked the steel door.
He was in his element, nothing could stop him. His forehead scar pulsed.

All of them wore lightweight but awkward, white coloured radiation suits and head hoods with face windows.
It could have been right out of the James Bond film and the madman in Dr No.

Tony anxiously gripped the sides of his chair, he watched the monitors intensely.
Bill did the preliminary checks then said "Ok, we do the ten second run at minimum thrust. I will start the count down for two minutes."

Outside the quiet was unusual; birds had stopped their vibrant symphony.
A fox and her cubs that normally passed through the farm courtyard had bypassed it and gone along the hedgerow instead.
Only the incessant hum of spring insects from the overgrown fields could be heard.

Seven, six, five, four…. a robot voice from the computer counted down the seconds until ignition.
Three, 'fuel feeds are go', two, 'pre-ignition sequence started', one………

Ignition…………

Bill was gripping the table edge so hard, he couldn't feel his fingers.

There was a slight crackling as the early explosion charges detonated, compressing and consuming the complex fuel mix in the tiny combustion chambers.
Then it happened.
A grating sound followed by a tiny roar that increased in volume.
The run countdown sounded out 'Nine, eight, seven, six …'
There was a sort of small bang. Bill looked up, anxiously scanning the display screens.
All indicators were on green for go.

Five, four….. The engine still ran, producing a sound like shredding steel… three, two one…………

Cut off.

A chugging sound could be heard to fade away, and then all quiet.

Bill spoke first, "Well that seemed to go very well, look at the thrust figures, well above what we expected for the first test."
He had a demon gleam in his eye.

Gustav hesitated, said "Yes, so good, so far.... I'm just going through the sensor data, looks ok, no red error conditions."
Tony was wet with perspiration. He said nothing, just hammered at his keyboard, operating the mouse at a crazy speed, his eyes glued to the screen.
The computer run processor chimed its completion and up came several windows of graphs and to the side, tables of numbers.

The three of them gazed intensely at the screens.
"Wow" said Gustav "It worked, see the fuel consumption quantities are in keeping with our estimates. Engine combustion chamber temperatures are a bit high but still in spec."
Bill leaned forward, "I like the thrust measurements, impressive and no real residual radiation. Good, GOOD!" he exclaimed.
In the dimly lit room, the gargoyle face was screwed up in glee.

After a little while the three of them exited the bunker, Bill first with a radiation measuring Geiger counter in his hand. As the engine cooled, a ticking sound could be heard.
They circled the smoking, dark silver canister, inspecting it like it was their first love, tentatively admiring, yet hypnotised by the attraction.
Gustav checked for fuel leaks or any failures of the systems that the computers had failed to spot.
Bill wandered over to a small blackened spot in the centre of the armoured absorption panel in the concrete wall.
His Geiger counter crackled a little.
Tony looked up, "Bill, that's scary man!"
Bill quickly retorted, "To be expected Tony, the thrust emissions are bound to create a little hot material."
He grinned like a Cheshire cat, pleased as punch.
Continuing he said, "No worries, I'll get this little lot extracted later and dealt with by a source at the Sellafield nuclear site."
Bill's network of contacts seemed unbelievable.

After a while, they concluded the first test was a resounding success.

Bill quickly said, "Right, let's proceed with test two."
While the other two were doing final checks outside the bunker, *Bill covertly turned off the control for automatic radioactive shutdown.*

Test two.
Again they huddled in the bunker anxiously watching the burn, integrity sensors remained green for good. The metal shredding noise rose in pitch and a hammering could be heard as the exhaust hit the armoured concrete.
A couple of amber warning lights came on towards the end.

However, it looked good, the engine continued to burn at a quarter thrust for twenty seconds. The barn and the bunker shook with the engine vibration. In addition, excessive heat in five out of the six compression chambers was flagged up.

Engine shut down.

After some results analysis, a haze of combusted smoke from the fuels greeted the three men as they gingerly came out of their bunker.
Tony sniffing and coughing, his nose twitching in the stench.

Bill was on cloud nine, he beamed from ear to ear.
"Just look at that, LOOK AT THAT, all intact and our test results are bloody brilliant."
He waved the Geiger counter around again. As before the odd radiation tick, until he went over to the concrete wall, where the engine blast had hit the thrust panel.
A harsh crackling rasp screamed from the counter.
"Hell, bit lively here!"

Gustav exclaimed "Bill, we need to stop now, the radiation levels are serious."

Tony his face very pale, was already in agreement, "Yes Bill, I think we have more than enough data to work with."
Bill wasn't convinced, he replied "No, we must have another test; those chambers are getting too hot, we just need to correct the cooling. Yes, another test with more thrust…"
Gustav looked at Tony.
Bill was already back in the bunker, applying some changes to the engine parameters.

A head looked in.
It was Tony.
"Bill, I go now. I have wife and children you know. I cannot take further risks…."

Before Bill could utter a word, Tony disappeared out of the barn.
"Tony, Tony my friend… we are so close….don't bottle out now…."

But Tony was gone.
He threw off the protective gear onto the ground.
In fact he walked quickly, nearly breaking into a run back to his car behind the farmhouse.
Not even retrieving his overnight gear from within.
In minutes, his car shot down the lane.
Bill looked pleadingly at Gustav, "Don't tell me you're going too?"

Gustav gave an amazing Labrador dog look. The silent pleading in his eyes, the internal conflict he was fighting, trying not to abandon his boss.
'Easy' he thought to return the very generous bonus residing in his bank account.
He started to walk away.
Bill got up to follow him.
"Bill, I …..I honour you as a boss and a colleague, but I feel one more test will be one too much. Something may go wrong. We have enough now to build a good orbital engine, no?"

Bill sighed, sat down on an old bench outside. "Gustav, go. Thank you for staying until now. I needed you guys, your expertise and support to get this far. Thank you again."
Before he could finish, Gustav grabbed Bill's arms and shouted at him "Bill, you know it is dangerous to go further, possibly lethal for you. Surely you can see this?"
Bill shook the grip away, "I have to go on, and don't you see? I have to ensure this engine will work at a minimum of three quarters thrust…."

He looked at Gustav.
The man was frozen on the spot, his hands held in the air, loyalties splitting him apart.
"Go Gustav, go now please. All remains as we agreed, keep your bonuses.
The back of this is already broken."
Bill turned and walked back into the barn.
Gustav stood still for a while, then discarded his radioactive protection and walked back to the farmhouse, muttering and swearing in German.

Bill's forehead scar had become pink, it throbbed again.
'Dammit' he thought, 'This is vital, we are so near.'

He worked for a long time, analysing the two previous burns, picking out small flaws in the graphs against predicted patterns. Then he applied little changes to the engine dynamics parameters, including cooling changes.
The one thing he could not change was the mix of exotic elements in the pellet feed.
They had worked long and hard to determine the correct quantities and composition of the pellets, including uranium 235. Each pellet was tiny, the size of a mustard seed. All of them held in lead lined fuel containers, preventing the radiation from escaping…….for now.

Bill stopped, wiped his wet forehead.
He said to himself "Well that's it. I've done all I can think of. Start with a slow burn, gradually increase to half thrust then see if it holds."
He felt confident.

Confidence is one thing; courage to carry through is another.....
Bill reached into his inner jacket pocket and pulled out the hip flask, thinking
'A little Dutch courage won't go amiss........' he raised the flask in a mock toast, with the sentiment "This is it. I believe in you Bill Craswell, if few others do.
Go for it Bill, do your thing....to infinity and beyond!"

Securing the cap after a rather large glug of Famous Grouse whisky, he moved closer to the battery of screens. In the bunker half light, his serious face was a flickering pattern of colours, catching the reflections from the bright computer displays.
An eerie picture, king gargoyle.

He started the program, one minute to the burn.

At twenty five seconds to go, the steel door opened, Gustav came in.
He slammed the door shut and peered at Bill through his clothing mask window. He held his thumb up. Bill grinned, slapped his shoulder and they sat down side by side watching the screens.

The engine fired a snorting rattling sound. At a third thrust, their bunker was vibrating again. The critical measurements of engine integrity all stayed green.
Bill shouted above the noise, "I have to go to manual Gustav, the program will not allow more thrust on automatic." Gustav nodded.
Bill slowly, ever so slowly increased the engine power.

Towards half power, the engine did its stuff. The thrust combustion gases were starting to make the central armour panel glow bright red in the concrete wall.
The whole barn seemed to be shrieking and vibrating together with the bunker.

A shaking reverberating came right through the floor under their feet.
Gustav looked at Bill with a grim pale face.
Bill returned it with his gargoyle grin.
It said nothing is going to stop me now.
He turned the control and watched the engine thrust go to three quarters.
Outside the bunker, the barn interior was a fog of smoke and gas.
The engine nozzle glowed orange, its mounting frame vibrating hard.
The noise was horrendous.

From the engine exhaust centre, white hot flames howled in a staccato of explosive gravitational reactions. A roaring searing beam flew out, a fierce inferno of gravity defying plasma.

The armour panel in the concrete had caught fire ……radioactive fire.

Bill shouted as loud as he could, "Look at the gauges Gustav, everything is holding! Cooling is good. Fantastic! look at the bloody thrust measurements, unbelievable! Means the fuel will go loads further……"
Gustav's eyes were bulging out of their sockets.

Then Bill increased the thrust.

Gustav hadn't heard a thing, the noise was deafening. He had bit his lip making it start to bleed. He turned to Bill shaking his head, his hand motioning for Bill to shut down the engine.

Bill gleefully cried "Look, LOOK! nearly full thrust and good integrity ! GREEN FOR GO!" He became oblivious to Gustav's frantic sleeve pulling.

The bunker steel door had started to leak around its seal, smoke curled inwards.
The gravity engine screamed and vented its wrath.
Outside the bunker was a scene from hell.

A red warning indicator came up on the display.
Then something utterly strange happened.
It was as though somebody had switched the microphone off.

A gulp of silence.

Lasting maybe a second, then WHUUUUMMMP ! a huge thudding crash.
Followed by a massive grating sound, together with a wailing ear splitting screech.
Metal tearing and shredding.

Bill looked at Gustav, their faces shocked to white.

Something outside crashed against the steel door bursting it inwards.
Bill was flung against the far wall. Gustav was shoved hard and pinned against the computer displays as their glass screens burst into myriads of fragments.

Everything went dark.

Chapter 9

5.30 pm Saturday 17th March
Bill Craswell's farm, Norfolk

After the monstrous cacophony of noise, the silence was total. A bad smell of burning engulfed them.

Gustav prised himself off the cluster of shattered display screens. He coughed in the swirling smoke and dust.
Finally he found Bill lying on the floor in the corner of the bunker and pulled off their protective head masks.
Then Gustav dragged a semi conscious Bill out of the bunker through swirling masses of smoke and powdered debris. White snow fell from the roof.
Visibility was two yards at best.
Bill shook his head, part staggered on one knee, shouted "God, it's snowing, what the hell?"

Gustav struggled to see, making out the pale light from blown open side doors of the barn. He pulled and half dragged his boss outside until they were clear of the smouldering barn.
Quickly running his hands over Bill's arms and legs, Gustav shouted asking if he had any back pain or injuries.
Bill shook his head.

Gustav shook off his garment together with fragments of glass. They both rubbed their ears, trying to get rid of the ringing sounds still present, shaking their hair which was matted with soot and dust.
Gustav between gasps of air, said "Not snow Bill, just roof insulation breaking up and coming down. Something shredded it into fine pieces. You are very lucky not to have any injuries."
"Ah didn't quite escape Gustav."
He winced at a couple of nasty cuts, bleeding from the back of his hand.

Despite smoke virtually engulfing the barn area, there were no signs of flames.
Just in case, Bill grabbed a fire extinguisher from amongst several stacked at the entrance. He staggered back into the barn.
The smoke was clearing.
Then Bill gasped in horror.

"Oh shit….Gustav!..... Good God ... The bloody engine has gone!"

The absent engine complete with frame, had torn itself clean off the floor anchors leaving ragged holes in the concrete.
Instinctively he looked up at the roof. He sighed with a little relief, no hole, the roof was pretty much intact still, and just bits of insulation panel drifting down.

Gustav walked in, nearly tripping over a downed roof strut.
"Gott im Himmel, look Bill, LOOK!" he pointed to a massive hole beyond the bunker.
At the rear of the barn opposite the burn end, the steel wall had been peeled away like an open tin can.
Bill ran across to the yawning hole and looked through.
There in the field about fifty yards away, was the smouldering, but intact gravity engine. Upside down with its buckled frame legs stuck up in the air at crazy angles.
It looked like some giant dead insect.
The surrounding grass had caught fire sending smidgens of grey black smoke curling up into the air.
Something made him glance slightly to the side and towards the back end of the field.

Bill went ice cold.
There at the far hedgerow was a little shimmering man in white.

"Oh gawd!... oh my gawd…….what the hell …..him again?"
He went to sort of wave, when Gustav shouted at him.

"BILL, Look here!"

Still dazed, Bill turned around to look at where Gustav was gesticulating.
He gasped again, this time at the other end of the barn.
The concrete wall to contain the exhaust blast was still there, well the sides remained, they were cracked and deformed.
The middle was completely gone and so was most of the steel barn wall behind it.
The engine thrust had completely ripped out the centre of the concrete containment shell. Together with a very hot central panel …gone.
Maybe not so temperature hot, as dangerously radioactive hot.

"Strike me dead!" exclaimed Bill.
He turned and glanced back through the hole in the steel wall.
The man in white was gone.
Bill rubbed his face, closing then opening his eyes, yes the man was gone.
He took a ragged breath and gestured to Gustav to follow him outside.

After dowsing the grass fire around the engine, they discovered the remains of the concrete wall scattered wide some dozens of yards away. The Geiger counter crackled away, Bill grimaced. Gustav walked around shaking his head, uttering German profanities. Then he fetched the first aid box and bandaged Bill's hand.

Back in the farmhouse, they hooked up the retrieved computer server to a laptop.
The server had been tucked under the bench in the bunker and miraculously it had survived intact. Gustav's protective clothing had several blast shreds, but he uncannily came away virtually unharmed, just a few bruises.
Their eyes were glued to the laptop display, scanning the last engine burn and readings, made just before the catastrophe.

Bill said "See that, my word do you know what Gustav?"
Bill was shaking a little.
"Go on Bill."
"It looks like the engine remained operational even when the frame was tearing out the floor mountings. Only when some of the cables sheared did the systems detect a problem and quickly shut power to the engine. Then as the cooling had been shut down prematurely, the fire started."
Gustav sternly replied, "Ah yes, that is good. Now I think we should clear up soon Bill, and then get out of here."
Bill's eyes flicked around, he looked out of the window across to wisps of smoke hanging around the damaged barn. He grimaced, his hand was sore.
He focussed back on Gustav, "Yes, we better get this place sorted and the radioactive residue bagged and shipped out somehow."

He turned back to the laptop and started pulling up more result figures.
Bill's eyes popped wide "My word, the thrust is way higher than we predicted.
Like, hang on let me do the numbers..........yes, cripes like, no can't be..." his voice tailed away.
He muttered "No wonder the wall got blown out and the engine broke its frame mounts. I estimate the final thrust reached perhaps five hundred percent over what we expected. Incredible! What do you think Gustav, secondary reactions after leaving the compression chambers?"
Gustav was scribbling some calculations on a pad.
He quickly inserted the results into several equations on the computer. Shaking his head slightly, he said "Hard to say Bill, we need more analysis. According to the temperature sensors we had, no....Mein Gott ! They have gone off the scale!" he quickly scribbled some numbers.
"Bill Craswell!"
Bill looked at him strangely, Gustav never used his surname.
Gustav had the look of a man possessed.

He grabbed Bill's sleeve and said "If you project the sensor readings, I make it five to six thousand degrees centigrade in the centre of the combustion chambers. It is only momentarily within each of the drive explosions, just a fraction of a second, but which means……"
Bill cut in, "Holy Hell Gustav… that's…. that's FUSION temperatures!"
Gustav carried on, "Yes …. It appears at the central core of the combustion explosions, a small fusion interaction happens. It is incredible Bill!"

Bill's heart leapt, he grabbed Gustav's shoulders, grinning, trembling.
They stared at each other sharing a maniacal look.
Their hearts were pounding, their bodies and minds still shaken from the near catastrophe.

Bill's thoughts wandered back to the image at the end of the field. He suddenly felt he badly needed to talk to Karen. Somehow she would know who or what the man was.

It took what was left of the evening and the next morning to clear up the debris that they could lift.
Great big lumps of concrete remained perched at odd angles in the field like some ancient religious site. Some were "a bit radioactive", according to Bill.
"No way can they be moved by us. Have to leave them there for now."
He had a little guilt twinge, then pulled the gargoyle face thinking, 'No problem the farm is off limits to people anyway…'
With the farm tractor they winched the battered engine onto a trailer.
Then donning protective suits they bagged up as much of the radioactive debris as they could find and move. Burying it in an old cesspit hole, they covered the radioactive debris with earth. Finally with the engine and major bits inside the barn, Bill padlocked the battered barn doors.

Gustav started laughing, a nervous deep laugh. "What are you locking it for?
There are two huge holes at both ends!"
Bill said between heavy breaths, "Yeah well, we'll have to get them plugged somehow. But that will have to do for now, I'll come back and arrange a proper clean up, soon as."
They quickly removed their protective suits and buried those as well in the cesspit, finally closing the large rusty iron covers on top.
Gustav had sunk down and sat on the ground, "I am exhausted Bill…."
Bill replied "Yes, bloody hard work mate. Glad you came back. Thanks."
Gustav "I had to Bill, to see it through. It needed two to run it… and someone to pull you out of that bunker." He smiled at his boss.

Bill nodded, "Thanks a million Gustav. Come on we must shower now, get ride of any residue."
His mind was aglow with a new pride.
Despite the end catastrophe at the barn, the engine had worked and in the final test, worked flawlessly.

What hadn't really sunk home due to the partial state of shock they were both in, was the criminal seriousness of the radioactive matter they had created on the farm.

Bill kept thinking about the manifestation of the glowing man again, down at the bottom of the field. Someone or something was keeping an eye on him.
He shuddered.

Later that afternoon they drove out of the farm's winding entrance lane and onto the main road. After about two miles they were flagged down by a policeman. Another got out from the patrol car.

He beckoned Bill to wind down the window. "Sir, have you some ID? And where are you going and where have you come from?"
"Afternoon Officer, we are Ministry of Defence scientists returning from our Norfolk installation near PartleDown. Our destination is in Hampshire."
The policeman checked both their MOD passes and driving licences.
Bill as casually as he could, asked "May I ask what is the problem Officer?"

"We had reports of loud explosion like noises, early yesterday evening. Several of the locals phoned in. You know anything about that?" He looked intently at Bill and Gustav, especially at Bill's bandaged hand.
The other policeman had walked over to join him.

Bill caught the suspicious mood and put on his best innocent smile, "Wouldn't know Officer. We were working all day yesterday and night in our laboratories over in PartleDown, heard nothing." He turned to Gustav. Gustav nodded a couple of times.

With a smile, Bill raised his injured hand slightly and said "In case you wondered, bloody sharp edges on one of the computer frames, you'd think manufacturing would know how to de-burr these days. But I'm a scientist, we take the risks in our stride."

Bill looked at the copper, grimaced and quickly continued, "I bloody hate working weekends, but it's the only time you can take down some computers, so you can work on the damn things."
The policeman smiled cynically, "We all have our late hours Sir, duty you know and look after that hand. Thank you. Have a safe journey."

The policeman waved them on.
He looked at the rear of their disappearing car for a while and then reached for his collar mike.

Midday Sunday 18th March.
Los Cancajos, The island of La Palma, Canary Islands.

The fruity sangria was rich and ice cold.
It slipped down too easily.

John looked out from the café frontage and up at the sky.
His mind wondering how and why that object in space had suddenly expanded hugely in size.

John turned and looked at Karen as she said, "We ought to get a little villa out here, and I love this place."
"Yes, it would be grand. A lottery win would help."

Karen spoke, "Well now that I am the sole inheritor of Mum and Dad's estate, I……" she didn't finish, she remembered, "Well I was the sole inheritor, now there is a complication."
John frowned, "Like what?"

Karen paused, breathed in the cool sea air, watching the surf crashing on the black rocky lava coast. "You see I have a brother now, well a half brother. When I went through Dad's things I found a letter from a guy named Angelo."
She then took John through the contact made by him and the birth mark he, herself and her Dad shared.
Pretty conclusive.
Somehow, when her Dad was in the Mediterranean he had fathered Angelo. She thought 'but he was married to Mum then, oh Dad… how could you?'

John leaned back on his chair, pondered then said "Wow, so have you met him?"
"No, but I must contact him. You see he told me about his parents, his Pa being the Mayor of Skiathos. So I did some research.
In fact I spoke to the receptionist at the Skiathos Greek Antiquities Museum and I learnt some interesting stuff, especially about an American shipping agent there."

John took another gulp of the sangria, a cool, fruit laden taste, ice cubes clinked.
He swallowed and said "Go on, sounds like the plot is thickening."
"Well, apparently Silenos Drivas, that's Angelo's Greek father umm step-father, has a joint manufacturing and distribution company with a chap named Irving Dekker.
This company makes reproduction high quality Greek and other 'artefacts' and ships them all round the world. The company has a turnover in the high millions of Euros.
I believe my Dad had business links with them, but he never confided in me. He always was a bit secretive."

John had a puzzled look, his eyes then widened, "Of course, I remember now."
Karen continued, "Yes that's where your ex-wife met Dekker's son Orlando, at the antiquities fair in London back then, when I was helping Dad on his stand."
John grimaced for a fraction of a second remembering his ex-wife Theresa and her affair with Orlando Dekker. It resulted in their divorce, but he quickly smiled, "And where I met a beautiful woman who completely dominates my life, thank you."
Karen laughed "So glad we met John. Strange, fate that is. They say there is much more to coincidences then we care to believe."

Then she had that far away look again.

"So what else did you find out?"

Karen turned back to him, "Yes, well there is more. I pretended to the receptionist that you, my husband, were looking for unusual, exceptionally, rare objects. These would be ancient and possibly Persian. You see Dad in his will mentioned a third ancient artefact, a helmet, with powers like the cross and the sword, and that Irving Dekker might have found it. So I was doing a bit of fishing."
John smiled with a chuckle and said "your husband now, sounds interesting!"

Grinning, Karen took a sip of her drink, ducking round the cluster of little umbrellas decorating it.
She then continued “The receptionist started taking a particular interest in that she said she could introduce me to someone who may be able to satisfy our search.
I casually dropped into the conversation about some press cutting I read that mentioned an Irving Dekker finding ah…yes quote ‘a magnificent Kylix drinking bowl set which was a centre piece in the Greek Museum.’”

John looked around the little café waterfront, quiet, peaceful. Far out the ocean waves murmured their song. A hand full of people were paddling on the dark sand amongst some rocks near the water’s edge.
An old local lady, with nut brown skin and long grey hair, was hunched over a magazine drinking her coffee in the corner of the café.

Karen carried on “With that the receptionist dropped her voice to a whisper and said yes that is the man and he may delight you.”
“Delight you! Say no more!” John winked naughtily.
Karen lightly punched him in the arm, she exclaimed with a big smile,
“Silly.”
Then she said, “So I told her I will call again in a week or two, to arrange a date for a trip to Skiathos, for when we could meet up with Dekker.”
“Sounds very interesting. Maybe meet Angelo at the same time?”
“That’s exactly what I was thinking.”

John’s phone buzzed, a Fleetwood Mac tune rang out; the track Second Hand News.
“John Creeson?”

“Yes, hi Richard.”
“Hi John, something serious has come up and it cannot wait until you get back.”

Karen was frowning, she thought 'This is our holiday. Damn, we should have left our mobiles at home and picked up temporary ones here.'
Richard Armitage continued in John's ear.
"…. where the anomaly Crackwell is now, as I said, we have become aware of a large area of distorted space. I have this first hand from Colonel Mondone. He said it was important that we have this information straight away."

John took on a serious look, "And what do they think this distortion is?"
Armitage's voice became very serious, "From our early analysis, it looks like a huge single object moving slowly. It's practically invisible. I would have liked to have Bill to do some in depth analysis using the Gravity Array, but he is away this weekend, working on the Norfolk Gravity Array upgrade."
John's mouth opened, no words initially came out. Then he said "So what are the powers that be doing? I guess the government have plans in place?"
Armitage spoke slowly, "John, we need you and Karen to go to the European telescope complex on the peak of the volcano where you are staying. Quite handy you're there actually. I have arranged for you to be met by a couple of leading cosmologists. They have already done some quite astonishing observations, and I think speed is of the essence."
John "I see."
Armitage "I have booked both of you in at the accommodation onsite. You'll need warm clothing as it is perishing up there at that height. I think if you can make it today that would be prudent."
John "Today? Hmm ok Richard."
Karen having caught the gist of the conversation grabbed John's arm motioning for the phone.
"Richard?"
"Yes, that you Karen?"
"Yes, we are supposed to be on holiday here. Just how important is this? Surely it can wait until we return home?"

Armitage took a deep breath, "I wish it could Karen. Trouble is the military are mobilising......."
He let that sink in. "Already our armed forces are on high alert as are several other nations' forces. You see the trajectory of this invisible object is on course for the Earth. The very nature of its invisibility gives the impression it does not want to be discovered."
Stuff of science fiction, but really happening and bizarre events starting to happen.
"So I need you guys to have a close look at that object as soon as possible, using the very powerful telescopes there at the.... hang on let me check.......yes the Roque de los Muchachos installation. I will get Bill and his team here to monitor it via our gravity arrays when they are back up. Glean whatever we can."
He signed out.

Karen looked dejectedly at John, then she pulled a face and said "Oh God...."

The same day, early evening.
Somewhere just south of London, UK.

Gustav was at the wheel doing his share of the driving.
Bill had just switched his phone back on.
"Hmmm, loads of texts and three missed calls."
He spent a while reading the texts, then looked at Gustav.
"Trouble in store. Looks like Armitage has been trying to get hold of me.
Something about Crackwell, the anomaly."

He called Richard Armitage.
Armitage glanced at his phone, merrily playing the Jerusalem hymn, *'and did those men in ancient times...'*
"Ah Bill, where the hell have you been, I've been trying to get hold of you all day!"
Bill smiled and thought to himself, 'Yeah and whatever you want, I've been doing and achieving ten times more than that '

"Richard. The Norfolk Array server upgrade is complete, couple of hiccups, but we got there." He had a crooked smirk on his face.

"Glad to hear that Bill. I tried to call PartleDown but the bloody phone system seems to have packed up there…again. Did you try any calls while you were onsite?"
Bill "No, just used our mobiles."
"Damn strange Bill as I couldn't get yours or the other guys' phones either."
"I think they had a partial phone network breakdown in the area. Anyway what's up Richard, you sound a bit stressed man?"

Richard took a deep silent sigh, thinking 'the bloody camera system was out too, again. It seemed to be flaky as well. Or was it a Craswell doing, something going on up there in PartleDown?'
He replied "Yes to the point. Something huge has come out of Crackwell."

Silently he let the implication sink in.
"WHAT? Please repeat Richard, I'm not sure I heard that clearly."
"Bill, I repeat A HUGE OBJECT HAS COME OUT OF CRACKWELL and what's more it is INVISIBLE."

Bill gasped, said "Oh Lord!"
Armitage continued, "Can you guys come straight to ESS at East Meon tonight?
I think we need to bring the Gravity arrays back online and look at this point in space and mighty quick. The Ministry are leaning hard on us."

"Right you are Richard, I reckon ETA in about… an hour?" he glanced at Gustav who nodded in agreement. "Yes an hour. Hold the fort Richard."
The call ended.

Richard Armitage was muttering and cursing, "Mind the bloody fort, mind the bloody fort! Once a godforsaken backwater putting my illustrious career on hold. Now the centre of the world and I can't keep track of my people!"

He got up and walked over to the coffee machine, still moaning.

The pipe came out. He ploughed tobacco into the pipe bowl and then punched buttons on the machine as though it had personally offended him.

Much later still at ESS, East Meon

They were on their second coffee.
Midnight was long past.
As tired as they were, yawning didn't come. There are times when the brain learns to remain sharp. This was one of them.

Bill leaned back in his chair scratching his head.

"Beats me Richard, damn thing is as you said invisible. Apart from that minute propulsion trail, the gravity arrays cannot see anything else."
Both Richard Armitage and Gustav Huck sat close by, their eyes glued to the wall displays.
One showed a video stream from La Palma, courtesy of the Roque de los Muchachos telescope observatory systems. The invisible black patch moved slowly across the screen.

Gustav said "It is incredible, the size of it, massive!"
Armitage pulled out his still warm pipe and started to load more tobacco in.
Smoking in his office was against regulations as was the entire site.
He glanced at Bill's bandaged hand and had not failed to notice the slight nervousness of both the men.
Armitage pondered looking at them both, noticing red marks in various places on their necks, their faces.

Earlier he had called Tony Cressada to see how he was doing, but the man's wife said he was asleep, having come home quite unwell.

Today had been especially demanding.
He put the unlit pipe to his mouth and took little draws. A quiet intermittent sucking action broke the silence.

After some minutes, Bill exclaimed, "Bugger this, I'll call John and Karen and put them on speaker phone here. We need to know more of what is happening."

Armitage nodded, it was time he had a little investigation of his own.

Chapter 10

7pm Sunday 18th March
2000 metres high and heading towards the volcano summit.
Destination: Roque de los Muchachos European Observatory, La Palma

The sun was setting.
Huge orange streaks fanned out in the sky from the west.
Ragged snow covered edges of the volcano top, sparkled golden with the last of the sun's rays and the deep blue sky was slowly turning dark purple.

John drove the four wheel drive Nissan up the winding mountain road.
A thick forest of pine trees hugged the steep slopes, some teetering over almost a vertical drop.
As they rounded a very tight bend about two thirds up the volcano road, for a moment they faced south west. Looking across at what was left of the collapsed southern wall of the huge ancient volcanic crater.

He said "There see that old ridge running down? There is something ominous about it."
Karen "Yes I do. Tell me more."
John "Well back in I think it was 2004, a BBC Horizon programme depicted a horrific tsunami scenario right there."
Karen's eyes widened, "Really?"

"Yes and it was quite scientific. Apparently there had been a massive land slip in the late nineteen forties at the same time as the volcano last erupted. The BBC scientists predicted another landslip was going to happen at some time in the future. When it does happen, it will be humungous. An enormous chunk of mountain will slide into the sea creating a giant tsunami."

She replied “and so is this really possible?”

He glanced at her as the car came out of the bend into a straight bit of road.
“Well other learned scholars hammered the BBC programme saying the evidence didn’t exist and scared people unnecessarily. Frightened not only the locals in the collapse path here on the island, but people living on the American east seaboard.”

Karen quickly “America! But how, that is so far way?”

John looked serious, “Apparently the prediction was that with such a giant rock mass breaking away and sliding quickly into the sea here, a tsunami wave in the deeps of the Atlantic would only be, what, a couple of metres high.
However, with the enormous energy of such a wave, by the time it reached New York and running into shallower water, it could rise to about fifty metres high.”
Karen “Good God, that’s scary.”
John “...and locally around the Canary islands in the shallows here, maybe a hundred metres high.”
Her eyes took in the scenario.
He joked “Well it has been fourteen years since and the old rock hasn’t budged an inch.”
She sighed “Glad about that John. I was just thinking of Ming’s experience and her boyfriend when they were caught up in that Hawaiian tsunami.”
John said “Yeah that was pretty awful. I believe sometime ago they installed seismic sensors here along that rocky ridge. So no worries, we’ll get plenty of warning.”
He laughed as he saw Karen’s worried face.
She smiled back, “Yes, we are too much doom and gloom these days! ….must look more on the bright side.”

Near the summit the road ran along the edge of the crater top.
Karen shouted “Ooh John… pull over into that lay-by; let’s take some photos before the light goes completely.”

Standing on the roadside, it seemed as though they were on top of the Earth.
The peak of the ridge seemed to be surrounded by blue sky as far as the eye could see.
Way below them was the cloud level.
The clusters of barren cold rocks on either side of the road gave way within a few tens of metres to gigantic drops.
Carved out of the high edge of the volcano rim, the clean tarmac road had replaced an old footpath. Scattered patches of snow and ice clung to the roadside strata.

Karen got out and said, “Coo…bit chilly up here.”
As they peered over and down through the mist, clouds hovered around the dark green forest clad sides of the volcano. Ground level was nine thousand feet below.

They snapped a few photos, and then Karen turned to John and said, “John, you don’t say much about your family?”
They had sat down on a couple of smooth rocks near the road.
John surprised looked at her; he replied “What brings you to ask me here?”
Karen “Oh my mind wandered. This place, it feels near the top of the world, just us, the clean fresh air, and the endless blue sky. Then I thought of my mum Jenny, dad Edward and your dad Reg, somewhere far away up there in the blue yonder.”
“Yeah, he’s been gone, what must be five years now. He was a radar expert in the war you know.”

John’s dad Reginald Creeson had worked with the British team to develop early warning radar. During the second world war, they were able to spot the German planes coming across the English Channel, laden with death and destruction.
He continued, “You know our parents would have lived very different lives if the Germans had invaded England. They were within two weeks of doing that.”

Karen watched him; she moved closer, took his hand.

"Yes, must have been a very worrying time for everybody."
John said, "Well if they had, it was discovered in the captured archives later, that they planned to ship every British male up to the age of fifty, back to the German war factories in Europe."
"God is that right? Just shows John, how little periods in time can be so life changing."
She glanced across the ragged edged rocks and across to the few clouds in the sky, thinking to herself 'Fight. Fight for what we have, our freedom, and our families.
Awful thing war. There must be another way….'
Continuing John become sombre, "It would have gutted this country for decades and probably you and I would not be around now. Europe descending into the Dark Ages for heaven knows how long. Thank god for Dad and the radar guys, the RAF and everybody else in their defiance of a common threat."

He then said, "Yeah our parents went through a lot. I spoke to Mum the other day. She's becoming a little forgetful and that old cottage is becoming too much for her.
I did suggest she sold up and bought one of those modern apartments attached to a complex for retired people. You know an onsite restaurant if you want it, a warden around to help and a new social life meeting people her own age."
"And did Audrey warm to that?"
He laughed "She wanted none of it! Independent to the end, that's my Mum. Your mum Jenny, I remember you saying she was a nurse?"
Karen was far away, she replied, "Yes she was. Afterwards she started her own business in acupuncture healing."
"Ah."
"While she was very good at it, it also allowed her to apply her own 'healing techniques'."
"Karen, what do you mean?"
"She had a gift you know. A real healer, but she shunned any publicity, so she used acupuncture as a front. Don't get me wrong, acupuncture is a real science and she used it in tandem with

her gift. My mum Jenny spent some years in China you know, learning the ancient techniques and their spiritual cultures."

John became silent, thinking about his own beliefs, the strong spiritualism that oozed from Karen. Then the weird test they had conducted with the ancient artefacts. Somehow Karen connected to those old relics, each seemingly to contain a miniature technology that was way beyond mankind's understanding. The scientist in him struggled internally; he wanted to understand how it all ticked.

Karen at length said, "Do you know, my mum told me of one particular patient she had who suffered from bad sciatica. It was a longish acupuncture session in her clinic and she also applied some of her healing techniques."
John turned to her.
She continued "Well the session was successful, but when she got home the sciatica had transferred across from the patient, *into her own arm.* Temporary, but it was very painful for the next couple of days."
"Incredible." exclaimed John.
"Yes it was amazing John. There seems to be no answer as why that happens."

What was left of the blue sky was turning to black. The odd star twinkled. No aircraft exhaust trails could be seen.

Aircraft were not permitted to fly over the European Space Telescope Centre on La Palma. As well as no gas or particle pollution, absolutely no light pollution was permitted either. Even the airport was situated down below on the edge of the island shore, with aircraft strictly following arrival and exit routes from the sea board, avoiding the telescope complex on the mountain top.

Karen shivered, zipping up her jacket, "It's so cold John."
He replied "Yes, they said it would be about one degree up here… brrr… it gets into your bones. Let's go."

The accommodation complex was a little way down from the telescope installations. It had been specially designed to emit very little heat and no light at night.
Telescopes need clean, stable cold air and no excess light.
In reception a young guy in his late twenties had been waiting for them.
His long black hair tied back in a pony tail, Latin complexion.
Carlos Rodriguez greeted them both with a warm smile.

"Hello, Mr Creeson and Miss Durgas, such an honour to meet you guys!"
Karen blushed a little "Oh please first names… Karen and John."
They both shook hands with Carlos and he familiarised them with the complex layout, showing them to their room. "Once you've freshened up and sorted your bags, please join me in the Hubble Lounge for coffee, ah have you eaten?"
Karen replied, "Yes, sort of, we had sandwiches on the way, but a snack would be welcome."

Fifteen minutes later.

They were sat in a corner alcove with a pile of hot savoury offerings, little meat pastries, sliced spicy sausage and a bowl of salad.
Steam rose in swirls from hot tea and coffee.
Carlos went straight to the point "As you know we have been asked by our governments to investigate a strange occurrence out at the object, Crackwell I believe you call it. Using the new VLT (Very Large Telescope) we have analysed a huge area where the light from those stars appears slightly distorted. As a result we have detected a very large object moving slowly. By all accounts it would seem invisible."

John was the first to reply, "Have you any more data on it?"
Carlos said "Yesterday the Americans told our governments about it, so an emergency government directive here, commandeered several telescopes to be made available immediately. I and

another astronomer Louis Remond, have been asked to drop our research work and look at this issue."
Karen quickly said "That is serious, I know in the past, when I booked time for remote access on one of these instruments, the procedure was quite daunting and I had to ensure well in advance, to book my requested viewing dates and times."
Carlos pulled a frown, "Yes, unfortunately as a result of this commandeering, many astronomers are upset at their lost schedules, some quite angry."
Karen, "I can understand that."

Another man appeared at their table.
Carlos stood up "Ah... please let me introduce Louis Redmond, our resident galaxy expert."
Karen immediately looked at Louis with intense interest.
He was probably about forty.
Stunningly handsome, with a dark complexion and almost black hair, darting vivid blue eyes.
They shook hands.
Louis spoke "I am very interested in your gravity work with the supernova."

Feverish discussions followed, and then Karen said something, "Louis? Have you looked at the Andromeda galaxy lately?"
Louis stared at Karen, his sapphire eyes locking on her, "Why yes in fact I have. Why do you ask me?"

Karen looked around, she felt a little exposed, a bit nervous.
She was about to broach the subject of the 'dark menace' that she had felt with her spirituality and her sensing the origin to be Andromeda.

She slowly replied, "Well I have been doing some analysis on the object Crackwell, to try and determine the nature of the portal construction. The data I have seems to correlate with a path of sorts that goes back to the star cluster Omega Centauri."
Louis frowned, "So where does the Andromeda galaxy fit in?"

Karen knew she had a golden opportunity here, but careful, careful.
Surrounded by the scientific community, for now she needed to keep her other talents secret.
She sort of fabricated her approach.
"Well…I.. Well…..let us say I have detected another path that breaches the portal corridor, but comes from the direction of the Andromeda galaxy. It is most strange."

Louis just looked at her, but his eyes were slightly glazed, his mind working hard.
John and Carlos listened as the discussion evolved.
At length Louis spoke slowly and cautiously.
He said "There is something very odd. Unique I would say."

Karen puzzled, leaned forward; John couldn't help noticing her bosom resting on the high table. His mind became distracted and wandered away to nice thoughts.
Her eye caught his, and a tiny smile fleeted her lips.

She said "Tell us Louis, please, no matter how odd it may appear."
"Ok, what we have is a very interesting transmission from the European satellite Aurora. Recently it flew by the planet Saturn. It is on course for the planets Uranus and Neptune. In doing a course correction, the X-Ray and Gamma Ray telescopes on board, briefly faced the Andromeda galaxy.
It was a unique moment with the satellite way over to the side of our solar system to get a more sideways look at this galaxy, particularly the black hole at its centre."

"…..and something beautiful if you like, staggering and huge was discovered."
The silence as he took a breath was cloying.

"A jet emanating from the centre of the galaxy. A giant jet of extremely hot gases and X-rays, pouring out from disintegrating stars as they are being dragged into the massive gravity of the spinning black hole. But what is magnificent, and Karen, John, maybe you can turn your Gravity Array to look at it, is what I believe is a stable energy cortex snaking out along the route of the jet."

Karen was turning very pale; goose bumps crawled on her arms. He continued "You see the direction of this cortex is interesting. I extrapolated the direction and it lines up sideways and points to the orbit of your anomaly, the object Crackwell. What is incredible is that the cortex snakes right out of that galaxy across to ours. Colossal energies are involved. We believe this cortex will remain in position for many years."

What he said next produced an unease that cut the air.

"My observations hint at this cortex providing a corridor-like path."

Karen looked at John, her eyes contained fear.
John had snapped back to the present, he spoke "My god Louis, you have stumbled, sorry, discovered something extremely important!"
Louis chuckled "I think stumbled is more accurate."
Then he puzzlingly said "...and what is strange is that we are unable to see clearly where this cortex enters our solar system. It sort of fades out."

Karen said nothing, and then she wasn't there in mind anymore, only body.

Late that night in the large monitor hall.

A hubbub of noise greeted them.
Over on the far side, huge wall sized display screens dominated the room.

'Much like our lab set up, only bigger.' thought John.

Batteries of computer stations, each with their own large display, lay in rows in front of the wall screens.
Each desk position a luxury work space, with a bunch of what looked like joysticks and little control handles to the side of each work station.
Many seats were occupied.
Carlos “Those large screens can display images directly from our telescopes. Also we can show images in the X-Ray and Gamma ray domains.”
Karen, “That is excellent.”

Then a smartly suited man entered and walked directly over to them.
Carlos turned and introduced him.
“Please may I introduce our site director, Mr Claude Guillermin.”
They all turned and got up to shake hands.

Claude Guillermin was not popular at the Roques de los Muchachos Centre.
He was a rules and regulations man, stickler for procedures, yet bending them as and when it suited him.
Of medium height, short brownish hair, brown eyes, probably late forties and displaying an odd short patchy beard, which refused to grow in some places.
Guillermin grinned a ragged cemetery of stained smoker’s teeth.

He spoke in a slightly high pitched whiny voice.

“Very, very happy to have you people here. As you can see matters are becoming extremely serious.”
He looked hesitantly at Karen. Suddenly she felt awkward, and turned to Carlos who completed the introduction.
Karen “Yes you certainly have a wonderful facility here Mr Guillermin. Carlos was just showing us some of the capabilities.”
Guillermin replied with a little arrogance, “Thank you. We lead the world in cosmology here. I like to think others follow where we go.”

John carefully eyed the guy making an instant judgement. Some people you naturally warm to, others you need to get to know more……and then some that instantly put you on your guard. Claude Guillermin fell into the last category.

Guillermin spoke with a commanding, authoritive voice, "Now there are certain arrangements shall we say that need to be understood right from the start.
Carlos first let me thank you for quickly setting up the live feeds from your scopes to main control.
This will give various people in our governments, a direct visual on the proceedings."

He continued, "With the present situation likely to change very quickly, I need to be informed on a half hourly basis, even if you have nothing to report. We need you guys with your special expertise, to work as long hours as possible. Catch sleep where you can, but I have authority from the Spanish, French and British governments to maximise our monitoring of just what is happening out there…meaning you must stay onsite for as long as is necessary." his hand pointed up to the ceiling and then to the wall screens.
Guillermin paused for a breath.
'God ' thought Karen, 'This guy could be Richard Armitage's brother and it looks like our holiday is about to change.'
She realised the wonderful opportunity to work here, but these observations could be false alarms, telescope errors and so on. They needed this holiday badly, to rest, to recuperate, to spend time together without science getting in the way.

Their Wales episode still recent and very raw.

She interrupted, "I would like to say that we have volunteered part of our holiday to be here and we are under no authority to be compelled to stay. However, I am very keen to help in the investigation staying one maybe two nights."

She glanced at John who had moved close to her, he nodded his concurrence.

Guillermin, gave a sickly smile. "Please, I do not wish to how do you say it, 'strong arm ' people into working on this phenomenon." The pitch of his voice had lowered.
"You see the matter has been decided above my head by your government. There is now a military presence on site, not only to protect it, but to….to..."
Karen quickly interjected, "To keep people prisoners here."

Again the half smile, the uneven row of yellow teeth. "Of course not, you are free to come and go as you please. You are professionals, but as you know in situations of emergency, professionals do what is necessary. Thank you, please enjoy your stay."
With that he left abruptly.

"I didn't like that one bit, or him." whispered Karen to John.
Carlos had an apologetic face said "I am sorry, he is not very diplomatic at times."
John replied "Gees…. I think things are getting very warm, much more is happening than we think we know. I must speak to Bill. Get the Gravity Arrays aligned, although at the range of this object their sensitivity will be very weak."
He continued, thinking as he was going, "Also unless this giant craft or whatever it may be, uses some sort of gravitational thrust, we may not see anything."

They didn't need coffee to keep them awake tonight.
"Ok everybody I am switching the VLT to the screen."
All eyes swivelled to the wall as the huge screen burst into a myriad of coloured stars and nebula.
Carlos said "There, see the distortion? We have it on automatic track. The systems are monitoring the distortion and calculating the movement from the distorted star positions. We get this sort of

fuzzy outline. Then we have programmed the systems to remove all those stars within this outline and hey presto."

He keyed a command and said, "Our craft or asteroid is no longer invisible."

Gasps could be heard.
Sure enough a large black mass appeared slowly moving, stars winking out in front of its path and stars reappearing behind it.
"Flippin eck" exclaimed John, "What the hell is it?"

Carlos looked around at them all, said "It is at about fifteen million miles from the Earth and travelling at around one hundred thousand miles an hour. The direction of travel is not clear, but it seems to be travelling in an arc that would bring it to the Earth. If it maintains that course and speed, it will arrive here in approximately one hundred and fifty hours, about six days."

They were all spellbound, their imaginations rampant.

He continued "We estimate the size to be approximately five hundred miles in diameter."

Karen felt strange, but she said nothing despite her mind sensing imminent danger. All of a sudden holidaying seemed secondary.
Louis whistled "If it is a spacecraft, the size of it is immense."

He then turned to a second giant wall display mounted alongside the one showing the invisible craft. Here Louis brought up a picture of the Andromeda Galaxy.
He magnified as much as the systems resolution could give. Then he keyed in commands to highlight its black hole jet.
X-Rays and Gamma rays were converted to visible colours.
Louis slowly spoke, "There, that is what the Aurora satellite recorded."
A very tiny thin line came snaking out the galaxy centre. It was a brilliant orange, tinged with yellows and a lot of blue.

Louis operated the on screen pointer.
"There is Andromeda in the X-Ray spectrum shown as that bright orange orb in the top left hand corner. The bluish spike is a huge plasma jet from the black hole in the centre of that galaxy. There inside, that is our cortex jet, possibly a million miles wide."
Fabricated in wispy x-rays within the blue jet, was a hair thin white line.

Karen felt shivery; she had been standing, but quickly sat down.
John was quick to notice. He said quietly "You ok Karen?"
She nodded yes.

The hall filled with more people.
A uniformed man with cropped hair approached them.
"Hello, I am Commander Richmond, attached to NATO forces in the Atlantic arena."
Carlos turned round, he quickly introduced everybody.
The commander continued, "I do not represent the onsite security force, well not directly, but more I am the liaison for the EQUIRF."
John puzzled said, "Sorry never heard of it, please enlighten us?"

Richmond replied "European Quick Response Force. I have instructions to pass on all the information you have to my superiors, in real time as you receive it."

John said "Ok, I understand you. But remember we are civilians and not in the armed forces."
Richmond countered politely, "I respect that, but you must understand that the situation is changing rapidly. Your particular skills are invaluable here."
He paused then said, "My seniors have issued directives to restrict the information so as not to alarm the general public. We are already aware of heightened public anxiety. Also there have been and are, increasing episodes of violence around the world, some are terrorist activities. Some installations as of necessity will come under military jurisdiction and protection."

Nobody spoke; they listened as the Commander continued.
"You see in the last few hours, there has been an unusual ramp up in world wide criminal activities, especially mindless attacks. We monitor this information through all our sources, media, military, and as you can imagine, more covert methods."

John spoke, "So what do you think is happening Commander?"

The Commander replied, "I think you know as much as we do. Somehow it is not coincidental that as this object in space appeared and we are talking only a few hours, we are seeing that violent acts throughout the world have accelerated alarmingly in number. Some of the public may get a sense of impending doom. If it is just an asteroid, already the military are looking at ways to launch a missile to knock it off its Earthly course."

Karen whispered to John, "I feel…um a premonition…that it is as though the human race is being slowly… infiltrated, yes possessed even."

Her mind seemed to link to Anne Whitfield's, was that possible? Far, far off yet clear, was a quiet voice in her mind, yes a warning, then she had it.
Then some feeling or voice said 'something so frightening was about to happen, beyond anything that could be comprehended.'
She involuntarily shuddered, cold waves travelled down her neck and along her arms.

"Sorry I didn't catch that, Miss Durgas." Richmond looked directly at her.

She had a face of stone, said curtly "Oh just a feeling I have, as though some unknown energies are already here on Earth. Scientist thoughts you know."
Louis looked at her.

Richmond nodded, and then continued, "So I will be here for the next few hours, but I'll not stand in the way of your work, but if you can brief me regularly, thanks."

At that moment John's phone rang.
He saw it was Bill Craswell.
"Bill, good to see you mate, are you hooked up to our video feed here in La Palma?"
Bill replied, "Yes we are, bloody amazing and a bit scary John."
John "Do our arrays show anything more?"
"No I'm afraid not John, but we are closely monitoring the thing. Hey, have you heard they're talking about curfews back here in England?"
John's eyebrows rose "You're joking?"
"Nope, they have asked for a voluntary curfew, so that the armed forces can better monitor the country at night and they are saying a state of emergency is in the wings."
John frowned "Christ, seems like a little over reaction, I know be prepared and all that, but what if whatever is out there… is friendly?"
Armitage cut in "John, Karen, Richard here. I think all contingences must be considered.
We need you guys to stay in touch. I have full visibility of the video feeds here anyway, but if something extraordinary comes up, call us."

With that the call ended.

Karen got up, grabbed John's arm, said to the others "We're going to take a break, drop of fresh air; we'll be just outside there." She pointed to one of the lounge restaurant doors.

After a couple of minutes walking, they stood on a small hill.
The night was dark and cold.
Karen said "Just needed to get away from all that madness in there and up there." she glanced at the immense starry black sky.

A massive inky void pin-pricked with thousands of tiny spots of light.
Looking at John she squeezed him tight, she needed to hold him close, to….then she exclaimed "what's that bulky thing in your pocket?"

John felt her pull away a little and put her hand against the bulge in his coat.
He laughed, reached in and pulled out a wrapped object. Removing the cloth he held up the sword, the ancient corroded sword that Karen's Dad had found in Anglesey.
"Oh John! I wondered what that was! Why have you brought it with us?
But, then maybe I understand……"
John pondered for a moment, said "I had this feeling, not to leave it behind you know. Not only that it might get stolen, but more of a sense of protection I guess."

They both looked up at the jet black sky, filled with myriads of bright star constellations. It was a magnificent sight. Then they looked for the approximate place where the giant object was located. Difficult to see with the naked eye, even if it was visible…..
The silence was total, their breath faintly illuminated in the cold frosty air.
A light wind blew.
Karen said, "I need to try something John, to dream a connection with Anne, Sabrina and maybe some of the others. I noticed on my phone a text some while back about a circle meeting they are having tonight. Including linking up with those unable to actually be there, like me for instance.
It starts, let me see….hmmm…. yes in about ten minutes. Can you stay near me?"
John "Of course. Glad we grabbed extra layers to wear."

Karen lay on the ground, eyes shut. She was lying on her back and face up on the blanket she carried in her rucksack. John sat on a nearby rock gazing through his pocket binoculars at the brilliant starlit sky, then moving over to where he knew the anomaly Crackwell was.

The dreaming session had commenced.
Karen although conscious, had been able to enter a state of deep relaxation.
A single candle flickered in a hollow in the ground.
She was breathing slowly and deeply.
John smiled, thinking 'bet she's fallen asleep'.
He wondered about this spiritual stuff, not a disbeliever, 'but how on Earth can it exist scientifically in the universe?'

He was jolted out of his star gazing by a little moan from Karen. Instinctively he tried to look at were the invisible object would roughly be.
He squinted through the lens, and murmured to himself 'Nothing only the stars…. yet…. …..no wait, …what is that ?......I see tiny red flashes…'
There in the sky where something demonic lurked, dozens of miniature sparkling red lights could be seen, all twinkling on and off.

Suddenly Karen sat up with a jerk, with her eyes still closed she gave a blood curdling moan, "Uuuurrr….it's started, oh my God……no, please …NO !!!

John ran over, knelt close, "What Karen? What is happening?"
She opened her eyes wide, she was trembling.
John felt something insidious trying to envelop them, something faint, intangible, yet there. His skin went cold, his heart thumped. He stammered, "Oh lord, what the hell?"

Karen unclipped her sacred cross from underneath her blouse and held it out.

“Quick!” she cried,

“QUICK JOHN, GET THE SWORD OUT NOW ! KNEEL CLOSE TO ME!”

Chapter 11

Very late at night. Sunday 18th March
Outside the European Space Telescope Complex Building, on the volcano mountain top.
La Palma, Canary Islands.

For the first time in his life John Creeson felt spiritual, huge waves of shivery cold flowed through him. The hairs on the back of his neck became taught wires, tugging, pulling.
Karen shouted again, "THE SWORD… JOHN! QUICK…. BRING IT CLOSE!"

He fought, feeling something trying to come in, to suppress, to absorb.

The pair of them were being targeted.

A horrible feeling of utter helplessness was being insidiously impinged on his psyche.
He drew on a new strength and with a huge effort, he pulled out the sword and held it towards the cross.

Karen started to quietly moan… and then it happened.

The blue beams shot across linking the old artefacts. The beams became a thick wand of colour. The cross and sword locked into position.
Karen stared straight at the sky, her concentration intense, then she closed her eyes, thinking 'focus and repel'.

Immediately something incredible happened, not entirely new to them, but much more significant this time.
Both John and Karen became enveloped in a large faint purple sphere.
It glistened and rippled like a balloon.

Staggeringly extraordinary events followed.

The pale moon high in the sky seemed to change colour, or rather part of it did.
It started as a tiny purple spot on its surface. Very quickly it grew in diameter and forged a line, a tiny purple beam arcing out and reaching towards the Earth.
The whole sky took on a slight glow, a pale purple tinge, even in the blackness of night.

John had been watching it all.
Karen shook with her eyes closed tightly.
He gaped open mouthed at the proceedings. That awful invading presence in his mind, whatever it was, suddenly vanished, pushed back, away, gone.

Karen opened her eyes vampire like, staring, bloody.
She stood up holding the cross still linked to the sword, she was rock still. Her gaze slowly turned to meet John's.

He felt helpless, losing control.
Powers beyond what any Earthly physics could explain.
He looked at Karen "God…. Karen, oh hell … are you….are you ok?"
John stammered to finish the sentence, his mouth was bone dry.

At that moment, Karen gave an enormous sigh; she broke into a wide smile.
"Oh John, it's gone, we've repelled it somehow!"
The sky became jet black again.
He turned and looked in the direction of the invisible object.
The tiny flashing red lights had vanished.
They stood for a moment, trying to comprehend, to understand.

After some minutes, John spoke, "Karen I saw something fantastic. Something connected our moon to the Earth. It lasted maybe twenty seconds."

Karen was now fully out of Dreaming mode, she replied "Yes, I felt it. Like being surrounded by a motherly love, inside a womb."

John started to shiver, "I………. I saw a….. A purple line from the moon and I know roughly where. It's close to where the Chinese moon base is."
He said "That was the most incredible feeling I have ever had."

Karen had a growing feeling of strength, the power to deflect, to protect.
She thought 'Who am I? What am I?'
She was still frowning when John gathered his senses and commanded, "Come on Karen we need to get back inside, see what's going on."
He grabbed her hand and putting away the sacred objects, they both stumbled back to the control complex building.

As they burst through the inside doors, they met pandemonium. People shouting and gesticulating, clustering around the huge wall screens. The room lighting had been doused. The full brightness and colour of the screens bathed the audience in an eerie glow. Karen noticed the still forms of a few people lying on the floor, others hovering over attending them.

Carlos saw them, his voice rising, "Ah there you are, something incredible has happened, is STILL HAPPENING, LOOK!"

They joined the circle of people around the screens. Commander Richmond was to one side, rapidly talking to the smart phone stuck to his ear. The site director Guillermin was sitting at the front, his hands frantically gripping and un-gripping the chair arms. He had a headset on and was gabbling non-stop into the microphone.
John looked at the screen and what he saw made him sit down and gasp.

The previously invisible object had taken on a fuzzy form, like a large crinkly black asteroid. Pock marked like volcanic rock. It was just enormous, but no more red flashes occurred.
Carlos shouted "It's changing, it's turning. The course is changing."

Phenomenal events continued to happen. Everybody was rooted to the spot, frozen by things that seemed right out of science fiction.

The black object developed a tiny red glow at the centre.

Louis screamed "OH MON DIEU, LOOK EVERYONE, LOOK AT CRACKWELL, SOMETHING ELSE HAS COME OUT OF IT!!"

All heads swivelled to the second giant wall screen.
Something was indeed manifesting itself, something again quite huge, but not quite invisible.
At that moment the black asteroid object would seem to become aggressive.
Its central red glow brightened to a searing brilliance and detached itself quickly from the black spacecraft. Because that is what it was, no doubt in anybody's mind now.
A ball of red fire hurtled at the new massive object just embarking from Crackwell.

Carlos called out the size of the new object, "It is about four hundred miles in diameter and it's….. It's changing shape..... Demonio ! they are commencing battle."

They all watched the scenario unfold.

Karen thought and felt ' humanity was teetering on the edge, the edge of what?'
Deep thoughts, deeper go deeper, she closed her eyes.

The dread suddenly hit her, 'Oh no, please go away, we are insignificant in this universe. Why us?' very clearly she saw in her mind the threat. Some sort of rabid intelligence bent on the utter vanquishing of humanity into a zombie like existence…..

….. and there was something else….far worse….difficult to comprehend.

She paled, feeling numb. People around her seemed far away.

She started to see a more serious threat, something totally beyond comprehension, a threat to all that humanity held dear.
A fear some of us only see in our nightmares….

Her mum was close; she felt it more than ever. "Oh mum, mum." Tears streamed down Karen's cheeks.

Extreme events continued.

As people were glued watching the giant displays, shouts of incredulity rang out.
The red ball of fire seemed to expand outwards as it hit the new object, almost certainly some sort of spacecraft.
For a moment, a glittering, firework show surrounded the new spacecraft, and then the red disappeared.
Claude Guillermin and Commander Richmond mouths wide open, had momentarily paused, no longer speaking into their phones. What was about to happen had everybody's attention.

Louis shouted "LOOK, the new ship is changing shape again, it's so damn hazy, cannot we acquire a clearer picture?"
He was talking to one of the technicians.
The guy shook his head, "No, that is the best we have. There is some sort of distortion. There are enormous energies emanating from it."

Louis again "Oh mon Dieu, the centre is.....it is glowing, the intensity is increasing..."
A smaller support screen showed the area of the two ships bathed in energies with colours across the spectrum.

The new object at best could be described as an enormous set of complex fuzzy spherical mesh cages, one inside another. At the very centre was something extremely bright.
One of the other technicians sitting at a console exclaimed loudly, "There are powerful X-Ray, Gamma and Beta ray emissions from the new object. The measurements show massive distortions in these emissions.
We are seeing energies of a colossal magnitude."

Cries and shouts rang out as the conflict escalated.

Very, very quickly, a shaft of blinding white light appeared to emanate from the new object. It flashed and stabbed directly across space towards the black ship about a million miles away.
A distance of approximately four times that between the moon and the Earth.

In a nutshell, a four hundred mile diameter 'new ship' was directing what appeared to be a white hot beam of energy directly at a five hundred mile diameter 'black ship'.

Two gargantuan beasts dancing a conflict to the death.

The prize seemed to be us, the Earth.

Screams and yells echoed around the hall.
Then a deathly quiet, the seconds ticking by.

With enormous speed, the searingly white hot beam hit the dark ship. For a moment a fuzzy orange flare appeared just off centre of the black mass. Tiny red orbs were seen ejecting just before the beam impact.

Then the dark object started to break up, brilliant sparkles of light rippled through fracture cracks in the dying disintegrating black spacecraft.

To Karen it was a furnace of evil.
In the large room forty five breaths were held in unison.

Suddenly their building shook, displays rattled on tables, charts fell off the walls.
John looked at Karen. They shared the same thought
.
A gravity wave had hit them.

Barely a second later, an enormous flash erupted on the large wall screens, blotting out the entire sky. A distant sharp crack and rumble could be heard.
Quickly the white glare reduced to a yellow glow and then the inky blackness of space. The black asteroid ship had been obliterated in a colossal explosion.

Everybody joined in the confusion, holding onto tables, each other or even falling to the floor.

Then the lights went out.

The ground shook violently again, people fell to their hands and knees, scrabbling in the darkness for the exits.

An hour later

With emergency lighting on, some semblance of normality had returned.
It was three o'clock in the morning.
From what they could glean using the remaining working computer and telescope systems, was that the smaller victorious spaceship had disappeared, possibly back into Crackwell.

The accommodation and control building had withstood the earthquake, with senior security and site executives attempting to restore some sort of order.
Medical teams were attending to several people either injured or in shock.
The earthquake accounted for some injuries, but before the black spaceship destruction, others had been struck down by an unknown loss of consciousness.
People sat outside in the freezing cold rather than risk injury from more quakes inside the building.

Emergency generators had kicked in, covering for some severed power cables to the telescope site.

Fifty metres from the building, Carlos his eyes white, looked across at John and Karen, he said,
"I cannot understand what has happened tonight, it is unbelievable."
John was shivering; he replied "This may just be the beginning."

Karen had just sent a text to Colonel Mondone in the USA. She felt strongly he needed to know what John and she had just been through. No longer could they keep the artefacts capabilities to themselves. Someone they could trust must be told and it wasn't their boss Richard Armitage.

Karen said, "We cannot stay here long, we will freeze. John let's get the car and try to get down the mountain."
Louis spoke up, "You run a great risk, the police have radioed to say that the road you came up on has fallen away. The mountain ridge has collapsed there, so you cannot go back that way. The only other route is the western side and that may be out as well. Best wait for the emergency services."

Karen stood up, "We could wait for ever, need to get away and understand this."
Suddenly she was no longer on holiday.

She glanced at John, then Carlos.
"Come on John, let's see if the Nissan is still ok. Carlos we'll take a chance on the western road. Join us."
Carlos raised his hands apologetically, "Sorry, I have to stay here."
John got up and followed.

A man appeared close, waving his hands.
It was Claude Guillermin, the site director, "Stop, you two stop, I order you!"

Karen turned around, glared at the man; she said "I'm sorry. We need to get out of here."
Guillerman stood with his hands on his hips. "I am afraid that is not permitted, we have a state of emergency now. The government has decreed no one leaves the island."
Karen exploded, "Go to hell, you have no jurisdiction over us. We are British scientists and we are needed back in England."

John was taken aback, Karen rarely became angry. She had some fire for sure.
She continued, "And we have three spare seats, anyone who wants to come with us, do so now!"

Guillermin was still spluttering, he cursed with his hands in the air and walked back to the building.

Only Louis joined them.
He spoke "What happened with you guys outside back there, just before the explosion?"
John turned and said, "Something incredible Louis, something beyond my understanding."
They both looked at Karen. She was trance-like, she stared back at them saying,
"Yes it was life changing."
She turned to the dark sky, "and what happened up there will be life changing for everybody…"

She faltered, and then continued, “Louis I cannot explain now, and this may seem presumptuous but somehow John and I just repelled an awful menace.”

Louis stared back open mouthed, his face a puzzled expression.

Karen’s phone played a quiet fanfare, she took it out.
Text from Sabrina.
It read ‘Call me soon as. Thanks Sabrina.”
Time was running out.

John spoke, “Let’s go……..NOW!”

Some people had already taken their cars, as far down the mountain, tiny bright headlight beams could be seen travelling along the road.
It was inky dark, the only illumination being the massive sprinkle of stars in the sky.
Karen drove carefully, the car beams sweeping ahead around the bends.
Illuminating a pine forest one minute and then as they rounded a mountain bend, the headlights shot straight over into the darkness, huge vertical drops just off the edge of the road.

After the evening’s events, the night blackness was creepy beyond words.

The three of them, though tired through lack of sleep, stayed awake, anxious and scared, frequently looking out the car side and back windows.
Louis asked Karen a question, “Your Andromeda curiosity, the jet and the cortex.
I feel you know more? Please enlighten me.”
She glanced across, her hands tight on the wheel, “Yes I have a hypothesis. You may not agree, but I feel that the black craft which was destroyed, somehow came along that jet cortex from the Andromeda galaxy straight into our galaxy.

It then intercepted the corridor that creates Crackwell. Giving it the means to travel quickly to the Earth."

"Karen, that is some statement. It is a colossal distance to travel, like about two million light years. How do you substantiate this?"

A surreal expression dominated her face; she replied "In science terms, the jet creates a corridor, which is the cortex. From what you have shown us, this cortex tunnel appears somewhat stable and itis generated by the enormous gravitational field of the black hole in Andromeda. It may have temporal and dimensional properties, outside of galaxy time and space."
Louis started to nod.
She continued, "So that awful spaceship somehow entered the jet corridor, and was propelled along it, travelling the enormous distance in a comparatively short space of time, bending space. Likewise with the Crackwell corridor it could travel quickly to us. Only a theory of mine, but I believe time and space dimensions are being crossed. I have to do the maths when I get a chance."

Louis said "Sounds like a long shot to me, why Andromeda, why not a populated star system nearer us?"
Karen bit her lip, "Because I feel it Louis. I get a sensation of immense danger emanating from that galaxy. You see I have an ability if you like…."
She momentarily stared at Louis.
He nodded, said "Ah…" and then turned and looked out of the window.

Forty five minutes later they had travelled half way down the mountain.

Louis took a phone call.
He looked at John and Karen with a new fear.
"I have just received some worrying information from the seismic team. The crater southern wall has moved here in La Palma."

Karen just stared at Louis. John exclaimed "Oh god that means the prediction could be happening. How much movement do they have Louis?"
"The sensors indicate about a centimetre drop right along the ridge. This is very serious as that means the complete section of the southern wall has dropped slightly. The whole south face of the volcano could collapse at anytime."

John was deep in thought.
He then said, "The gravity wave from the asteroid explosion in deep space may have triggered this. Possibly the beginnings of an earthquake."

Karen suddenly uttered, "And we are driving right towards it…"

Louis said, "I know the island's roads, the safest would be the coast road around the north and then the east coast route, but it will take hours. Or we can head for say the coastal port of Tazacorte on this road, then get some breakfast and keep going. OR…we take the shortest and riskiest route back to Santa Cruz and Los Cancajos, where your apartment is, which means we head straight for that southern wall and over it…before it moves again."

Three minds said 'Holy crap!' Each in a different language, English, Latin and French.
They had a diabolical dilemma.

At length John said, "Ok, let's head for that coastal town and wait for your friend's next report. If no movement, we make a dash across the southern wall, over the edge of the crater and down to Santa Cruz. Is that a good plan?"

Karen nodded, said "Yes, but why not stay a day or so in that town, to see if the wall does move anymore? At least we would be safe there. I'm scared you know."

Louis replied, “If the southern wall descends into the sea, that coastal town may disappear under water from the resultant tsunami.”
Silence.

Karen felt ill, she said “Oh god, maybe just stop here where we are high up and wait it out?”
John had been rummaging in the back of the Nissan.
“Hmmm, not much in the way of provisions, a litre of water and some chocolate bars.”
Karen continued to drive. Something told her that they had to keep moving.
The headlamps penetrated the gloom ahead, no wildlife running across the road, no twinkly animal eye reflections from the road side forest.

Every living thing had felt the warning and was keeping low…… hidden.

3 a.m. Greenwich Mean Time that night.
Droxford, UK

Bill Craswell had carefully driven home.
He was exhausted, leaving Richard Armitage still monitoring events at the ESS establishment in East Meon.
On their remotely connected wall displays, Bill had seen the momentous clash of titan objects in outer space, possibly giant spacecraft. The total vanquishing of one and the utter disappearance of the other.

He swore at intervals thinking ‘Every bloody thing happens at once…’
Then Bill smiled the gargoyle grin, thinking about his successful yet near catastrophic engine test. He laughed out loud “Haaa…. ride on Bill.”

His mind again moved back to that event in the sky and the fact that it had created gravity waves. Yes, their arrays had detected them, but he was too tired to do any analysis.
A large glass of whisky would do nicely soon…….

He had to admit his nerves were a bit ragged, this living and working at the edge was bloody telling. Stopping on the house driveway, he got out and slammed the door, noticing that his wife's car was parked alongside.

'Oh god, another row looming….'

He winced inwardly.

Bill walked through the hall and into the lounge, and he instantly froze.
There sprawled on the carpet was the still form of his wife, July.
Red wine was splattered on the carpet, a glass lay nearby, broken at the stem.

He quickly lifted her upper body and turned her face towards him.
Rosy cheeks, a red mark around her left eye. He took her pulse and noticed her shallow breathing.
"Oh thank God." He whispered.
Her right eye had a nasty bruise, he thought. 'That's going to be a shiner.
Had she been, was she drunk?'
July stirred, groaned and slowly opened her eyes. She shook as she realised she was being helped.
"Oh Bill, oh thank heavens you're here. I had an awful sensation, like a bad nightmare."
Bill watched her carefully, having remembered the odd dark halo that seemed to follow her on that hell of a morning.
It wasn't there.

"July, you ok?"

"Yes Bill, I seem to have come out of something, like I have been sort of….. Sort of trapped, yes locked into my mind, unable to fight…."
Her voice tailed off, she started to cry into his shoulder.
Bill thought of the divorce she was pushing for, her affair with a RealRouge executive.
He wondered 'Maybe hope yet, maybe she would change her mind…..'
"July, you've hurt your head. Are you dizzy?" he felt her forehead, no fever.

She drew a shaky sob and said, "No, I think I'm ok, just very weary now, think bed to sleep Bill. I'm so sorry I've been a shit to you."
Bill took a long breath and slowly said, "That's ok. I've been through some crappy stuff myself lately. I love you July…"

She replied "I know you do, but things have changed for me. You know I am seeing someone else and I do want a divorce. But I want us to split as friends.
Is this possible Bill?"

He was desperately tired with the strain of the last few weeks bearing down on him.
And then…

Suddenly poor Bill was in that place, the little dark locked room where he cried and cried as a boy in the orphanage.
He was back there now.

"Oh July, if there is something I have done or not done, just say. I…."
She interrupted him, "It's not you Bill. We just grew apart and I need a different life now. Please understand."

Bill's heart felt like an orange being squeezed of all its juice. A lump of concrete formed inside his stomach. He said nothing.
Then July fell asleep in his arms.
He looked at her and thought of all the years they had been together, the fun, the laughter, the beautiful passion they had enjoyed.
His little bit of fame nearly two years ago now.
She had loved the media attention, the flashing cameras.

Now all gone.

He carried her up the stairs and laid her on the bed fully clothed, drawing a thin quilt over her. She was in a deep sleep, dead to the world. Bill couldn't bring himself to undress her for bed. Something between them had died. Somehow things were different now, a change, no going back.
A tear fell down his cheek.

Slowly he walked back down the stairs, his legs were leaden.
He slumped on the lounge sofa with a glass of scotch and flicked the television on with the remote, going straight to the late news channels.

"*.....take your BodyScan vitamins today and live years longer. Proven in clinical trials...*"

The advert finished and a red head woman newsreader came on.

"We now have a further NewsFlash."

Bill warmed to her voice.

"*The latest we have on the space battle is that neither spacecraft is there anymore.*
Information on the exact details is still sketchy. What we do have is that the resultant explosion waves caused much damage

to electronic systems here. Satellites, networks, even people's televisions have been damaged.
The whole world is waiting for the next instalment of this unique episode in Earth's history. All nations are already initiating military preparations for a direct attack on the Earth and world leaders are in emergency talks."

Bill's sleepiness seemed to evaporate, he watched goggle eyed as the news program carried on.

"*What is more, during the night's events, many people around the world suffered amnesia or a loss of consciousness. Scientists are trying to make sense of the energies released far out in space and how they have affected our planet."*

What she said next, made Bill sit bolt upright.

"*In addition, an earthquake has been detected around the Island of La Palma in the Canaries. This group of islands far out in the Atlantic are volcanic in nature and La Palma has a potential and uniquely dormant catastrophe, waiting in the wings. Essentially the whole southern flank of the volcano could slide into the sea creating a huge tsunami. The experts say if this happens, New York will go under water from the massive resultant tidal wave travelling across the Atlantic Ocean."*

"Good God!" exclaimed Bill.
Knowing full well both John and Karen were out there.

He glanced across at the side table and picked up a bulky envelope addressed to him.
Bill opened the envelope and frowned, pulling out a little cloth bag.
No accompanying letter, he thought 'what the hell is this?'
He unravelled the package.

"Aaaarh !"
He dropped the object on the floor and jumped back.

It rolled to a stop.
There on the floor was a rather deteriorated shrunken head, with the letters 'BC' crudely etched using dye on its forehead.
It wasn't the one in Richard Armitage's glass paperweight.
This one had a lighter skin.
'Poor devil…' he thought.

It was that final straw, Bill sunk to his knees clutching the side of the table.
"Holy shit…. Who on earth would send me this?"

In an instant he already guessed at possibly two or three people.

Maybe his called in favours were starting to seriously backfire.

Monday late afternoon 19th March
Long Beach, New York - Eastern USA seaboard

Theresa Dekker strolled arm in arm with her husband, Orlando Dekker.
She laughed at a quip he made about some quirky screeching seagulls fighting for scraps from a fisherman throwing his bait away. Not a good fishing day.

She looked at Orlando and replied, "Not like your Dad Irving, he's good at fishing. Fishing for treasure!"
He smiled.

Theresa had only just started to laugh again after their frightening near miss in Hawaii, from the tsunami wave.

One moment she was lying on the beach sipping a pina colada, the next her husband screaming at her and dragging her fast and furiously up the beach.

Behind a huge wall of surging, roaring, churning water rapidly chased them up the sands.
'Dreadful' she had thought, 'came from nowhere…'

Here at Long Beach, they had just checked out of their holiday chalet and were walking to their car.
She glanced at Orlando, "Orl?"
"Yes sweetest."
"Do they really think a giant wave is going to hit here? You know from that tsunami in the Canary Islands?"

"Well I reckon it will be a tiddler when it gets here, but we're getting out now, taking no chances."
She turned and looked out to sea. The sky was steel grey, the horizon misty.
Still some traces of snow on the ground. Snow this late, but not unheard of.

Orlando stopped, his hand shielding his eyes. He was frowning.
"Hmmm, look just in front of the horizon, there's a sort of white line."

Theresa's eyes widened, she muttered, "What the hell, is it, do you know?"
Quickly he pulled out his pocket binoculars and looked out to sea for some time.

Suddenly he grabbed her hand and broke into a run, the car park just yards ahead.
"Goddammit! That's a wave. Let's get the fuck outa here!"

Their car churned the car park dust and screeched out, flying down the road.

Chapter 12

Tuesday morning 20th March
CIA Headquarters, Langley, Virginia

Colonel Arrack Mondone was motioned to sit down.
He faced a stern grey haired man across the desk, wearing a uniform with a NASA insignia emblazoned on it.

"Colonel, with the sudden change in situation which I know you are fully aware of, a directive from on high has been issued. With immediate effect NASA has taken full control of JPL Special Projects, especially your jet engine rocket project."

Mondone tried to speak. The man raised his hand and continued, "This is as a direct intervention from the Government office. This means you are now reporting to me, Michael Swaine, Director of NASA Space Technology."

"I see. Would this be temporary or a permanent change Director?"

"That is an unknown Colonel. The current situation is unprecedented. As you know there are to be several missions next year to the anomaly out there. These need to be coordinated centrally."
He paused looked at Mondone, and then said, "Your projects will continue as per plan for now. I shall arrange a full project meeting here at our Langley Research Centre shortly after today's meeting with the CIA and deputy Chiefs of Staff, which you will be attending. Thank you Colonel."

Conference Room 5

The emergency meeting was heavily attended, not only by several senior CIA people but also by the deputy chiefs of staffs from the Navy, Army and Air Force.

Adding to the group was the cosmologist Heinreich Stuttland, Brad Bannerman from the US Gravity Array group, plus Colonel Mondone, Ming Zhao his technical staff PA and Gail Letchford, his new PA.

Completing the attendees, Michael Swaine, NASA.

As Ming had discovered, Gail was her new compulsory colleague and possibly Mondone's lover. The US Vice President had been forced to resign in a corruption scandal and the services of his PA Gail were no longer required, but she had latched onto Arrack Mondone very quickly.

Gail's body language with Mondone had Ming wondering.

Bob Redford CIA, started the meeting, welcoming and introducing everyone.
Then he said "Gentlemen and ladies, time is not on our side.
As you are all aware, the events of Sunday and yesterday have taken the whole world by surprise.
Nations are confused, some are preparing for hostilities, others a welcome.
The recent alien space conflict witnessed by many, changes everything.
We have seen power beyond man's imagination.
General Tristam please, the floor is yours."
He sat down.

General Martin Tristam, USAF, promptly stood and spoke in a loud solemn tone.
"Thank you."
He slowly looked around, all eyes keenly on him.
"As you know yesterday's science fiction has become today's sobering reality.
Our top people are working hard to analyse the data we have, and data that is still pouring in from other agencies around the globe.
Taking Mr Redford's introduction, we need to work fast and

prepare for the return of the anomaly. It is far behind the Earth now, but will return when our orbit next January reaches that spot again.
As observed, whatever came out of that portal has weapons of a power that we cannot match. We detected hostile moves during the early stages. Hostile to Earth.
The risk of doing nothing is not an option."

He stopped then said loudly,

"At any time new vehicles of destruction may emerge from the portal."

Heinreich Stuttland, the President's cosmological and space advisor, spoke up in his deep guttural accent, "Precisely General, we know the portal is now too far away for us to reach it easily by rocket. What does the military plan to do if something hostile does emerge before next January?"
The Army General replied, "Then we use our nuclear arsenal to provide close range defence of the Earth."
Stuttland scoffed, "Against an adversary that commands giant invisible spacecraft with technologies we can hardly imagine?"
Tristam replied "It is all we have. We must hang in there until January when this portal is close again, then we use our only hope."

He paused, glancing around.

"Next year we will use one or more nuclear devices, the most potent we have, to try and close the portal. However, we have reason to believe that just before the black spacecraft was destroyed, it launched small projectiles. These could be escape craft, robot missiles, anything you care to imagine ladies and gentlemen."

They all hung on his words.

A pitiful plan at best. Quiet descended around the table.

Tristam continued, "The best information to date is that a very large invisible spacecraft exited from the portal. Before it was intercepted by the second craft, it had started to proceed on an Earth bound course.
During this period, unusual occurrences happened here on the ground."

He stopped, tapping his fingers on the table edge. "This meeting is not for speculation but what we have is a sharp ramp up of negative human activities around the planet. Let us say terrorist and also unprovoked incidents happened on a scale that is significant.
Needless to say, we have used all resources at our disposal, satellite based telescopes, ground based telescopes, radar to get a glimpse of what sort of technologies these craft might use. Indeed we have looked right across the electromagnetic spectrum."

Heinreich spoke up, "How about our new gravity arrays, did they see anything?"

Brad Bannerman quickly replied, "Unfortunately our LIGO system was offline undergoing maintenance at the time. The new gravity arrays are still under construction using British technical guidance and are not operational until next week. Although we have reason to believe that a powerful gravity wave from the craft's destruction caused an earthquake on or near the island of La Palma in the Atlantic Canary group.
We are waiting for the British to process their gravity array data and release it to us within hours. As you are aware the expected tsunami did happen, but fortunately a prediction about the wave travelling across the Atlantic and submerging New York proved incorrect.
Instead they have experienced a two metre high swell, which only caused a little damage."

Mondone interjected, "Sir, if I may speak ?"
Tristam nodded.
Mondone stood, "As you have mentioned, it would appear that we are observing energies and let me say 'powers' that seem to be beyond human knowledge. I have just received a confidential update from my British scientist colleagues who are at the La Palma observatories. It was sent in the early hours of Monday morning, not long after the second craft appeared and destroyed the invisible spacecraft."

He waited for a reaction, none.
Tristam said, "Please enlighten us Colonel."

Mondone hesitated, he didn't want to put his career on the line, but he utterly trusted the information he was about to impart.
"Well, as you said, an unprecedented hike has occurred in how shall I say it, criminal acts? In the light of this knowledge I would like to convey what the physicists John Creeson and Karen Durgas observed just before the second spacecraft appeared."

They watched Mondone like hawks.
Hardened military men.

He had gone a little pale. His distant but fierce Mongolian background was coming to the fore. Ming had noticed Mondone's rigid posture and knew what he was about to divulge. After he had briefed her earlier on, she realised how courageous he was to bring this ethereal like information to the table.
Raw incredibility and denial would be certain and possibly Mondone's credibility.
Gail had a puzzled look on her face, her mouth open in amazement as she followed the discussion.
Mondone breathed in sharply, said "Something tangible happened, ladies and gentlemen, something I believe John and Karen instigated.
Probably saved our skins and possibly more than we know.

Maybe gave us just enough time before the second spaceship appeared and did the business."

Heinreich interrupted "What mumbo jumbo is this?"
The Navy deputy Chief of Staff, Admiral Coburn, cut in "Colonel Mondone, just what are you saying? Clarify please."
Mondone became curt, "Your consideration is essential. I would not bring this to the table unless I believed it was of vital importance."

He waited a moment, then continued, "There are, shall we say devices that are in the hands of these British people, that during the period of high threat, initiated or started something or some machine based device in the moon. We recorded a tunnel of light from the moon creating an aurora around Earth's atmosphere."

There were gasps of incredulity from several of the people in the room.
Some of the deputy Chiefs of Staff were shaking their heads.
Somebody said "Crazy stuff. Sit down Mondone, stop making a fool of yourself…"

Mondone said "I have evidence, please watch."

He quickly doused the lights, bringing up a huge wall display showing our blue Earth's curvature against the ink blackness of space.
He continued "Now the ISS (International Space Station) was out of line of sight with our rogue spacecraft and the conflict, but it took these videos."
Mondone operated the pan control, so the moon came in at the right hand corner.
He then started the recording.

For a while nothing happened.
He said, "Look at the moon and the actual time display."

All eyes turned to the right hand corner.
Then something very odd happened.
A little bright purple spot appeared on the moon. Instantly a thin faint purple light beam seemed to twist and thicken into what looked like a fibrous rope. It stabbed across to the Earth.
As it reached our planet, it widened dramatically, thinning and enveloping our home planet in a faint purple sphere.
The planet's edge became fuzzy, a pink-purple glow seemed to appear right around the very top of the atmosphere.
It remained for some minutes.
Audible gasps could be heard.
Mondone allowed the video to continue.
Then obscured behind the Earth, the death of the invisible craft created an almighty flash that corona'd our dear planet, briefly illuminating space and our moon.
After the explosion, the scene rapidly returned to a normal Earth image, with the dark starry universe behind and the grey moon hanging over to the right. The purple lines had vanished.

Mondone switched off the screen, switched up the lights and turned to his audience.
He now had everybody's attention and quietly he said, "I know it seems unreal, but there is your evidence. Also the Chinese moon base happens to be right in the vicinity of that purple spot. We could assume the placement was a coincidence, but it is something for us to address, perhaps directly with the Chinese."
He glanced around and sat down. "Thank you for your patience."

Tristam was the first to speak.
"Thank you Colonel, a most incredible observation and how shall I say? An option in our possible salvation. We must track down the Brits and their devices as soon as."
He looked across at Bob Redford. "This is a top CIA responsibility Bob, see me afterwards."
Bob nodded

Ming gave Mondone a worried look, thinking of her friends John and Karen, now the subject of a cloak and dagger hunt.
She also realised hers and Arrack's knowledge of the Chinese moon base saga and the invisible objects they had seen, *was still not common knowledge with the US military, even here.*
That proof had been erased, by someone or something.

Bob Redford spoke up again, he said "and what about the Chinese, now that their moon base is manned again, what are they up to?"
Tristam replied, "Well you are best placed to know Bob. Our own intell has yet to reveal any substantial update on what we know."
Mondone quickly interjected, "I have made contact with a senior Chinese industrialist who has close contacts with the Chinese government. We are due to meet them within the month. They want our gravity wave or rather the British gravity wave technology.
In return for substantial information on their moon base operations, I intend to reciprocate a little, but it is dependent on how our discussion progresses.
Naturally sensitive material may have to be authorised by our more senior staff."

He had more to say and raising his hand he glanced at Michael Swaine.
Nothing must be held back, pertinent information was vital to this meeting.
The man nodded for him to go ahead.

Mondone took a deep breath.
"Finally I need to convey an incidence to this meeting."
He coughed, cleared his throat and continued, "Early last February we detected a brief incurrence at the moon base by almost invisible intelligent objects. I suggest these may be related to one or other of the portal spaceships. At the time the astronauts in the base were believed dead, for quite some time, as a result of a very close meteor strike last year."

Ming noticed how close Gail was to Mondone.
Gail's lips were tightly shut as she stared sequentially around at the attendees.
Her demeanor was one of anxious concern for her boss.
Tristam took up the issue, "Yes I have seen your report Colonel. If and when these return we need to know immediately."
"Yes Sir."

With that Arrack Mondone plus Ming and Gail left the meeting. There were other parts of the agenda they were not privy to.
Mondone turned to Ming, "We'll meet tomorrow morning at the NASA office here, 9am sharp."

"Yes Sir."

The Metropole Hotel, Langley

Late that evening back in Mondone's room, Gail slowly sipped her vodka tonic, clinking the ice cubes as she rotated the glass, slices of lime dancing in the liquid.

She eyed him as he walked out of the steamy bathroom wearing his white bath towel.
"Nice shower Arrack?"
He smiled and looked at Gail in her thin silken bathrobe, her bosom barely covered, the robe parting at her thighs.
She flicked back her blond wavy hair.
A change from brunette, a new look, a new her.
A simple pearl necklace was complemented by a tiny pearl ankle chain, both enhanced by the flimsy dark blue bathrobe which left little to the imagination.
He thought she was a gorgeous creature.

Temptation beyond most men's will power.

"Yeah, felt good." He sat down beside her, grabbing the drink she had made him.

He took a long cool gulp and swallowed slowly, then another. Licking his lips he returned the empty glass to the side table. He continued to look at it, just ice cubes left in the bottom.

"That …I needed. Today was tough. Did you follow some of the technical stuff?"
She nodded "Yes mostly."
Then Gail leaned towards Mondone and their eyes met.
They kissed briefly, then a little longer.
Her luxuriant perfume engulfed him.

He smiled again, "Feel so good to have you here Gail. I just hate business trips alone. Sanity is two people knowing what they want, not like the crazy meeting this afternoon."
Gail cocked her head, "Yes Arrack, I cannot believe that space stuff. Like a refill?"
"Now that is a silly question." he laughed.
She handed him the newly filled vodka tonic and in a moment it was half gone.
A catchy rhythm wafted across from the radio.
Arrack suddenly got up and started to dance on the carpet, holding on to his towel.
"Yeah…..Here right now, right here, right now."
He did a crazy wiggle dance, arms jerking in and out sideways like some mad puppet.

Gail screamed "Ha!" and smiled a beautiful set of teeth. Then as he sat down she smoothed his inner thigh and said "So good to be with you Arrack, you do make me laugh."
Her bathrobe had parted.
Mondone again was totally mesmerised, aroused.
The fishing adage came to mind: he was gone, hook, line and sinker!

She was the dominant sexual partner, usually wearing some jewellery and not much else. Gail took his glass placing it on the

table, then pushing him back on the sofa and pulling his towel away, she swiftly mounted him.
Her physical stamina and technique wore him out every time.

“Gail, you sure are sweet…” he kissed her lips gently and slowly.

Arrack Mondone had not known such pleasure and yes a degree of happiness, for the first time in years. He gripped her buttocks and lay back feeling happy and wondrous.

The following morning, NASA meeting room, Langley.

Arrack Mondone was twenty minutes late, unusual for him.

Bing… a text arrived.

‘I will be slightly delayed, Mondone.’

Ming was thinking about her cat Jimmy. He was now based with her at JPL in California, but this time through official channels. She couldn’t bear to leave him back at her apartment in Hawaii, even with Akoni’s mum Lekika offering to look after him. Trouble was he liked the JPL canteen titbits too much, putting on weight again. But now he was a very sick pussy cat, having eaten something very disagreeable. Normally Angela one of the chefs there, looked after him when Ming was not around.
Maybe he had eaten a mouse or something too gross to mention. Ming grimaced, thinking cats do this a lot; make themselves ill catching and eating things they shouldn’t.
Then she thought about Akoni, missing him badly, thinking how the time might drag before they could meet up again.
She had winged off a text a few minutes ago.

Bing…. text reply.

‘Hi gorgeous, miss you too… Loads.

Good news my holiday request for Easter has been cleared. How are you?'

She quickly sent another, *'Akoni, That's great! I can't wait for Easter. Yes I'm fine. You meeting my folks will be wonderful, a lovely break and they always make a big fuss. We'll be able to spend some time together, just us, afterwards. With the rest of my leave I've booked us in at a little romantic hotel near Santa Monica beach.'*

Her dreaming was broken by Arrack coming in from the side door.
"Morning Ming! Slight delay, traffic accident on the main highway."

But he was beaming from ear to ear.
"Good morning Arrack, you seem to be on top of the world today."

She was thinking that Gail must have seen to him good and proper last night.

"Yes feel good. Another day, another challenge." he sort of chuckled.

She looked at him. He had his 'office' uniform on, white shirt, tie and the appropriate insignia on his jacket.
As he turned Ming spotted a red and purple mark on his neck just above his shirt collar.
She sort of smirked, Arrack noticed her attention and Ming quickly adopted a more serious countenance. "So Sir, what have we in store for today?"

Mondone took a deep breath and sat down on the other side of the table. Behind him on the wall were a couple of framed photos, military groups of people all smiling with American pride. The rest of the meeting room was rather sparse.

Stacks of chairs in the corner.
A large long black mahogany table dominated the centre. In another corner a tall green potted tatty fern sagged sideways showing a few withered brown leaves.
It was gasping for water.

Ming's laptop pinged with some message.
She half went to look at it, when Mondone cleared his throat and said a little haltingly.

"Firstly Ming, I need to get something straight. Let me say that your assignment to me remains the same, your technical skills I cannot do without. Gail is now my administrative PA. She does the paperwork, arranges meetings, and books my travel you know. Sort of stuff you wouldn't want as responsibilities yourself really?"

"Very true Sir and thank you for clarifying the roles."
He carried on, "Also I want you to remain my technical confidant."
Ming nodded.
Mondone picked up a pen and twiddled it in his fingers, then slowly said.
"I guess you know about Gail and me.
I won't pretend. She is my girlfriend.
Thing is when we're on duty, it is strictly duty. No personal stuff can get in the way."

He sternly looked at her, but she caught a tiny melting in his eyes.
A sort of ok was needed.
Ming replied "Sure Sir, I understand no problem. Think we'll all get along just fine."
She grinned and he inwardly gave a sigh of relief.
At length, he put the pen into his top pocket and said "Yes, we sure will. Now as you heard there is some concern about secondary ETs."

Ming looked at Mondone, then she cottoned on, "Ah yes the objects that left that craft just before it was destroyed. Where are they now?"
"Exactly Ming, we don't know. They became invisible to our eyes and radar."
She exclaimed "Oh hell. God, what a worry. They could be anywhere, even here somewhere."
Mondone replied, "Well the security forces are on full alert, not just ours but across the world. This neatly leads me onto the next item."
Then he turned to the side door and said, "Benji? You can come in now."
With that a tall, well built, uniformed guy walked rigidly in and saluted the Colonel.
He stood absolutely still. No mouth movement, his steel grey eyes locked looking forward. A slight whirring could be heard.

He wasn't human.

"Oh my, he's been repaired?" she exclaimed.
"Ah no Ming. This is the fourth generation, one of two actually. I'm afraid the original was damaged beyond repair."
"Oh..."
Ming thought back to the fire fight in the Wales Gravity Array building, with the original Benji robot, hurling himself at the Chinese machine gunners, discharging Mondone's pistol. He took out a few of them, and then he disintegrated in a savage missile explosion.

Mondone carried on, "Yes there are some improvements to his autonomous software, plus new sensors, new armour and weapons pods."
Ming frowned a little, "and these can protect against fast missiles?"

"To some extent, yes. You see we have taken the hand held expanding armoured shield and created a body layer that can be worn by Benji. This armour layer moves on a micro support frame that covers the vulnerable areas of his body. When he detects objects such as large calibre shells or missiles coming towards him, the layer moves incredibly quickly outwards. Basically the armour shield is then rigidly held about two centimetres from his own body. This way the armour absorbs the main blast, and may disintegrate but hopefully saves Benji."

"Sounds impressive Sir."
"Also the sensors allow monitoring in the light spectrum beyond the range of human eyesight. Together with advanced radar, and a new radio technique, he is able to look through non-metal walls and to some extent inside and around buildings."
Mondone paused then said, "Also he has new weapons technology, which includes a rail gun and a pulse laser weapon."
Ming frowned and said, "Rail gun? I've heard of those Colonel."
"A rail gun is like a rifle in that it fires bullets of a kind. However, it uses linear magnetic technology to hurl tiny projectiles along a magnetic rail... *many times faster than any bullet.*
It uses huge pulses of electrical magnetic energy to fire a hardened metal arrow head at the target. Because of the speed, it has several times the destructive power of a bullet."
"He sounds remarkable Sir."
"Yes. We had to incorporate a small special power generation unit.
You see between spurts of fire, Benji needs large amounts of power to recharge the rail gun battery source."
She nodded.
Mondone added "The laser weapon is a one-time very high energy beam pulse of about five seconds. Enough to go through thin metal at medium range. It is chemically recharged in about a minute. He has ordnance sufficient for two shots."

Ming's eyes were glued to the robot.
Her mind wandered.
'Shades of the old Terminator films, just hope we never give them the flawed human psyche......'

Mondone continued, "I need much more field testing. We have a battalion of these being manufactured. Very top secret at the moment."
He paused then said "Ming?"

She looked back at Mondone, "Sir?"
"How do you feel about Benji accompanying you now and again? Try him out so to speak. You see with your observation skills, you could spot his limitations and so forth, providing feedback to the development guys."
"Well, yes sure Sir. Uumm… what about off duty you know, my recreational time?"
"Up to you Ming. Obviously the more time he has with you, the better."
"Bit freaky Sir, if you don't mind me saying so."

Mondone smiled "I'll give you full command mode, so you can shut him down at any time, just with a spoken phrase. Thing is Ming, with your talents and the latest events I feel you could do with some protection."
"Protection? God Sir! Am I being hunted?" her mind wandered to the elusive alien escape crafts.
She already had a feeling of surveillance, though nothing tangible, probably human.
'Probably! Hell what am I thinking' cursed Ming in her thoughts. 'Now I would even welcome human surveillance…. rather than something else…something horrible…..'

Mondone replied "Sorry, I didn't mean to alarm you. I'm a bit on edge myself.
I guess millions of people around the world are. We just don't know what may happen next. I have a gut feeling and with your knowledge of the earlier cloaked happenings, I guess that you need to be looked after."

"Ah ok. Well it is some reassurance and I am game to see how it goes Sir.

Like uum… when do want to start this 'testing'?"

"Today would be good."
Ming gulped.

Mondone cleared his throat, paused and looked at Ming a little strangely.
She returned the questioning look.
"Ming, there is more."
"I'm all ears Sir."
"As I disclosed at the security meeting, both Karen Durgas and John Creeson invoked something, some… how shall I say it without it sounding fantastical? … let us say they connected with a device that produced a controlled beam or field that seemed to deflect the energies from the dark asteroid craft."
Ming's eyes widened, "As you demonstrated at the meeting, it looked incredible."
Mondone continued, "Yes and I believe they need help, now. We are in a threat scenario with these goddam offshoot craft wherever they are. I am convinced that Karen and John may be one of their targets."

Ming went cold, she thought back to when Karen lay shot, bleeding and unconscious on the floor in the Wales Gravity Array building.
She herself frozen in shock.

Mondone spoke again "I have dispatched another Benji, latest spec, to the British. Officially it is a new test model for them to evaluate, but I have sent it direct to their ESS establishment in East Meon. Under the guise of helping them with a robotic interface to their ReachThru virtual reality systems and their gravity array setup."

Ming still had the puzzled look, "Can Benji really help them…."
Mondone smiled "Well the robot is quite capable of processing at high speed the video data presented by the ReachThru headset.

As we know the amount of gravitional data they have in their databases is huge and Benji will be quite an asset to them."
Ming replied "Ah… I see."
Mondone quickly said, "However, THAT is the official line. What I'm about to tell you is confidential Ming. Their Benji has programming to seek out John and Karen and then monitor their surroundings on a subtle basis.
Specifically to spot danger.
He can then offer some rapid protection."

Ming was not convinced.
Again she cast her mind back to the catastrophic battle in that Wales warehouse. They had come across John Stoneham the ex-SAS man, their so called protection, lying dead on the building floor. Then all of them ducking and diving trying to avoid the Chinese bullets. Karen hit near her heart, Arrack in the shoulder, the British scientist Amit dying on the floor. John knocked out cold from a rifle butt.
Their only chance Benji the robot, exploding into pieces as he took a direct hit from a shoulder launched missile.
Finally all of them being bundled into a van and then taken out to an offshore submarine.

Ming thought 'That was against human opponents……… what could he possibly do against a very advanced alien civilisation?'

The door rapped.
Mondone looked up, shouted "Come in!"

His PA, Gail walked in.
Mondone's eyes clamped to the slight wiggle of her hips.

"Good morning Sir. Hello Ming." A brilliant white smile adorned Gail's face.
Perfect hair and red lipstick freshly applied.

She took full advantage of Mondone’s one hundred percent attention. “Sir, here are your meeting minutes from yesterday and your travel itinerary for the next week and yours too Ming. Already in your diaries, but hardcopy for your reference.”
She handed out some paper.

Ming raised her eyebrows and thought ‘Interesting times ahead…..’

Chapter 13

A day previously.
7am Monday 19th March
The village of Tijarafe, the island of La Palma, Atlantic Ocean.

They had shared the driving and it had been non-stop, going as fast as they could during the dark hours.
Karen was wincing from the ache in her chest, the almost healed bullet wound from the Wales episode.

Now persuading a café owner to open up early, they sat outside drinking large mugs of coffee and scoffing stale croissants left over from the previous day.
Hungrily they devoured the dry buns lubricated with jam or generous dollops of honey.

No one had really slept last night, only the odd doze.
Circumstance forcing them to stay awake and a clammy apprehension prickled the air.
Tiredness was a luxury.

The café's few wooden tables and chairs were sprawled across the pavement next to the main road which gave way beyond to a view of a sea bay.
Tazacorte was now off the plan. The main road had reports of subsidence, so they had taken a small winding mountain road down to this town, Tijarafe.
In a while they would bypass the coastal town of Tazacorte and instead head straight for the southern volcano wall.

Here in Tijarafe alongside the café, ran a line of large squat palm trees, parallel to the road. On the other side were broken groupings of dry stone walls.

Together with a sprinkling of multi coloured apartments and terra cotta roofed houses that peeked out between trees on craggy hill slopes.
Quaint colours and deceptive peace.
Far away and below them, the blue sea glistened a million mirrors to the rising sun.

John was dreaming, 'Lovely place this. Honeymoon material.'
He inwardly glowed thinking about a proposal of marriage to Karen.

Louis looked at John and spoke. "You know those objects that escaped from the black craft? I wonder if we can check out news sites, our contacts and so forth to see if they have reached the Earth?"
John murmured, "Yes…track the damn things down."
Karen was already on her tablet wirelessly connected, scanning the news pages.
She said, "Nothing reported yet. Though the space explosion has knocked out some satellites and ground based systems like phone networks."
John pondered, replied "Yes keep a close eye on the newsfeeds. With a bit of luck those little craft whatever they are, may have been destroyed out there."
He nodded towards the sky. "If they weren't, then the trouble we have is that these damn things are likely to be invisible again."
Karen looked up, her eyes nervously glancing one eighty degrees around, said "Scary times guys."
Her phone started to ring. They all jumped.
She glanced at the caller.
"Jane … ah… hi Jane."
Jane Horsham was sitting in the lab in ESS, it was 8.10am UK time, coincidently the same time zone as La Palma.
"KAREN! How are you? John ok? after last night's events we are so worried."

Karen said "Yes we're ok. Scary, scary stuff. The world will never be the same."
Jane quickly replied "The news reported an earthquake in the Canary Islands, what happened at La Palma?"
"Yes there was a large tremor and the south wall of the crater has moved slightly, but all quiet now."

Jane "I know we can't discuss confidential stuff on the phone, but what did you make of the sky battle? Incredible don't you think?"
Karen slowly spoke considering every word "Something else happened. Both John and I were involved and best not discuss any detail here over this open connection.
To be honest we are in awe, no… I think shock as to what is happening. We're now in Tijarafe having breakfast and plan to make a run for it on the road over the south wall before any movement happens again."
"Oh god Karen, that sounds dangerous, do take care."

Karen frowned and said "Is Bill in yet?"
Jane "No, Richard said they had a very late night watching the events unfold. I guess Bill will be in pretty soon, you know how excited he gets. Richard is in and he looks like death warmed up!"
Karen laughed a little and said "No change there then?"
She heard Jane roar with laughter at the other end.

Karen giggled "Ha ha..yeah. …. by the way did the gravity arrays pick up any data from the anomaly or those massive objects last night."

Jane replied "Funny you should mention that, because Richard said Bill was up at the Norfolk array the weekend doing some updates. We expected the whole array system to be offline until Monday sometime. However, I checked this morning and the arrays were back up Sunday afternoon and well the results….." she tailed off.
Karen snapped "What Jane? what did the arrays see?"

"Amazing detail Karen, as you mentioned with this unsecure line can't talk about detail, but masses of weird measurements. The first pass processing of display data was mind boggling. We have a second more comprehensive analysis run in process. Bill will be able to unravel it when he comes in. The arrays are down now, looks like the space explosion took out the orbital arm of our array system."

"Thanks for the update Jane, that's a shame about the array. Keep us posted."
"and you guys take care out there. We need you back in one piece."
"Thanks Jane, bye….. bye."

Karen turned to Louis and John, said "Jane said the arrays have recorded a lot of gravity details from last night's clash, but the orbital unit is damaged now."
Her phone rang again. She saw it was Sabrina. Her eyes stared at the screen for a second. "Guys, I need to take this call outside."
They both nodded.

Karen walked through the café door, "Hi Sabrina."
"What happened Karen?"
She described to Sabrina the previous night's events, her dreaming connection with Sabrina's group and their purple sphere experience.
Karen stopped, there was silence at the other end of the phone.
"You still there Sabrina?"
"Yes, I was pondering……thinking."
Sabrina gave all her answers in a considered way, full of meaning both literal and hidden.
"Karen, with what you and John have achieved, you are both in great danger now."
"Oh dear." exclaimed Karen.
"As soon as you return to England, please can we get together? I…umm…I…"

Karen frowned, Sabrina her spiritual oracle was hesitating, out of character.
Sabrina continued "Karen, during our circle session and just before you invoked your shield, I'll call it that, but it is much more… yes before that happened, I was able to make a link."
"A link? to what?"
"To that awful huge object in space that was eventually destroyed."

Karen suddenly felt very cold, shivery, she said "Oh Sabrina, I hate to think what you've seen or felt?"
"Terrible Karen, I will tell you more when you return, but even with all my spiritual strength I became very, very afraid. You see the threat I mentioned comes from these objects and a very distant place where they originate from. If we cannot counter it somehow, everything and everyone we know and love will disappear…. forever."

Karen went deathly quiet.

"I must go Karen, just remain very vigilant and use those artefacts again if you have to. Speak soon."
"Ok Sabrina. You stay safe too, bye."

Two police cars raced by their sirens blaring.
Outside the town was waking up, a few cars passing.
Some pedestrians walked by a little too briskly. News travels fast.
Two old men sitting on the table outside were waving their arms, gesticulating at what is happening now. Not like the 'good' old days, reliable human conflicts …..

Karen went back inside, "Come on guys, let's make a run for the south and get over that ridge while we can."
John "Yup, good idea. I feel this is the lull before the storm."

This time Louis drove. They headed down the LP-1 highway to Los Llanos and beyond.

Everything around was dry, the trees drooped their thirsty dull green and yellowed leaves toward the dusty red ground.
As they passed through some small hamlets and villages, Karen said, "Oh look at those houses, the colours, right out of a child's paint box.
Pastels, blue, red-brown and there yellow. Such a contrast to white.
Look even pink ! and I love those deep orange terra cotta roofs. "
John exclaimed, "It seems just about everybody who has a patch of land is growing bananas. Wouldn't mind a little shack here."
Karen looked at him and pulled a face. John nervously laughed, "Well after that landslip, maybe not!"

They passed through a hamlet, El Jesus.
Karen smiled at the sign.
The Spanish invaders who came to the island in the fifteen century had left their Catholic influence.
Her mind flashed momentarily to Lei Zhao and Steve Crowley.
'Something about her? No maybe him…' her intuition was strong. 'something way back in time…'

Thump. The car hit a pothole jarring everybody.
Her thought train disappeared.
The road meandered around the volcano slopes, revealing lush lower areas terraced with banana plantations.

After a couple of slow hours in crawling traffic, they moved past an accident between a lorry and a truck, Louis accelerated hard.
The road snaked along the mountainous country, the sea ever present on their right.

A sharp bend to the left approached. Right at the bend was a café perched on the edge of a cliff. Louis said "Merde…. How about some more coffee and a pee stop……… guys?"
John woke up and murmured "Yep…… good idea."

Their Nissan stopped with a lurch.

Karen who was semi-dozing, came to. “Ah....oh...where are we?”
Louis turned around to look at them in the back seats.
“This is the Mirador el Time or the ‘Café on the Edge’.
It is perched on the edge of a precipice and see the road continuing around there? Well to the right of it, is a sheer drop of maybe two hundred metres straight down and look you can view the entire valley from here.”
He smiled.
John “Wow, what a place. Cracking view!”
Louis “I sometimes come here for lunch on my return to the other side of the island and sit for a while enjoying the scenery.”

They took a table outside. John tentatively standing with his hand stretched out to the rail. He wasn’t very good with heights. “Cor, some view, reckon I can see for.....umm.. probably ten miles. There, there is the southern wall.”
The valley spread out far down below in a green haze. Little hamlets of houses dotted here and there. To the right a bright shiny sea stretched to the hazy horizon.
To the left, dark green forest carpeted the steep rock as it rose high inside the towering volcano wall.
A slight cleft in the walls at this angle, revealed the path to the inner pit of the crater, now thick with forest and lush greenery.

His pointing made Karen and Louis look to the far south. A misty haze was partly obscuring a huge wall of dark rock rising above the valley.
The south wall.

Lunch was slightly hurried, the schedule not far from their minds. The hot steak sandwiches were very welcome.
John “Louis where is your home in France?”
Louis “In Marseilles, I live in the suburbs with my wife and daughter. I hope to return within a day or two. Soon as I can get a flight I guess. I have been here on the island, two months now.”

Karen "You must miss them and with those strange off world events, I think people just want to be with family."
Louis smiled, "I do miss them terribly, and it will be good to be back in France for a while. Luckily I can work from home at times, so it is a good arrangement."

Louis paid the bill and they wandered to the door.

Something happened.

John went to step outside but his leg seemed to stay in mid air.
Karen lost her balance and grabbed the door frame.
Louis uttered a shout "Mon Dieu, what is happening?"

The café shook violently, some tables fell over, dishes, plates, cups fell breaking in a crash and clatter of noise. Glasses rolled over and smashed behind the counter. People stood up swaying trying to grab something to hold.

"Earthquake!" shouted John.
He turned and grabbed Karen who pulled Louis and together they staggered outside.
Wide eyed they quickly looked all around, trying to keep their balance subconsciously knowing the cliff edge was just yards away.

A large tourist coach was rounding the bend. As it lurched down the cliff side road, the brakes screeched on, churning clouds of dust from the sandy tarmac.
The vehicle started to slide……..
Too late the driver had spotted that the road ahead of it was completely breaking away, tumbling over the cliff, plummeting way down into the valley.

Louis looked on horrified as the coach slammed into the steel barrier at the cliff edge, buckling it.

People inside clutched the seat backs in terror, with wailing screams and cries coming from some open windows.
Tyres started to drag.
Black rubber smoke billowed out as the brakes locked.
The big coach started to slide along the barrier generating a screech of rending metal. Then the barrier gave way.

Karen "Oh god no, NO!"
John ran a few steps, then stopped frozen to the spot.
They watched as the coach started to slide slowly and grindingly over the cliff edge.
Somehow it didn't fall, but hung precariously on the edge, balancing, rocks and debris crashing and falling in a cloud far below.

Louis was already running to their Nissan truck. "Come on…. QUICK!"
Karen and John dove inside and clutched the car side stanchions as Louis gunned the car down the road towards the coach.

The screaming from inside the coach was horrifying….. that of the doomed.
The exit door was up front, with nothing but fresh air below it for six hundred feet.

Death close at hand.

As the Nissan screeched to a stop on the left hand side of the road against the rising rock wall, the coach driver could be seen to rev the engine and slowly try to reverse using the rear wheels. The front cabin, wheels and almost half the coach was hanging over the edge of the abyss. The rear tyres turned, scuffing and moaning clouds of dust into the air.

Louis turned the rear of the Nissan to face the coach.
Karen just got out and stared, "Oh my god, … what can we do?"

John was already flinging open the rear doors, remembering the electric winch mounted at the rear of their truck. Louis held a thick coiled rope from the vehicle tow kit; he was frantically looking along at some steel reinforcing bars in the rock face. 'There must be one that has a gap around it. MUST BE......'

Then the coach lurched, some more road broke away under it.
Its engine moaning loudly with the rear wheels spinning frantically in reverse.
Dust rose in a huge haze around the vehicle.

In what seemed like minutes, Louis had the rope around a rock face support and linked to their vehicle front tow bar.
John had raced across the road with the winch cable to the coach. He scrabbled underneath the back of the coach looking for somewhere to hook it on.
Choking dust enveloped him.
Karen ran to the coach, she could just hear him coughing above the engine noise.

Then the high rear cabin window burst out of the coach, the glass shattered as it hit the ground. People lunged themselves out.
Amidst the din John shouted "OK. USE THE WINCH!"
Instantly Louis threw the winch drive switch and the cable went tight.

Then Louis ran to the coach rear, throwing the end of another coiled rope up and into the open window hole. Frantic hands clutched it. He shouted "Secure that end, around anything you have, a seat base, whatever......QUICKLY!"
Karen undid the large snap clips holding the engine bay cover of the coach.
It swung open. Hot air hit her. Ignoring the proximity of dangerous rotating engine belts near her body, she lifted herself up and stood on the bottom rim of the engine bay.
Already people were coming down the rope, she grabbed them,

pushing, holding until they could jump the last bit. Her chest throbbed with pain.
Louis was back at the truck, frantically nursing the Nissan's electric winch.
It screeched and whined pulling rigid the cable that John had attached under the coach. The wind action gave a shuddering noise, bad news, far too much load for it.

The big coach was far beyond the winch's maximum torque.
Smoke poured from the winch motor, a sickly smell of electric burning gave its message.
He shouted "It's no good, the winch cannot hold!"
He threw the cable lock on to try and grip what they had.

Dust and clouds of blue exhaust smoke rose around the coach.
People continued to climb from the rear window.
Karen grabbing each person, steadying them down.
She was exhausted.

A creaking, moaning sound vibrated from the coach.
Inexorably, it was moving slowly over the cliff.

Louis screamed to Karen, "KAREN GET OFF NOW! THE COACH IS GOING OVER!!"
All of a sudden no more people came out.
The dying winch had given them vital tens of seconds.
The driver remained in his seat, head out the window looking at the coach rear as the coach engine whined trying to make the rear wheels grip.
He was losing the battle.

Karen leapt off the coach, coughing in the dust, she shouted "Where is John ! Oh GOD, I can't see him. LOUIS! …JOHN'S TRAPPED UNDER THE COACH!"

Louis Remond had been in one or two scrapes in his life, but this topped it.

Suddenly he realised not only was the coach going over, but a low wrenching sound heralded the demise of the Nissan cable attached to the wall.
The cable strands began to fray and snap.

The Nissan was going over too.

He screamed at everyone to move away, frantically waving his arms.
Karen stood with her hands across her mouth, she tried to look, duck down, see under the coach.
Amidst the engine smoke, clouds of dust from the revolving, scraping rear wheels obscured the whole underneath of the coach.

She whispered "No…no,no,no…..oh John, my love, my precious man……….oh God."
Then it happened, probably all of four seconds, no more.

The whole lot, coach, cables and the Nissan were moving. The car plucked from the side wall twisted and slithered gratingly on to its side, following the coach. They slid over and down the cliff.
A moment later a distant series of crashing and rumbling sounds were heard far below.
A brave coach driver had sacrificed himself to give everybody else onboard a chance.

Silence.

Standing in a huddle on what was left of the road, the coach passengers, mainly women and children were frozen in utter shock. They held each other, mesmerised by their desperate and lucky escape.

Karen knelt down on the road near the cliff edge.
Clouds of dust and smoke drifting by her.
She was crying a prayer, tears streamed down her face.

Louis ran up to her and knelt alongside; he put his arm on her shoulder.
"He was a very brave man Karen, saving many people."
She just cried and sobbed.

Some cars had pulled up, their drivers getting out gawping at the scene and also that the cliff road had gone. Louis glanced across at the distant south wall.
"MON DIEU!" he exclaimed.
A huge cloud of dust was rising right along its base.
A massive section of mountain was sliding into the sea.

And then something extraordinary happened.

As the dust cleared around the cliff edge where the coach had gone over, one dust shape refused to dissipate.

It then moved, slowly.
The dust shape fell down a couple of times and moved perilously towards the edge.
Louis was lightning quick.
He sprinted, slid and almost fell over the edge and then he grabbed an arm.

John's arm.

Karen stood and whispered a "oh…John…..thank you God."
She cried her face wet with tears.

Later

Back down in Tazacorte the ambulance crews had their hands full.
At the small hospital people were being ferried into the A&E department.
Nurses running in and out, other staff on mobiles as they dealt with earthquake casualties coming in from many directions.

John sat outside wearing an oxygen respirator, he was still coughing from the dust and exhaust fumes still in his lungs. His clothes were matted with dirt.
Karen fretting and helping him to breath, turning her head looking anxiously for support.

None.

The doctors had more critical cases from the earthquake to deal with.
Louis had disappeared some twenty minutes ago.

John tore off the respirator and coughed heavily, vomiting and discharging the debris from his lungs. He knelt down, hands on the ground.
Karen on her knees holding him, she said "Oh John…. I'll get some help, get your lungs cleared somehow."
She desperately looked around.
He cried, "Water, need some water……….."
She threw off her rucksack and gave him the last of the water bottle.
He coughed and spat after the first gulp, then drank the rest and stood up.
He was pale as a white sheet.
"Ah….God that was awful, but think it is clearing a bit."

John looked around, said "I'm ok, bit shaken but ok…..did all the passengers…" he became racked with coughing again "phoew… ah….did they get out ok?"
Karen replied "Thanks to you and Louis, they all did bar the brave driver. He stayed at the wheel to give them a chance."
Her face was sad, "He gave his life for them."

John just looked at Karen and gripped her arm, "Louis saved me you know. I couldn't see a thing in that dust and I was just about to walk over the cliff edge."

Karen managed a smile, "Thank god he moved so quickly, ah here he is."
Louis strode up a little out of breath and with a pained look asked John, "How are you John?"
"Uum…yeah…ok, think my lungs need lubrication."
He started to laugh then broke into a coughing fit.

Louis looked closely at John and grabbed his shoulder. He paused looking around, then quickly replied, "Good. I have chartered a fishing boat to take us round the island and close to the airport. The captain wanted far too much money but I had no choice. We need to go now."

Karen suddenly spoke, "What about the south wall and the tsunami it will create?"
Louis "strangely it appears that this part of the island only saw a metre wave, the bulk of the wave front is travelling along the western Atlantic. Have you seen the volcano southern valley?"
She looked at John, Karen "No, we had our hands full."

Louis in a sombre tone said "The wall took down with it some of the valley. It is not a total collapse, although some towns there have vanished and many people have lost their lives. That huge rock pushed a subterranean hole underneath.
Thrusting through the island's side and into the sea, it has caused a tsunami wave."
Karen wide eyed uttered "and the USA eastern seaboard?"
Louis "I have no idea how big that wave will be when it reaches them. Come, we must leave now to get this boat."

John, his clothes discoloured and filthy, his face smeared with black soot, said "Pray no more secondary quakes come."

Chapter 14

8.50 am Wednesday 21st March
Richard Armitage's office, ESS, East Meon, UK.

He paced up and down his spacious office, clutching the unlit pipe.
All his people were due here at 9 am.
His mind was seething.

Finally a full showing of his team, after some of them gallivanting up in Norfolk, another off sick, and John and Karen holidaying in the Canary Islands.

He had been stuck here, fuming at the lack of information from his people.
Bill Craswell was acting very odd, a bit like a grinning Cheshire cat with secrets, but he seemed jumpy at the same time.
Jane remained distant, fully occupied with her work.
A dark horse that girl.

Tony Cressada complaining of a stomach virus that he picked up in Norfolk.
Gustav Huck with some strange marks dotting his face, 'again having an air of what? yes, an air of elation.'
'Something is out of kilter.' thought Armitage.

His thoughts wandered to John and Karen's incredible diversion, first to the telescope arrays and then saving the lives of nearly thirty people from a coach plunging down a cliff.

He frowned; there was another aspect that he struggled with.
Nothing tangible only that he felt very angry 'at….. at what?'
'Them… yes they were involved in something that was not reported.'
John and especially Karen, she seemed to have skills, yes skills beyond her scientist talents.

His back grew stiff and he clenched his jaw as an insidious feeling took over.

A faint black mist clung to the rear of his neck.

He banged the pipe on the table with a clatter. Some tobacco spilled out.
Over the past couple of days the Ministry in London had given him at lot of stick.
Subtle hints about his career, future direction changes and 'emergency' senior staff arriving to help out.
His grimace turned into a sickly smile as he remembered his little joke on Bill with the shrunken head.
Bill possibly not having any idea who sent it, 'or even if he suspected me' thought Armitage, 'so much the better.'

He thought 'This meeting will sort the wheat from the chaff……'

Just outside the room

Bill grabbed John then hugged Karen, "Sooo happy to see you guys, glad you came through ok, what a scrape!" he beamed from ear to ear.

Karen replied, "Things just keep happening Bill. I'm supposed to be on convalescence leave but Richard asked if I could come in today."
She winced a little from her chest pain.
Jane hurried up and hugged Karen, "Well done Kaz! God you guys were brilliant saving all those people!...oh Karen…you ok?"
"Yes I'm not bad really. Just my wound aches a bit."

Jane squeezed her hand, "You need some down time."

John smiled and turned to the closed office door, "Thanks Jane. Well we were on holiday, it was just something we had to do. Come on let's see what his lordship has for us today."

By 9.05 am they were all in the office and seated.

Bill Craswell, rested his bandaged hand on the table, he had a little smirk on his face.
He had reason to feel very pleased with himself, well mostly.
That horrible package through the post had thrown him. His mind went back over his connections and favours he had pressed from them, some close to blackmail.
But Bill was honourable; he knew he would never shop the people who he had worked with.
The secret gravity engine test was most present in his mind. Already he had story, a plan to ensure Richard did not catch on, but which would justify a number of engine improvements.

Then his mind wandered to the brief analysis of gravity data he and Jane had looked at from Sunday's momentous clash of gargantuan spacecraft.
He still couldn't believe the results.
Jane and Bill had done a quick virtual reality session with their ReachThru goggles, analysing the clash of titans in space. Their initial discoveries from the gravitational data, were mind boggling.
John was itching to get on the ReachThru to realise their glee.

Tony Cressada could not sit still. He played with his hands as though trying to wring some invisible towel. He glanced repeatedly at his mobile phone.
Gustav Huck sat back on his seat with a slight smug expression, twiddling a pencil over his pad.

Jane studiously watching everybody, scrolling her tablet now and then.

Karen stared into free space, clutching her coffee, her mind far away.

Her and John had both managed to get a flight home yesterday Tuesday, after much delay and a very rough sea voyage around La Palma. Their boat captain had more than earned his money battling through numerous small tsunami swells as they headed around the island.
Thank god for a seasoned sailor.

Armitage had not yet been briefed by Bill about the ReachThru discoveries.
They said more analysis was needed.
He would not be put off, continuing to huff and puff.

Their boss had put away his own shrunken head glass paperweight for this meeting.
It was not popular, numerous comments stuck in his mind.
Petty people he thought. They need to get into the real world.

Constance his secretary, sat nearby, ready to take minutes.

Armitage slowly looked around the room and then said,
"Thank you all for attending today. As you know events have gripped the world by storm. We are central once more, our magnificent technical resources available to keep our leaders fully informed as to the ongoing situation."
Jane smirked thinking 'Richard the preening peacock, grabbing the limelight as much as he can.'
Armitage continued, "Firstly the world is now a different place, each nation has set up alert levels and mobilised their military forces. The western nations are pretty much together here. I believe our friends in the east, are similarly galvanised although they are not dealing with us directly. There is much suspicion around the world, with even some less informed nations suggesting the space spectacular is an American staged diversion."
He paused, no one interrupted.

Karen stared at Armitage, he seemed not to be quite in focus.

‘God’ she thought ‘I must still be very tired from our Canary Island escapades.’

He caught her glance and did something peculiar, unnatural for him.
He scratched his left shoulder and shook his head a little.
She watched him closely.

Grunting Armitage continued, “ESS is now a fully protected military base. Armed guards govern entry and exit. In addition we have covert surveillance around the site. As we know there may be other parties or even unidentified craft or objects from space that may be very interested in what we do here.”

His smile was a little macabre.

Bill Craswell interrupted, “Surely Richard, if these things emanated from the large craft which was destroyed, we must be up against very sophisticated technology and weapons that are almost unimaginable?”

Armitage stared at Bill, “Exactly, but man must muster what he can. Hence all services are on high alert. The powers that be are preparing for any eventuality.
If I may continue.... our Array system is now out of action due to the orbital arm failing as a result of the space explosion blast waves. Our Wales, Norfolk and Oban installations are still operational but no longer effective and as you said John, the neutrino link cannot work without the orbital array station. However, we managed to acquire a huge amount of data from Sunday night’s events and I am very keen for you guys to get on it, soon as. I suggest straight after this meeting.”
Karen looked at John, then Bill.
You could almost taste the excitement in the air.

Armitage ploughed on, “Also as the anomaly Crackwell is only really measurable properly from the southern hemisphere now

and to keep our capability, the Australians have kindly offered on a shared technology basis, to construct a Gravity Array there. It is now well advanced, with them doing a satellite launch next week to get their orbital array up in space."
Bill "Impressive."
"Yes, we initiated plans with them in early February. Thanks to Bill for highlighting that the anomaly Crackwell following on in its orbit, would disappear from our own view."

It was not quite true. The UK gravity arrays can see gravitational waves coming right through the Earth, but with the Earth not in their path, the data would be a lot cleaner.
Armitage now looked first at Jane and then at Bill.
"As a result I would like you Bill to go to Australia and help them configure and test their array as soon as possible. Jane too, with your experience and knowledge, I would like you to accompany Bill and support the array testing and commissioning.
I would expect you both to be there sometime next week."

Jane was open mouthed, her heart leapt. 'Travel already… yippee!'
Bill was taken aback, his mind started to go over everything here. Need to tie up loose ends, especially his engine.
He spoke up, "Sounds excellent Richard. Just need to complete some engine mods. We have recently generated some new modified computer models for the gravity engine and after some early runs, certain engine updates are required.
I'm sure Gustav and Tony are more than able to carry on without me."

Both his colleagues nodded their concurrence.
Little did any of them let on about the near catastrophic secret test of their miniature gravity engine in Norfolk.

Bill quickly reflected on the white man at the end of the field.
He felt a chill.

Armitage still had his suspicions; they had been up to something in Norfolk, but what? Pursing his lips he continued, "Excellent. Sounds like you guys have containment in place. Now onto other business."

Gustav thought 'Containment! Hell, all that radioactive material was still up there…'

"Other business, ah yes, I must congratulate John and Karen for their amazing experience and the rescue of those people from that coach in La Palma. I…."
A round of clapping started.
Bill the loudest, exclaimed "You two have the protection of saints!"
Karen smiled and looked at John, she thought 'Mr Craswell, you don't know how close you may be….'

Armitage held up his hand, the clapping died away. "Well done and of course you are in the media again."
This time John beamed, fame was not such a bad thing.
Then Armitage's demeanour became very stern, his face quite pale.
Karen saw a wisp of something at the back of his body.
Like a tiny dark aura.
She quickly glanced at the others. Nobody was seeing what she saw.
He seemed to shudder a little.

Karen gripped her pen so hard it broke, she felt very uneasy.
In fact, she sensed danger.

Armitage spoke, his voice seemed to have a slight distant echo, "Karen, John tell me, something happened as those two craft engaged in conflict.
I'm told that you guys left the telescope systems building at that time.

Something that you both did or were engaged in that …. that…..” he stammered slightly trying to find the right words.

Richard Armitage was staring at Karen, his eyes piercing into her with a pain like a blade.
“RICHARD!” Karen just shouted at him. She broke to a whisper. “Are you ok?”
“Yes I am fine.” His voice had adopted a low grating tone, “Tell me more about those artefacts and where they are now?”

“Richard what do you mean?”
Her hand quickly went to her cross under her blouse, her thoughts driving at him.
John wasn’t slow.
He had also sensed the situation and was bent over to the side of his chair, his hand gripping and preparing to withdraw the ancient sword from his briefcase.

Armitage appeared to sway, he uttered a little moan, his hands pushing in front of him as though to try and push something invisible away. Then he fainted, falling and striking his head on the table.

Bill rarely swore, but said “What the fuck happened there? Jesus, someone get the nurse!”
Jane raced over to Armitage’s still form on the floor.
Blood oozed from a gash high up on his cheek.
She checked his pulse and lifted his head onto one of the loose seat cushions

For Karen, she saw that the black mist had disappeared.

Later, the paramedics resuscitated Armitage. Still in a daze, he was taken to hospital.
Bill spoke to Karen and John. Jane joined them.
Bill quietly said, “There are weird things going on and I want

to talk to you Karen as I think maybe only you may have the answers."

All four of them went down to the Newton lab and shut the door. Bill said, "First let's get a strong coffee. I bloody need it, that's for sure."

They all sat around one of the lab tables.
Jane watched Bill closely, she thought about him and his awful divorce. He had mentioned July's fall late Sunday night and how when she came round, she was more amenable and apologetic. Bill had said she still wanted a divorce, but he had an undertone in his voice, a hope maybe.
Jane pondered 'What did she feel…a twinge of heart strings? Hell no. Well maybe….' She tried to understand her feelings. She liked Bill, especially working with him. He was a do-er. not a talker, one of those people that really achieved progress.
And travel to Australia now. Her heart leapt, more exciting times. She glanced back at Bill and smiled.
He looked at her and returned it a little.

Bill tapped the table with the two fingers he had on his left hand and then spoke.
"There are some bloody strange things happening not only out there…" he gesticulated towards the window, "but around here too. What the hell was wrong with Richard? He looked like a demon possessed."

Karen replied, "I think he may have been just that."

Bill looked sharply at Karen, "You think so? Well I have had experiences too that I want to share with you guys."
He nodded at John and Jane.
"It's about time that you knew. We are a close knit team and things are getting out of hand. We need to level with each other concerning everything that happens.

However, until we can establish trust with others, I suggest a closed circle here, just us?"
Their eyes met with approval, silence nodded its agreement.
John became serious, "So what do you know Bill?"

He paused, took a long deep breath.
"Firstly Gustav, Tony and I were only briefly at the Norfolk Array in Partledown.
You see I had managed to do most of the software upgrades remotely, prior to then."

Bill hesitated, and then said.
"Instead at a secret location of mine we tested a miniature of the gravity engine."

John burst out "YOU DID WHAT?"

Bill replied, "Yes a gravity engine we had secretly constructed."
There were gasps from both Karen and Jane. They knew the dangers of any Earth bound testing.
Jane stared incredulously at Bill, the man she admired for being a doer, a go getter. Now he may have spread dangerous radiation around Norfolk.
John was speechless.

Bill quickly continued, "It's ok, the engine performed fine, in fact better than expected. The thrust was double what we estimated. We did get a little radioactive fallout, but cleaned up as best we could. A follow up operation to finish the removal of the radioactive matter will get under way as soon as."
Karen's face became purple, "You reckless idiot! You endanger not only yourself but our country and more by doing this!"
"Sorry Karen I know how you must feel. You see the engine did break its mountings and go through the barn wall into the field, but the contamination is local to the farm.
We had to do this test otherwise our much larger orbital engine would have failed.

The tests allowed valuable modifications to be made ensuring the engine's stability. What's more I saw….."
He didn't finish.

"Double the thrust you said. Double?" John spoke up.
Bill turned to John, "Yes double, there may have been secondary reactions we believe, possibly micro fusion."
John's eyes became glazed, he was deep in thought.
Karen interjected "Well I hope you got what you want, because as sure as hell I want to report this."
Bill "Please, please wait there is more. Let me explain the white robed man."

He then went on to tell them, but concentrating on Karen, about his so called dream in the countryside near ESS, where a white cloaked man had warned him about the explosion particle and that he needed to modify the gravity engine. Bill then described the moment he discovered the gravity engine in the field at his Norfolk farm and the white robed man appearing again at the very end of that field.

Bill "What the hell is he Karen? It was not a hallucination or dream, I actually saw him."
Karen's anger had subsided; she slowly stood up and walked around the room, stopping to look out of the window and across the thinly grassed fields.
Out there in the earth furrows, a gaggle of crows did their awkward walk, jerkily looking for worms and insects.

At length she wandered back to the table putting her hands on it and looked around at everybody.
"I too need to tell you guys…." She looked directly at Bill, then Jane "…about our experience at La Palma. The one that Richard seemed to sense but not knowing what it was."
She conveyed her dreaming session and that it was interrupted by a desperate attempt to fend off an unseen menace by using their

ancient artefacts. She described the cross and the sword and how they seemed to work.
Jane was in awe, "Oh Karen, John this is incredible…. Are they man made?"
John with a solemn look said, "No, we believe they are of a technology that we can only imagine…."

Bill slightly shook his head "This is crazy, but I like it, amazing ….amazing."
Karen spoke "What's more it is very likely that myself and John are in great danger from this…. this unseen menace. Bill, I feel that your white man is here to help. Possibly he represents the beings from the second craft that came out of the portal.
I cannot be sure, just a strong feeling I have….."

Bill, "To be honest this is so surreal."

Karen spoke, "During our, I guess you could call it a 'spiritual conflict', I can't think of any other description, I sensed clearly a repulsive, vile species.
Insect like, devouring without feeling or emotion. I glimpsed powers beyond our imagination, ethereal abilities that can reach far across space and violate our souls. Spooky and scary."

Jane had her hand over her mouth, said quietly "What the hell? Seems unbelievable, what is happening, is our imagination running away?"
Karen caught the whisper.
She said "At times, I so wish it was. Why oh why have WE been fated to be so involved with this stuff?"
Jane replied, "Well out there, Mr God or whoever they are, have in their supreme wisdom picked you guys for some special reason."
A little sarcasm crept into her voice.
Karen looked at John for guidance.

He spoke up "Ok. So let's put these facts together, I'll call them that. To summarise, we have a particle caused by our explosion

last year, which is embedded in the moon. Its extreme impact velocity unfortunately caused the death of the Chinese astronauts in their moon base."
Bill's face puckered into a guilty frown.

"and then Bill has had some sort of warning that his gravity engine is unstable and he made steps to rectify this."

He looked at Bill, who nodded vigorously. "Then we have this colossal conflict out there in space, by spacecraft of technologies far beyond our capabilities. In the meantime an unseen but measurable attack happened to the Earth, which by the grace of God, Karen and I seem to have thwarted.
It seems incredible that we have been, what.... selected? Or fate has somehow intervened allowing us to discover the capabilities of these old objects.
I still haven't the faintest idea how they worked or where to go from here."

Karen caught John's arm as he slumped into a chair.
She said looking at the others, "You see this thing is bigger than all of us, yet how do we safely tell the world?"
Bill pulled a gargoyle face. He said "We have to; we cannot be expected to carry on like this. Unless we have been singled out somehow......you know to carry on in secret?"

His voice faded away and he started to dream he was on the podium receiving a Nobel award, the accolades, the fame, shaking hands with world leaders........

Bill jumped as Jane's phone made a loud bing.
Jane turned and frowned at her phone.
'Oh Gavin...what do you want?' she thought.
Text received.
'Jane. I need to see you urgently. I'm in trouble. Love Gavin x'

The room became deathly silent.

Karen glanced around then said, "Think we ought to look at that conflict through the gravity array data. Give Richard something to……" she stopped took a deep breath and continued. "You know what? I have a feeling that Richard was possessed by something…um….something very sinister."
They all hung on her words.

Bill replied, "Then we need to keep Richard out of the loop and be on our guard."

Karen said, "I have an idea. Something that I have learnt that can bind us closer together against whatever may threaten us."

A little while later…

Early on Karen had suggested the other three participate in a relaxation session and try some meditation.
They all sat in a circle on cushions with eyes closed.
Four candles burning and flickering on a small central floor mat.
A small stone object occupied the centre of the mat.
They had locked the lab door from the inside to prevent or warn of any outside interruptions.
Window blinds pulled and the discreet observation cameras disconnected.
So called 'safety' cameras.

Both Bill and Jane were apprehensive, not knowing what to expect.
What they did know was that Karen had a gift to help them all.

She spoke "Relaaa..x …totally. Take long slow deep breaths. On the intake draw the breath as though it starts from your groin and passes upwards through your body, your vital organs and then passes out through the top of your head. On exhaling reverse this path. Do it slowly and meditatively."

After a long pause she said, "We shall go directly to the stone, the altar and travel upwards to the upper world. Climb, go up until you are there."

Her phone was playing a quiet drumming sound.
"Breathe in... breathe out. Go deep within your subconscious. Ignore everything outside of this. Just let it happen. Relax."

Bill's mind was churning, too much thinking.
Karen said "Empty your minds, just be. Look for your guides. May be a bird or animal."

Then she adopted a deep thought motion herself, attempting to reach out, to feel and sense each of the others in turn.
Our spiritual orientation, something deep within all of us, if only we would let it.

After twenty minutes, Karen changed the drumming to a more frequent rhythm and let the others slowly come out of their dreaming states.

John, "Ah um... I nearly fell asleep there."
Jane "Karen, that was so amazing for me, I did drift for a moment into I guess your world?"
"It's not my world, but a vast new environment of peace and enlightenment."
Bill "Bit weird if you ask me, but I did see a couple of creatures."

Water got sipped, it was essential.

Karen, "Enough for now. Take it easy and come to slowly, hold on to your visions."

After some time John piped up, "Ok. Let's get the system cranked up. Have a real close look at Sunday."

Much Later.
The ReachThru Virtual Reality System, ESS

Totally blind to their lab surroundings, they now wore ReachThru headsets.
Sitting in an arc on reclining chairs gave them all a comfortable viewing posture.

Inside the ReachThru goggles were twin built-in screens, giving a view of virtual reality or as in this case, actual reality recorded.
John initiated the sequence to set up their viewing positions close to Crackwell.
As always the effect was almost unnerving, with real stars and deep black space totally surrounding the viewer, *in all directions.*

Once they were all 'floating in space' John activated a slow motion sequence prior to the expansion of the anomaly object Crackwell.
This was constructed from their gravity array data and visible observations from telescopes. Each person had been 'placed' in physical space around Crackwell.
There to his right was Jane, a little red cat symbol. To his left Bill the lion and further left was Karen a white eagle.

They had all adopted animal symbols they had sensed during their brief dreaming session earlier.
Himself an owl.

Tiny thumbs up from close to each symbol gave the 'go for launch'.
A huge superimposed 3D micro grid consisting of very thin criss-cross lines, formed right through their view. This faint yellow mesh represented real space and time.

Jane although not her first time, still gasped at how real it felt.
Just floating, nothing supporting you in a vast universe of black and stars.

The ReachThru goggles gave her an almost full vision as though she was actually in this world of outer space. Real telescope feeds of the inky black sky Sunday night had been superimposed into their view. She could see myriads of stars, white, yellow, some orange-red.
Far away clusters of suns, even faint coloured patches that were nebulae.
Nebulae, the distributed hot gases and material from some ancient exploding star.

Jane drew a sharp intake of breath as she looked down between her legs, to see deep black, star pricked space as far as the eye could make out.

Nothing underneath her, nothing supporting her body.

Instinctively her free hand gripped the chair arm even tighter.
Then around and up above her head, an endless dense splatter of stars that reached back enormous distances into the black universe.
"Whoa!" She felt a little giddy.

A natural sensation at over two million miles from Earth.
Synthesised with real data, but very, very lifelike.

John spoke through their headsets, "Ok the anomaly is over to the right, see the very slight buckling of the grid pattern around it. I have highlighted the area with a blue circle."

The apprehension mounted, as somewhere out there was that invisible object, the cause of so much attention and mystery.
"Now I will start the sequence, just before Crackwell expanded in size on Sunday."

He inched on the time.
They all watched intensely, not wanting to miss anything.
Crackwell the mysterious portal.

Suddenly a little shimmer of the grid occurred right at the blue circle.

A little flexing and then it happened. Like a stone dropping into a still pond, tiny ripples started from the centre and fanned outwards. Only the faint yellow gravity array grid showed it, because Crackwell remained invisible.

After a few minutes, hours in real time, the grid ripples surrounding Crackwell expanded to hundreds of miles in diameter. Finally stopping at nearly ten thousand miles wide. John adjusted the blue circle to match.

Karen exclaimed "That is incredible. Now I guess we wait for that black asteroid thing to exit from it?"
"Yup. Now watch closely." John fast forwarded the recording.

Heart rates increased.
When you are about to see something that is a really scary, despite being a recording, it galvanises your adrenalin rush.

It would have been some hours in real time, but here covered in only tens of seconds as the video was played in fast forward. Crackwell seemed to glow, little flashes appearing at the periphery of the blue circle.

Crackwell, that unexplained hole, a rift in space and time.

All four of them watched closely, the tension was electric.
Karen thought 'Oh God, this is it. We're about to see what frightened Sabrina so much.'

They almost missed it.

The grid around Crackwell buckled for a split second, then the glow was gone and the grid reverted to normal.

John froze the recording; he said "There, the alien craft has exited, totally unseen. Look to the far left of Crackwell, see those tiny ripples along the grid? That is gravity distortions from its propulsion drive."
Bill gasped "Good lord, the bloody thing is invisible!"

Karen interjected "I am now manipulating the background stars behind this craft. The program will remove all those with slight light distortions from normal, then replace them when the distortions disappear. Just like they did at the La Palma observatory."

Bill's eyes were wide with disbelief.
Jane shivered a little.
Virtually sitting there in space seemed just too damn real.

"There…" said Karen "Now the craft should be track-able, John can you release the recording?"

The star fields blipped a moment, and then it happened.
A huge black roughly circular shape traversed slowly across the background star field.
"Holy crap!" exclaimed Bill, "That thing gives me the shivers, the size of it."
John looked at the numbers on the periphery of his display. "Yes, it matches the La Palma estimates; it is about five hundred miles in diameter."

Bill was sweating profusely. His short black hair was wet with perspiration.
His forehead scar pulsed.
Jane just repeated very quietly "Oh my god….."
For a little while they watched the black 'asteroid' traverse across space.
John accelerated time and then slowed it down. "There, see? Multiple red flashes.
I saw those from the La Palma mountain top."

The asteroid flickered with dozens of tiny red sparks.
Karen felt her heart pulse, feeling again the scary moment they endured as an unseen force tried to subdue them.

John froze the recording.
"Comments anyone?"

Karen was first to speak, "Incredible. All we know is that coincident with those red flashes, John and I had to use our artefacts and generate some sort of shield."
Jane asked "Do you believe it is a robotic craft or manned by aliens?"
"God knows…"
Bill said "Let's see what happens next. John?"

John incremented the time on until the second craft started to emerge from Crackwell.
As it came into sight, John magnified their view by moving them all very close to the second object.

Four people 'floating' in deep space, the Earth and moon small and far behind them.
Jane gave a little cry; she gripped the sides of her chair tightly.
Bill went quiet and started to whisper "What the hell is that? What on earth is happening?"
Karen was using her quantum physics knowledge.
Her perception of the new craft deepened in utter amazement.
At four hundred miles wide, it too was huge.

It seemed to be composed of numerous revolving cages with something very bright at the centre. But none of it was in focus.
All of a sudden a giant red ball of light enveloped this craft.
John spoke, "There, the attack from the black asteroid."
A massive beam of energy had been launched at the new craft as it exited Crackwell.

As the red light dissipated around it, possibly deflected or absorbed, the new craft became much more visible.
Suddenly in their view, the gravity grid twisted in multiple tiny spots, hundreds of little points, all bending and pulling the grid.
John shouted "LOOK, look at that.... What the hell are they?"

Karen was furiously manipulating the view processor, she magnified, panned across, magnified again. Checking a readout of energies she swore, "Bloody hell, the energies are colossal and yet they are pin points, what are they?"

Then she realised what was almost impossible to comprehend.

She exclaimed "This is incredible, let me pull you in. Hundreds of black holes, no thousands of them. Very, very small.
Micro black holes, each with enormous gravity I reckon. Yes look at those rotating cages. They must be....no can't be... but yes they are.....they are magnetic or gravity devices of unimaginable power. They lock and control the tiny black holes!"

Black holes, those very small objects at the centre of galaxies and no doubt lone ones wandering throughout the universe as well.
Pulling any nearby matter, be it rocks, gas, planets or even stars into their immense gravitational fields. No one knows where all this material goes. The black hole is so dense and with such a huge gravity pull, it cannot actually be seen......even light cannot escape.

Sure enough the second craft was a mass of revolving rings and odd shapes, containing and manipulating probably hundreds of thousands of tiny black holes.
Total mass control, an awesome technology way beyond man's imagination.
John allowed the scene recording to proceed very slowly.

Then something amazing happened.

The whole shape of the craft changed, it seemed to stretch into a long pod. The black holes were depicted by thousands of tiny pulsing distortions on the 3D gravity grid matrix.
There were so many that at times, the grid could only display a huge blur of activity.

The revolving rings became distorted, misshapen. Huge forces controlled the twisting, deadly energies emanating from the maelstrom of writhing black holes.
The bright object in the centre was a tiny star, white hot.

Karen frowned at the measurements. She gasped out loud "That star has….wait …crikey…fierce X-rays coming from it as well. I'd say it is a neutron star, huge amount of extremely dense matter, way beyond what its tiny size implies!"

The astonishing scenario continued.

Bill gasped "LOOK! the bloody thing is distorting. That little star is changing shape….Jesus! Now what the devil?"
John had slowed the recorded sequence right down, as in real time things were happening very quickly.
Before Bill could finish, the giant spherical spacecraft created a tunnel made up of the tiny black holes. These then closed and stretched around the star. A sort of spout formed at the end. Then the grid at that point blurred, seemed to revolve fast towards its end and vibrated violently.
A cyclic action of tiny black holes moved at dizzying speed along the tunnel from one end to the other. The enormous gravity of each one focussing on the neutron star, as it passed by

Instantly, molten matter was dragged out of the star at a colossal speed.
Blindingly, a white hot focussed stream of brilliant plasma shot out at almost the speed of light.

A million miles away, and brief seconds later, the deadly plasma beam struck the black alien asteroid
Very high velocity liquid death at six thousand degrees centigrade.

For an instant their view showed the black asteroid craft splitting apart. Then a blinding flash announced its destruction.
Bill just mouthed 'Oh my gawd…' over and over.

John stopped the playback and called everybody to disengage and remove their ReachThru headsets.
Written on all their faces was incredulity and astonishment.
He said "Steady. Take your time to re-adjust."

Then he said "You see that? A technology that can control thousands, probably millions of micro black holes………..flippin incredible."
Bill was spellbound, he just shook his head.
All of them streamed perspiration.

Karen similarly was soaked through, her blouse damp, clingy.
She exclaimed "So, so extraordinary. They use moving black holes with their huge gravity to drag matter out of that little sun at near light speed and fire it at the black ship. They must have been searching for and harvesting tiny black holes for millennia. Maybe millions of years…………" her voice faded as the scale kicked in.

John added, "I try to imagine how it can be done. Just imagine giant super efficient gravity magnets of compact yet enormous power. Only something like that could control a micro black hole."
Karen commented "And that plasma must have been extremely hot, what thousands of degrees centigrade?"

In his mind Bill was galloping ahead, ……wondrous stuff without a doubt.

Then he had one of his rare moments of inspiration.
His thinking ploughed on 'White hot plasma, the product of fusion in the star and indeed our sun……and my God!....like some of the stuff that the gravity engine must have spewed out……'
His hand covered his mouth.

Jane looked at Bill, said "What Bill?... what's up?"
He sort of shook his head, replied, "Uh, well I have a theory, but I must check it out first….perhaps you can help me with the maths?"
Jane said "Course Bill…" but thinking 'What is he up to now?'

No one said much after that.
They were all overwhelmed by the sheer technological scale of what they had just observed.

After a while, John gave a little smile.
"Well, it seems that we have some sort of guardian beings with capabilities that are beyond belief. I guess one can garner some sort of relief from that……"

Bill at length said. "This is just too important to keep to ourselves."
He reached for the phone and rang a Ministry number.
After a while he said "Bill Craswell, ESS Director of Special Projects. I need to speak to Sir George Ratcliffe immediately….."

He waited then raised his voice "I don't care if he is in a meeting, this call is of extreme national importance, get him to this phone NOW….. please."

Much later in another lab at ESS

The three of them sat around the stainless steel table.
Gustav looked at Jane and Bill, saying "So what have you guys got for me?"
He smiled in that serious German way.

Bill hesitated then said, “Well Gustav, you know our little engine experiment and your fusion temperature calculations?”

Gustav frowned, “Yes, I finished what I could with the data we had and it is indeed fusion, albeit only briefly. Hence the higher than expected levels of thrust and the extra heat produced.”
Bill said “Plasma heat I think. I have asked Jane to help you with more analysis.”

Gustav gave a puzzled look, “There is more?”
Bill “Yes, what design changes do we need to make to concentrate and narrow the exhaust output and increase the thrust, to say double or more?”
Gustav gave a shocked reply, “Mein Gott Bill! Haven’t we got close, how do say it? Yes, too close to the edge already?”
Bill said, “This is important Gustav.”

Gustav’s eyes widened, he smiled, “We will definitely die this time……”

It was a joke that nobody laughed at.

Chapter 15

7.30 pm Wednesday 21st March
The Bird In Hand Pub
Lovedean, UK

Jane didn't want to go.

She had wanted time apart from Gavin.
Indeed she had effectively dumped him.

His phone call was pleading, he sounded desperate.
Needing to see her, just a quick drink he said.
She had declined until she sensed pain and anguish in his voice, and fear underneath.

Conservatively dressed, Jane Horsham ambled into the pub, wearing a roll neck navy jumper and blue jeans. Her long red hair was combed straight and clipped back.

The pub was busy for mid week with hot food aromas drifting from the kitchen.

She scanned the customers first for Gavin and then for Roger or maybe Luke his son.
Roger, the crooked sixty year old now in jail, charged with assisting a foreign spy.

Negative, none of the usual suspects were there.

Going to the bar she ordered a white wine.
Yes a Chadonnay with an ice cube.

She wandered through the dimly lit place, people chatting and drinking.
A log fire was dying, the staff too busy to refuel it.

People crowded the bar area, all trying to talk over one another. Painfully noisy.

Jane really didn't want to be here.
Then there was Gavin sitting in the corner, slumped over his beer.

Suddenly on seeing Jane, he jerkily straightened up, smiled and waved.

She walked over and sat down, said "Ok Gavin, I'm here just for the one. What's on your mind? And how are you………god Gavin you ok?"
Gavin looked at her, he had a puppy dog face, reddened with the odd bruise.
"Yeah not too bad."
He had a slight wheeze in his voice.
"So glad to see you Jane."

She looked at him sternly, "Gavin what's up?...you hurt?"
He paused and his eyes became a little watery.
"Jane I'm sorry I fucked up. I wouldn't have asked you but things have got a bit serious."
"Serious?...couldn't be more serious lately Gavin!"
He pulled a face, he was in pain.
She asked again "Gavin?... show me."

He looked around to ensure nobody was looking directly over into their corner.
Then he raised his T-shirt.
Jane gasped, "Oh God Gavin… you poor man… how did that happen?"
She gave him a stern look, "Not another of Crowley's pranks gone wrong?"

Gavin shook his head.
His lower body was a mass of red marks and large ugly purple bruises.

"Ugh… WHO did this?"

"Roger is out on bail. He got his heavies to work me over…….. it hurts Jane."
"Bastard. Have you been to the doctors or hospital?"
"Nah…. I'll be ok."
Jane looked hard at him, she bit her lip.
Gavin was not in a good place. He owed Roger eight and half grand plus interest.
Owing that sort of money on extortionate interest was bad enough, but defaulting to the likes of Roger meant it was extremely bad news.

Jane gulped her wine then caught her breath as it went down the wrong way.
She coughed and spluttered.
Gavin half got up and leaned over to her rub her back gently. He pulled a face and winced as somewhere his body cried out in pain. He nearly made it back to his chair but slid onto the floor holding his side.
"Oh Gavin…cough... God… you can't go on like this. That bloody car and Roger's shitty loan."

"I'll pay him Jane, I will. Job's still good at the abattoir, but I had to take today off sick."
He paused, wincing.
"They got me last night."

A couple at the bar looked across as Gavin struggled back into his chair.
Jane looked around letting out a long slow breath; nobody else was paying any interest.
She said "So what's next? Have they given you an ultimatum or something?"
Gavin looked scared; he glanced out the pub window.
His eyes were bloodshot, one with a nasty shade of purple around it.

At length Gavin quietly said "Sorry Jane, I've no right getting you involved. I did wrong with all that tekkie stuff Roger wanted and getting you and your workmates in trouble. I'm so sorry. He was I guess, yes……um…what do they call it? Ah yes, blackmailing me."

Jane was softening, although he had screwed up, he was still a bit of a lovable rogue.
Gavin continued "They gave me till midnight, and then they're going to empty my mum and sisters' place. Maybe rough them up a little ….not good."
His face showed he had nowhere else to try.

Jane thought long and hard, her face became solemn.
She said "Right Gavin you listen to me and you listen well. I will lend you the money to pay Roger off…with conditions.
I will be there with you when you pay him, a witness……and you set up a direct debit to repay me regularly…." She glared at him.

Gavin suddenly had a look of salvation, of thanks, of yes… relief.
He brightened, nodded, mouth firmly shut.

"Gavin!"
A shout from over the other side of the pub made them both freeze.

It was a smiling Shane waving from the bar; he had just come in and was ordering a drink.
Gavin waved back, and then Shane turned to the bar to get his beer.

Suddenly near where they were sitting, from an outside door close by, two dark shapes slowly appeared.
Gavin froze. He quietly said "Holy shit….I….ah"
Jane turned to look.
Two burly men had approached their table; one had something in his pocket.

They wore dark jerseys and black jeans. Heavy steel boots grated on the wood floor.

In a flash one had leaped across to Gavin, picking him up bodily by the front of his jacket. The other pushed the table away and with his arm brushed Jane back into her chair as she tried to rise. A deep burr of a voice spoke "Now we don't want no trouble Gav, so just come outside with us. Roger wants a little chat...... YOU!" he pointed and looked straight at Jane with a grizzled unshaven face and dark eyes, "YOU stay right here if you know what's good for you and don't do anything stupid like calling the law."

She shrunk back in shock.
Her mind raced.
Jane quickly looked at the bar; people facing away, nobody had noticed the kafuffle in their corner. Shane had disappeared.

Gavin was sort of dragged, half pushed through the door and then he was gone, with the two heavies.
Still in the pub Jane fumbled with her phone. She dropped it. It came apart and the back, together with the battery flew across the floor. "Oh bugger... oh Gavin!"

Outside, along an obscured wall near the pub car park.

A stocky bearded man stood with gloved hands, rubbing a fist into the palm of the other.
"Hello Gavin, I've decided not to waste anymore time. I'll ask you now, for the last time, HAVE YOU GOT MY MONEY?"
Gavin was held by both the heavies, they levered his arms behind his back.
"Aah....ugh...Roger please. Good you're...um..out of jail. I'll get it for you ....just....just need a little time. You'll get it all I promise ....tonight."

Roger spat then said "You've said that for the last three weeks Gavin.
Wearing a bit thin now. And was it you that got me arrested? Eh EH? They've charged me with treason Gavin, FUCKIN TREASON, taken my passport.
I'm on bail, cost a packet.
I'm not in a good place, GAVIN!"

Roger closed in and punched Gavin in the stomach.
Gavin just folded in huge pain.

The door burst open and Jane came running out. She leapt on one of the heavies from behind tearing at what hair he had, kicking him in the side and punching the side of his face. Her Tae Kwando coming back.

He swatted the slim girl off as though she had been a fly.
Jane gasped falling and rolling onto the gravel.
Roger turned and looked at her.
"Ah my pretty sweet, you're the cause of all this investigation with the army and the police. Time you had a little something to remember too."

He started to move towards her, taking out a short stubby billy club from a long trouser side pocket.
She screamed.
Gavin was on his knees still pinned by the heavies.
He was sobbing.

Unexpectedly, a gut wrenching roar came from behind Roger.

Something hard slammed into Roger's back with a crunching thump.
He fell like a bowling ninepin, slumping to the ground.
Pulling back and rotating a motorcycle chain with a hideous lump of teethed metal on the end, was Shane in full fury.
Six foot and sixteen stone of uncouth anger is ugly.

The heavies dropped Gavin and started to move forward.
Shane roared again ducking a swinging punch and then wielding the metal into the first one's face.
A squishy thump resounded. Blood and teeth came out.
The man crumpled, gurgling, holding his face. He fell to the ground, still.

With that the other big guy decided things were not going well. He turned, scrabbled his feet on the loose gravel and ran fast out of the car park.
Shane roared again, "Come 'ere you bastard!" he started to follow then stopped.
Gavin staggered up, he gasped "Oh Shane man, thank god…. Thank god!"
Shane ran back and checked the heavy and Roger on the floor.
Roger laid twisting and groaning on the gravel. "Think I broke his back."
He leaned over Roger and shouted at him "And there's more like this if I see you again, you coward!"
Then Shane looked over at the other heavy. A huge bloody gash in the man's face was apparent. He was quite still, possibly dead.

Jane sat on the gravel, pale and shaking. She said, "Christ what a mess! Gavin, Shane…..oh my god!"

Shane replied "Come on let's get out of here now, Gav can you walk?"
"Yeah, just feel like shit….ah….ouch…..thanks Shane mate, you're a lifesaver."

Shane stood there, the motorcycle chain slowly swinging to and fro in his right hand like a pendulum.
A little blood dripped from the large gear wheel attached to the end.
With one hand on her mouth, Jane pushed herself to stand up, brushing grit off her clothes. Small chunks of gravel still stuck painfully to her palms where she fell.

"Oh my god........Shane... they were bad men, but what have you done?"

"They had it coming. Roughing up Gavin here. Good mates look after each other, eh Gav?"
With Shane gripping his hand, Gavin had very slowly got up and stammered "I owe you big time Shane........"

Shane winked and folded up the motorcycle chain weapon, wiped the business end with a dirty rag and put it in his coat pocket.
Jane looked at Gavin's mountain bike lying against the side wall. It was smashed.
Roger lay on the ground quietly moaning.
She grabbed Gavin's arm. "Come on Gavin, let's get you to the hospital. Thanks Shane, god I feel awful....oh Jesus ...."
Looking frantically around she took a deep gulp of air....and half pulled, dragged Gavin to her car.
She shouted, "Shane, want a lift?"
Shane broke into a running trot down the lane, shouted "Nah thanks. Na problem. See ya...."

After ten minutes in her car, Jane pulled over and stopped. She looked at Gavin.
Shakily she said, "Oh god.... Things just don't stop happening.... what...whatever next. We should call the police...."

She said "I'm going to drop you at the hospital A&E, you might have internal injuries. Then we talk about if and how to pay Roger off ...if he survives.
Seems he wants more than the money now."

Gavin meekly said "Ok Jane thanks a million. I don't know what to say."
She pulled up outside the hospital and turned to face him.
Gavin said "Thanks Jane. I'll do good you know and......I still love you."

He creased a painful smile, then got out and limped to the A&E entrance, turning and waving back.

She smiled a little and nodded, then gunned the car back onto the main road.
Jane thought back to their crazy relationship, now suspended, in fact back then she in her mind had ended it. 'Gavin, oh Gavin…..'
Paying Gavin's debts would halve her precious savings.

And yet petty stuff really.
The whole world seems to turn on trivial matters, which in some cases become awful conflicts and wars exaggerated beyond comprehension.
Compared to the enormity of what they saw in the lab this afternoon, everything else seemed so diminished.

She hit the brakes hard and swerved into a lay by, putting the car in neutral.
Jane put her head in her hands and started to weep.
After a little while she nervously looked up and around through the car windows.
She had come onto Catherington Lane.
Thinking, 'Oh hell… the police will be after us. What with Roger and his henchman badly injured back there.'
Jane sat bolt upright with a start. An ambulance would take them to the same hospital Accident & Emergency department, as Gavin had just entered. "Damn" she blurted out loud.
Quickly she sent a text to Gavin.
Then another to Karen Durgas.

She took a long gulp from a water bottle.
Her hand hurt from hitting that guy in the face.
A text reply came in, it was Karen, 'Yes I'm in, please come round.'

Verbena Crescent, Cowplain

The door opened, Karen said "Jane you ok? What's happened?"
Jane wearily said, "More trouble with Gavin. I just had to see you. Hope you don't mind?"
"Please come in. You hurt?"
"I'm ok. Just shaken up."

Over a couple of large glasses of wine, Jane had explained to Karen the night's awful events.
"Oh Jane you must feel terrible. Don't blame yourself for all of it. I think Roger might just be out of commission for a while. Reckon Gavin ought to get his Mum and sisters to a safe house somewhere."
Jane quickly retorted, "Not my place!"
Karen, "Oh sorry, God no." she smiled, "You know we just seem to attract calamity."
She squeezed Jane's hand.
Jane stayed silent giving a little smile to Karen, but her mind was not in a good place.

At length Karen grabbed the remote and switched the television on and selected the local news channel.
They watched for ten minutes, there was nothing about the Bird in Hand fight.
Then Karen switched to the BBC continuous News channel.

Immediately, pictures of panic buying in supermarkets appeared.
Karen spoke, "Why do they do show that on TV? Now even more people will go out and empty the shelves."
Then the newsreader switched to St Peter's Square in the Vatican, Rome.
The Pope was booming out through the loudspeaker system.
His hands were held high and wide.
A translation from his Latin speech appeared as rolling text at the bottom of the screen.

"…………and I stress to you all………be calm but vigilant."

His arms remained in the air, he slowly looked from right to left, then the middle.

"I speak not only for our faith but out to all the world's faiths. We must be strong and join together against temptation and evil forces that are present not only here but out there."

He pointed to the sky. The packed square remained deathly silent.

"When Jesus came as our saviour it changed our world. Now is the time to gather all his teachings. When he died, he had started the preparations for this challenge we face today."

A low hum started amongst the crowd. People whispered.

Jane looked at Karen, checking for a sign, something that she felt Karen could give.
Karen's stare remained on the screen.
The Pope continued.

"We see good AND evil. When you are sure, welcome the good. If evil presents itself and ONLY then, take refuge in your church, your mosque, your temple, wherever your place of prayer is. Here you will find protection."

With that the Pope dropped one arm, waved the other in a respectful sign and disappeared inside.
Karen put her hand to her mouth and audibly gasped.
She frowned.
Jane turned saying "What's up Karen? Did he say something that I've missed?"
"No, it's to do with something my Dad said in his will….um… about churches."
Now intrigued, Jane leaned forward, "What did he say Karen?"

Karen squinted, and then brightened up, "We must pay a visit to Quentin, my Dad's friend Quentin Huxley. He may have the answers."
Karen glanced at the clock.
"Jane, we must visit him tomorrow morning. He resides in an old people's home in Hambledon. I'm officially still convalescing, but it would be good to have someone with me, can you come?"
"Ok, I'll take the morning off ill. Richard is out and I'm sure Bill will be ok with it. Think maybe a little 'women's trouble'." She smiled.

Karen replied "Thank you. But I must go in first thing to ESS. There is a delivery for me to pick up."
She looked at Jane in a jocular way.
Jane cocked her head and then gulped down the last of her wine.
"Go on…."

Karen continued "The US guys have sent John and me, a personal Benji."
Jane laughed cynically "Really? Ha, why? The last robot was hopeless trying to protect us against that Chinese attack."

Karen paused, looking at her glass as she twirled the wine around inside.
She watched the red liquid cling to the sides then fall back into the body of the wine.

"I have a feeling we may need him. Just a feeling Jane, you know like an insurance policy I guess. He did take out a few of the enemy before they got him."
She paused, then said "and also this one has a few interesting upgrades…."

Jane's eyebrows rose just for a second, a mischievous look on her face.

"I trust your feelings Karen. Hopefully we won't need his services. Um…is he, you know complete?"
Karen burst out laughing, "What fully functional in all ways?"
Jane grinned, "Well?"
Karen replied "I believe he has his tackle, but I don't know if it works."
Jane laughed, "Well if I get bored I might just check him out!"

They both burst out laughing.

Then their attention was diverted back to the TV screen as a man appeared behind a podium.
He wore a smart dark suit, white shirt and a green motif tie.
Slicked back short blonde hair contrasted radiant green eyes.
A booming voice came out.
Karen gasped, "Good Lord, that's Maxwell! Maxwell Blackwood the Scientologist. He's married to John's sister Christine."

Blackwood had a look of supreme confidence, an arrogant air.
He spoke slowly, loudly and deliberately.

"It has come, the moment we The Church of Scientology welcome. It is time to realise the legacy of a long distant past."

He paused, his hands visibly grasping the edges of the podium.

"We have instructed our members to accelerate our procedures. These will empower humanity to acknowledge their ancestors."

His voice dropped an octave and increased in volume, *"Ancestors that have now manifested themselves close to our planet."*

Jane had eyes like saucers "Hell, are these people right?"
Karen sighed "Maybe, they believe that we humanity, were let's say 'seeded' by them, many tens of millions of years ago. And yet .."

Karen gave a little laugh "Um….perhaps we were…"

Then they both turned to the screen again as a newsflash came up. A solemn newsreader quickly spoke,

"*A strange tragic event has occurred near a sacred temple in the Chinese City of Qufu. It is believed that it is linked to Sunday's off world conflict. A giant spherical object that was almost invisible and described as 'living death', rolled through a crowd of worshippers, killing possibly as many as sixty people. It seemed impervious to gunfire from the soldiers on duty there. However, it has been reported that when a group of chanting Buddist monks approached, the object disappeared. Some of the monks perished. We are unable to bring you any recording of this incident at the moment.* "

Then the news program turned to other events.
Shortly after the adverts followed.

Karen paled, turned the TV off and said "God that awful thing. They're here…."
She gripped her cross, she felt shivery, clammy.
Jane exclaimed suddenly catching Karen's arm, "Oh Karen, it's unbelievable. Karen? You alright?"
Karen regained her composure, replied "Yeah….I'm ok, just felt something horrible for a moment. I reckon that thing landed in China after escaping from the black asteroid. In fact my gut feeling is that I know it did and it is the most repulsive menace."

9.30 am Thursday 22nd March
The Riverside Rest Home, Hambledon

Benji remained in the car. They didn't want him to alarm the residents.

He looked quite human. Casual shirt and slacks. Brown suede shoes.

Below his fair hair, he had a slight tanned face and wore semi dark glasses.
Even his occasional head movements to look out of the side window, were smooth.
He pretended to read the newspaper he was holding.

The Mark II version robot was visibly almost indistinguishable from the human he was copied from. Only close up could you hear the quiet hum of servo motors when he moved.

Inside the Riverside Rest Home, a very old man in a wheelchair was attended by a nurse. She whispered into his ear, "You have some visitors Quentin."
His eyes opened from a slight doze, to see Karen and Jane standing a little way off.

"Ah hello, nice to have some new company! Oh is that… is that Karen, yes! What a lovely surprise."

Karen quickly came over and said "Oh Uncle Quentin, it has been so long, what? Many years I guess?"
She kissed him on the cheek.
"Don't worry child, You haven't changed at all. Just wonderful to see you and who is this?"
"My friend Jane."

"Hello Professor, I've heard a lot about you." exclaimed Jane.
"Oh dear, I hope not all bad? And please just Quentin is fine."
He smiled through a grey shaggy beard.
"Karen tells me you are one fascinating scientist."
Quentin croaked a laugh, "Ha…. Well I have had my moments."

They sat down and the nurse went off to get some tea.
"Well, well what brings you girls here? Such a pleasant surprise for an eighty four year old, you know."

Karen wasn't sure were to start, she coughed, cleared her throat and said, "It's about my Dad." She glumly looked at Quentin, "Some sad news, did you know he passed away recently?"

"OH... my word, no I did not! When did he leave us?"

Karen replied "I'm afraid it was pneumonia Uncle Quentin. Dad had a chest infection and he aggravated it in Anglesey, Wales. He died there......so hard to bear."
Quentin turned the wheels of his chair a little towards Karen. "Oh my dear, it must have been an awful shock. He was a wonderful man. But Anglesey? What was he doing there?"

Jane followed every word.
Karen "Something happened, he found an incredible artefact.....a sword."
Quentin's eyes nearly popped out of his head, "THE SWORD! How wonderful."
Karen "You know of this object?"
"Yes I do. During my researches many years ago I had determined that it existed."
He eyed her blouse and the bump the cross made.
Quentin gave her a puzzled look, said "and if I am not mistaken you now have the cross? And have you discovered the power of these objects?"
"Why yes I have the cross and recently during that outer world conflict we used the cross and the sword to ....um.. well, they provided some sort of protection. How do you know these things?"

Quentin looked at Jane then Karen, he took a deep breath.
Karen said, "My friend Jane is completely trustworthy, anything you say will be kept in confidence."
Jane nodded.
He spoke slowly, "Until now I have kept certain facts very secret. I spent a lifetime researching not only about these objects, but other shall we say, more obscure things."

Quentin looked around as the nurse carried a tray of tea over to them.
"Ah.... Good you remembered the biscuits." he gave her a great big grin.

She gave a lovely smile and said "But of course Professor, I would be a bad girl to forget them, wouldn't I?"
He laughed as she walked away. Old as he was, there was still a little devilish gleam in his eye.
"Where was I? ah yes." He looked intensely at Karen.

"Karen, when your father Edward, returned many years ago from Greece with your cross artefact, he started me on a quest. What was curiosity became an obsession with me and as you have seen with your father too. You may already know that these objects are not man made. They are extremely sophisticated devices that contain a technology that is millions of years ahead of mankind's knowledge."

Karen gasped "Oh my. I *thought* they were extra terrestrial........."
Jane's eyes stayed wide open, non blinking. She said "So who has made them?"

Quentin creased a smile, "Indeed who? Well I have a good idea and what I am about to tell you now, you may choose to disbelieve, it is your right. You see I am an old man and I need to pass this information on."

Karen "So what do you know Professor?"

Quentin sipped his tea and crunched a biscuit.
After a few minutes, he continued with a croaky voice, "Where to start? Well maybe a long time ago. I believe that we have mentors, people from another place in our galaxy, who were instrumental in man's early development on this planet.
An intelligent species far, far away; who have possibly been around for hundreds of millions of years."

Jane inwardly became a little sceptical. "What evidence do you have Quentin? Apart from what happened Sunday night."
"Yes evidence. Well it is there; very well hidden I might add. Otherwise man would have known a long time ago. His ancestors probably did. You see ancient drawings and sketches can be very revealing if interpreted in the right way."

Karen replied, "I have had some shocking experiences and my work with our gravity arrays has revealed some of what you say. It is very scary Uncle Quentin. We need …um…we…" she faltered.
Jane chipped in, "We need help Quentin. We need support from the right kind of people."

Quentin gripped Karen's sleeve, he had a look of extreme compulsion.
"You must believe what I am about to tell you. Humanity is on the verge of extinction.
When I say extinction, I suspect something far more horrible, like imprisoned painfully… for ever…" his voice tailed away, he looked out of the window.

Karen caught her hand on her mouth, "Oh Uncle, what do you mean?"

Quentin continued, "You see over the millennia, man has always fought wars, big and small. He never seems to learn from the awful lesson of the suffering, the murder and the pointless deaths of many people. During man's existence many millions of people have died needlessly. Why is this?"

Jane tried to interrupt, but Quentin held his hand up.

"*It is because it is not man's fault. It is not our fault.*"

The women sat open mouthed hanging on his every word.

"It is because of a horrid influence far beyond our galaxy that over time has grown in power and capability. This influence reaches from a colossal distance and penetrates every fibre of our society. If evil and hell do exist then that is where it is.

This is why despite the massive efforts of the few good leaders of the world, peace and happiness for everyone has not been realised. It is so strange, ask yourselves, why do these awful persecutions of people continue to happen today, in this age of enlightenment, tolerance and a growing world wide moral awareness?"

He coughed and shuddered a little.
Karen quickly said "You ok Professor?"
"Yes my dear, although I think my time is not far off."

Karen "Oh Professor, don't say that. You are just tired, you don't need to talk now, and perhaps we can come back?"
He leaned over and grabbed her arm firmly.
"No, I must tell you now. It is so important."

They were sitting by a large bay window overlooking the rear gardens, a tall fan shaped pampas grass waved in the breeze. Quentin briefly peered out, as though he expected someone or something to be watching.

He continued, "And yet we have been protected to some extent by these mentors. You see they have implemented devices, very clever, very discreet tiny devices in all the world's churches, mosques, temples, you name it. In many places of worship."

"No?" exclaimed Jane, "This seems so fantastical, but…how do you know?"

Quentin sighed, "Yes it does seem extraordinary, but I assure you I have done my homework. You see I have come across two of these devices in my lifetime. One deteriorated before my eyes, slowly breaking down into powder. The other was embedded in a large building block from a demolished church here in England. If the devices are investigated in any way, they sort of self destruct, fragmenting into powder in a subtle but quick way. Stops any attempt to analyse them."

He seemed to shrink slightly, and then Quentin shook his head. "I….I must apologise, my health is not what it was."

He reached across to a glass of water which Jane quickly passed to him.

Karen spoke, "Uncle Quentin, these objects, can you describe them?"
At length he spoke, gathering his energy, "They are tiny stones, looking like, perhaps the Lapiz Lazuli stone in your cross, dull in colour and the size of a small grape. They are a conduit to a giant machine which I believe is buried in the moon. Indeed the whole moon may be this machine. An extraordinary proposition."
He wheezed and coughed, but struggled on.

"It…it is possible that it harvests its energy from the sun side of the moon.
I believe this machine is a good thing. Implemented by our mentors to protect us over thousands of years from an awful menace. Hence church buildings, mosques and the like have, I guess a sphere of protection generated by these tiny devices. They link somehow to some sort of powerhouse machine in the moon."
He smiled at the two women and spoke quietly.
"Think about the feeling you have when one walks into a church or cathedral. Don't you suddenly feel humble, safe? One gets a sense of awe and peace. A deep comfort and reassurance?"

With a sigh he flopped back in his wheel chair seemingly exhausted.
Karen "Oh Uncle. This is amazing. But how do the devices appear in new mosques and churches? Who puts them there?"

"The invisible ones."

Jane frowned said "How on Earth?….I struggle to follow this Quentin."

Quentin replied "You don't have to. Just listen to what I have said and maybe reflect on it later. You see I have been in touch with Lei Zhao who enlightened me with her Chinese research. She discovered the presence of this object in the moon."
Karen spluttered, "Lei, the girl with Steven Crowley?"
Quentin gave a little chuckle, "Yes. I know both of them quite well. Steven is an old friend who is on his own crusade to save our world. He is very much in tune with what is happening right now. Which leads me to tell you about another device, a bracelet that he asked me to look at. It is indeed similar to your cross and the sword.

Whoever maintains these devices has most probably the power of cloaking, you know to become sort of invisible….and there is…"
His voice faded, he gave a little snort and half closed his eyes.

Suddenly Quentin's head lolled a little and he started to snore, fast asleep.
Karen looked at Jane and smiled, "I think that is the end of our interview!"

Leaving the rest home, their shoes crunched on the gravel road as they walked back to the car through an avenue of tall, spindly trees.
Karen turned to Jane and said, "Well pretty damn incredible eh? I sense you don't believe him?"
Jane replied, "Hell, it's a lot to stomach Karen. I need proof I guess and what did he mean by invisibility?"
Karen frowned, "Don't know. Maybe invisible mentors?" she paused then said, "We know that the giant black ship had some sort of invisibility too. God, we know so little."

Then Jane thought about her parents in Scotland, their cottage near Loch Ness.
A deep need to be with them overcame her.
She walked on in silence.
Karen looked over to the car, now twenty yards away.
Benji had got out, he stood near the car intensely looking back over her shoulder.

She shouted "Benji, what's up? What can you see?..Report!"

A near perfect human voice came out, slightly staccato.
"Karen, there is danger near the house behind you."
Karen quickly turned and looked at the two storey high Riverside Home, about a hundred yards behind them now.

All quiet, no earthquakes, no machine guns opening fire, no explosions.

Just quiet.
And yet….the birdsong had stopped.

She glanced around the house. There were some tall fir trees to the left of the building, a large oak to the right.
Although the sun was shining, there seemed to be a large darker shadow than could be cast by the house and the nearer trees.
On the edge, the furthest left fir tree cast a lighter shadow.
Karen was perplexed, she said to Jane "See the shadows are inconsistent."
Jane's pulse increased, she stuttered, "Ah no…oh wait maybe…. yes there is something odd."

Karen replied "LOOK, look now see the second fir tree has a lighter shadow too.
The house shadow is moving. Can't be the sun, it's far too slow. See it's only slightly different, there…..over there the lawn, see a fuzzy line between light and dark? What's more it's moving too quickly for a sun shadow."

They walked back slowly, puzzled at what they couldn't see, compelled to find out.

Jane slowly walked to the right side of the house.
She looked pensively towards the rear of the place.

Benji was already out of the car and running.
He gave a low shout, "Warning, please retreat back. Warning!"
His under arm weapon pods were clicking and opening.

Jane then abruptly stopped, frozen to the spot, her eyes locked to the lawn, "Oh my god……and it's not the sun."
A very large patch of grass a little distance away was squashed flat.
The flattened patch seemed to move, to grow.

"Whatever is creating the shadow is massive..and ..oh the grass… look!…God it's invisible. Oh my GOD!"

She cocked her head to an odd noise.
Sort of a slithering, squashy sound.

The robot moved quickly running along the lawn, placing himself between Karen, Jane and whatever was on the lawn.
Karen commanded "Benji, what do you detect?"

Unusually Benji did not reply straight away.
He sort of gurgled, then said,
"Extreme danger! My systems are defending against radio energy attacks.
Please retreat immediately."

Time was very short.
Suddenly his right hand weapon pod displayed a short stubby barrel.
As Benji ran between Jane and the house, he pointed the tubular weapon and fired a one shot high energy laser pulse.

Enough to melt and go through metal plate at short range.

The air crackled as an extremely bright glob of a beam stabbed out into what looked like thin air. It was aimed up into apparently nothing, at about fifty feet high and maybe fifty yards behind the house.

With a thud, something invisible stopped the laser pulse. From a central point, blinding light briefly starred out from the impact. For a short moment, a huge shimmering image was illuminated.

There the gargantuan menace quivered.
A giant spherical object pulsing and twitching.
It writhed with black and grey tubers, whispering odd noises and repulsive odours.
The damn thing came closer.

Jane gasped, then screamed and turning to run she lost her footing and fell.
Karen ran over to see more of what was happening.
She cried, stopped and knelt down.
Thrusting her hand down the neck of her blouse, she pulled out her cross.
Her hand shook as she held it out.
She squeezed her eyes shut in concentration.

Quicker than the eye could follow, Benji's primary armour expanded from his body.

Almost at the same time, a flash of something hit him.
The whole of Benji's body flickered in a set of tiny sparks.
A sizzling noise could be heard.
He staggered slightly, taking a step backwards, his armour poured smoke.
The alien stopped as it was hit by a fury of bullets from Benji's machine gun.
Then it seemed to fade and vanish.

Suddenly the air cleared, shadows lifted.

It was over.

Benji closed his weapon pod and retracted the smouldering movable armour, back inwards against his mechanical body.

On another command, the robot walked over to the women and stopped.
He said "The danger has moved away and I estimate travelling at approximately fifteen miles an hour southwards. All systems are functional, I have sustained only minor damage."
Karen just looked at him, his armour seemed intact although it seemed to be speckled and still smoking. She looked closer and felt a shiver. The speckles were myriads of tiny holes in the metal exposed under his shredded shirt.

"Oh hell what did that?.... it's melted….maybe acid? Ok let's get out of here.
So, so scary. Is it still there?"
She glanced again at the house.
Benji replied, pointing "No, it has gone south across those fields."
"What the hell was it Benji?"
He paused then replied, "Unknown entity. I am monitored not to expand further."
"What!"

The robot remained silent.

Both the women stood shocked, rooted to where they stood, eyes looking all around.

Invisible adversaries are hard to see.

Karen turned quickly shouting at Jane, "Let's get the hell out of here!"
Jane said "What about the people in the rest home?"

Karen replied "Well the damn thing has retreated for now. This is a police matter. NO… military I reckon."

With hearts pounding, both women ran fast to the car park in shock, Karen already on her mobile to the police, then she called John at ESS.

Survival instincts made them move very quickly.

Karen stuttered as she drove, "That bloody awful thing was the same as the one in China, don't you reckon?"
Jane her face white and lips tightly drawn, just said "Yeah."

Their car hurtled down the gravel drive. Benji sat in the back, twisting to face the rear window, his systems still on high alert.

Back at Riverside, a nurse shouted for support.

Quentin Huxley had stopped breathing, that snooze had been his last.

Chapter 16

That afternoon Thursday 22nd March
Karen Durgas's house.

Earlier Karen had frantically called John.
He dropped everything at work, driving fast to her place.

Shakily Karen explained their frightening encounter.
John spoke, "So Benji, was he successful, did he confront the beast?"

Karen glowered, but at no one in particular, then said, "Yes he used his laser weapon which illuminated the thing and then his automatic gun. I'm not sure whether he stopped it or just provoked the thing. I used my cross John, to force it back. This gruesome entity seems to have immense energy and maybe I just confused it enough for us to get away."

Glancing across at Benji, John took a couple of strides to face the robot.
Benji jigged his head up and said, "Sir, I responded to danger earlier, my automatic defence systems were partly successful in repelling the threat."

John curtly replied, "Define the threat."
The robot remained silent.
John repeated, "Benji please describe the threat. I command you."
Benji paused then said, "I have been monitored not to release sensitive data.
My creators have the information. I can request that they contact you?"

John cursed under his breath and muttered to Karen, "Bloody American military. I'll call Mondone directly." He then said loudly to Benji, "Not needed Benji, we will do that directly, just remain alert and in a protective mode."

“Yes Sir.” replied the robot.
“And Benji, next time you encounter this type of threat, I want you to deploy ALL your weapons’ resources in order to disable or destroy the adversary.”
“Understood Sir.”

Jane grabbed John’s arm and said, “John, I am so scared, that thing was monstrous.
So, so evil. I could sense an aura surrounding it that seemed to ….to soak up and oh hell, I think to null life itself…”
She looked desperately at John then turned to Karen.
John replied “Sounds the same as the one in China…… alien beyond words.”

Earlier at the Rest Home gates, the police had arrived, with both Karen and Jane trying to describe what they had encountered.
Lead officer, “You have stated that what you saw was unearthly, like nothing you have ever seen before. Quote ‘a large scary opaque object’?”
Karen with a face like thunder, “Officer. It was huge, maybe forty feet high and I…”
She broke down.
“Alright love, take your time. This is very important.”

They already knew of the threat.
Jane was white and in some shock.
The other policemen returning from the back of the rest home, got her to sit, providing a little water.
Suddenly she shouted, “They’re here! You’ve got to believe us.”
“Ok, just tell us all you can.”

At that moment a large black SUV pulled up.
Two men in combats got out, one obviously a senior officer.

After some discussion the men came back to Karen and Jane.
The senior army guy said, “Colonel Drayton. This is what you must do. Do not repeat this episode to anybody. We have the

situation in hand…and HIM." Pointing at Benji the robot, "Comes with us."

Karen vehemently stood her ground, "I think not Colonel. He is MOD property and on loan from the US JPL Exotic Projects group. I have personal responsibility for him. He remains with us."

The Colonel pursed his lips and then made a phone call.
After a while he turned to Karen, "Very well. You will hear directly through senior management at ESS for guidance. I suggest you keep your robot within those premises' grounds from now on."

She nodded, but inwardly discounting his advice.

Afterwards, they drove very slowly and carefully back to Karen's house.

Later

John looked up from his smartphone inside the house, he commented "Helicopters are flying low again. Really noisy today."
Karen turned to speak to Jane, but the noise was deafening.
They moved cautiously into Karen's back garden to see the tail end of two Apache helicopter gunships flying low in the direction of Hambledon.

John surprised, said "Looks like they've taken you seriously Karen, thank God."
but he frowned and thought 'Flying Men O'War here in Hampshire……hells bells.'

The Apaches had armoured cockpits to protect the pilots and an array of dazzling weaponry including heavy armour piercing missiles.

Enough to take out almost any of the world's best tanks.

Karen spoke, "All of us and that includes Bill, must have a meeting with my friend and shamanic group leader Sabrina very soon. She warned me of this."

Jane felt cold, clammy. The back of her neck was crawling.
She said, "I really want to stay right here with you folks, if that's ok? I would just feel a bit safer."
Karen smiled, "Sure, no problem Jane. If you wish to stay here tonight, I'll get the spare room ready."
"Oh thank you Karen. After this morning's events I just want to be safe and close to you guys." She smiled a thank you.

Karen "John have you the sword?"
"Yes, it is in my coat inside pocket."
She sighed, "The combined power of the artefacts is reassuring."

He continued, "It would seem that the beast whatever it was is focussing its hunt on you Karen, or maybe Quentin who has enlightened us all. Damn… what's the home's number?"
Karen opened her mobile and read out the number.
He quickly got out his phone and made a call.

"Riverside? I am John Creeson, a friend of Karen's. She visited a resident of yours, a Quentin Huxley this morning. If he's awake may I speak to him?"
The line went quiet, then a low voice spoke to John.
His eyes widened, he said "How did he die?"
Again a pause.
"Oh dear, please offer my deepest sympathies to his family. Thank you."

Jane and Karen had stopped talking, hanging on John's words.
"Quentin Huxley passed away around 11.30 this morning….. It seems he died in his sleep."

Karen welled up, "Oh poor Uncle Quentin……he was such a lovely man."

That evening John and Karen were sitting in her garden, watching the sky darken with the night. Up high were aircraft exhaust trails glowing orange, catching the sun as it set over the horizon.
A bottle of red wine was open, glasses still half full.
Stars had started to appear.
A light breeze swayed the fir trees in the neighbour's garden.

Despite the dry quiet evening nobody could relax.
The alcohol was having no effect.

"Mum is that you?" Jane looked out of the kitchen window clutching her phone.
Her eyes scanned right and left and then upwards to the sky.
"Yes dear, how are you?"
"Well…um…something has happened here and I want to come up and see you and Dad for a few days….soon."
Her mum caught Jane's sombre tone.
"Oh honey, you sound a wee bit distressed?"
"Yes I am a bit shook up, but ok. Can't really tell you over the phone. It's just that I miss Scotland so much, and of course you and Dad."
"Anytime my love, it would be lovely to see you. I expect your new job is keeping you busy?"
"Yes just a bit Mum. Also I will be travelling to Australia soon with my work, how cool is that?"
"Sounds marvellous dear. When do you think you'll come?"
Jane paused, the sky was becoming quite black, the oncoming night approached. Bringing with it all humanity's myths and fears of the darkness.

She shivered trying to cast the day's events to the corner of her mind.
"Soon Mum, maybe in a day or two. I'll call you as soon as I know I can get some leave."

"Ooh that'll be nice!"
In the garden, Karen waved her to come over.
Jane, "Mum I've got to go now, I'll let you know, take care."
"Ok Jane, love you, byeee."
"Bye Mum."

Karen, "Jane I'll make your bed up in the middle room. You'll be pretty safe here, John and I will be right next door and Benji will be awake all night. He has been commanded to monitor the house perimeter. Think of a heavily armed night watchman, ha!"
She allowed herself a nervous laugh.
Jane smiled, "That's good. Um….what if they or it somehow take control of him? and…and make Benji attack us?"
Karen replied, "That is a possibility, but I doubt it. Colonel Mondone said that certain safeguards have been built in. If Benji's software or systems are tampered with, he has a subroutine that plays the track 'Road to Hell' by Chris Rea to warn us and then he does a forced self shutdown.
Jane laughed "No way!"

They all struggled to get to sleep that night.
Jane tossing and turning, then finding a science fiction book in Karen's library, 'Childhood's End' by Arthur C Clarke. She had read a summary and it seemed a fitting preparation for whatever the future might hold………

Karen stayed tight in John's arms, eventually falling into a fitful sleep.

Benji sat in the lounge, quite still, eyes open.
Spooky.

He was so human to look at.
Blue eyes, fair hair, all synthetic. They had replaced his ruined shirt with a jumper, also his jeans too with some of John's, luckily the sizes more or less matched.

They had speculated on what caused the myriads of tiny holes in his metal over body.
Now he had various sensors deployed. With 360 degree vision, courtesy of not only his 'human' eyes, but tiny lenses circulating his head and his body, he could monitor all around. His vision expanded to infra red heat detection to enable him to pick up moving objects in the dark of night.
In addition he had been equipped with an Ultra Wide Band Radio processor.
These weak but cleverly coded pulses of radio were mixed with very low levels of normal radio noise and so very hard to detect by an adversary.
By blanketing an area like a building with these coded radio pulses and checking their reflections and delays, the robot was able to look behind walls and other objects.
Outside the night was black, the moon had gone.

About 2.15 am something entered the rear garden.

Benji jerked his head to one side, stood rapidly, then clicked his arm.
It opened to reveal the rail gun.
A weapon capable of firing a stream of hardened metal projectiles, three times faster than normal bullets.

He quickly opened the lounge doors to the garden and went outside.

Very late Thursday 22nd March
Jet Propulsion Laboratory, Pasadena, California.

In the darkened office, a single lamp illuminated the metal desk. Shadows flickered as the display screen changed.
A large man, his hand cupped around his chin was muttering profanities.
He keyed some instructions, clicking the mouse rapidly.

Then Colonel Arrack Mondone reached for the phone.

The ringing went on and on, finally a sleepy voice said, "Yeah… Ming."
"Ming, it's Colonel Mondone. Apologies for waking you at this hour."
"Ah…uummm…that's ok Sir…ah…um…what's up?"
"I need you to come into the office, something important has happened."
"Um..now Sir?"
"Yes Ming. Sorry to get you out of bed, but you need to see what I have just received from Karen's Benji."
"That's ok Sir, on my way."
She yawned.

Mondone had been alerted by a covert transmission from the robot.

After two strong coffees and an hour later.

Ming's Benji sat still on the spare chair in the office corner.
He didn't like coffee but was very partial to machine grade oil.
Ming had commanded him to accompany her.
Travelling at 1am alone in the dark was spooky enough, but with the present turn of events…… it was unthinkable.

She turned from the display, gave a low moan and stared at Mondone.

"oh ….Jeepers Sir, just what do you make of that?"

He scratched his unshaven chin giving an audible rasp.

"God, what awful ugly bastards they are and damn weird too. Well Ming, now we know. They are here on this planet. I wanted you to comment first hand before I raise this with our people. We believe there are three of these that escaped the giant black spaceship before it was destroyed. One has appeared in China and killed many people and now the same or another has popped up in England."
He tapped his fingers on the desk continuing,
"There were others but our telescopes show that they probably perished in the mother craft explosion."

She was deep in thought and pursing her lips, she reran the brief video again.
Ming had used her talents to enhance the short video and after some considerable time she had managed to process it sharpening the very brief illumination.
There it was huge and menacing.

What they looked at was not stable or a solid physical object.
She had slowed down the video to stretch the brief second of the object illumination to several seconds viewing.
They saw through Karen's Benji, via his cameras, the discharge of the laser weapon and its impact on nothing.
To be precise, a mid air nothing.
And then a massive dark glistening bubble appeared.

The giant image was mobile, writhing.
In a very large roughly shaped sphere, they observed a continuous movement of hundreds of black eel like tubers amongst mushroom like fans.
Ming cried quietly "Aah…oh dear look at that….it's so gross."

There in the sphere liquid, she saw brief flashes of gaunt and squirming alien faces.

Then the image disappeared as the laser pulse was absorbed, fading to invisibility.
In tandem the house rear lawn re-appeared as the background and the extra giant shadow had gone.

"Ugh…" Mondone reached for his phone and made a call.
Ming felt cold, uneasy.
Her mind pictured various scenarios of what this thing might do…….
She shivered, stammered "God that is something……something from our worst nightmares…."
Mondone grimaced "Yeah, a satanic beast if ever I saw one."

"Air Force Command, Rogers."
"Sir, Colonel Mondone. Apologies for calling you so late but I have an urgent situation regarding our extra terrestrial interlopers."
"Go on Mondone."
"I have a video recording of an entity seen in England, the UK. It is large, probably four stories high and about the same wide. We have just a brief snapshot. Our automan, Benji II by name, attempted a defence against it."

"And?"
"He deployed the one shot hi-pulse laser, which illuminated what we believe was a near invisible adversary. Followed by a short burst from his automatic gun."

"Effective?"

"The being seemed to move away and then travel south. Benji sustained some damage to his armour. Also the log shows he received an intense burst of radio energy.
His shielding was enough to protect him. It would appear that the alien is mostly undamaged."

There was a silence at the other end, then General Rogers spoke slowly and articulately, "Mondone, send me what you have. I will contact the UK chiefs immediately."
"Yes Sir."

After that Mondone reluctantly called his new boss.
A rather irritated voice replied "Swaine."
"Sir, Mondone here. Sorry for such a late call but I have an urgent update to the Red Objects Hunt."

"Mondone, this had better be good, you disturbed my wife's sleep as well. What news?"
Mondone explained the robot's recorded transmission.
"I am transmitting you the data now."
He added, "I have taken the initiative to inform USAF Command, General Rogers."
"What! circumventing your chain of command?"
"No disrespect Sir. No, just needed to move very quickly. Rogers had asked me to call him immediately on anything to do with the Red Objects project….Sir."

Michael Swaine, Director of NASA Space Technology swore under his breath.
"Ok Colonel. BUT next time I would appreciate being involved first."
His voice boomed out of the speaker end of Mondone's phone.
"Understood Sir."
"That's all Mondone. Keep me posted."
Click.

Mondone pulled a face at Ming, which grew into a mischievous grin.

He tapped the biro on his pad and turning off the computer said, "You know Ming, there's an awful lot of people getting involved in this now. I am becoming a smaller cog as our military and indeed persons of every persuasion and prominence become the reactionary forces."

"May I call you Arrack again Sir?"
"Of course." he smiled.

They had a rapport, a friendship which extended beyond their military duty.
"Well Arrack, I have been feeling very uneasy lately. I guess I want to be close to my folks and Akoni. My gut feel is not good."
He watched her closely.
Ming carried on, "You see I have a belief that things, you know the situation will deteriorate before we launch next year. Even then what can we really achieve?"

Mondone looked sombre, his eyes were tired.
He rubbed his aching shoulder, the subject of a bullet wound he sustained in Wales back then in January.
"We must do all we can. What has happened is beyond mankind's comprehension. However, there seems to be something or somebody willing to protect us."

Ming's perception was sharp, she replied, "What if the do-gooders are not powerful enough? Look, why have they let these awful beings, whatever they are, get so damn close to Earth? Surely they should have been intercepted many light years away?"

"Good point Ming."

She paused then said, "Is my leave for Easter with my folks still good or do you need me here?"
Ming had a pleading in her eyes.
Mondone was tapping the biro hard on his notepad. It split and ink flew out.
Ming laughed "You seem to have an issue with pens."
He grinned, "Yeah, damn things… you'd think they would have perfected them by now." he grabbed a tissue from a box and

wiped his hands, then continued, "Sure take your holiday Ming. I will endeavour to ensure that you get a break. Whatever happens with the exception of a full alien invasion, I'm sure we can handle things without you."
She smiled, "Thank you. That's good Sir."
"Just stay available, you know phone, email etc."

His mobile rang.
Mondone looked and saw it was Gail.
"Gail, yup….yes I know it's very late. Something came up that couldn't wait. Yeah I'm finishing up now, be home soon honey…. bye."

Mondone ended the call, said "Well guess that closes out my evening here Ming."
Ming smiled, she said, "Sir, it may not be my business, but Gail sure makes demands on you. Not only…um I mean personal, but she…um seemed to …"

"What Ming?" Mondone gave her an indignant look.

"Sorry Sir, Just concerned for you." said Ming thoughtfully.
He became brusque, "Well don't be. Time to go. Thanks for coming in."

"You're welcome Sir. When duty calls I'll be there."

He nodded and nearly smiled.

Early morning Friday 23rd March
ESS, East Meon, UK

The black Jaguar had rocketed out of Whitehall in London.
Sir George Ratcliffe instructed the chauffeur to drive fast, doing the run to Hampshire in quick time.

Now he now sat in Richard Armitage's office sniffing the air, sort of stale smell.
He grimaced thinking 'Yes bloody pipe tobacco. Flaunting health and safety.'

He thought 'Damn nuisance Armitage being confined to hospital. Forces me to run things directly.'
Accompanying him in the car was his new bodyguard Barry Westland, now in the cafeteria having a spot of breakfast.
Ratcliffe had asked Constance, Armitage's secretary, to fetch some breakfast to him in his new office.
Constance unused to providing breakfast was a little put out, but said nothing.
She thought 'I'm an executive secretary, not his skivvy.'

Ratcliffe mused on. 'Barry Westland an ex-Marine commando, decorated for services in Iraq, Afghanistan and lately undercover in Syria, had come highly recommended.'
Ratcliffe pondered on the demise of Barry's erstwhile predecessor Roger Stoneham. 'Murdered by the Chinese squad in Wales. Too easily.'

His mind wandered back to Armitage. 'the man had some sort of nervous breakdown, now heavily sedated in a hospital ward, but he didn't seem under undue pressure?'

Ratcliffe frowned, he doodled on the pad.
He smiled as he rotated the glass paperweight in his hand, looking at the shrunken head inside. The glass distorted the view, but better that way he thought.

A most ugly object, a typical Armitage toy.

Ratcliffe stretched his legs out under the desk and spread his arm out on the leather chair side arm, thinking ‘I could make this room a lot cosier, maybe a new assistant, female, youngish, short skirt maybe, shapely…..yes.. lots of admin would keep her busy.’

His reverie was broken by a knock on the door.
“Come in.”

John Creeson walked in, saying “Hello Sir George, I saw your car pull up and guessed you might be here. Have you a minute?”
Bill Craswell followed, said “Morning Sir George.”

Ratcliffe motioned John and Bill to sit down.
“Good to see you John, Bill. I was just about to seek you guys out. My word haven’t a lot of things happened lately?”
Bill replied “You could say that.”
“John, are you well, you look a shade pale old boy?”

John laughed nervously, “Yes, fine. I think all this fast action is affecting my diet. Maybe another holiday is in order, a real break this time.”

Ratcliffe’s demeanour remained serious, “Think that might be a while now.”

Before that meeting

Earlier John had mentioned to Bill the awful apparition that Jane and Karen had encountered.
Bill became deep in thought, but at length said, “These manifestations are becoming all too frequent. Maybe we should run it by Ratcliffe?”

John replied, “Maybe Bill. I think Ratcliffe and the Ministry will need concrete proof. Apparently there is a recording that the Benji made. Karen is trying to extract the data but she says it has some sort of lock on it.”
Bill replied “Yeah, weird that. Typical controlling Yanks I reckon. Still must be a good feeling to have a mechanical bodyguard.”

John laughed out loud and made Bill jump.
Bill “What?”
“Bloody jumpy Benji. God…. last night he woke us all up in the early hours and guess what?”
Bill looked at him oddly.

“He disintegrated a large fox that was prowling in the back garden!”

Bill smiled and chuckled, “Could have been an alien disguised as a fox.”
John went to laugh and then caught himself, he said “You know Bill, we can’t discount anything these days.”

Bill then exclaimed, “Whoa!”
He was looking at his phone. “Bloody hell John, see here on the Ministry stream, it says those two helicopters of yours have gone AWOL. They just disappeared, crews and all.”

John looked at him, staring, frowning. He said “Really? …. Things are getting out of hand. Well that will get the big wigs moving. Oh Bill, Apaches….. they are supposed to be tough birds.”

The present snapped back.

Ratcliffe smiled, cleared his throat and then asked them to describe in detail the Sunday night array data capture.
He was picking at the corner of the ink blotter pad, scuffing the paper edge into a thick puffy lump. He listened to John intently.

At length he spoke, slowly and hesitantly. John had only covered Sunday night's space conflict and the ReachThru visualisations. He didn't mention Karen's encounter with the monster at the rest home.
"Thank you John, most extraordinary."
Ratcliffe paused, and then he said.
"With immediate effect, I am taking over directly Richard Armitage's responsibilities. Also several staff from the Ministry will be arriving here in the next few days to bolster your team. As you know the world stage is changing dramatically as these significant events unfold. Thank you Bill for your very prompt heads up."

Bill nodded, said "Well our data was, to be honest mind blowing. A non-scientific term I know, but what we saw was astounding, beyond credibility. Cannot even begin to compare with anything we can even understand. It is a supreme chance to learn so much."
Bill's face contorted into joyous glee, the gargoyle evident.
Ratcliffe continued "Yes, yes sobering times. The spacecrafts' conflict in terms of your gravity data, is of incredible value.
After seeing your conflict preview video clip Bill, the Cobra team have put in place certain plans."

COBRA: The government's emergency response committee.

John Creeson was all ears, "and are we privy to these Sir?"
Ratcliffe curtly replied "Usual stuff national security, military on orange alert.
I cannot divulge any detail, but you will be informed if the situation deems your awareness."

Bill thought 'Then I guess that's a definite bugger off.'

Ratcliffe took a long deep breath, then said, "Bill, as part of the close knit team here, you will need to know about this. John how is your fitness these days?"

John frowned, said "Well, pretty good I guess. Swimming every week, running and mountain biking when I can. Quite a bit of hill walking when I get the time. Some gym. Why?"

Ratcliffe had half a smile, "Good, GOOD. You see your fitness is going to take a few hikes, because John Creeson, NASA has asked specifically that you join them to train as an astronaut engineer for inclusion in one of their launches early next year."

John Creeson almost fell off his seat. He broke into laughter, "Me? An astronaut!"
Bill had a look of surprise, said "Good lord John, your wings have come."

Ratcliffe was unfazed, he carried on "Yes, they are serious and so are we. I do hope you take this opportunity John. It is almost an imperative, your nation calling you, I would say."

No way out, was what he meant.
John sat still in his chair, his heart was beating strangely.

Ratcliffe continued, "the Americans are building an entirely space based gravity array, using our technology. They will launch and deploy this before Crackwell the anomaly, returns on its orbit."

John Creeson realised Ratcliffe was serious, he felt a little queasy, thinking 'Launching into outer space, my God. Weightlessness!'

His new boss said "and they want you on hand, there in their command vehicle in far Earth orbit, to run and control this array in real time. Rapid response, tuning and achieving the maximum data extraction and then streaming it live for the teams on the ground to respond to."
He looked at Bill, "and yourself Bill, we want you and your team on the ground to support John and the NASA guys plus monitor the gravity engine telemetry, to ensure optimal operation of the JPL rocket."

John became puzzled, said "Why cannot I do this from the ground? Is it signal delay? And what do you mean by 'respond'?" Ratcliffe relied "Partly, but events may happen very quickly. They want you up there, to control and adjust the position of the arrays dynamically to achieve maximum clarity. Events may happen very quickly and our responses may have to be equally rapid. Your real time information will provide maximum advantage. In addition, if any of the space based gravity arrays develops a problem, they want you to space walk and repair it."

John felt his stomach turn.

Bill said "Sounds a mite dangerous to me. Look what happened Sunday night.
Within a thousand miles of those craft, the energies from them were lethal. Not to mention that huge explosion which was deadly to anything within a million miles of it."

Ratcliffe's hand drummed quietly on the desk.
He said "There are significant risks. The Americans will deploy a number of tactical nuclear devices. John you do have the option to refuse this. It's just that you are in an almost unique position to help and well.........."
He looked directly at John, "Well your country has already offered this help to the Americans."

A fait accompli.

John stared at Ratcliffe then glanced out of the window. The beautiful, serene rolling countryside of Hampshire, the place he loved.
There fading into the distance were brown earth fields, with the early green signs of a crop appearing. Some birds swooped nearby.
A vale of yew trees dipped to the west of his view.
Those craggy dark, thin leaved ancients of the natural world.
Nearly always found in churchyards.

John felt odd.
His comfort zone had deserted him. His mind contemplated floating in deep space. Scary.

He did not have a say in the matter. 'What would Karen think?' As if he didn't know.
His heart leapt to try and comprehend his new career change. 'Wow…' and then 'Holy Cow!" was all he could think.

Ratcliffe ploughed on, "Another matter and somewhat evasive is the issue of these so called alien craft that detached themselves from that exploding black mother craft.
The Americans have some information on the whereabouts of one or two of them, yet they seem reluctant to let us have it?"

John started to say, but Ratcliffe carried on talking, "So guys, did our gravity arrays pick up any trajectories of these things heading, say for the Earth?"

Bill looked at John. It was the look that said we have to do this.
John turned to Ratcliffe and spoke firmly and deliberately, taking the other man's attention completely.
"Sir George. We were unable to see any trails of these escape craft, but I want to bring to your attention some occurrences here on Earth. There have been at least one or maybe two occasions that we have witnessed something unearthly. Karen Durgas and myself that is. Bill has had an experience too…" he glanced at Bill for an ok. "They are not, how shall we say, easy to comprehend. You may not believe what I am going to tell you, but you need to know so that the authorities can act."
Bill pulled a face, almost the gargoyle as he wrestled with the 'white man' image thing.

Ratcliffe's eyes opened fully, his demeanour took on a very serious look.

"Go on."

John paused, then took a slow silent deep breath.
"Back on the mountain top in La Palma, Karen and I used some ancient artefacts to repel a menacing force. These devices invoked a protective shield of sorts from a giant machine buried in the moon."
Damn he thought, sounds like far fetched science fiction.

Well all or nothing now, he carried on.
Ratcliffe grasped the glass paperweight and slowly rolled it in his hand, his eyes locked on John.
"Yesterday, Karen and Jane encountered what we believe is one of those craft you mention, or something from the craft. The robot attached to Karen defended them and made a recording of this alien. I guess you can call it that. Apparently they are invisible."
Ratcliffe interjected, "Yes the American loan of the Benji auto man for your gravity researches, seems to have been sidelined. I didn't realise he had been fitted with weapons? and the security forces, what did they uncover?"
John hesitated, "Well by the time they were on the scene, the thing had disappeared.
You know they've lost two attack helicopters in the vicinity? no trace of them at all.
I believe arming of the robot may have been deliberate, a protection which saved the women's lives."
He studied Sir George Ratcliffe to see if the man was trustworthy ....difficult.

Ratcliffe started to smirk in a cynical way, said "Yes the Apaches have temporarily gone AWOL, but I have it to fact that their flights were altered at the last minute.
Top security and so on."

John felt uneasy, unsure of any headway, he struck with some facts.
"So, George what do make of the Chinese temple incident with all those people killed?"

Ratcliffe pondered, taking a breath he closed his hands together and said, "Unusual, most odd. Thing is everybody is taking to the world stage, propaganda and so on. One must be careful what to believe."
Then he sort of scoffed, "So John, your stories are incredible. Evidence is paramount. What do you have?"
Bill watched Ratcliffe and thought 'The bugger doesn't believe John.'

John was not going to be put off, but he was oblivious to Ratcliffe's subtle scorn.
He continued "The evidence was in front of our eyes…yes, but we have nothing really concrete to show you. It's a case of trust… and what's more during some remote testing, Bill saw……"
John caught Bill's facial expression, a tiny nod was saying ….SAY NOTHING.

He turned fully to face Ratcliffe. The man had a sly smile.
"Please John, do explain."
"As I thought Sir George, you are not convinced?"

"Damn right John, all this airy fairy stuff doesn't belong in this room. BUT and it is a big but, if there is some evidence in what you say, let me have it and I will follow up. That's all for now. Thank you both."

With that they were abruptly dismissed from Armitage's office, leaving Ratcliffe to ponder the meeting's discussions.
As the door closed shut Bill turned to John and swore, "How the fuck are we going to convince anybody about this stuff?"

John just replied, "When people start dying….reckon he knows more than he's letting on."
Bill grimaced, the gargoyle appearing, "I'll be in the lab John."

John nodded as they parted company.

Pascal Lab, ESS

The lab doors burst open.
Jane looked up "Bill…"
Bill had a dark look, almost clouting himself as the doors swung shut.
As he bumped through, his coffee slopped over onto the floor.

"Ah shit… yes hi Jane."

Grabbing some tissues he mopped the floor.
After, he went over to the giant wall display and sat heavily down at the nearest computer desk. Jane frowned, said nothing and turned back to her screen, leafing through a pile of papers.

"You ok Bill?"

"No, I'm not. We seem to be walking through treacle, slowly far too slowly. Sir George has some sort of hidden agenda."
She replied "I guess he doesn't see the entire picture?"
Bill turned to Jane, "After what you and Karen have seen and without Benji, you guys might not be here. Hell things are damn serious, scary. Yet it seems we cannot confide in the authorities. Looks like a conspiracy against us. Bloody strange."
His scar was throbbing.
She replied "With all this going on, I think our Australia trip is just the escape we need."
Bill smiled, he warmed as he caught sight of Jane's slender crossed legs. "Yeah, be a nice break."
She eyed him slowly then replied, "But first I'm going to take some holiday and spend a few days back home in Scotland, with my folks. Touch base with my roots, sanctuary, you know. After all this, this...madness."

Jane paused, her mind was working the options. "Bill what do you think about this meeting Karen's arranging with Sabrina?"
"My initial feeling is that it's a total waste of time, but because

things have happened to me as you know with the apparitions I have seen. I.....well... I have a feeling that we have become central to something of huge importance." he hesitated, stopped and looked despairingly at Jane.

"Oh Bill...I feel the same. Here I am investigating gravity distortions by our 'friends' in space out there and yet our very lives are in peril by something awful that looks like it is hunting us right now here on Earth. I keep thinking about those alien artefacts of Karen and John's. Are they really working with us or maybe just controlled by the Omega Centauri race?" she was trying to be humorous, yet analysing any possibility.

Bill's eyebrows hiked, he retorted, "God knows. What I do know is that we must take things into our own hands and do something drastic."
He quickly got up off his chair.

A deep voice from the door.

"Good questions and I wouldn't do anything hasty, Mr Craswell."

They both swung round to look at the entrance door.
Barry Westland, Armitage's bodyguard, stood there, his right hand holding the open door.

His left hand slid into his jacket and onto the gun holster.

Chapter 17

Saturday evening 24th March 2018
Scotland UK, near Urquhart Castle, Loch Ness

The game stew was rich, tasty and thick.
It was complimented by a steaming dish of potatoes and vegetables.

Jane took a large swig of her Dad's special ale, a brew he had obtained from the Fyne Ales Brewery. "Cor, nice beer Dad."
He grinned, "Drop of Scotland lassie."
She reached for the Arran mustard cream sauce, saying,
"Ooh it's so good to be home, I love this dinner."

Jane's father Andrew replied, "Tis your mother's cooking, the best."
He smiled, his forester tanned face breaking into multiple creases. Andrew was in his late fifties and slightly overweight, probably from her mum's savoury delights. He flicked back a shock of his unkempt black hair.
"Och, your always saying that Andy. Wanting to badge favours, eh? You reckon Jane?"
Her mum Kay was a round woman, bright eyes and long ginger hair tied in a ponytail.
"Yeah I reckon he is Mum."
She winked at her Dad.
"How's your job at the reception centre?"
Kay Horsham worked at the Castle Urquhart tourist office.

Urquhart Castle is situated right on the shores of Loch Ness and is steeped in history.
Commanding stunning views over the Loch waters, it has been the scene of many historic battles. The English under Edward I seized it during his invasion of Scotland. Then Robert the Bruce reclaimed it for Scotland in the 14th century. During the 15th and

16th centuries it saw more action and as a result, today it lies in ruins.

Kay replied "Aye, business as usual. Getting busy as the spring season gets going.
It's amazing how much the tour prices have shot up, but folks still pay 'em."
She added "Mostly the daft English."
They all laughed.

Their cottage near Drumnadrochit, was small, simply furnished and cosy.
A log fire burnt brightly at the end of the long room. Here a motley assortment of sofas and chairs clustered around the fireplace, while the other end opened into an old fashioned kitchen. The light green cupboard doors hinting at their contents through obscure glass panels. A row of just about every kitchen utensil hung above the worktops. Dozens of jars containing home made pickles, jams, eggs and other tasties, adorned the rough shelving along the back kitchen wall.
In the middle they sat around the family heirloom, a battered oak table, coloured with dark hues and wood knots.
Against the wall and between the worktops was a well worn solid fuel Aga cooking stove, its oven window peeking glowing logs.
It was from a previous era.

Kay looked over at Jane with a big rosy smile, "We kept your wee room just as you left it. It's all ready."
"Thanks Mum."
"I wish you were staying longer, but you say you are awa Monday?"
Jane chewed some pheasant and swallowed, she sighed, "Yes I'm afraid so. Work and stuff is becoming crazy. Mmm…this stew is so nice."

Andrew looked up from his plate, wiping his beard with his napkin.

"Jane? You said you worked for a research place in the Ministry and you've got a new job there now, how's that going?"
"Ah yes. It's very exciting, but secret stuff."
Her mind drifted to the apparition at the Riverside Home and her face could not hide her fear.
Her Dad missed nothing, he said "What's up sweetie? You seem a tad unhappy?"
Kay looked concernedly at her daughter.
Jane's eyes had filled up and all at once she burst into tears.
"I'm sorry, Mum, Dad. I've been through some frightening things. I….I just had to come home."
Her Dad had got up and hugged Jane as she rose from the table. He said "No worries, you're here now, safe. Stay as long as ye want. Tell us what's troubling ye?"

Jane took a long shuddering breath, she let out a sigh.
"Where to start? Well this stuff is supposed to be secret, but it should be made public."
Her Mum frowned.
Jane continued, "I guess you've seen in the News about the outer space conflict and the explosion that happened?"
Andrew followed, his eyes unblinking, "Yes lassie, we have, what does it all mean?"
"It means Dad, that there are serious threats to our way of life. As you might have seen on the News, the military forces in all countries are preparing for the worst. Maybe an alien invasion."

Her mum had eyes like saucers, "Aliens here on Earth! God save us all. What ever next?"
Andrew's face became sombre, he said, "So tell us more Jane."

"Oh Dad, Mum. This stuff is so secret but you just need to know, everybody should know, yet just a few of us have this huge burden of responsibility. Although I guess there are many other scientists like us around the world involved in similar activities, preparing for the worst."

She paused. They looked at her keenly, waiting.
Jane then said, "I'm afraid after the explosion, some really bad spacecraft escaped and are now here on Earth... somewhere. Also I know a couple of my group have special... um...abilities... really, really important abilities."
"So what scared you Jane?" her Dad moved close, touched her hand.

"Ok, what I'm about to tell you now is because I don't know how to handle this stuff. I don't know what to do next. Guess this is one of the reasons I'm here."

She went on to explain the detail of the space conflict. The 'saviour' ship destroying the evil black 'asteroid' craft. Then Karen and John's artefacts that were used to invoke some huge machine under the moon's surface to protect them, possibly the whole of humanity.
Finally at the home where they visited Quentin and the episode with Benji the robot firing his weapons and illuminating the huge monster.
Her mum kept saying, "Oh my......oh my Lord!"

Andrew said, "Tis unbelievable Lassie, you're sure now? You're not jus aving some bad dreams like?"
She shook her head and continued,
"Someone new has appeared at work, perhaps a new ally I guess, a confidant I think, I hope. You see Bill and I were discussing stuff in the laboratory when Barry Westland walked in."

Her Dad had a slight puzzled look.
"Oh, he's... um... a body guard to the Ministry of Defence guy that has taken over from my old boss. We thought he was going to arrest us or worse, but he sat down and confided that he is an under cover agent working for MI6, and Sir George Ratcliffe, that's my new boss at the moment, knows nothing about that."

"Ooh dearie. Secret service and all that!" her Mum's eyes still large.

Jane then went quiet watching her parents.
Her Dad was the first to speak.

"You did the right thing my girl, coming here."
He stared out of the cottage window, a view of meadowland reaching to a nearby forest.
Jane stuttered "Did I? I may have brought that thing here. It could be lurking close by!"
Her Dad stood up, went over to a long corner shelf and reached up bringing down his shotgun. He checked the barrels and inserted two live cartridges.
Jane cried "That won't stop it Dad."
He turned to her saying, "Well better than nothing. I'm sure both barrels will give it something to think about."
He replaced the gun.

Jane's mother Kay interrupted, "Ok you two, I'm sure the authorities will deal with whatever you are on about Jane. Father, get some drinks out will ye?"

They settled down to playing gin rummy, her Mum's favourite.
The glowing log fire cracked and sparked a few embers into the fire guard.
Her Dad fetched a bottle from his malt whisky store. Special occasions such as these deserved a treat.
After a few glasses, Jane finally relaxed, the first time in weeks.
She talked and talked, telling them just about everything that had happened.
Karen and John's escapades in La Palma, Bill's near catastrophic engine test and much more. She thought 'bugger the Official Secrets Act!'

Time and life is precious. She adored her parents, the closeness they had was something so special.

Sunday morning - early

The three of them had taken the old Daihatsu four wheel drive truck, down through the forest track to the waters edge at Loch Ness.
There a little sand and shingle beach nestled east of the castle.
A clutch of fishing rods were propped up with stays and were already enticing the salmon.
They had skipped breakfast to catch the brilliant sunrise as it rose, basking the Loch waters in a glittering cabaret. Long dark shadows slowly marched along the hilly forested sides of the Loch.

Jane's Dad sat turning the sizzling bacon on the little portable gas stove.
He broke a few eggs and added them to the large frying pan.
"God that smells good." said Jane.
Her Mum was unpacking all sorts of yummy delicacies from a holdall.
Oat cakes, a haggis, courgettes and some fried potatoes from the night before.
They sat in collapsible chairs munching bacon, eggs, haggis and veggies looking out over the shiny, still waters of the lake.
Steam rose in swirls from hot mugs of tea.

The air was chilly with a slow mist drifting across the Loch waters.
Streaming sunlight making bright pockets in the mist.
It was an eerie sight and no birds were about.

No bites. The fishing rods remained upright and still.
And Nessie the Loch Ness monster, decided not to make a show.

Jane stopped chewing and looked over to the far southern side of the Loch.
The flat water gave a ripple.

Then a rattling ringing broke the silence

.

Andrew's fishing rod was twitching, its alarm bell wiggling back and forwards.
He dropped everything and rushed over picking up his rod and pulling back in one motion.

Minutes later he landed a glorious salmon.
Waving his arm back to Jane and her Mum, with a big grin he shouted "Lunch!"

Droxford, Hampshire, UK. That same Sunday morning.

Bill Craswell ran his spoon around the cereal. No appetite.
The last few days had been unnerving, unreal.

He thought about Barry Westland, who abruptly appeared in their lab.
Odd that the man had suddenly warmed to them, a complete stranger.
Westland had confided to Bill and Jane about his disguise and even more incredible, some plans that the government had.
Bill muttered "Who to trust, that is the question…"

Bill drummed the wooden tabletop with the two good fingers on his left hand.
He looked around, the dishwasher was gone, the expensive coffee machine too.
Well July did buy that.

She had gone, completely, for good.
An empty wardrobe, various DVDs gone, a number of ornaments too and some more.
"Why…"
The house echoed its emptiness.
He felt so, so lonely.

His mind wandered to the Australian business trip.
'Helping the Aussies to set up a gravity array should be good for his career, more contacts. More visibility. Yes…and Jane.'

Bill liked her, more than he would admit even to himself.
She was very bright, her Maths and Metallurgy skills excellent, but she did have a short fuse. 'God' thought Bill, 'July was bad enough…'
However, Jane did warm to him, sympathetic with his woes and there was something more. She seemed to have … 'What was it?... an interest, yes she was quite excitable at times.'
Pretty girl, bright eyes, and even more amazing legs.

Then Bill scolded himself, 'Silly bugger Craswell, she's just had a lot of shit with her boyfriend. What was his name? …. Graham… um..no…Gavin... don't go there.
She's too young for me…by far.'

His mind then wandered to hotels, single rooms of course. 'Make sure their rooms were side by side……look after her, ensure she's ok, that sort of thing.'

He had heard about her being pestered by her previous boss Gary, when she worked in the Instruments Group. Bill thought 'Bloody pervert Gary had been reprimanded some time back for groping a woman. Apparently not the first time although nothing could be proved.'

Did he need this? These thoughts?
'Hell what a mess my mind is in lately. First the anomaly, then my gravity engine test, then the huge conflict in space, oh yes and that weird man in white………where the hell is HE from?'

He managed a couple of spoons of muesli, then thought about John Creeson up in orbit next year.
He smiled then spluttered a laugh "Bloody Creeson an astronaut! Well he'd better pack his brown corduroy trousers."

He sighed then drank the rest of his tea.
The breakfast TV news was full of mob stirring, ego maniacs. Obscure politicians rising from some murky past, now proclaiming they can see the way for mankind, waving their hands up high, shouting they will show the light for a new era.
'Utter tosh' thought Bill.

He rang John Creeson.
"Hello."
"John? it's Bill, weather looks favourable today. Fancy an early walk in the country, chew the cud and so forth, maybe a pub lunch after?"

"Yeah, sounds like an idea. My mind has been playing havoc, slept awful last night."
Bill replied "I'm not sleeping well either, how about we meet up at the car park just south of South Harting church, and take that walk over the hill. End up back at the White Hart pub for Sunday roast and a pint? If you've nothing else on?"
"Sure, Karen is here with me, hang on…"
Some voices, then,
"Yes great idea. We'll probably ride there on my BSA motorcycle, give it a blow."

Bill smiled, "Ok, see you at the car park, what 10am?"
John, "Ah…yes 10 it is then. See you there."

They took a long way round, hurtling along country lanes a shade faster than usual.
The exhaust crackled as John opened up the BSA 650cc Spitfire. A beautiful classic motorcycle twin, a thrill between one's legs. Karen thought so too.
She clung to John as they flew between the trees, then leaning into the corner right side then left as the bike took an S bend.

South Harting

Locking their helmets via straps under the seat, they left the bike in the car park and joined Bill. In a moment all three of them had disappeared along the footpath that led to a large field. Passing a children's play area to their right, they then disappeared into a thick clump of trees on the left that parted to reveal a leaf covered uphill stony footpath.

About two hundred yards behind them two middle aged men appeared ambling along at a slow pace. One wearing a dark green, waxed jacket, walking trousers and high ankle laced boots. The other had what looked like short green wellington boots, jeans and a navy Berghaus waterproof top.

They had a keen interest in the party ahead.
Karen turned to John, "God I need this, fresh air and exercise."
John smiled, replied "Yes it's great."

Bill had walked ahead a little up the steep rocky track.
Trees soared up each side, the branches meeting at times high in the middle.
Little coloured buds dotted and thickened the trees and twiggy bushes.
Amongst the dampness and clumps of brilliant green moss, life was beginning again with spring finally arriving. The ground was sprinkled with new shoots and on occasion a small green leaf braved to come out.
Going up the slope, the wet, brown, decaying leaves proved a bit slippery, as Bill nearly came a cropper, but managed to keep his balance. "Whoa!"

After ten minutes Bill was panting heavily, they caught up with him.
Karen laughed, "You need to pace yourself up this bit Bill. At least it levels out further on."

The track wound up and up, crossing a road and then widening into a worn rutted, stony path, a favourite for the mountain cyclists. Then the path teetered along the edge of a steep slope, sandwiched between huge tall trees.
After half an hour the trees gave way to large shrubs and then they walked on into open rich green grassland approaching the top of South Harting hill.
Stopping, taking in the north view of South Harting village far below, John said “Look at that, always such a pleasant picture, a typical English country village.”
Bill exclaimed, “Yeah and monsters lurking somewhere!”

They both just glared at him and strolled on.
John and Karen closed together walking arm in arm, but Bill had dropped back a bit.
At one point he stooped to pluck a tiny flower and nonchalantly but briefly looked behind.

As they passed the small clump of trees at the hill summit, they walked eastwards along the path, dropping down the hill.
Bill had a quick glance behind and said “Quick John, Karen. Crouch and get to our down hill path across the grass here, NOW!”

Both of them gave him a startled look, but did as he said.
They found the obscured path, reaching a large scrubby thorn bush on its left.
Bill said quietly “Duck here, all of us. We’re being followed.”
Karen’s eyes went wide.
The three of them squatted behind the bush.

The two gentlemen seemed to be in a hurry as they came into view up on the eastwards track. They were hurriedly glancing around, even turning to look back, as though they had lost somebody.
Very few people knew of the almost hidden return track going down the steep and shadowed north side of the hill.

Twenty minutes later after they neared the bottom of the track which approached a stile into the woods, Karen exclaimed breathlessly "Who the hell were they?"
Bill gasping between breaths said "American agents."
John stopped, gulped and said "How do know that?"
"CIA John. I briefly looked back and saw those two guys had stopped, one to pick something up. It was a contrived movement and I thought their body language was hiding something. ….then I'm sure I recognised one of them as Bob Redford.
John, remember him at our meeting in the USA?"
"Damn, Bill you've a good memory and cracking eyesight."

Karen quickened her walk, "Come on let's make sure we lose them."
Bill had a frown, his forehead scar was throbbing a little.
He touched it, and then said, "Now why would the CIA be following us? Surely Colonel Mondone could give them everything we know? I mean they already have our gravity wave technology."
John replied, "Maybe they are on to our artefacts?"
Karen was livid, "God no, NO! no way can I give up my cross, nor we the sword John."
Bill was watching them both in a strange way. He thought, surely these objects are far too valuable to be in the hands of Karen and John, more likely they should be in the hands of ……..

Then the cynicism kicked in. The military would use them first to research and then use the artefacts for their own ends. The politicians would suppress that the artefacts even existed, and then secretly evaluating them in some high security establishment. Perhaps they would also hold Karen and John for whatever purpose.
'Good lord what am I thinking!' struck Bill.

Karen and John were some yards ahead at the stile.
Karen shouted "Come on Bill, we need to make distance."
They descended the steep wooden steps.

Bill turned to look back up at the huge shadow of the hill.
The two men had disappeared, possibly scouring the south side, as they would have deduced that as the mostly likely escape route.

Bill stumbled a little. He glanced sideways down the hill, at the meadow and the sparse shrubs they had just come through.

Something glowed.

Then, there between some bushes, the man in white watched him and gently waved.

Bill shuddered, glued to the spot.
His neck hairs prickled.
He hoarsely shouted, turning to where Karen and John had been, "Look, LOOK he's back again!.....oh my GAWD!"

But they had disappeared down a steep slope traversing some wooden reinforced steps to cross the road at the bottom.

Then Bill caught his footing in some brambles and fell over.
"Aarh!"
He scrambled to his knees and saw that the man was upon him, not three metres away.
"Oh my gawd, oh my gawd..... For Christ's sake who are you?"
At that moment having heard Bill's shout, Karen re-appeared, having run back up the steps, she gasped and stopped just behind Bill.
John followed closely.
All three of them stared, speechless, open mouthed......holding onto one another.

The man looked old, with grey hair and a wispy beard.
His face was a little red but full of wisdom.
He wore a white robe and in his right hand was a short staff.
The strangest thing was a bright corona around him, glowing and rippling.

He opened his mouth.

A crystal clear voice rang out. It was sort of in their heads too.

"*Karen Durgas, John Creeson and Bill Craswell, please don't be afraid. Time is short and I have much to say to you here and now.*"

Karen felt tingly, her cross became warm against her skin.
John reached for the old sword in his rucksack.

The man held his hand up, "*No need for those, I am your friend and your artefacts actually belong to us.*"

Us?

Bill frowned, he said "I repeat who are you and where are you from?"
He continued, "And please explain what the hell is happening!"

The man smiled and said, "*I understand your frustration. What I am about to tell you may seem strange and unreal, so please just listen and be patient.*"

They waited. No one came down the hill track.

Just as well, this was a once in a thousand years event.....

He boomed out again, they all nearly jumped out of their skins.
John hastily looking around, wondering what or who might appear next.

"*You Karen and you John, are key to a future event early next year which may decide the fate of mankind, your species. I do not put this burden on you lightly. We will endeavour to protect you as much as possible. Karen, at that time you must convene in your*

friend Sabrina's circle. She in fact is already aware and making preparations.
There is a third artefact that you must obtain, the helmet. It is in possession of a man who has been assimilated by the evil forces that you are encountering.
We cannot provide extra artefacts as some of the knowledge to create them has been lost. Even our ability to maintain the device in your moon is limited."

Bill started to speak, "What are you?"
The man in white held up his hand.

"*As I said before, I represent a very advanced and very old race from far, far away in your galaxy. My name is irrelevant to you and my being, my essence is actually spread through several of my people.*
We have been, let us say in your language, that of benefactors and mentors.
It is not our place to meddle, but to gently and subtly intervene at crucial moments in your species history."

Karen's mind was furiously working. She felt an enormous enlightening feeling and then she suddenly stammered, "You mean…..oh my…I can see now. Did one of you appear here on Earth a long time ago?"

"Yes approximately two thousand years ago, we needed to guide man onto a certain path, to ensure his faith, his continuance and destiny. One of us sacrificed his mortal body to do this."

John held his hand to his mouth, he turned to look at Karen.
She was wide eyed too.
He exclaimed, "Why us? This is so important; you should share this with the whole world!"
The man replied *"We will in time, the world is not ready yet. Sacrifices will need to be made."*

Karen went cold, she realised where this might be going.

The man waved to say he needed to speak more.

"We have powers beyond what you could believe, but even our society, our existence back in Omega Centauri is threatened. The fabric of our civilisation is changing, devolving."

Bill quietly said, "By the black asteroid beings?"

"Yes indirectly. They have harnessed the arcane powers of the universe, dark powers that we do not understand. We are able, as you have seen, to manipulate the greatest forces of the galaxy. Yet they have mastered an underlying potency derived somehow from dark matter. We have tried for several million years to understand and fight this menace. Tried and failed.
Huge numbers of us have tried and died.

Many times we have endeavoured to make contact with these beings, but to no avail.
They are so alien and different, that despite our technological skills, there appears no way to speak with them, to negotiate some sort of truce or understanding.
As a result we have taken alternative and extreme methods.
This has temporarily brought hope. For your species and others, we did back in our past develop a way to deter and confuse these beings, and so repel them. This you see as the device in your moon, the power it has, is initiated by your artefacts."

Karen uttered, "Then what can WE possibly do?"

The white robe shimmered as the man replied,
"You must prepare, there is time and there is a way. These creatures of the dark are using a freak corridor from their galaxy to our galaxy. It is being generated purely by chance, by the huge black hole in their galaxy, sending out a plasma jet with an unusually stable cortex corridor within it. They are now able to

travel through this corridor. This very jet is forced under colossal energy right out of their galaxy and across about two million light years to arrive right here near your solar system. Over thousands of years, these beings have at a huge distance influenced your race in a bad way. They are the cause of much of the 'evil' that your planet endures."

"Oh my goodness...." exclaimed John.
Karen was shaking slightly. She found she was just able to cope. John felt it through her hand. She stammered "This is so hard...... the black hole jet, that's what Louis discovered back in La Palma!"

The man continued, *"Yes, the alignment of this jet will continue for maybe a thousand years. What you need to know is that this evil race has already launched an armada of giant spaceships along this corridor. They will reach the exit near here, by early next year. A hundred or more of these craft will arrive.*
We are preparing to engage this fleet, but the outcome is not certain."

Bill moaned "An armada, oh my god...."
Karen spoke, "So the anomaly, the portal? did they create that?... and why do you wait for them to arrive here? Why not intercept them back at the origin where they come from?"
The man paused looking at the three of them.
A strong wind had arrived, bending the small trees and shrubs around the group.
The grasses flattened in the wind. His robe remained uncannily still.
Bill nervously looked around.

Eventually the man in white looked at Bill and said.

"We created the portal to travel quickly and fix the damage to our machine in the moon. This damage was caused by the impact of the particle that was created in your laboratory explosion."

Bill moaned and sagged to his knees, one hand on his queasy stomach.

"Unfortunately the creatures of the dark used our portal to travel the final leg to reach your planet. This is why we had to react quickly and destroy their ship. But as you know some small craft managed to escape. We are not able to traverse the vast distance across to Andromeda, in time to stop the armada. The cortex corridor they are travelling in has an energy that will only allow outward travel. If we attempt to enter this corridor, it will disrupt our spaceships. We can create a new portal but it cannot reach that far across to the Andromeda galaxy. It requires energies of a magnitude that even we find extremely difficult to create."

At this point Bill, holding his head in his hands, muttered "Oh my gawd, it's all my fault, my entire fault…..heaven help us."

The man started to fade, he said *"No Bill Craswell, it would have happened anyway. Their galaxy jet portal is shifting closer. Please all of you, discuss and plan with Sabrina and the other circle groups. Then wait for my further instructions."*

With that the glow and the man seemed to dissipate away. Just a fine mist shrouded the area and then he was gone.

Bill was almost crying, his eyes were watery. "Oh hell, what do we do?"
Karen replied shakily "As he says we must convene as soon as possible with Sabrina, she will be our oracle. The man mentioned nothing about going to the authorities, which is so worrying."

John looking up and around, said through the strong wind, "Let's get out of here."

With that the three of them ran, jogged, paused for breath, walked fast until they were in the village again.
People were going about their business.

The White Hart pub was open and a couple of old timers sat outside drinking beer and smoking.
A family of walkers strolled by, children, mum and dad, an uncle perhaps and a grandfather, all talking and laughing.

Karen watched them ponderously and thought, 'Our whole way of life will disappear unless we fight this awful menace.'

Then she felt very depressed. 'What can we really do, if even these mentors, our so-called saviours with all their vast powers, are unable to save us?'

Bill had gone on ahead to get the drinks.

There he downed a double scotch very quickly, ordering for the others as they walked in.

Chapter 18

Noon - Easter Sunday April 1st
Little Venice, Los Angeles, USA

Ling Zhao glowed inside, her family complete for Easter.
She watched her eldest daughter Ming sip a large iced Cosmopolitan martini.
Together in the bright sunlit kitchen, they were making final preparations to the lunch.

Outside on the veranda, Akoni glugged a bottle of cold Michelob. He watched people ambling along the canal pathways, and then turning to Ming's father Ju-long said, "Ming talks very highly of you and your Air Force career, Sir."
Ju-long smiled, saying "Yes, I have had a wonderful but challenging life in the service, but now I am enjoying retirement and you Akoni, I hear you had a miraculous escape during the Hawaiian tsunami?"

"Hell yes, though I remember little and as you know I was in a coma for some weeks."
"Have you recovered now?"
Akoni paused, smiling, "No, not fully, my memory has gaps, but your wonderful daughter has pulled me through. I owe her a lot."
Ju-long eyed Akoni, weighing up the Hawaiian.

The proud father replied, his eyes enquiring. "She's a tough nut. Been through some hard times, you know?"
Akoni chuckled, "Yeah, she has. I was near death's door myself and if it wasn't for your daughter I wouldn't be here now. She is so special."
Ju-long grinned at him, squeezing Akoni's shoulder.

Their house was unique, as was every other place in Little Venice. The front of each residence adjoined a tidal canal.

Years ago during their construction, the network of canals had been cut so as to form a symmetrical lattice. Along the canal bank most houses had their own little coloured boat tied up to a jetty or mooring post. As the tide came up, one could motor out to the estuary in Los Angeles.
Many years ago Ju-long and Ling-long had acquired a piece of land at the end of one of the canal strips, very early in its development. It was at a price he could afford then on his Air Force pay. They built their own house adding little oriental touches.

All the canal houses had a unique character.
This prime piece of real estate over time has become much in demand.
Every house in Little Venice was different, all of an egotistical design, shape and colour.
Millionaires, famous artists, fashion gurus, pop stars, film directors, recluses..... they all wanted their place to be different, naturally.

To make a statement.
Of one desire, was a metal framed blocky house with a huge glass veranda, framed on either side by stainless steel columns and overlooking the canal. Another would be sandy brick and stone to match the Egyptian era, sprouting palm trees all around.
Next door a Swiss chalet.
Then another residence made of solid dark wood walls, ominous and closeted, with little barred windows and steel doors.

A full tide and stiff breeze bobbed the pastel coloured dinghies up and down.

Suddenly a sound resembling loud wind pipes came from the front door chime, announcing more guests arriving at the Zhao residence.

Ju-long got up and turned, walking down the hall and then opened the door.

"Ah my other lovely daughter Lei, you look well, so long since we've seen you!"
He hugged her tight.
Lei grinned "Oh Pa, it's been too long, so good to be here…" then said "…and oh please let me introduce Steven."

Her father turned to the tall fair haired bearded stranger.
Steven Crowley was dressed in black jeans, white open neck shirt, tan jacket and his long hair tied back in a pony tail.
He gripped Mr Zhao's hand and shook it firmly.
"Wow!" exclaimed Ju-long, "Pleased to meet you Steven. That is some grip you have there. Call me Ju-long."
He returned the strong handshake two fold.

Steven did a slight bow, "Very pleased to meet you Mr Zhao. Ju-long."
Ju-long thought, 'Where are my daughters finding these characters?'

The lunch was sumptuous, roast lamb, green bean casserole and maple syrup roasted vegetables. It was followed by pumpkin pie and custard.

Then they all exchanged little Easter baskets, containing cookies, sweets, small chocolate eggs and more. Steven received one with a little tiny motor boat in it, showing a tiny reproduction of the UPC flag of the United Peoples Church.

He roared out a laugh, "Ha! Very good, I love it!"
Lei grinned and said, "Thought you would."

Benji sat outside on the veranda alone.
Earlier he had provoked a lot of interest, particularly from her pilot Pa.
Now he was relegated to outside by Ming's command.
The robot had been reluctantly brought along despite Ming's protestations.

Back at JPL, Colonel Mondone had strongly insisted that Benji accompany Ming.
What swung it was when she mentioned her sister Lei would also be at her parents.

"In that case Benji must and would protect both of you. He is necessary."
Ming had been puzzled by this, she said "Why?"
Mondone had coldly replied, "Both you and Lei have special talents that enable the pair of you to uncover and understand strange issues. It is difficult for me to explain more clearly, but precisely because of that, I believe you both maybe be in great danger."
Ming was taken aback, "I think I understand, Sir."
He quickly replied, "The Joint Forces are slow to recognise this, hence I have taken the responsibility on myself to ensure that you have some sort of protection."

Later on at Little Venice, the wine had started to loosen a few tongues.
Ming and Lei were close together deep in whispered conversation.
Her father cleared his throat, and grinned "Say you two? Mind sharing the news?"

Lei "Sure Pa, sorry we just have so much to catch up on."
Ming, "We were talking about my submarine exploits and our amazing rescue by Steven and Lei."

Ju-long looked across at Steven Crowley, "A man of action. I like it. With events unfolding in outer space and on the ground everybody needs to make a contribution.
Folks have seen either with their own eyes or through the news media, the incredible events out there. Naturally they are suspicious of how well or how poorly their respective governments are looking after them. Governments want to avoid panic at all costs, and they may treat us like mushrooms."

Akoni frowned.
Ming quietly said to him, "You know, fed bullshit and kept in the dark."
He nearly burst out laughing, managing a restrained "Aarh…"
The others looked up.

Ling looked around the table, "Anybody for more pie?"
To which everybody except Steven, shook their heads.
The big man pushed his empty bowl across. "Thank you." he smiled.

Ling then raised a question, "So now we have a fine gathering of minds, tell me, what does one make of the recent events in outer space and here on Earth? Do they have a *religious* significance?"

Lei glanced at her sister then spoke, "Who knows Ma? There is some historical research I have done on ancient China that indicates….. Well pretty much proves that an extraterrestrial presence was here thousands of years ago.
Probably more than once. Possibly even millions of years ago."

Ling was not convinced, she replied "If it were true our Good Lord would have told us, surely?"

Ming looked at her mother, "Well Ma, National Security precludes me from telling you very much, and in a way you know as much as we do, but I believe Lei is right.
We need to keep a broad view; *religion is important*. Although, how it fits in I just don't know."

Ling would not be put off, she continued, "All this stargazing is all very well, but surely we the public ought to be told by our respective governments and our ministers of the churches, exactly what is happening? I mean the Reverend here in our church gave a most worrying sermon. He said there is nothing to fear from recent events and the truth is at hand….we can gain solace and comfort by attending church more often.

He said the church would be open everyday of the week."

Steven's loud voice interrupted her in mid-sentence, "Pardon my interruption Mrs Zhao, but if the public did know there could be mass panic which may result in many people's deaths."

Ling stared at him, "Please explain Steven."
All eyes were on Steven Crowley.
The showman rose to the occasion, the preacher Druid, the GunWharf Houdini.

He paused, looked at everyone in turn and slowly said, "Do you all really want me to tell you what I believe? ...something that you might not want to hear?"

Ju-long piped up, "Steven, I think we know the gravity of the situation. As I see it Earth is possibly under threat. I may be retired but my Air Force contacts are very current.
What I believe we need to watch are the world's religions turning on each other, apportioning blame for all that has happened.
Look how people panic so quickly. What with the President's speech trying to quell panic buying and now armed guards in the supermarkets."
Ling spoke up, "Yes...and one food bag per person only, how ridiculous."

Steven spoke again "Even your great country Ju-long, with its entire military might, may be ineffective against an adversary with unknown and powerful capabilities."

Ju-long was a little restless.
Lei watched her lover Steven closely as he commanded attention.
He had that mystic quality.

Ming started to think about Benji and how pathetic his response could be.
Not even a thousand Benjis would cut it.

Her mind drifted to automation.
'Benjis building Benjis.
Now maybe if there are enough robots building robots and with a vast supply of materials, we could have a sustainable army.
Yes, one that could replenish itself fast enough to overwhelm its attackers.'

Then a cold thought.
She shivered, 'What if the attackers manage to gain control of such a robot army and turn it on us. Hell…a nightmare scenario.'

Steven then said, "The saviour spacecraft that destroyed the dark craft, seems all powerful." He glanced at Lei, "But it is not. These mentors of ours whoever they are have provided us on Earth with some limited protection. My understanding through my contacts with the Church of Scientology, is that we AND these saviours face the gravest threat."

Ming felt uneasy, she took Akoni's hand.
Akoni suddenly intervened, "Steven, may I suggest that we are strong, strong in our own beliefs. Humanity can prevail, *we are survivors*. For instance look at the military capability right across the world that humanity has.
At least the cold war and all the other conflicts have given man enough firepower to wipe out us all out, so why not focus it against whatever threat that may come from outer space?"

Steven waited then said, "It would be on a different level, this threat has capabilities beyond our imagination."

Akoni frowned, "Are you saying that all of mankind on Earth could be wiped out that easily?"

Steven replied, "This threat comes as far as we know, from the distant Andromeda galaxy. It threatens our entire galaxy, the Milky Way.

If allowed, this evil will bring a dark era for ever… to humanity.
I will call it evil.
I believe it is the most depraved and emotionless alien existence.
Utterly without love as we know it.
Its empire could be so massive that it can absorb and destroy everything in this galaxy.
EVERYTHING I stress. Life in all forms will cease to exist as we know it.
Instead, from what I have found out, life here and across our galaxy, will be enslaved and made to suffer in the most macabre way……for all eternity."

Lei had a slight frown. In her mind she thought 'How does he know this? '

Ming started to say the Lord's Prayer in her head, 'Our Lord in Heaven… give us our daily bread…'

Akoni almost shouted, "How can you say this Steven? What proof do you have?
I mean another galaxy, surely that is so far away? How can they travel the vast distance?"
Steven acknowledged Akoni, "Very true the distance is huge, and the Andromeda galaxy is maybe two million light years from ours. But somehow they have found a way to traverse this distance quickly.
Maybe a wormhole or the like.
Proof you say? well my information has been gleaned over the years from many sources. Astronomical and scientific groups. Numerous government transmissions.
It is more a judgement, assimilating the information I have obtained over a long time."
Lei had a slight frown, she sensed Steven knew more.

At this juncture Ju-long slapped his hand on the table.
Steven Crowley sat down and everybody turned to Ming's father.

"Steven, what you say may have some truth, but it doesn't give you the right to dominate this Easter family lunch with such sombre conjecture.
Let us see what comes.
I have the utmost faith in our armed forces. Let us drink to that."
He stood and raised his glass.

Ming fleetingly shot a sly, resigned look to Lei, as they all raised their drinks.

Later, the men sat in the lounge smoking cigars and drinking brandy.
Akoni was struggling with his cigar.
In fact his first ever. Not wanting to be impolite he didn't refuse it.
Now he was turning a little green, intermittently coughing in the haze of blue smoke.
Steven had declined, puffing on his smuggled Greek cigarettes instead.
They were deep in conversation.

Out on the veranda Lei and Ming looked out over the still canal waters, now exposing the muddy sides as the tide went out. Their mum was inside clearing up, insisting she needed no help. Lei was the first to speak, "So nice being home, I feel so safe here."
Ming was deep in thought, "Uh…oh yeah definitely. I wish I could see Ma and Pa more, the military seem to own me lately."
Lei "You know I've been away a while. Life seems to take one in different directions, go with the flow, go …."
Ming interjected, "Go with your love."

Lei laughed, then became pensive. At length she said, "It's more an infatuation Ming. Love doesn't come easy, but I am very fond of Steven, he's fun, interesting and we travel a lot."
"As long as you're happy Lei? He does seem a bit mad, with those preacher eyes of his."
Lei smiled "Ha! I love his blue eyes and he does have a soft centre you know."

They became silent, looking up as the odd star appeared in the deep blue sky.
A couple of tiny bats flitted around the trees in the garden.

"Ming, have you found out anymore about those cloaked objects that you discovered near the Chinese moon base?"
Ming took a deep breath and sighed. "Not really, as I said our recordings were cleverly wiped. But the Colonel and I have talked much about them. What with the space battle, there seems to be a link."

Lei became serious, "You mentioned about some craft escaping from the giant explosion, is that thing in China one of them?"
Ming could not hide her fear as she looked into her sister's eyes.
"Yes it is. We know where two of them are. The China appearance and the other is in England somewhere. They are grotesque."
Lei went wide-eyed, "You've seen it?"
"Through the camera eyes of our robot Benji, that was on the scene. A most ghastly, macabre entity, the size of…oh god it was huge, maybe a large four storey house."
"Gees...What happened?"
"Well, you know Karen Durgas and her friend Jane Horsham?"
Lei nodded.

"They had just visited a friend in a care home and this entity, this awful alien was detected by her Benji robot. To begin with the damn thing was invisible.
Then Benji deployed a pulse laser weapon which illuminated the alien.
What I saw on the video was the most repulsive, scary object I have ever seen."
Lei said "Oh Sis…"

"Then it retaliated and Benji received some damage, but somehow the evil thing was repulsed, because after that it disappeared. Along with two British Apache helicopters that were scrambled later to intercept it. Lost, two aircraft and their crews, no sign

of them. Kept all very hush, hush.......the British public are unaware, can you imagine? Crazy as I'm sure there must have been leaks, you know people nearby who saw something?"
Lei exclaimed "Hmm perhaps not, you say it was in the countryside? God, this is so scary Ming and do you know what?"
"What?"
"I believe that those people, our so called saviours with the star craft, may struggle to help us?
Ming just looked at her sister with a growing feeling of unease.

A call from the door, "You two, like some Easter cake?"
"Thanks Ma but I'm still full from your lovely lunch."
Ming "Me too Ma."
"Ok."
Ling disappeared back inside.

Ming picked up their conversation, "These 'saviours' you say, what makes you think they cannot help us?"
Lei replied, "I have discovered something extraordinary during my recent researches.
When I was in China, as you know I visited several museums and quite a few ancient and historical sites. I covertly took many photographs. Very risky though.
They can be really funny about people taking pictures, like they lock you up, sometimes for years."
"I can imagine. So what do you know?"

"I revisited some pictures of a number of three thousand year old tablets I saw in a museum, plus I looked at a whole load of inscriptions on various ancient stone buildings and a couple of very old monuments. Only when I viewed them through ultra violet filters did I see particular symbols that stood out."

Ming became fascinated, "So what have you found out dear sister?"
Lei the younger, didn't miss the very slight scepticism in Ming's voice.

She paused, and then slowly spoke. "You see I determined a sequence. Not a sequence for a map or even the written word."
Ming frowned, said "Sorry Lei, do go on."
Lei caught the change of Ming's mood, serious.
"It's a mind pattern Ming."
She let the statement sink in.
Lei continued, "It's a series of images you must conjure up in the correct sequence in your mind, while concentrating on nothing else."
Ming with surprise said, "How on Earth is that useful?"
Lei "I suspect they are to be used with a technology that is now in its infancy here on Earth. Mind reading and being able through a yet to be invented transmission system, to project a coded message."

Ming frowned again, "For what reason Lei? To communicate with these 'saviours'?"

"No. It is to be used to access an entrance into their moon machine."
Ming's eyes opened wide, "You reckon?"
Lei "Yes, the symbols and hieroglyphs definitely show this and what's more it gives the impression that our saviours might not be around in the future and are giving us, humanity, this access, so that we at sometime in the future, can maintain the machine ourselves."

"Holy Smoke Lei, if what you say is true........." her voice faded as she worked out the dreadful odds. "If true, then we will become alone and have to defend ourselves against the monsters."

That night proved fitful and sleepless for most of the household, except Ming's Pa.

As he prepared for bed, Ju-long looked at the photo of a proud, medal adorned, uniformed Air Force pilot.
His beautiful wife stood beside him.

It had been taken just after he received one of America's top military awards.

Ju-long nodded off quickly, sleeping soundly as he had done for years.

Next day

The morning's breakfast was a subdued affair, until Akoni cracked a joke about Hawaiian life. After the laughter had subsided, Ming's Ma, Ling said, "So you guys are off to Shutters for a few days? You must have won the lottery!"

Shutters on the Beach, a luxury hotel on the Santa Monica coast, oozing with style and opulence.
Romantic heaven.
Ming laughed and said "Yep, I've been saving my service pay for Akoni and me to have a little break there."
She grinned from ear to ear.
Akoni squeezed her in a hug, "I'm such a lucky guy."
Ming continued, "and you must join us for dinner tomorrow night, all on me."
Smiling she looked at her parents, then Lei and Steven, reinforcing the invitation to them all.

"Ah…" exclaimed Ju-long, "love to, but I've an Air Force reunion tomorrow evening."
Ling couldn't quite hide her disappointment.
She looked across said "Sorry Ming."

Steven spoke up, "Thank you, we would love to see how the other half lives."

Early evening - Tuesday April 3rd
Shutters on the Beach Hotel, Santa Monica

Ocean View Restaurant

Just the two of them sat at a polished mahogany table, drinking Californian red from shiny crinkly crystal wine goblets.
Missing were Lei and Steven, who agreed to join them the next day for breakfast instead.
Something about Steven wanting to see the famous Little Venice canals walk that evening.

The crystal glasses caught and twinkled in the light from the overhead chandeliers.
A long stemmed candle burned in the centre of the table.
It was mounted in a bottle, of which the neck was covered in long multi-coloured rivulets of solidified wax.
A piece of art in its own right.

Brilliant orange light from the sunset, streaked through the ornate windows and across the wooden decked floor.
To complete the scene, some tinkling piano music ebbed through the air, caressing a crooning Dean Martin vocal.
"…taaake one fresh and tender kiss………..memories are made of this…."

The view looked out across to the far sandy beach line, the setting sun reflecting a dazzling path across the waters towards them.
A waiter behind the bar was shaking, with a rattling shoosh, some exotic cocktail.

Akoni raised his glass again, "To the woman I love, thank you for everything, life has become wonderful since you crashed into my coach."
Ming laughed, clinking her glass against his, "Yeah, my fault in the end. Fate I reckon… love you Akoni."
She pursed her lips and blew him a kiss across the table.

The restaurant was not busy.
Most diners were next door in the Pico Restaurant watching a live show.
Not for Ming and Akoni.
Here only a few people dined.
They had something quiet, together and peaceful.

She was looking out the window, the sunset oranges and reds reflecting on her face, her eyes like glistening jewels in the fading light.
Akoni thought 'God, she is the most beautiful woman.'
He fumbled in his pocket.
There were tears in the corners of his eyes.

"Ming?"

She turned around to his chair, but he was not there.
Turning a little further and there he was down on one knee.
Akoni held open a little velvet lined box.
Inside was a gold ring.

"Ming, I adore you and I love you. Please will you marry me?"

She gasped, "Oh Akoni, oh how lovely…."
Ming stooped and took his hands and the box in hers, looking at the gold ring.

It had a large diamond, encircled by two slim silver humpback whales, one at the top, the other underneath.
She paused for what seemed like a lifetime, looking into his watery eyes.

He waited and waited. His heart was pounding and his right leg started to quiver.

Then Ming got down on both knees.

Across at the bar the waiter had missed nothing, having stopped his drink mixing and now watching discreetly.

"Yes, YES AKONI , I WILL ! and with all my heart. Such a beautiful ring, the whales. So lovely."
She grabbed his arms pulling him close and kissed him passionately.

He stifled a cry.
They sat back at their table, Akoni dabbing his eyes with a napkin. Ming had a glow that outshone the sunset, staring in wonder at the sparkling jewel on her finger.

"Compliments of the house!"

From nowhere, the waiter wheeled an ice bucket into view and popped a bottle of champagne.
He flourished two slim beautiful crystal glasses and deftly filled them.

They both exclaimed "Thank you!"
Ming "What a surprise."

Parting with a glorious smile he said "Enjoy".

A marvellous toast.

Shutters.
The following morning.
Breakfast on the beach terrace.

All four of them tucked in.
Bacon, eggs, hash browns, tomatoes, mushrooms, refried beans followed by raspberry jam filled croissants.

They had a dreamy view of sand and sea, a few people wandering along at the far water's edge.

Some tall, craggy palm trees dotted here and there. The trees were mature, having olive green leaves. At the lower branches the older leaves had been fraying for ever.
Down on the sand, a tanned man leant sideways in a speeding sand yacht , its green-white sail bulging in the wind. Wheels spinning up puffs of sand, as it careered along the edge of the beach.

Steven was the first to speak, "Apologies for not being able to make it last night, but your Ma and Pa insisted we stay for dinner yesterday which turned into an amazing walk along the canals. Also we sensed you guys wanted to be on your own?"
He winked at Lei.
"But thank you for the breakfast invite. What a lovely place this is."
Lei added, smiling "Think Ma wanted to make the most of me. I have been away a long time."

Ming coyly replied, "That's ok, and with just the two of us, something wonderful happened last night."
Both sisters glanced at the shiny new addition to Ming's left hand finger.
Akoni had a Hawaiian grin, ear to ear.

At the rear, Benji the robot had been relegated behind the dark tinted windows of their Toyota in the back car park.

Only Colonel Mondone's insistence that he accompany Ming and Lei had persuaded them to bring him.
Ming knew of Benji's survelliance abilities and the fact that Mondone could watch them through him.
Bit creepy really.

Lei "This is so lovely, such a gorgeous hotel and the setting is wow."
Akoni replied "You've not been here before? Having lived just a short distance away?"

Lei smiled "No. Being close to the beach, we never needed to stay in a posh hotel like this and when we ate along here, Pa always said we could eat better for less at other places. Think he liked to keep hold of his service pay."
"Ha!"

Akoni dipped his croissant in his coffee and then he turned to address Steven.
"Steven, may I ask you about your Druid connections? Ming mentioned you have a special circle of friends?"
They all watched keenly as Steven went to answer.
He lay back in his chair and took a deep breath.
"What do you want to know?"
Akoni jokingly "Well if it's secret than I best not ask, eh?"
Steven smiled, brushing his beard with his hand. His hair was tied back in a pony tail. "Well it's a long story. I have been on shall we say a crusade for some years now. For a bit of background, I used to work in the intelligence community in the UK Government."

A waiter hovered.
Ming gently waved him away.

He continued "I realised that there was a lot of important information being withheld from the public. Some was dynamite and I guess people would be better off not knowing. But other stuff, decisions involving the lives of hundreds or thousands of people were kept secret. Even those people, didn't know about the moves being made that so seriously affected their lives."

Akoni, "Like?"
Steven paused, he replied "Well I can tell you of one example. A major pharmaceutical company was pushing for the rubber stamp on a new anti-malaria drug for the armed forces. A number of trials and results were suppressed. However later, some very good reports were, shall we say released. Then the company looked after some senior figures in the government."

Ming "You mean paid off?"
"Basically yes. Very subtle though. Stuff like giving them keys to luxury holiday homes abroad. Tickets to top events.
Free use of yachts, plus crews and whatever entertainment was required, you know the sort."
Ming interjected, "I hate the corruption in this world."

"So then the drug went out for general distribution to our guys in the field."
Akoni replied "And the veterans returned ill?"
"You got it, hundreds of them, with serious and permanent side effects. Their lawyers are still battling for compensation. It's hard to fight powerful closed door institutions."

Steven continued, "So I left the government and decided to set up an outside group of powerful, yet honest people, to change things."
Lei gave a quiet laugh.

Steven gave her a sharp look and quickly responded, "Yes well, to begin with, but it is never black and white, but shades of grey. As you know power can corrupt people….."
He hesitated, then said, "Not only monetary or plutocrat power but something else, power that until recently we were unaware of."
His mind was on the weird actions of Irving Dekker and July Craswell in the last meeting.
Steven then lied, "*As a result my Druid group is on hold until I can overcome these temporary issues.*"
He stopped and looked around for further questions.
None.

Akoni at length said, "Very enlightening Steven, thank you. It must be a hell of challenge to, shall we say, strike out on one's own?"
Lei interrupted, changing the subject, "I think breakfast is finished? Come on, let's go for a walk along that lovely seashore."

They all welcomed a chance to leave a tricky discussion.
Too many of these lately.

Three hundred yards out from the Shutters, the four of them strolled along the water's edge. Steven Crowley picked up the odd stone and skimmed it into the gentle surf.
The sun was bright and sharp, rising and peaking out amongst a drift of white stratus cloud.

Very few people about.

Benji strolled nonchalantly along the hotel front, watching them at a distance with his telescopic camera eyes. At a glance he looked quite human, his hand frequently holding onto his canvas hat, to stop it blowing off in the wind.
In his other was a rolled up newspaper.
He wore an oversize jacket with floppy sleeves, which disguised the large weapons pods he had mounted under his forearms. Plus he looked slightly hump backed, a disguise to hide the support backpack which was hidden under his jacket.
Covert stuff.
Even the local police were unaware of this walking weapon.

Colonel Mondone hummed as he watched the live scene remotely via the robot.
He had dragged himself into the Jet Propulsion Lab today after a rather sleepless, yet enjoyable night.
Then he spotted a tanned woman in a bikini, sunbathing on a hotel lounger nearby.

He thought of Gail, his insatiable lover.
She had seen to him again and again last night for several hours.
'Sleep what was that?' he chuckled inwardly.
What a woman he thought, 'She is amazing, fantastic sex. Hell, shall I marry her?'
He laughed at himself, his thoughts see-sawing, 'Whoa….man,

I need to get to know her better, know her as a person, ...could she be my soul mate? ...but she does twist me around her little finger...'
He inwardly felt so warm, and then scratched his unshaven chin.
'Back to the job, let's see.'

He felt tense, some distant fear nagged at the back of his mind.

Mondone scanned the horizon right to left, using the optical zoom controls of the robot's eyes.

He sighed at the tranquil scene, feeling intrusive.
A squad of young men and girl joggers ran by, laughing and puffing.
Then a slim girl in a close fitting tracksuit, wearing a headband and headphones, whizzed by on roller blades.
Yes, very intrusive.
He switched off the connection, leaving Benji on remote monitor.
Mondone walked off down to the cafeteria, some wake up juice needed.

He frowned, thinking 'Was it a waste of valuable resources? Am I overreacting?'

Some time later.

Ming held Akoni close as they ambled along the soft sand.
They followed Lei and Steven who walked on some yards ahead holding hands.
She cut a little diminutive figure against his tall frame.

Akoni said, "Think they might tie the knot?"
Ming gave a little chuckle, "Who knows? They certainly are a good match. Small as my sister is, she gives him a good run for his money."
"Money?.... ha yes the cigarette smuggling you mentioned. They still do that?"

"Yep, Greek ones. Apparently it is almost legal in Greece. The authorities there turn a blind eye. And the smokes are dirt cheap."

A jet ski way out in the water, thundered and bounced along, generating a white wake behind it.
A scattering of seagulls flew awkwardly up and down, swooping on a shoal of fish out in the water.

Then Ming saw them.

"Wow look at that!" she exclaimed, pointing to maybe five hundred yards out at sea.
Three, maybe four hump back whales swam together, and then they all dived, their huge tails standing up momentarily above the waves.

After a while two came up, blowing water and air upwards high above the waves.
Strangely the others didn't appear. Suddenly with an almighty splash the surfaced two vanished under the dark blue waves.

The seagulls flew off quickly too.
A chill wind seemed to come up from nowhere, and then the sun disappeared behind a clump of dark grey cloud.
The surf had turned greyish-green.

Lei shouted, "Seems a bit eerie, what happened to the whales?"
Ming replied above the wind, "I don't know, I don't know……."
She felt strange, some goose bumps on her arms.

Steven pointed to a black pinnacle far out, he said "Damned if I'm mistaken but hasn't that rock moved?"
Suddenly, he grabbed his forearm.
The ancient bracelet had started to tingle intermittently.
Ming exclaimed "I don't remember any big rocks here, certainly not like that….."

She watched the distant peak for a while.
Steven then said, "Perhaps it's one of those new Navy submarines they're testing? You know the weird shaped black stealth ones."

Akoni had the deepest frown on his face, he shouted "Aumakua! Look......LOOK THERE!"
He didn't mean out to sea, instead he pointed in the opposite direction.
They all looked away from the sea and back up the beach to where he meant.

With sand flying up from his heels, Benji the robot was running fast diagonally across the beach. He had discarded his jacket and his unnaturally large arms were apparent.

Ming caught her breath, hand on mouth. "Oh my God…….he's seen something!"
She turned to where the robot was heading.

"Aah…." moaned Steven as he clutched his arm again.
The bracelet was now throbbing.
His eyes frantically scanned around, and then back on the black object in the water.
Lei saw him holding his arm and then she looked out to sea.

The huge rock in the waves had quickly moved closer.
It became larger and something about it seemed extremely odd.
Its surface was moving,….. no, more than that….it was writhing.

Lei screamed.
All four of them just stopped, frozen to the spot in fear.
Their happy mood had evaporated.

Now it was being replaced by a growing sense of horror.

At JPL

The shrill alarm woke Mondone.
Even after a coffee he was so tired that a nap had been badly needed.
He staggered out of the makeshift couch-bed in his large office.
A computer screen had automatically come on, with flashing red symbols.

"Shit!" he made his eyes open as he clicked the mouse.
Looking through Benji's eyes he saw the moving rock close up, "Oh Hell, there it is…oh shit…..at last we have you……you ugly bastard…"

He grabbed the phone and punched a short number.

"Get me Strike Command……..QUICKLY!"

Santa Monica Beach

Back on the beach, time stood still for Ming, Akoni, Steven and Lei.
Something had glued them to the sand.

Then the sea parted as an enormous object rose and moved and slithered onto the shingled sand.
Ming felt absolute panic; her mind was like sludge, full off what? She couldn't think or even physically move.

Steven Crowley had managed to get his smart phone out. He was frantically talking to it, and then he fell onto one knee. Something invisible was pressing down on his shoulders.
Lei stood still, her eyes white, her face pale as milk.
She just said, "Oh what the fuck is that? Oh god…its one of them! …STEVEN!"
Like the others, she felt unable to move, rooted to the spot.

And then the thing came into focus, maybe a hundred yards from them.
As high as a forty foot building, it shimmered with its whole dark surface, writhing and twitching.

Close up they saw the awful reality.

Hundreds of clams, eels and fish were stuck to the periphery of the monster, their very life being sucked out.
It seemed to drift towards them, dispensing with the now dead Earth creatures and they fell off in clumps, to reveal a transparency as the creature or spacecraft, whatever it was, started to turn invisible again.

Something very unnatural and alien penetrated the immediate atmosphere.

Then almost at once a huge flash occurred on one side of the creature, followed by multiple explosions and thuds.
Benji came up quick, slowing and skidding in the sand.
He was furiously discharging several weapons at once.

The monster rose and ejected an oily black set of tendrils which snaked out rapidly towards the robot, now dizzily firing from both arm pods.
A nightmare shriek emanated from the alien.

Benji moved lightning quick, withdrawing his long thin motor sword from his backpack. It buzzed loudly, chainsaw-like, swinging in a cutting arc to meet the tendrils.

Ming gasped as she watched helplessly.
Benji's sword just dissolved, the tendrils melting it, as they snaked past his twisting body.
Steven watched on in a mix of awe and fear. He dropped his phone and clutched his bracelet in a deliberate movement.

The beast turned.
Its focus, the little robot.
Smoke surrounded the gargantuan Goliath and the little 'David' Benji.

A fight to the death.

Benji was fighting for his mechanical life, he was trying everything he had been programmed to do, ...*SAVE THE HUMANS.*

His outer body armour flipped out into position instantly.
Secondary weapons nosed out of his left hand pod.
Then his rail gun uttered a metallic scream as hundreds of tiny super hard projectiles hurled themselves outwards. Travelling at more than five times the speed of sound, they shot towards the grey quivering mass.
It started to disappear in a cloud of smoke.

Then he turned to the humans and barked 'GET DOWN!'
Finally, in a crackling roar, he launched several mini rocket grenades and let rip with his mini-chain gun. It gave a short spurting and haunting shrill rattle, spitting death at over a thousand rounds a minute.

Ammunition gone.

A loud, deep shrieking sound emitted from the beast as it disappeared in a blinding haze of explosions and smoke. Something like a black column appeared to rip out from it at enormous speed towards the beach.
There was a crash, more explosions.........then a sucking sound.

Steven Crowley had got to his knees and was screaming "Get back thou evil menace, ye of no faith, BE GONE WITH YOU!"
He held his arm with the bracelet out towards the beast.

After what seemed an age, the billowing haze of black smoke started to clear.
Acrid fumes drifted across.
Eyes watered.
Ming found she could move a little, slowly getting up on her knees.
She gasped at the scene.

Lei stared incredulously at Steven. He had a sort of faint purple shimmer rotating around him. He then staggered up to his full six and half feet height, with both arms extended, fingers splayed out towards the alien.
"GO, BE GONE…"

In moments the monster was back at the water's edge, rapidly becoming invisible again. It seemed as huge and real as ever.
Sitting on the sand, Ming gripped Akoni in panic, she shouted "Oh god, the bloody thing is still alive….."

Benji was quiet. She turned and looked to where he had been.
She let out a cry.
There distributed across a dozen square yards, was what had been a state of the art soldier robot.
His smashed body parts lay smoking and sparking. Above them a black wigwam of snaking curling spokes seemed to revolve, consuming and drawing energy from the remains. Then the wigwam faded and vanished.

Benji had done his job, distracting the monster for valuable minutes.

Ming turned to check the others. All of them seemed to be able to walk slowly now, stumbling, trying to move away. The oppressive force no longer there.

Lei shuddered, holding on to Steven.
They were all in some state of shock, except Steven.

Akoni waved his hand shouted "LOOK, IT'S MOVING AWAY……THERE!…and HERE THEY COME , thank the lord,…. oh praise be….."
He fell to his knees and grabbed handfuls of sand shaking them in the air.

Up above, a squadron of fighter jets screamed in.

Chapter 19

3pm – Tuesday April 3rd 2018
Edwards Air Force Base, California, USA.

The large room had no windows.

Several high ranking officers sat around a large oval polished oak table.
The lighting was subdued, with most of it coming from the large wall screen display.

Frozen on the wall monitor were numerous aircraft, some disintegrating in mid air. Dominating the middle of the display, was a huge nebulous apparition, swathed in fire and clouds of grey smoke.

A brisk knock at the door.

Colonel Arrack Mondone entered the room.
The guard saluted, retreated out and closed the door.
General Rogers motioned to Mondone, "Ah Colonel, please take a seat."

Mondone could not contain his astonishment at the galling screen display.
"My God….."

Continuing, Rogers gesticulating with his hand, spoke, "Present we have Air Force General Webern, our Navy deputy Chief of Staff, Admiral Draviston, the Army Chief of Staff, General Hayward and CIA director Bob Redford."

Mondone rose slightly, nodded and saluted.
The others that Rogers didn't introduce were almost certainly government people.

Rogers continued, "Gentlemen as I was saying, we have accounted for three objects that entered the Earth's atmosphere soon after the conflict in space. Our intelligence suggests that there are probably no more."

He paused looked right around the large table, then continued,

"From our early analysis, these objects are alien in just about every way we can imagine. It has been mooted that they are in fact an image projection of unknown energy, possibly a stasis field or a deflecting force that we do not understand.
Deep inside there may be a matter kernel, driving the sphere.
As you are all aware, the world's governments are working hard to counter what we now know could be a very serious threat to humanity. Unfortunately the media news has generated panic in China. Already our contact with this alien has been on the various news channels here. At Santa Monica Beach some people used smart phones and the like, to capture video and stills of what happened.
People are frightened. We have a duty."

Rogers scribbled something on his pad, tore it off and handed it to his aide, who immediately left the room. He spoke,
"The gravity of the situation deems I call the President right after this meeting. Then we take the appropriate action."

He turned to Mondone,
"Colonel Mondone please report."

Arrack Mondone stood upright and took a deep breath, his eyes glued again to the screen.
"My robot, a Mark II Benji, deployed every weapon he had... against this,...this beast. It appears all had no effect, bar a last ditch attempt using gun launched grenades and a chain gun mounted in his arm pod which fires small calibre depleted uranium bullets.

The robot was overwhelmed just after this and he was destroyed. However, the alien then retreated back into the sea."

"Thank you Mondone. To continue our discussion I need to understand how and why the Air Force squadron lost most of its aircraft?"

A pale faced Webern replied grimly, "We lost several very experienced pilots. As yet there is no wreckage or debris to be found. The remaining two aircraft reported that the lost planes had been, and they describe it as 'destroyed then absorbed' by the enemy."
He gripped the table with white knuckles, staring at everybody in turn around the table. "I can add that our missiles and heavy calibre automatic weapons failed to stop this adversary. A variety of warheads were used including high explosive, armour piercing, fragmentation and none, I repeat none, stopped this monster. Our radar, laser interrogation and other sensors failed to reveal the substance of the object. All energies are just absorbed, no reflection whatsoever."

"Thank you General."

Rogers surveyed the scene both on screen and in the room.
At length he spoke to the Navy man, "Admiral Draviston, have your people located the adversary presence?"

Draviston, a big man, about fifty, spoke in a deep, calm voice.
"Yes, initially by one of our submarines. Now we are tracking it via a weak heat signature, with the vessel staying at long range. The alien is approximately one hundred miles off the Californian seaboard and travelling south west.
Deployment of torpedoes was considered, but we needed to avoid the risk of the adversary returning, possibly coming ashore again. As you know our fleet capabilities are substantial and reflecting on the Air Forces losses, despite using some of the most powerful conventional weapons we have,

I want the President to authorise a tactical nuclear strike far out at sea."

You could hear a pin drop.
Cold military decision was imminent, spurned on by fear of the unknown.

Rogers calmly raised the question, "Admiral? Are your people certain that the energies deployed by a nuclear strike will destroy this adversary?"
Draviston replied, "Our calculations estimate that considering the relatively small size of the alien, it would need to have an extraordinary capability to withstand a direct nuclear hit. With little else in our arsenal to use, this opportunity to use a nuclear weapon may not present itself again. It would seem that there is a reduced risk out at sea. If we can achieve an underwater strike then also the EMP pulse will be muted."

Normally the Electro-Magnetic Pulse from a nuclear explosion is a fierce generation of magnetic electrical energy. Enough to render permanently useless, virtually all electronic devices within a radius of many miles.

Rogers licked his lips slowly then said, "Yes, I understand we have a moment now to tackle this threat and we should not let it slip away. The situation may deteriorate rapidly."
Arrack Mondone held his breath involuntarily, he finally breathed out with a sort of gasp, saying "Sir, are there alternatives?"

Rogers turned to him curtly, "Colonel, I'm afraid these creatures or whatever they are must be destroyed and if that means the nuclear option then we will take that path. The Chinese have lost track of the one that killed their people. The English have also lost sight of the second one. Let me remind you that they lost two Apache attack helicopters and crews, again without a trace of wreckage."

Mondone sighed inwardly, thinking 'Nobody was thinking out of the box'. Then he thought about Ming and her friends, now all in the secure hospital wing of the Air Force Base.

Secure, so they could not leave.

Hospital Clinic - Edwards Air Force Base

"What the hell is going on? I am a British citizen and I demand to be released from here at once!"
Steven Crowley was angry, red faced and threatening at six and a half feet tall.
He looked through the small reinforced window and banged on the locked steel door.

Totally ignoring him, an armed guard on the other side of the door, continued to face the other way.
The four of them, Steven Crowley, Lei Zhao, Ming Zhao and Akoni Kekoa were locked in what was a largish room. Some chairs and a table at one end. A bathroom accessed from the middle of the room and some loungers at the other end.
Bright wall pictures of desert flowers, sea shores and snow covered mountains seemed out of place right now.
Ming at length said, "Steven, it's no use. We need to wait, I'm sure it is just precautionary."

She reflected on the very recent past.
Soon after the monster disappeared back into the sea, roaring from the ineffective air attack, a number of Air Force vehicles tore down the beach. They screeched to a stop near the foursome. Some personnel in environment suits, disembarked, and not quite bundled, but manhandled the four of them into a truck. The only spoken sentence from the guy in charge was, "We need to put you guys in quarantine, please do not resist or attempt to escape. Thank you."

That was two hours ago. Now after some pretty thorough medical examinations including blood tests, they were all weary. The intensive individual interrogations had seemed overly harsh.
The fact that the whole of the Santa Monica water front had witnessed the conflict was sidelined.

Akoni was clearly in distress. He was still not fully recovered from his tsunami injuries and the coma that had followed.
Ming held him tightly.

Lei went over to Steven and tried to calm him.
He carried on ranting, "These buggers seem to do what they like! Well they don't know who they're dealing with.... huh!"

After that he wandered over to the window and sat down. His demeanour slowly relaxed. His hand was around the arm bracelet. Steven Crowley looked through the glass and upwards to the sky. He remained almost motionless for a long time.

Lei watched him.

Another hour and a half passed.
They sat wearily. Nothing to do. Their phones 'confiscated.'
On the low table now cold, were several half drunk cups of tea and coffee.
The door opened and Colonel Mondone walked in.

Ming sprang to her feet, giving a brief salute, "Colonel! What is happening, why have we been detained so long?"
"At ease Sergeant and I hope I can allay the anxiousness of the rest of you people."

Crowley got up and said, "You sure can Colonel, by getting us out of here."

Mondone looked at them all in turn, and then faced Steven Crowley, "I will in due course. You will all be free to go soon, except yourself Ming. I have just seen the medical results and nothing untoward was discovered."

Lei frowned, "Untoward? What do you mean?"

Mondone raised his hand in acknowledgement. "Please. Yes I'm sorry you have been put under duress but the powers that be, wanted to be sure that you guys were not contaminated or infected."

Lei went cold, she murmured "Oh Jesus…."
Mondone continued, "Obviously we cannot be one hundred percent certain. As of yet we know very little about the AnGax, the monster that confronted you guys and the robot."
An image of the smashed robot flashed through Ming's mind.
AnGax, the new name allocated to the aliens.
Surreal, like out of some computer game.

Ming said, "Sir, my fiancé Akoni is not well, he needs rest and out of here?"
Mondone raised an eyebrow,
He said, "Sure I see no reason for any of you to stay now, we are arranging your release. Ming I will leave you to arrange transport, once you've been finally debriefed."
He sort of winked, she couldn't be sure.

Crowley deftly held his arm bracelet with his other hand.
It had stopped all pulsing some time ago. Strangely the clinic doctors at the base had ignored it. 'Maybe they thought just some dull trinket to go with the mad Englishman.'
He smiled, having a little supreme feeling.

Later after her meeting with Mondone, Ming had requisitioned an Air Force Sedan, one of the lightly armoured ones and now drove the four of them back towards Los Angeles.
To their left, some sparse green vegetation dotted the hills and rocky outcrops.

After a while thicker clumps of trees announced the start of the Angeles National Forest.
She glanced over and said, "Do you know, normally I like to drive through the forest. It takes about twice as long on a good day, but the views and scenery are a joy."
Lei quipped, "Yeah but not today, huh? Funny but I just want to be back home with Ma and Pa right now."
Steven Crowley was cursing under his breath. The military had confiscated his phone. 'To be returned at some point….'
He had managed some video of the beach catastrophe.

Akoni grumbled, "We're US citizens and our rights seem to be walked over."
Lei replied "Yeah true, but they released us fairly quickly, which you not think is strange?"
Ming said, "Well in the films you see people sometimes held for days or weeks without any recourse to a phone call or lawyer. Guess the Colonel must have had some influence."

She looked out the cab window, glancing around and then up at the sky and continued. "I think we're pretty safe now. From what the Colonel told me the military are tracking that awful thing far out at sea. But….and this is a big but, he whispered under his breath to me that they, that is the Air Force, threw everything they had at the monster.
As we saw, the damn thing just repelled it all."

She sighed heavily.
A large queue of traffic came into view.

"Damn it! Let's get some country." she changed her mind and took the next exit, swinging off and driving up a small mountain road.
"I know this road. We'll do it for a bit then swing back for the highway, get round whatever is causing the holdup."

Lei at length spoke up, "Well I think something else saved us." She looked at Steven.
Akoni gazed at both of them curiously.
Ming cautiously glancing back in the rear mirror.

Lei said "Now is the time I think. Tell them Steven."

He squinted at the sun low in the sky and then as the car rounded a rocky bend, a panoramic view appeared showing the forest stretching away in a mottled wash of greens.
Towards the horizon he could just make out the sprawling Los Angeles skyline with tall buildings nudging up in the haze.
Then far in the distance off the coast, the bluish-white sea starting to glitter as the sun moved westwards to the horizon.

"Well, it seems some time ago I stumbled on an artefact that is not what it seems.
It is a sophisticated device, not of man's making."

He paused watching their faces; Ming had slowed down for the winding hilly roads.
Crowley added "It probably saved our lives on the beach."
He showed them the arm bracelet.
It didn't look more than a beaten greenish bronze trinket with a dull dark jewel in the centre.
Some little scrolls circled the stone.

Akoni frowned, "What the hell do you mean man?"
Crowley went on to explain about the huge machine in the moon and the power that seemed to emanate from there.
Ming took a sharp interest, "The moon? That's so interesting. But surely back at Edwards, they would have found your bracelet out?"
Crowley never had a chance to answer.
Something far away abruptly distracted them all.

Just as their view of Los Angeles vanished behind the next rocky bend, an enormous flash came from far out at sea.
For a second everything around them became twice as bright.
Then as their car moved into the rock shadow, a tremendous red glow briefly enveloped the area.

Ming screamed, "Oh hell, they've nuked it! EVERYBODY GET DOWN!"

The heat blast had quickly followed the explosion flash of intense light.

She swung the car against a rocky outcrop, to shield them and slammed on the brakes, pulling the handbrake hard until the handle nearly broke.
The sedan shuddered to a stop.

Seconds later, a powerful gust of wind hit the area.
For a brief moment, every tree and bunch of grass around the rocky outcrop, bent as the nuclear wind hit them.
After what seemed like an age, the four of them gingerly crept around the outcrop and just stared.

On the horizon meeting the sea, they could just make out a small mushroom cloud rising high into the atmosphere.
Crowley muttered, "How could they do that? So close to the city."
Ming grimaced, she said, "Well they did, they must have used a nuclear warhead, probably on a torpedo, but I reckon it was a surface hit. Downtown LA will have been damaged."

Lei started to cry. "Ma and Pa are down there…."
Akoni growled, "Well the price we will pay had better be worth it. I guess the monster couldn't have survived that."
He looked at his Air Force girlfriend Ming for acknowledgement.

Sergeant Ming Zhao sighed "That was a serious step to take. They would have explored all other options first and deploying nuclear weapons requires a Presidential order. With the thing out at sea, I guess there is minimum exposure to land based people. Trouble is my gut feel says the beast may not have been destroyed. Don't ask me why I feel that, I just do."

Steven Crowley was discreetly pressing his bracelet, his mind somewhere else.
With that their Sedan hurtled back down the highway towards the city.
The speed limits were of no consequence.
Back at Edwards Air Force Base
General Roger's office.

Bob Redford flexed out his joined hands. He had a smug look on his face.
Two other CIA operatives sat opposite the General.

General Rogers leaned forward and spoke quietly as though there might be eavesdroppers.
"Repeat to me again Bob, what you just said."

Inwardly Redford sighed, he thought 'Having to deal with some of the military top brass was like trying to walk through deep mud. However, no way round but to work together….. this time.'

"Of course Sir." He replied.

"We believe that the bracelet the English guy, Steven Crowley was wearing has some unusual significance. It appears to be a device of powers that we may not understand. After the medical clearance they went through, we allowed the four detainees to leave. I am under orders that we covertly monitor Steven Crowley."

Rogers nodded and motioned Redford to continue.
"It is similar in capability to an object that a one Karen Durgas is wearing. She is also English. We are currently tracking her and

her colleagues in England. They encountered the second alien entity in Hampshire there. As you know it also was repelled then it disappeared."

Rogers spread his hands palm down on the desk and said, "Capability? Please clarify Director Redford.....and I need more than moonshine purple spheres and lines.
Plus do you know that this Crowley character is some sort of mad preacher?"

The intonation was clear.
The subtle message was, leave the real stuff to the Military.

Redford paused, took a breath and replied, "Well Sir, there is as you know suggestion that a giant machine resides under the moon's surface. This machine appears to link to these …ahem… devices. What's more they seem to offer a kind of protection.
The President has already shown an interest in this avenue…I believe……"

He was interrupted in mid sentence.

"ENOUGH! We need to get a handle on this Redford, I'll get the science guys involved."

Before Redford could say any more, the phone rang.
"Yes….. Rogers."
A rapid loud voice was heard on the other end.
"Thank you."

Rogers craggy face took on a smug expression which became solemn.
He slowly put the phone down and said,
"Well events have overtaken us. We have just destroyed the alien entity."

Redford's face spread into a grin, "Excellent stuff General, how?"

Rogers pulled a dark but satisfied face, "They used a nuclear torpedo."
Redford became wide eyed and uttered "Good God…."

Later that night, on the outskirts of Pasadena, in Mondone's apartment.

A single lamp burned in his lounge-cum-office.
Arrack Mondone scrolled through the computer displays on his desk.
He had Steven Crowley's smart phone video on one screen and a mushroom cloud on the other.

"Hmmm….." he was deep in thought.
He enhanced the ultra violet on the phone file.
There it was. A purple sphere, faint but visible, surrounded all four of them, Ming, Akoni, Lei and Crowley.
He squinted at something else.
From Crowley there appeared to be a purple line going… 'yes going up into the sky.'

"Well I'll be damned…" he said quietly.

A voice from the bedroom, "You coming to bed soon honey?"
Gail was becoming restless. She knew what Arrack was going through and wanted to comfort him badly. Only, her idea of comfort was very physical.

And Arrack Mondone was desperately tired.
Making love was the last thing on his mind right now.
He needed some answers to what was going on.
"Soon babe. Five minutes."

Earlier he and Gail had talked about the forthcoming trip to France, travel arrangements and what a beautiful area they would be staying in.

Near a magnificent chateau in the town of Amboise on the banks of the river Loire.
A chance for both of them to have a couple more days after, maybe taking a boat trip down the river.
Gail then said "You need a break Arrack, you're tired honey. The France trip sounds lovely, could we not tack a bit of holiday on the end?"
"Yes I know. See how things pan out. Holiday is a luxury at the moment. Technically we are on a war alert which means all leave is cancelled, but you're right, a decent break would be good."

They briefly discussed the attendees and Gail's responsibilities. Usual stuff. Chicken feed to Gail.
After the responsibilities of PA to the Vice President, this was a walk in the park.

She dreamed back.
Gus Storrick, second in command to the most powerful man in the world.
He had plied her with jewellery and money.
She had absolutely adored the life style, all the razz a'matazz, the halls of Congress, senators steeped in testosterone. Not that she was distracted. Gus was an insatiable lover and she matched him.

'But love itself, no… that didn't figure in the equation.'

Now, thinking back to Arrack Mondone, she smiled.
He was a bit of a dark horse, handsomely endowed and a great lover.

"Ok Arrack honey. Don't be long."

Mondone then thought of Ming, his technical staff lady.
Her plight on the LA beach and the uncanny coincidence of the alien appearing right there. He turned again to the frozen video of the alien under attack from the robot.

How right he was to ensure that Ming, Lei and their partners had some sort of protection.
Although the strange addition of the purple glow made him think. Mondone frowned, 'Why are the authorities so reluctant to acknowledge our unusual discoveries? It's almost as though they know, but are covering it up or diminishing their significance in the grand scheme of events?'
He scratched his chin.

The robot had more than performed well.
A stunning defence that was overwhelmed by unknown forces, but it bought valuable time.

Then a message clicked on his phone.
"Sir, just to let you know my Ma and Pa are safe and unharmed. Thanks for asking. Ming."

Ming, Akoni, Lei and Crowley had returned to the Zhaos' in Little Venice.
Family and friends together.

He glanced at the wall pictures, military most of them.
Groups of smiling dashing men in uniform.
Then the one photo he really treasured, a shot of him and his daughter at Disneyland, 'taken, hell must be ten years ago now.'

His marriage had collapsed a long time before that.
He sighed, thinking when he might next see his daughter.
She worked over on the east coast, a small town bank manager in Kingston, New York State.
Twenty five years old and going places.

"Arrack?"
He glanced in the direction of the bedroom, got up and turned the shower on in the bathroom.
After he towelled himself, Arrack walked into the bedroom, his bare feet sinking into the soft pile carpet.

Gail lay naked on the bed, fast asleep.

Mondone inwardly gave a sigh of relief, and then chastised himself. 'Why should I be relieved that she is asleep? She is so beautiful and desires me all the time, I should count my blessings.'

He smiled and carefully crept into the bed, quietly pulling the covers over them both.
She moaned, turned and moved into his arms.

Sleep came so soon.

Chapter 20

3 pm – Sunday 15th April 2018
Flying at 45,000 feet
On route to Hotel Mecuna, Hong Kong Island

It's amazing how slowly one could look through the airline magazine.

Watches that cost a month's salary.
Perfume adverts with smug muscular men and sultry dominated women.
Dreamy exotic holiday locations.

Jane sighed and stuffed the magazine back in the seat pocket.
She drank the last of her Chardonnay wine, licking her lips, it was particularly good.

Their bumpy flight was taking them to a night stopover in Hong Kong.

On the plane, a couple of crying babies had prevented any real sleep.
Jane distracted and tired, had just cycled through the videos not really watching any.

She found even dozing impossible.

Sitting next to her, Bill had dropped off, snoring loudly.
He became restless in his sleep, and then Jane dug him in the ribs.
Indignant he got up and staggered to the toilet, trying to wake up.
On his way there, woozy Bill opened and closed his puffy eyes.

Then the plane suddenly lurched as it plied through the storm, Bill nearly falling into the next row of people.

He came back to Jane staring at him.

"What?... what's up?"
She curtly replied, "Don't you remember?"
He gave a look of surprise.
She quietly said "Your bloody hand wandering in my lap!"
"Oh shit Jane, I don't remember, must have been in my sleep, sorry!"
"Yeah right."
She turned and looked out the dark portal window.

The landing did not improve the atmosphere, with the plane bouncing three times, as it swerved in the cross wind.

Queasy stomachs.

Hotel Mecuna, Hong Kong

Now the steak dinner was finished, they had quietly retired to the hotel bar.
Bill gave a little schoolboy smile and said, "God I am tired, but that steak was just the ticket."
Jane glanced at him, nodded then returned to her tablet, scrolling through some social media site.
Gavin had tried to Skype her. Also some odd texts from him, '*Jane, I must speak with you, please. It's about the helicopters.*'

She frowned, then her countenance brightened as the truth dawned.
'Did he mean the lost Apaches?'
She sent a message.

Jane tried to be distant, far away.
She was weary, trying to think of anything but the awful event at the Riverside Care Home.
Bill too was struggling, still stuck mentally at South Harting, the image of the white robed man haunting him.

They both knew of the other's experience.

A lot of stuff was being shared between the four of them. A problem shared is a problem halved, or quartered in this case. Well that was the theory.

After an age and a couple of drinks each, Bill looked at Jane and said "You look tired Jane. Guess the rough flight didn't help?"
She looked up from gazing at the ice cubes in her vodka tonic, and sighed.
"Yeah, I'm shattered Bill. So many traumas lately."

Bill agreed "Yes. I keep thinking about what the man from Omega Centauri told us at South Harting. Really need to share it with the world you know."
Jane looked at him "Maybe it was some clever projection, an image you know. Someone screwing with you?"

"I don't think so. Ask Karen and John, they believe him. No reason not to."
He rubbed his face, "God I'm tired. Sleep doesn't come easy these days, what with my wife July gone."
She thought she sensed an innuendo. Let it go.

Bill said "How's your room? Comfortable?"
She quickly replied, "Very, just great."
He paused, hesitated "Mine's really nice, great big double bed. Fridge is full of good booze. Maybe..."
Jane cut him short, "Maybe what Bill?"
The look said everything.
He stuttered, "Um, I was thinking, sort of a night cap. Chat you know."
Her eyes looked at him unblinking.
"Bill it's been a long day, I'm very tired you know. Need to be in bed soon, what with that early flight tomorrow."
He felt a little disheartened, in his heart he wanted company. "Sure, ok. Guess we've pretty much talked about everything anyway."

Then Bill brightened up, "Well at least we're on a nice jolly and away from Ratcliffe's pontificating. Think we could be at least three weeks in Oz."
Jane managed a smile, "Three weeks? Well that's good. I hope we don't drive each other crazy during the time."
Bill became serious, "Hell no. Using your skills Jane is what I badly need to push our projects through. You see I tend to rush things a little and.....well and..."
She quickly added, "Yes I know."
She knowingly looked at him, their eyes locked briefly,
"And I'm your check and balance, a second pair of eyes and all that. Glad you believe in me Bill."
She yawned.

He nodded affectionately and looked at a large framed print on the wall.
It was Turner's famous 'The Fighting Temeraire' depicting a huge, old, valiant, wooden sailing ship. A large warship of the line from Nelson's era, circa 1800.
It was being towed to the breakers yard, by a then modern little steam tugboat.

For some reason he thought about his parents.
"You know Jane, that picture is very poignant. The new helping the old away."

She looked at him a bit strangely, stifling another yawn, then said "Bill, apart from July, you don't mention your family at all? ... um... are your mum and dad still alive?"
"I haven't a clue."
"Oh?"
Bill breathed in and then sighed, "You see I never knew them. I grew up in several orphanages. In fact when I was a young man, I did find out that my real parents were still alive. They did not die in some car accident, after all."
"Oh Bill..." Jane realised she had unwittingly stepped on a nerve.

“Yeah well as I see it, it doesn’t really matter whether they are still around or not, because they didn’t care about me.”

At that moment the little boy could be seen fleetingly on his face, the anguish and pain of never having a real mother’s or father’s love.

Jane leaned over and grabbed Bill’s arm, saying “I’m so sorry Bill, if I had known…what an awkward question to ask.”
He flooded in melancholy, his eyes a little watery, “That’s alright Jane, you didn’t know. It was a long time ago and it’s behind me now.”

Bill cleared his throat, swallowed and looked at the picture again. “You see I fancy myself as that steam boat, leading the way, dumping old technology with outdated methods and ploughing a new wave.”
He smiled at the analogy, and then looked at her, but in a workman like way, “So how are you and Gustav doing on the engine modification? I haven’t had a chance to ask you.”

He watched her reaction.
“Yes good, we have made a lot of progress. Although any testing like you did, will have to be on an official basis. Sir George has taken a particular interest.”
Bill pulled his slight gargoyle face, “Yep, he sure has and do you know why?”
Jane gave him a quizzical look.

“He knows about my secret engine test in Norfolk.”
“Oh God Bill, who told him? what was his reaction?”

Bill Craswell slowly rotated his glass of beer and then gulped the last drop, gesturing to the bar waiter for a refill. He glanced at Jane signalling if she wanted another.
“Uh uh.” shaking her head.

He peered around the lounge. The hotel bar was busy with a cosmopolitan selection of people. A multitude of race and colour. Over the other side of the room a large group of young Chinese men were having a heated discussion, hands gesticulating wildly in the air.

Bill nearly laughed, "I told him. You see I had nothing to lose and everything to gain. Much better than he eventually finding out through the grapevine and then using it in his own creepy way."

"So how did he take it?"

Bill smirked "He seemed rather cool about it all, wanting to know the details of what was a highly successful, but slightly messy test. He thinks he holds the ace card, having much to gain from this amazing achievement of ours. Yet believes he has me over a barrel because it was a blatant contravention of protocol. Not to mention the radioactivity, that still needs clearing up."
Jane said, "So what will happen?"

Bill smiled "All will be ok. I don't trust the guy but he has powerful leverage with senior politicians and people in the Defence Ministry.
He can be our door to fame and fortune."
Bill gave a little laugh, "If we don't all meet our doom first!"
"Oh Bill, please.... I am scared enough as it is."

He leaned across the table and whispered to her. "He is actually very supportive of further development of the gravity engine, especially your project with Gustav, Jane."
She leaned back, frowning a trifle, "Go on Bill tell me more."
"Well it was my idea and it could be a goer. This side project, which you are working on, is not really an engine."
He watched her puzzled face and then it dawned on her.
"I think you have guessed it?"
She hedged her curiosity and said, "I have an idea, but tell me Bill."

He quietly replied, “It is a prototype weapon. Something that we may be able to use against the aliens, you know like you and Karen encountered.”
Jane shuddered, some goose bumps came up on her arms. “Really?”

“We’re trying to replicate on a miniature level what that second spacecraft did, albeit not extracting plasma at high velocity from a star but using our piddly little engine.”
“Ah…I thought so Bill. Do you think the plasma exhaust output has enough energy to kill them?”
Bill grimaced then raised his eyebrows, “If we greatly increase the ratios of nuclear metals and accelerate the explosions throughput to…..ah, I reckon at least tenfold. Then the calculations and modelling, which you did I might add, show as you know a considerable concentration of very high temperature plasma exhaust.
Our only challenge is to somehow increase the plasma exit velocity.
Give the weapon some sort of range.”

“Cool Bill, I will try my utmost to ensure it has a chance of working.”

“That’s the ticket. Soon you will see more people join us to work on it.”

She pondered and then said, “Bill, so did you get the plasma idea from your engine test with Gustav?”
He took a long breath, pursed his lips, clasped and unclasped his hands.

Jane knew Bill was struggling with something.
“Tell me Bill, a problem shared is good.”
“Ok, you may think this is a bit weird and certainly coming from me. You see I don’t have much time for the spiritual stuff that Karen follows. However, after our white robed man experience

at South Harting, which was a life changing experience, I am becoming different…um…a different person."
He stopped, looking at her poignantly.
"Go on."

"Well during my dreams and I think when I was awake but very quiet, somebody was whispering into my ear. Nobody you could see, but I just knew it. Like when all of a sudden you get a feeling, an idea to do something or see someone."

Jane put her hand on Bill's.
He was needing reassurance.
He continued, "Where does that idea come from? You might say we generate it ourselves through our own rationalisation, our own knowledge. Well that's true to some extent. But I now feel that occasionally we get a little help."
Jane smiled and squeezed his arm, she said, "Like using the plasma output from your engine?"

"Yes exactly. It's possible that the white robed man or a spirit may have whispered that in my ear. Sounds a bit daft really, but I feel sure we're on the right path."

She watched him, and then turned her head as approaching movement caught her eye.

The waiter came across with Bill's beer.
Bill took a long slurp, slowly eyeing the bar's occupants.
Nobody looking at them.
His mind was thinking 'all this cloak and dagger stuff, Jesus.'

"You see Jane, this project is one of hundreds being initiated around the world.
To try and find weapons that we can use against these aliens. I saw some footage of the alien contact in Los Angeles. The Americans threw everything they had against it, then used a nuclear weapon far out at sea." He paused. "We don't know if

even the immense power of the nuclear strike did the trick. It is possible that somehow the alien countered the nuclear energy with some sort of shield."
She watched him with a little admiration.

He frowned, and then continued "I reckon this monster whatever it is, needs some sort of sophisticated distraction that stops it putting this shield up."
Finally he said "All I know is that a lot of money has been found to pursue these projects. Reckon our gravity plasma gun will get a lot of focus."

Jane knocked back her drink and cracked the glass a little too hard down on the table.
She said, "Sounds bloody risky to me Bill. How do we test it safely? Christ, a beam weapon! Just like in the science fiction films."
Her expression became deadly serious.
"Your original engine design is hairy enough! If there is any failure in this…uh..weapon, a catastrophic explosion is highly likely…..and your white man will return."
The gargoyle instantly appeared on Bill's face, "Fuck…. yeah….I know. Don't worry Jane we'll see this through to the other side."

She thought, 'Bill is a conundrum, yet so deserving of the recognition that eludes him, but there's something strange. Why can't these mentor people just provide us with their weapons to engage the aliens with?'

Bill's screwed up face disappeared as he daydreamed future fame again.
Jane was thinking about what lay ahead and yet suddenly for the first time she felt calmer.
Her phone binged.
She picked it up.
Message from Gavin with a short video.

After some seconds, she exclaimed, "Oh god....Gavin saw the monster as it fought the Apache helicopters........it's being illuminated by the missile explosions....oh hell..."
She turned her phone screen to Bill to share the short video.
Bill "Jesus Jane, it's awful, what a repulsive thing, where did Gavin take this?"
Jane's anxious voice raised an octave, "It was near the abattoir where he worked. Must have been the alien we saw at the rest home. See the helicopters are being overwhelmed by what looks like some sort of black webbing. Then he said the thing just vanished into thin air."

"Bloody invisible again. You know Jane; your work on the plasma beam weapon is becoming imperative."
"Yeah, and we're playing with fire........ literally."
Bill sighed, "I know".......yawn, "time for bed I reckon."

Later, he raided his room fridge and with glee found a couple of miniatures of Jameson whisky, topping them up with ginger ale and ice.

Meanwhile in her room Jane locked her window, pulled the curtains tight and stripped to her underwear. Pushing the chair and table as far as possible into a corner, she started on some Tae Kwando.
After a few stretches, she slowly went through some hand blows, kicks and mimicked throws. 'God!' she thought 'Rusty as hell, but at least I can remember the moves.'

She glanced at the pulled window curtain, as though something might be there.

2.15 am Bill's room

Hot, uncomfortable.
Bill woke up with a start, he was dripping wet with perspiration.

Throwing the thin quilt off, he reached for a glass of water on the bedside table.
His throat and mouth felt like the bottom floor of a dirty bird cage, dry and crunchy.

He glugged the water in great gulps, gasping then uttering, “Oh gawd, I feel awful…”

He nearly switched the bedside light on, but a faint glow caught his eye.
It was over the other side of the room near the curtained window.
His mind said ‘bloody hotel rooms, always bright street lights and noisy traffic outside…’

Bill turned to see and he shot straight up in bed, his back hard to the wall.

“OH MY GAWD !…….”

There he was, glimmering in the dark.

A pale white shape, just two eyes and a mouth could be made out.
Bill shivered trying to retain his composure, this time he wanted some answers to his questions.

But he never got to ask them.

Early am. Tuesday 17th April
Two thousand feet above Sydney airport, Australia.

"Ooooh Bill!... look at that!"

Bill glanced over Jane's shoulder and through the aircraft window. Down below was the Sydney harbour complex.
Arching across the harbour, the famous black bridge looked like a toy.
Facing it across the blue-green water, stood a multiple fan of giant white shells, the Sydney Opera House.
Boats criss-crossed leaving little wakes behind them.

"Bloody marvellous Jane, I've never had the chance to get to this part of the world before and now the government pay us to come. Fantastic!"

The landing was uneventful, although a tortuous drag through customs ensued.
No food, wooden objects that might harbour woodworm or the like, or even dirty walking boots allowed. Not even a Mars Bar.

Finally they dumped their bags at the Old Fitzroy Hotel in WoollooMooloo, a suburb of Sydney and went out for some fresh air.

Bill could see Jane slowly relaxing.
He was pleased; she had been through some crap.
The girl was technically brilliant and with her maths and metallurgy skills, Jane easily took on and completed the work he had given her so far.
He mused 'They were getting along fine….well mostly.'

She was still off hand with him. The wandering hand incident on the aircraft had unsettled her. 'God' he thought 'Why on Earth did I do that?'

Reaching the busy sea front, they now sat outside a waterfront café, Harry's Café de Wheels, drinking coffee and eating hot pies, the café speciality.

Above, a crystal clear blue sky was dominated by a brilliant warm sun.

Australia's autumn.

Jane between mouthfuls said, "This fish pie is amazing. How's yours?"

Bill whose mouth was utterly full of cheese and bacon pie, just grinned, and nodded with raised eyebrows, uttering a "mmm… yum."

Right in front of them magnificent boats and yachts lined the pontoon.

Jane piped up, "See that big motor yacht near the end of the pontoon? The catamaran with the aerials and the big radar dome on top."

"Ah yes very nice."

"Well it belongs to Russell Crowe the actor."

Bill said "Really? Wow what a lovely boat. He must be loaded, all those films I guess. You ever see Master and Commander?"

Jane glowed, her eyes twinkled, "Ah, not that one, but I thought he was lovely in Gladiator."

Bill smiled, the crows feet appearing around his eyes, "Well Master and Commander is a cracking film, set in the Napoleonic era. Naval battles and more. I liked Paul Bettany as Jack Aubrey's surgeon."

"Jack Aubrey?"

"Yeah, he is the frigate Commander played by Russell Crowe. Based on one of Patrick O'Brien's historical novels. Excellent historic writer."

Jane looked out over the water, shielding her eyes with her hand against the bright sunshine "Ah… must see it one day."

They continued to watch the estuary, people coming and going. The odd yacht going off into the hazy horizon.

Bill suddenly said, “Does The Fountains of Paradise mean anything to you?”
Jane looked round and raised her sunglasses, “Um…no. Why?”
He drew a long breath, and then said, “Well I had a funny dream last night and this bloke mentioned them…”
“Not the bloody white robed man again?”
“This is real Jane, you have got to listen, because….. Well because I swear it wasn’t a dream.”
Jane “Go on.” She was searching her tablet.

Bill remained silent, he looked out up the harbour.
Seagulls screamed and swooped near a moored fishing vessel. On board, men in yellow waterproofs were sorting and gutting the day’s catch.
A bunch of gawky pelicans waited patiently on the dockside for the odd thrown titbit.

Jane spoke, “Well it says here it’s a fiction novel by Arthur C.Clarke…um.. based in Ceylon, where is that?”
Bill “Oh, Ceylon yes that’s the old name for Sri Lanka, it’s in the Indian Ocean.”
Jane continued, “I’ll send a summary to your smart phone. Something about a geostationary gateway…. whatever that is…..”
“Hmmm.. geostationary gateway. Anything else besides the book?”
Jane read on, “No other hits. They mention something about a sacred place on a mountain, um.. they build an elevator right up into Earth’s orbit.
Sounds crazy to me.”

Bill’s mind drifted, thinking all these enigmas and puzzles.
“I might get the book. Bloody odd, can’t think what the meaning is….thanks Jane.”

The Sydney Institute of Physics

Later that afternoon, a taxi took them across Sydney until the urban sprawl softened into large grassy areas cordoned by short fencing and clumps of tall, tinder dry, green leaved gum trees.
A few hundred yards up a new tarmac road, the car stopped outside a large modern building. It had a giant white sign depicting 'Sydney Institute of Physics' in large scrolling stainless steel letters.
Looking at the steel columned, glass fronted building, Bill exclaimed with a little sarcasm, "Impressive place, let's see if the inside matches the exterior."
Jane just smiled at him.

Within minutes of their arrival in reception, a young stocky man with short fair hair and a ruddy complexion came through a side door. He wore an open neck blue shirt and dark blue chinos.
"Gu'day, I'm Jake Brown, Lead Scientist on the project and you must be the famous Bill Craswell."
He shook hands warmly with a grinning Bill, who loved the accolade.
"And this attractive young lady?"
Bill quickly introduced Jane, "Yes, please let me introduce our systems expert and my technical assistant Jane Horsham."

Jane beamed, she felt on top of a wave. Her eyes momentarily locked on Jake's as they shook hands. Then Jake said "Great to meet you guys, we are so excited about the gravity array, but please come through and let me introduce you to the rest of the team."

She thought 'Excited, now there's a word.'
Jane's mind wandered, she was sizing up Jake, 'yes…very fancy-able.'

Over fruit juice and tea, Jake introduced his colleagues Riley Wilson, specialising in astrophysics, Lucas Burke

the team's brilliant chemist and Bruce Jones specialising in telecommunciations.
They announced that the Australian gravity array complex was complete and semi-operational, including the orbital one.
A stunning achievement in a very short space of time.

It was a 'needs must' project which was now awaiting Bill and Jane's expertise to do the systems testing, calibration and commissioning of the array system.
A large interactive wall screen showed a map of the south east of New South Wales, with the triangle of ground based gravity arrays superimposed.
Bill spoke, "A superb piece of positioning, you should get a sensitivity and accuracy equal or possibly better than our UK installation. Marvellous."

Jake his eyes aglow replied "Thanks mate, we really appreciate your coming out to Oz. Hope we can show you a few sights and some local hospitality."

Jane had a large smile, "You guys ok working with engineering Sheilas?"
Lucas Burke broke into a chuckle, "That's pretty much old school these days. Love it, gives colour to our field. The more female engineers the better, that's what I reckon."
Jane blushed a little, then Jake took hold of the meeting, "Ok, tomorrow we want to take you to our main base which is where one of the gravity arrays is situated. It's in Kurragong Heights, in the Blue Mountains. Say about a hundred and twenty klicks from here.
Bill did the conversion in his head, thought 'about seventy five miles'.
Jake continued, "Like your setup we have remote access to the other points of the array from the base office. So I guess we need to talk about what we want to measure."

The room went silent, the three Aussies keenly waiting for Bill Craswell to speak.
He eyed them in sequence, and then glanced at Jane with a look that said 'where to begin…'

After a little while, he spoke quietly yet authoritatively.
"Yes um…. as well as the conflict in space, during which I might add we recorded incredible results, there are other issues that have manifested themselves."

"As you know the prime objective of this installation in Australia is to monitor the portal out there. Particularly in the next few months prior to it returning close to the Earth again. Our UK installation is somewhat blind now, with reduced sensitivity and will only be directly facing the portal very early next year. Then we will have yours and the American arrays up as well as ours, to provide comprehensive measuring but also redundancy. In case one of our installations goes down."

He paused and then with a solemn face added, "Or knocked out."

Bill stopped, looked at each of the Australians in turn then slowly said, "As you guys know, there have been objects detected that were dispatched to Earth from the dying alien spacecraft. Now as we speak I hope they are being tracked.
Part of your mission is to try and detect any more that arrive near or from the portal. In fact, arrival from anywhere in space.
All we can hope for is that they distort space enough with their propulsion systems, for us for us to detect the gravity waves."

This was a long shot. The authorities grabbing the array technology as a detecting facility, but not realising how narrow was the chance of detecting these small distortions.
Jake spoke, "Bill, I guess you've been briefed, but to clarify our responsibilities, we are under intense scrutiny and direction from our governments both here and in the UK."

Bill "Yes, I understand."
Jake continued, "What this means is that once the system is operational, it must be live around the clock, seven days a week. Absolute minimal down time is allowed for maintenance or repair slots. We have a guy from the........."

Before he could finish, the door swung open and a dark suited man, with a striped white open neck shirt marched in.
"Well hello to the Brits! Welcome."
His smile was full of white gappy teeth.
Beads of sweat clung to his forehead which preceded a bald pate.
"Angus McTrae, Australian Ministry of the Interior."
He shook hands strongly with Bill and Jane.
Jake paled a little, said "I was just going to mention you Angus."
Angus took command saying, "Thanks Jake."
He stared without blinking at Bill and Jane, firing the question, "We're hoping the arrays will be fully operational within a few days, what do ya reckon?"

Bill smiled; a glimmer of the gargoyle crossed his face, "Well if all things run smoothly I don't see why not."
Angus "Good, good, and great to see a lady on the team, beauty *and* brains no doubt?"

Jane felt a little uncomfortable, replied smiling "Thank you, I'm sure I can bring balance to the equation."
A sly dig at the male orientated engineering world.

The rest of the afternoon was spent with the two teams cross fertilizing their knowledge.
Angus became a little bored half way through and left the meeting. As he got up to go he exclaimed "I'll leave you experts to it, way beyond me. Jake please brief me afterwards, later tonight. Thanks."

With a wave he was gone.
Jake turned and gave a sickly smile to the rest of them.

The afternoon disappeared as they worked together, surrounded by wall screens and computers. The white board became covered in mathematical equations.

Taxiing back to their hotel, Bill turned to Jane saying, "Very good progress today. These Aussie guys have assembled their array in record time. Katoomba tomorrow, Blue Mountains eh?" he smiled at her.
Jane replied, "Yes, they are very skilled guys. I thought Bruce Jones was a bit distant?"

"Yeah, I enjoyed working with them today, they're a great team and your maths my girl, stunning! They were well impressed. Bruce, hmmm...quiet oddball character, but this business takes all sorts. Like me."

"Ha ha...yes. Thanks Bill, I just love this job."

She felt more relaxed, feeling in control, but something was bothering her.

Then she thought about Bill, 'Just what is he up to next?'

Chapter 21

Wednesday 18th April 2018
Australian Gravity Array – Base Control
Kurragong Heights, Blue Mountains, Australia

After their arrival, Bill and Jane had spent several long days commissioning all the ground array systems.
Finally they had, via a remote link, configured the orbital satellite up in outer space, containing the fourth gravity array.
The Aussie scientists had feverishly worked with them.
A severe schedule driven by their boss was at the back of their minds.

It was a schedule of necessity.

Bill felt good.
It was wonderful to be back on the array stuff.
His mind wandered to when Conrad Thursule was alive, prior to their disastrous experiment explosion which killed his colleague a year ago.
Prior to that, he thought 'Would be just over two years now.' that they made a once in a lifetime discovery.

What an incredible time. Following the first miniature explosion test, they had published a scientific paper that took the physics world by storm.
A new and very successful way to measure gravity waves.
He had hugged Conrad with glee when they had achieved the equation solving that had eluded Albert Einstein all his life.
The ability to measure gravity waves in huge detail and incorporate them into the world of physics.

The accolades had come in thick and fast.
Even Nobel awards were mooted.

At the same time his boss Richard Armitage had suddenly became intensely interested in the array project; instead of moaning constantly about how much it was all costing.
Bill had come out of a backwater and again become his embarrassing self to all those past colleagues.
He grimaced a little, remembering his time at Aldermaston, the nuclear bomb research establishment. He wanted to test controlled nuclear runaway and the strange energies it would generate. His bosses then had a dicky fit and banned him off the project.
He thought 'and what was wrong with nuclear runaway, as long as you had total control and able to stop it?'

Still stark in their minds was the dark legacy of nuclear runaway in the Russian Chernobyl Nuclear Power Station back in the nineties. What started as a routine experiment in managing a nuclear pile when switching to back-up cooling systems, went badly out of control.
They couldn't stop the reactor core dangerously overheating, producing thermal runaway at six thousand degrees centigrade. Uranium undergoing fission, hot enough to melt all metals, concrete, you name it and then travel downwards towards the Earth's core, dissolving everything in its path.
Plus, the enormous build up of hydrogen and extremely radioactive gases that blew out the reactor protective concrete dome at the power station, south of Kiev in Russia.
Shortly after, the radioactive particles killed many people onsite. Years later the resultant cancers hit thousands of other people where the radiation had spread not only in Russia, but wind born across Europe.

"Bill!"
He turned breaking out of his daydream.
Bruce Jones, the telecoms guy, almost shouted a question.
"Bill, can I ask you about access to your UK gravity array?"
Bill came back to the present and raised his eyebrows, "Sure Bruce, fire away."

Jones angled his tall thin body, leaning against the filing cabinet near the wall.
He was quite pale, his eyes seemed to lock on Bill.
Flicking back his long black hair, he slowly said, "Can you control your array systems, say from here? Like I hear any day now they are going to send up a repair crew to fix your damaged orbital array. We could then look through the UK eyes so to speak?"

His demeanour was a little odd.
Jane caught it, she tried to remember, to recollect.
'Was it Déjà Vu?'

Bill replied, "Yes we can, with the correct security logins of course. Also they have a replacement array satellite going up. It will be a lower cost than sending a manned crew up there and that can only be done with an American Orion launch and these have been suspended anyway."
He smiled the gargoyle, "… and we don't trust the Russians to launch for us.
So it will probably be a European launch."
"Aah I see." said Jones.

His body cast a shadow on the wall. It wasn't quite sharp despite the strong sunlight piercing the room.
Bill continued, "Well Bruce, in fact with the array data files I have copied to your systems, there are some test logons, so that you guys can remotely use our facilities if need be."
Jones, "That's excellent, soon as you can. Thanks."

Jane blinked her eyes, several times.
She was having difficulty focussing on Bruce Jones. She glanced at Bill who deftly noticed her uneasiness.
A laugh from the other side of the room broke the suspense.
Lucas Burke said sarcastically, "Ha! You wait until the Aussie Space program takes off, and then we'll show 'em."

Sometime later Jones disappeared complaining of a migraine.

After that the Australian team went to a status meeting, with Bill and Jane left to grab a coffee in the cafeteria.
They sat by the window with a stunning panoramic view.
Way down below the cliffs, dark green forests sprawled dozens of miles into the distance over a murky mountainous horizon.
Jungle really and hardly anybody lived there, except all those snakes, spiders and leeches.
You stick to the known tracks and wear ankle protectors and stuff. Just in case you accidently trod on a snake…
The Aussies were naturally blasé about the local animals. “No probs, we have the antidotes. With bites from the likes of the brown snake, you ought to get the jab within a couple of hours, or you might peg it!”

Behind them in the room, the Institute Cafeteria had various sculptures and objects on display. There were odd shapes of multi faceted metal in glass domes, hovering in the air with no obvious support. The rear wall adorned with pictures of laughing student faces.
Across on the facing wall a symbolic wall mural depicting Australian aboriginal history. Cleverly and tactfully merged in, was the arrival of some Dutch and then the English settlers.
Vivid colours roared out.

Bill sipped his coffee and at length spoke, “I love that metal toroid in the air, that’s focussed superconducting magnetic fields.”
Jane said, “I know.”
Bill quickly spluttered, “Course you do! What do you make of that over there?”
He pointed over to the corner where a huge model of twisting and orbital coloured balls, all different sizes, made up a tall thin vertical tower standing on a wooden base.
Curving around and between the balls were thin silver bands of varying thicknesses.
The whole display was set in a dense three dimensional matrix of wires, distorted at various points.
He had a slight smirk of enlightenment and not a little pride.

Jane smiled and replied, “It is the latest interpretation of quantum mechanics and its relationship with gravity waves. Karen would love this place.”

Bill did not reply straight away, he acknowledged her with a little nod.
“Yeah, they are certainly pouring the money into these sorts of establishments. You know Australia is such an upbeat place. You can feel the momentum and vibrancy of the people here. They all have that get up and go for it attitude.”

‘Just like me’ he thought.
Jane changed the subject, “You notice anything strange about Bruce Jones today?”
Bill frowned a little, “Yes, he seemed a little odd. Can’t put my finger on quite what though.”
Jane scowled and said, “Reminds me of what happened to Richard Armitage before he had that seizure.”
“Yes, you’re right.... bloody weird.”

Silence enveloped them as they stared out of the window.
The orange sun just above the horizon was blanching the clouds into a deep red.

Mid morning – Monday 23rd April
Approaching Echo Point, Katoomba in the Blue Mountains

Their main work was almost complete.
Australian gravity arrays were operational and producing extremely good results.

As Bill had mooted, their system was way more sensitive than the UK setup.
He was slightly envious, but happy that he and Jane had been pivotal in the testing and commissioning.

One installation had initially proved troublesome and Jake had suggested they go on site to verify the setup. It was now operational, but needed some onsite work.
Situated about two hundred miles south of Sydney, the array was built in an area named The Rock, in New South Wales.
Bruce Jones had offered to drive them there.

Just time now to snatch a brief couple of days holiday before this last piece of work.

Jane had been somewhat miffed, at 'the three weeks' initial projection by Bill.
Looked more like two weeks at most now and the drive to Katoomba had been uneventful.
The air was warm, dusty and humid.
Thank god for the car air-con.

They pulled into the motel.
Bill "Hello there!"
A grizzled proprietor greeted them with a huge grin, "G'Day to you folks! All the way from the mother country eh?"
He then grabbed and carried their bags to their rooms.

Bill slipped a ten dollar note into the man's hand.
"Yes and loving it, I must say. Thanks mate. Where can we find a good place to eat?"
"There's Smokey Joes down the way, good tucker there."
He disappeared into his office and then came out with two fistfuls of cold beers.
"There ya go."
Jane, "Wow! That's very kind of you. Thank you."
Bill smiled, "Man, that's just what we need after that dusty drive, thanks again."

Smokey Joes didn't disappoint.
Beef steaks with a sauce to die for and chips with gravy, Aussie style.

Later they strolled towards Echo Point, a famous lookout perched on the edge of a cliff.
Jane put her arm through Bill's as they walked down the road.
He looked round at her in a surprised way.

"Bill Craswell, I want to walk with you, not just side by side. It's a long way from home and a bit lonely out here. I'm a bit nervy you know. Do you mind?"
She looked at him to indicate an understanding, colleague to colleague and the friends that they had become.

Bill replied, "Sure. Course no problem. Understand how you feel. Still it's nice to have a young lady on my arm."
He grinned cheerfully.
She smiled thinking 'He's not a bad old sort really… and not old, just needs to work on his paunch a bit.'

Together they entered a large flat stone paved area.
Right around the perimeter ran a stainless steel railing at waist height, panelled in thick transparent glass. There were about two dozen people dotted along the railing, amongst them a group of Japanese camera clicking tourists.

Beyond the railing there was nothing.

As the two of them reached the rail, Jane gasped.
"Coo, look at that Bill, amazing."
He just said, "Streauth!"

Just underneath them, the cliff dropped sheer for maybe a thousand feet.
Arcing to each side of the platform were mountain cliffs that rose vertically out of the forest floor.
Straight ahead and far down below stretched a dark green tree forest.
It sprawled all the way maybe twenty miles to the purple horizon and sure enough a range of blue tinged mountains intercepted the forest about half way there

To their right, the side of the distant cliff gleamed orange copper in the sun's rays.
On their left, rising from deep below and out of thick clinging mist, were several very tall knobbly pinnacles of rock.
The Three Sisters.

Bill just stood and took it all in.

.

At length he said, "It is unbelievably beautiful. Almost primordial."
Jane beamed "So cool Bill, so tranquil. Glad we came."
She squeezed a little closer to him.

She shivered for some reason, but it wasn't cold.
The mist surrounding the Three Sisters rocks had risen and started to swirl above the steel parapet like a white cloud.

Bill shuddered and sneezed.
Suddenly he cried out loud "Aaarh!"

The bullet had hit him hard, his jacket front perforating in a little cloud of bits.

He staggered backwards, clutching his chest, his eyes rolling white.
Falling to the ground, he went quite still.

Jane turned looking for their assailant. She ducked and quickly grabbed the railing as she partly lost her balance.
A second shot rang out. It seared through her arm sleeve and wanged off the steel railing with a metal shriek.

"Oh my GOD! We're being shot at ….oh Bill, BILL!"

Now she too lay on the floor, behind a group of disorientated Japanese tourists, some who had seen him fall.

The last thing going through Bill's mind was the song 'I'm Turning Japanese, I'm Turning Japanese Now....' he dimly wondered why?

Then a crack, crack, crack. A different sound.
The Japanese group parted, running in all directions.

Jane peered up slightly and screamed again.

"oh Mum, Dad.........oh there, THERE ..... hell...what the ?"
She paused, her stricken face frowning, "God... someone has shot him."

About sixty yards away on the wrong side of the railings, a man could be seen rolling and tumbling through the scrub bushes and then he fell down over the cliff.
Slipping out of his hand was a long rifle with a telescopic sight.

She frantically looked for black clad Chinese soldiers, their attackers in Wales back in January.

Jane turned wide-eyed looking further down the way and saw a man was running full pelt towards them with a pistol in his hand.

She had moved over to Bill, her arm holding his head up, but leaning over to try and reduce their target profile.
Jane frantically looked around, her thoughts screaming 'somebody, anybody help us!'

Bill was coughing violently, his legs shaking.

Jane looked to the sky, "Oh Lord....please help us." was all she could stammer.

Chapter 22

Noon – Monday 23rd April
Echo Point, Katoomba in the Blue Mountains

As the man drew close, he glanced over the rail and then lowered his revolver.

Jane wide eyed, her pulse near bursting point, exclaimed,
"Barry Westland! Thank god...."

The British agent stopped abruptly, replacing his gun in his shoulder holster.
The last time they had seen him was when he surprised them both back in the ESS lab.
He glanced back at the cliff edge, and then said, "Your assassin is dead, keep calm."

Barry knelt down and quickly opened Jane's tattered bloody sleeve where the bullet had hit.
"Um...let's have a look. Yes, my word you're lucky. Just a flesh wound, the bullet has passed clean through. You ok?"
Jane was shaking like a leaf, she nodded. Shock events had come again, and then she turned to look at the limp form of Bill Craswell.
"Yeah, sure I'm ok, but poor Bill... oh god Barry is he dying?"

She gasped and looked at a prostrate Bill who started to cough.
He was wheezing desperately to get his breath, his face was milk white, drained of all colour.
Instinctively Jane glanced over to where the assassin had fallen down the cliff, half expecting him to somehow have climbed back up.
She pained a thought, 'Never, never assume anything.'

Her mind kept zigzagging to their Wales attack and then back here.

Quickly Westland opened up Bill's jacket and ripped his shirt apart.

"Strange, …I can't find an entrance wound. Just this huge, red bruise mark."

Very surprisingly, Bill sat half up, shook his head and rubbed his chest, breathing heavily.
"Winded me…..ugh…." he took a deep breath… "Couldn't breath, the pain is not so bad now…what hit me?"

Westland reached into Bill's inside jacket pocket and sort of laughed, sighing with relief.
He took out the remains of a sturdy little book.
The front cover had a round hole just off centre. The rear cover had a large bulge protruding from the back.
As bits of paper fell out, Barry flipped through a tatter of pages, and then with a very sharp tug pulled out a deformed bullet.

Bill's eyes locked onto the bullet and he cried, "Oh my gawd! ….come hell and high water I would never have believed it. Oh Jesus…what a stroke of luck, but my little Physics book is ruined….."

Jane exclaimed, "Well don't mourn its loss Bill, because it just saved your life!"
He noticed Jane was holding her arm, the sleeve bloody.
Bill coughed then took her arm.
"Jane, you're hurt?"
"It's ok, just a graze. The bleeding seems to have stopped now."
Barry tore Bill's shirt sleeve off and split it to make a bandage for Jane's arm.

He then continued to examine Bill's little shattered book.
"My word, it has quite thick metal front and rear covers, no wonder it stopped the bullet."

Bill grimaced and groaned, then said "Have a look towards the rear at the bottom, there is a secret compartment."
Barry opened what was left of the back and there a tiny square hole had been cut to contain an object. The pages surrounding the hole were jagged, torn.
He said, "Nothing Bill, just a little empty compartment."
"Oh no!"
Bill turned looking around across the ground where he lay, wincing at the pain in his chest.
"Can't see it.....oh hell...was so important...must have gone over the side."
Jane frowned, "What Bill? What was it?"
Bill gave a sickly smile, the hint of the schoolboy.

"A piece of Kryptonite."

Barry Westland broke into a hoarse laugh, he caught himself.
"Yeah right Bill. A piece of Superman's home planet!"

Jane's face became contorted, half way to a laugh.

Bill had a pained expression, his hand holding his bruised chest.
"You may scoff, but it really is from a planet maybe like Krypton. A meteorite with unusual properties you know. Of course nothing to do with the fictitious Superman.....ouch."

His face contorted as he breathed heavily.
"I carried that little piece of rock everywhere with me, sort of a lucky charm."

Barry Westland stood up said "Lucky, damn right Bill. Ok, come on let's get both of you to hospital."
At that moment a blare of sirens announced the arrival of two police cars and an ambulance.

Later that evening, back at Echo Point

Jane held Bill's arm with her good one. The other in a sling.

They stood at almost the exact spot where earlier they had nearly lost their lives.
Now almost dark, the vast hidden forest expanse dropped away beneath and in front of them.
The air was cool, eerie. Thick damp mist clung to the tops of the cliffs.
Across amongst the bushes on the cliff edge, fat beetle like Cicadas buzzed their noisy symphony.
Bill had suggested that they must come back and overcome their fears.
Previously in the afternoon, the hospital had bandaged Jane's arm and checked them both over. Bill happily letting the nurses fuss over him.
Famous British scientist and all that.

Luckily he had got away with just a severe winding and bruising from the bullet impact. Much to his annoyance the police had retained the remains of his little book.
'God, what a life saver' he thought.
After they initially arrested the secret service agent, Barry Westland had remained at the station helping the Katoomba Police.

Then Bill looked over to the yellow tape around the cordoned off area.

The place where the sniper had locked onto them through his telescopic sights.

'Bastard.' thought Bill.
The police had quickly recovered the body, some abseiling down the cliff, others following the labyrinth footpath through the forest.

Jane was the first to speak.
"You know Bill; I can't believe Westland was shadowing us all the way out?"
"Yeah. Gives you the creeps. Why are governments so secretive?"

Further down in the shadows, the Aussie armed policeman had discreetly kept his distance, but was no doubt highly alert.

Bill sighed, "And the bloody sniper, Bruce Jones! Who would have believed it?"
Jane "No wonder he was acting odd back at the array building."
Bill then said, "And now we have Him."
He gestured with his head towards the policeman. "I spoke to Barry before he left with the police and he said that they knew about Jones before we arrived here.
God, why didn't they intervene before he had a go at us?"

"Maybe Bruce Jones was ahead of them, ready to pounce.
We are valuable targets you know. What with our gravity array knowledge and the plasma weapon project."
Bill nodded, "You're so right Jane. Bloody scary times. I reckon we could do with round the clock protection."

Jane held his arm a little tighter, she said, "I think I know who is really after us."
Bill turned to her, his eyes probing, "More Chinese?"
"No, don't you see. People are being affected, gullible people.
To do things that they normally wouldn't. Extreme things Bill."
"Yes…you've got something there. The world has never seen so much terrorist activity."
"What I mean Bill, is that I have come to the realisation that some malevolent force is at work. Do you not think that it is linked to those monster entities and is targeting us through people here."
Bill murmured "Does seem that way. Weird powers maybe?
Perhaps telepathic control?"

Darkness had fallen; the black sky was peppered with stars.

The cicadas' cacophony was rising to a crescendo.
Close up their rasping, scraping noise was almost unbearable.
Zigzagging in the air, tiny bats flitted their haphazard acrobatic paths.

Bill's aftershave drifted across.
She inhaled deeply, enjoying the closeness of a man.

He felt warm and emotional.
A young woman holding his arm made him feel wanted and needed.
He wasn't needy by any means, but the warmth and scent of a pretty lady was such a nice feeling.

"Come on let's get back to the hotel and have a drink." smiled Jane.

Two days later in the afternoon.

The morning was brilliantly sunny with an intense deep ultramarine blue sky.
Very warm.

A large powerful cruise boat leapt away from the dock in Sydney.
Within a minute the magnificent Sidney Harbour Bridge rose high to their left.

Jane pointed to the very top of the arch on the bridge.
"There they are, see all those little dots close together, that's people up there walking the top of the bridge."
Bill grimaced, "Bloody daft. Ha! You won't get me up there and how much did you say they each paid, two hundred dollars."

"Reckon I could get you up there." She had a crafty look.
"No chance."

The boat surged ahead, leaving a curving foam wake as it turned and passed the white shell like roofs of the Grand Sydney Opera House.

Jane kept saying, "Ooh so cool, so cool." holding her phone to video all around.
FaceBook would get a lot of activity tonight.
The vessel continued up the harbour towards the estuary entrance and just fifteen minutes later swung in towards the town of Manly, on a spit of land.
Top-market real estate, millionaires' pads.
The walk from the pier took them through the Manly shopping precinct.

Bill not taking much notice of the shops, just strolled on.
A cool glass of beer foremost in his mind.
Jane tugged his arm making him step sideways.
"Ugh."
"Bill, let's have a look in here for your book."

With that they entered a trendy second-hand bookshop, the windows splattered with posters of cabarets and gigs in town.

Inside, their noses twitched at the musty books smell.

Half an hour passed as they looked through a maze of shelving and corners, with the usual sidetracking, picking up all sorts of books and flicking through them.
Bill gave a large sigh. "No, I don't think they've got it. I've been through all the science fiction. Can't see it."

At that moment a small bespectacled woman appeared from what seemed nowhere.
"Maybe I can help? What are you looking for?"
Jane turned and replied, "It's an old science fiction novel by Arthur C. Clarke, called The Fountains of Paradise."
The woman frowned, "Hmmm rings a distant bell. Let me see…"

She went over and tapped away on a computer at a cluttered desk. It was piled with papers, odd stacks of books and periodicals.
Then she went out back.
Bill gave Jane a look to say 'let's go'.

After an age, the woman appeared grasping a faded paperback.
"There the only copy we have."
Jane "Wow! Thank you, we'll have it. How much would it be?"
"Oh, say a dollar fifty?"

Leaving the bookshop, Bill grinned at Jane. "Well done you. Now I'll see what the fuss is all about."
Secretly he was pleased as punch.
He knew this book held some sort of key to a mission he somehow had to accomplish.

They wandered on towards the wide beach on the other side of town.

Bill stopped to read a sign.
Jane eyed him.
His pallor was better, more of a ruddy glow again now. 'Had he lost weight?'
She opened her clutch bag and looking in the little mirror re-applied her lipstick, purple-red. A striking vibrant colour contrasting her deep auburn hair.

She reflected again on their past few months' experiences and how it had told on each of them individually. For her, appetite as strong as ever, but loss of sleep was dragging her down.
Unable to go to bed peacefully anymore.
Just before closing the bag, she sighed as she caught sight of the huge dark shadows under her own eyes.

A long row of tall, thick trunked fir trees lined the parade, parallel to the beach road.

They seemed to reach up to the sky and then between the trees and the sea shore stood some roofed huts dotting the sands. Welcome shade to counter the harsh Australian sun. Barbeque heaven with fitted gas supply and grills. All free to use including gas; a handsome Aussie gesture to locals and tourists alike.

Far out the waves gently rolled onto the sandy beach, a distant swash and crash.

Bill his hand shading his eyes, squinted as he looked out to sea, the water was so bright and glittery from the sun's reflection. Pale blue with patches of green, a sea that drew you. It murmured, come swim in me. Only a few people were about. One or two at the waters edge, the odd swimmer bobbing in the waves.

Peaceful, serene.

"This is a smashing place." uttered Bill, grinning as he glanced one hundred and eighty degrees around. The fir trees stretched in a line, vanishing towards the distant Queens Cliff headland. A flock of seagulls squealed and whirled above the sea waves. Jane replied, "Yes it is. Mmmm. Pity we still have our tail."

One hundred and fifty yards behind them, two plain clothes armed policemen were pretending to read a restaurant window menu.

Bill looked at Jane, "I know, but it is reassuring, given recent events."

They had endured not only police attention back at Echo Point but the press were now onto the famous duo. Local papers had them as front page news.

"*Ground breaking British scientists in assassination attempt.*"

Down near the sea, they were again arm in arm.
As they strolled along the water's edge, white surf crashed and foamed near their bare feet.
The damp sand was scrummy underneath, firm yet a bit squidgy enough for toes to sink in.

Bill turned to Jane and smiled a little, he said "Jane, this is great. Makes me feel so alive."
She smiled at him, "Pity we have to go home soon. I'm getting to love Australia."
They wandered on some more.
"Bill, I know you are very upset over July leaving you and with me, you know I dumped Gavin?"
Bill slowed his walk. He waited for more, saying a slow 'yes'.
"Well I...um…like you quite a bit. But I think we must stay friends.
Just friends. It's important. Makes things uncomplicated… you know."

His eyes probed her.
"Sure Jane, I feel the same."
As his heart dipped a little, he thought 'Complication seems to pile on at the moment.
A nice quiet nine to five working existence did have its appeal. A hot dinner and wine in the evening, banter with the woman you love.'
He pondered some more, '…seems just a distant memory now.'

Replying he said.
"I'm sorry about that episode on the plane, my hand you know. It was in my sleep AND I wasn't dreaming about you. I didn't mean…"

She cut him short.
"I know Bill, you didn't mean anything by it. Don't worry. We have so much else on our plates, it's the least worrisome thing."
She laughed out loud.

Bill smirked, "You'll just have to tie my hands together."
Jane raised her eyebrows and smiled.

He joined in and chuckled with her as they strolled slowly, arm in arm down the shoreline.

After replacing their socks and shoes, they walked back towards the high street.
Bill exclaimed, "Fancy a drink, bite to eat too? I'm famished."
Jane smiled, "Good idea." Her eyes in shadow under her peaked cap.

The Hotel Steine was right on the street corner by the seafront.
A sprawling three storey, red brick establishment that went on and on.
Rooms higgle-di-piggle, some fully furnished, others empty and bare with peeling paintwork as though waiting for the builders to come in.
Stairways wrinkling upwards and opening to dusty walls and floors.
All very quiet with hardly any staff around.
Bill exclaimed "I reckon it's an old colonial building, bit of interesting history I bet."

Upstairs, they eventually found a dark cosy bar, with soft piano music tinkling in the background.
It was filled with mixed dark furniture and a row of brown leather cubicles against the wall. The whole ceiling had exposed heavy wood beams.
Hanging lamps illuminated the bar. Their reflections from the mirrors on the large wall sending a glow that filled the room.

Bill chuckled at a large charcoal sketch on the pale brick wall.
It depicted a busy inn scene in what must have been early eighteenth century Australia. Everybody wearing their finest, or not so finest clothes.

Bill had a glass of Fat Yak in his hand.
He exclaimed, "Love this ale, goes down a treat. Didn't know you liked this stuff Jane?"
Drinking the same, she replied "Yeah It's a bit like malty English ale. I like it."

Then she pulled a face at a sign on the wall, saying "Why is that?"
In large letters it said 'DO NOT USE THE TOILET WHILE THE TRAIN IS STANDING IN THE STATION.'
Bill smiled "I think it's to do with older trains not having any collection tank. It just gets dumped on the tracks and not very pleasant in a station. Ha!"
She pulled a face, "Oh yuk…"

They were the only ones in the bar.
Bill sighed, "About time for us to relax. So glad we didn't need to be physically on site at The Rock. Just shows how with a little skill on our part and remote systems control what can be achieved."
He winked at Jane.
"I wasn't happy about our plans to travel out there Jane. Bit jumpy as you can imagine after Echo Point."
"Me too."

Now and then a middle aged woman with her hair tied up, appeared behind the illuminated counter, stacking glasses and tidying things.

Jane became engrossed in her tablet, scrolling through obscure news sites, looking for anything weird or unexplainable. She suspected the mainstream news sites were already under open or probably covert scrutiny and control. Anything 'alien' would be suppressed on the premise of causing public panic.
She sighed.

Bill leaned across to Jane, said "You ok?"
She slowly looked up, "No. No I'm not Bill. What with Wales, the alien at the rest home and then being bloody shot at, again! Here in Australia. Got the shakes you know."

He nodded. “Yeah I feel it too. Could do with some quiet down time.”
She “And that bloody discussion about a possible black hole buried in the flippin moon!”

Tears were in her eyes.
“Oh Jane.” He got up and hugged her. They held each other tight for some minutes.

Just before parting she kissed him on the cheek. “Thanks Bill. I am tempted to go back to my parents place in Scotland, escape for a while.”
She looked at him pensively. Bill shrugged his shoulders and said “I would like to say do what your heart tells you Jane. Trouble is we need you at ESS badly right now.”
She sighed again.

Later he was flipping through the battered novel, interspacing his reading with a couple of ‘ahs’ and ‘I get it.’
He pulled a face at one point, looking first at Jane who was still eyes down on her tablet and then he looked across to the bar.

The bar lady was staring straight at him.

‘Oh gawd, what is she gawping at?’ he thought.
She broke into a toothy grin, “You guys want another beer?”
Bill half laughed, his was empty, “Yes please!”

Fat Yak flowed throughout the afternoon.

Jane after a long silent period said “Bill, would you have access to satellite pictures of say specific areas on the planet that may not be available generally, you know military stuff?”
He frowned, “Um yes I have certain access for our gravity array work, geographic positioning and so on which does have limited MoD access to military satellites. Why?”
“I want to look at the seaboard to California.”

“Ah…. The nuked monster?”
“Yes. I want to see if the US navy did destroy it or if not, maybe I can spot some heat trails.”
Bill replied, “Might be able to get a logon through my laptop back at the hotel.”

More Fat Yak ale.

Bill suddenly pulled a slight gargoyle face.
He exclaimed, “HE said ‘seek the Fountains of Paradise with your new element’…and you know what Jane?”
“No, go on clever clogs.”
She studied the man.
The enigma that was Bill Craswell.

“Well in the novel they erect a cable that goes straight up from that mountain in Sri Lanka, right up into the sky and then into orbit. A cable that is about two hundred miles long and attached to a stationary orbital platfrom.”
“How the hell do they keep it up there Bill?”
“That’s the trouble and they struggled in the story to stop the cable from breaking again and again. But when they fixed it, an elevator system was attached and they just winched things up into outer space from the ground. You see to begin with, they fire a rocket up laying out a long thin, but very strong nylon cable. At the ground station they then attach a stronger cable to the end of the nylon one and the orbital station winches that up. Repeating with stronger and thicker cables each time. ”

Jane was puzzled then her face brightened, “Of course to a platform in geostationary orbit, maintaining an exact position with the ground station. Bit like Sat-Nav satellites staying in the same place as well.”

Bill was on a roll. “Yup. Although today there is not a cable strong enough.”

He continued, "We need to go back and search our metallurgy data records on the two explosions. I know Amit did some analysis, but he missed something…*like possibly a new element.* We were all focussed so much on the particle that escaped."

Jane was putting things together fast.
"Wow. Like a new material to reinforce the cable?"

Bill glowed with a schoolboy grin from ear to ear.
"Yes."

As if they didn't have enough to contend with already.

Back at the Old Fitzroy hotel in WoollooMooloo

After returning late afternoon, they both crashed to their separate rooms for a nap.
Score: Fat Yak 1 Bill & Jane 0

The evening was a slow affair.
Jane, her hair still damp from a shower, was already at a table with a bottle of red, when a woozy Bill came down. His shower not so effective.
He spotted her and smiled, working his way through the crowded bar.
Laughter and merriment drifted across.
From the other side of the long room, a two piece band on guitar and drums, were knocking out a catchy riff.
Bill tapped his feet and gave Jane a sly glance.
He said, "When we get back I want to get some more prototype plasma guns under way. Not the great big howitzer size they want, but miniature versions you know."
Jane turned to look at Bill. She had been watching a group of inebriated women, all giggling and laughing.
She smiled, "Miniature?"
"Yes. I'm thinking something a soldier could hold at waist level, akin to a medium sized machine gun, but keep it quiet. Ratcliffe's

budget has been directed towards development of the large version only. You know tank mounted sort of size."
Jane said, "Ah I see."
She wasn't really that interested.

Time for play not work.

Their table glimmered in the flickering light from a single candle. Its flame dodging the breeze coming through an open window.

After dinner they opened a second bottle of red wine.
Jane burst out laughing, "Ha… your nose has gone quite a plum colour!"

Bill became a little embarrassed; he glanced around the bar then pulled a face at Jane.
She couldn't stop laughing. He chuckled quietly.
The airplane hand incident long since forgotten.

"Christ I'm pissed Bill. But it so helps to smooth out the sharp edges of our experiences. You know what I mean."
Bill plunged in, the alcohol taking over. "You know Jane we ought to be in the same room tonight."
Jane's eyes locked on Bill's, she went to say something.
He quickly continued "Of course I mean separate beds you know, but together.
Just that we can take comfort in being close in case anything was to happen.
Strength in numbers that sort of thing. What with bloody aliens and assassins."

His passion for her was overwhelming.

She knew it and smiled, "I know Bill, that's sounds a good idea, but I'm not sure about the beds."
He frowned thinking 'oh crap…put my foot in it again…'
Jane leaned over, touched his hand and whispered quietly,

“What I feel is that we should share the double bed, you know?”

Winking at him she grew a wicked little smile.
Bill’s pulse leapt.

It was one of those moments when two people desperately crave that human closeness.
The desire to be hugged, kissed and more.

They switched to one of the larger condi-rooms in the hotel.

Early am Thursday 26th April
Old Fitzroy hotel

Bill sat in the little kitchenette supping hot tea.
His demeanour was one of serene happiness.
A beautiful and fulfilling aftermath to an intensive night of love making.
Followed by the best night’s sleep in many weeks.

In his mind his estranged wife July was now permanent history.

Jane was still in the bedroom fast asleep, her naked torso partly covered by a jinzy coloured bed sheet.

He was scribbling on his notepad, occasionally referring to his laptop.
Bill thought about the plasma weapon project and what a long shot it really was, but great in that they were trying to use his technology.

But not half as exciting as this Fountains of Paradise stuff.

He pulled up an analysis spreadsheet from the explosion database, thinking.
‘Damn, not enough to go on. We’ll have to wait until we get back. Maybe revisit the samples under new spectroscopic tests.’

His reverie was broken by a shout from the bedroom.
"Can I hear the kettle?"
Bill smiled, replied "Sure. Tea?"
"Please."

A few minutes later still in his boxer shorts, he leaned over and placed the cup on the bedside table.
Jane sat up in bed, her long red hair partly covering her breasts.
Her large nipples poked through.
Bill gulped, thinking 'My God, she is so gorgeous.'
He felt an arousal.

She took a big slurp of tea, and then plonked the cup back on the table.

Jane hadn't failed to notice how tight Bill's boxers had suddenly become.
They left little to the imagination.

"Bill Craswell. Come here Romeo."

He did as he was told.

Jane had a lovely grin, she pulled his boxers down and giggled.
"Do what you did to me last night. Only slowly and more this time."

Bill was already there, his tongue and passion turbo-charged.

Shortly, through the rather thin hotel walls, her cries and moans penetrated far.

Chapter 23

Several weeks onwards.
A summer's morning - June 2018
Chez Nous, Denmead, UK – Durgas residence

Karen had been distracted.
Do anything but the chore of clearing the house.
Her subconscious kept tugging her in different directions.

Now on her laptop, she was checking some draft gravity equations against their array data from the colossal space clash.
She focussed on a couple of the larger black holes that the Omega Centauri people had controlled with their space craft.
Ships that were over three hundred miles in diameter.

She frowned. 'How can a craft so small control the huge gravitational energies of these black holes? Small as they are, these black holes are still monsters, dragging all matter that veers too close straight into their domain….
Unless the spacecraft draws invisible energy from the portal corridor?'

Her mind went through all options she could envisage.
A huge physics puzzle.
On the visual display she zoomed in on the killer plasma beam drawn out of the little neutron star and then fired at the black alien spacecraft.
'There…'
Tiny spikes of plasma were spilling from the main beam and circling towards these larger black holes. Again she zoomed on the gravity measurements.
As the spilled plasma flew and accelerated to each of the black holes' event horizon, she could see that the massive pull of the black hole was causing the plasma to reach light speed.

The event horizon, an invisible circle around the black hole. Deemed to be the point where matter sucked in by the enormous gravitational pull, just disappears.
At the edge of this circle, even light cannot escape this pull. Hence the name, black hole. You cannot see it.

A black hole that started life as a collapsed star.

'Einstein's theory of relativity was right all along...' she thought.

The variables in her equations were automatically updated from the new data.
She watched and worked through them closely, then Karen's countenance changed, her eyes grew wide.
'There just as those tiny offshoots of plasma disappear into the black hole arena near the event horizon, they seem to split into several streams.'
She could see a sort of spillage, the plasma was flaring and burning into its component elements. Karen analysed their tiny gravity distortions.

She went cold, *"Good Lord..."*
Changes in space and time.
Briefly her heart missed a beat.
It reflected the moment when one is on the brink of a momentous discovery.
Her mind raced.
"That's it! Of course it is so obvious!" she shouted it out loud.

Benji the robot glanced up from his sitting position in her Dad's library.
"Obvious?"
"Yes Benji. Some things are just staring you in the face but you never know it."
She had a massive grin.
Benji was perplexed, "I cannot see anything staring?"

Karen smirked, replied "Guess it's a bit too subtle for robots."
He went back to his reading.

She closed the laptop and sighed, looking around the dusty room.
But her utter elation continued inside.
She thought, 'Oh my…need to check and recheck, maybe get John to help.'

Back to work here.

Karen had been emptying her parent's house, bit by bit.
It was a tearful experience with memories everywhere.
In the home she grew up in, the photographs were the hardest to bear.
Her huge, sad grief at the loss of her Dad recently and her Mum last year.

Dad's funeral had been a low key affair, only a few relatives, herself, John, Bill and Jane.

Her thoughts 'Oh Dad, oh Mum. I need you more than ever now.'
She sighed.

What's more John had gone to the USA for his astronaut engineer training with NASA.
She missed him terribly.
It seemed hard to believe that her quiet, scientist boyfriend was destined for a launch into outer space early next year.

Medically he had only recently been discharged from the head injury he sustained when the Chinese mercenaries rifle butted him in the Wales Gravity building back in January. His searing headaches had finally subsided.

Karen picked up the Blue Sky envelope again.
It had been hidden in the folder containing Dad's will. She was supposed to have destroyed it months ago.

A hidden cache of a million pounds, well one point two million to be precise.
Buried in secret places, only to be found by codes her Dad had left her, inserted in a dummy stone in the walls of Colchester castle.
She thought 'God. Dad was paranoid about this stuff, but now I see why.'
Karen slowly looked around, past the dried up potted plants, the cluttered open writing bureau and her eyes stopped at a wall shelf.
There sat a dusty figurine of the Madonna holding the Christ child, similar to the one she had at home.
Something tugged at the back of her mind.
Destiny beckoned.

Piles of clothes occupied one corner, most would go to charity.
All the small movable furniture items were assembled in the dining room, again for charity.
A few valuable pieces she kept here in the lounge for now.
The house needed to be sold; she couldn't bear to move back here.

Karen then looked down the long lounge and out into the rear garden.
Without attention everything had grown wild.
Unkempt shrubs desperate for a pruning and then the grass now too high for the little mower in the shed.
Hanging motionless was the rusty play swing at the bottom of the lawn.
Half way down, an empty rabbit hutch had long grass and weeds growing through the half open door.

Too many memories.

Then she thought about the 'known' estate and inheritance.
Her mind flitted to her half brother Angelo, whom she had yet to meet.
He had been fathered by her Dad Edward in Skiathos, Greece, before she was born.

Angelo, son of Sarra who was married to Silenos Drivas, Mayor of Skiathos.

'The island of Skiathos, where there had been secret wreck salvage by, ah yes Irving Dekker, the person who may have the third artefact, the ancient helmet.'
'Hell…' she thought, 'circles within circles.
Complexity, all these people connected in some way…'

Then Karen frowned, she remembered Lei Zhao emailing her about a secret meeting where Dekker had behaved most oddly.
Then she shivered, a tingle.
Deep inside, her spiritual strength gave a warning.

Shaking and clearing her head she turned to the robot.
His face and hair gave a human-like appearance. His synthetic skin was not quite the texture or flexibility of the real thing, especially when he spoke.
Just small minimal mouth movements gave it away.

"Well Benji what do make of that? I have a half brother in Skiathos and I have never met him."

The robot looked up from a text book he was scanning and replied, "Mistress Karen, I am unable to comment really, but maybe you should meet him?"

Benji had some human dialogue programs, which used neural learning. He would improve as he experienced more human interaction.
His main programming was military, his specific directive to protect Karen.

"Well that's a given! But when Benji?"

The robot froze for a moment, pausing as though running a long decision based program. At length he spoke, “Maybe you should have a holiday in Skiathos?”
“Damn Benji! That sounds a great idea. Only I would rather go with John, no offence you know. But he is in America now.”

Benji replied, “Non taken.”

Karen could still not get used to her body guard robot.
His damaged outer armour had been replaced and she had managed after some fierce phone calls to prise the Benji video out of Colonel Arrack Mondone.
She had watched this video of the horrific apparition that she, Jane and Benji encountered at the Riverside Rest Home. He had attacked it, but she felt sure her ancient cross somehow had been pre-eminent in repelling that awful monstrosity.
All trace of the monster had vanished along with the two Apache helicopter gunships sent to attack it and their crews lost too.

She was worried, anxious but dogged in her determination to see things through.
The authorities had slammed shut any enquiry routes. Secrets, secrets.
As well as her team, she damn well knew about the thing and the image frequently haunted her.

Soon she was to attend a major spiritual meeting with Sabrina and a gathering of Elders.
With trepidation she wondered what awful future they might reveal.
Karen eyes flitted across to the chest of drawers on the far wall.
The top draw contained the ancient sword relic.

On top of the drawers, a photo of her as a girl on a sandy beach laughing with her Mum and Dad.

It was on the beach at White Cliff Bay, situated on the south side of the Isle of Wight.
She reminisced on that wonderful time building multi-walled sandcastles with her Dad.
They had tried to keep out the advancing tide.
Salt water streaming through the moats that they had dug around their sand fortress. Sea encircling them as they laughed and screamed, madly trying to rebuild flooding walls.

She smiled.
Fun times.

Benji spoke, “Karen, can you explain the emotion ‘maternal’ to me? I am aware of most human emotions even though I am not able to experience them.”
She smiled, “Ah yes, well for you it is irrelevant. It is to do with human birth and children being emotionally attached to their parents. You see, a good example is a mother’s love.”

Benji just watched her, his pale blue eyes unblinking.
Karen continued “Difficult to explain as it is something that I don’t think you could experience.”

“I believe I understand. Perhaps I can construct a robot myself and help it to learn.”
“Very good, that could well help, but I doubt if you could form a *maternal* relationship with it.”

He nodded but did not reply.

Robots building robots. Already a fact.
Creepy in a way.

Benji jerked up and looked towards the front window; he said “Warning Karen, I sense something outside that may be a threat.”

She quickly went over and looked through the window.

Strolling down the front path was a stout postman with a large Alsatian dog on a lead.
'Strange' she thought, 'Not our regular postman and I don't think he has a dog.'
Karen nonchalantly replied, "It's the postman. Guess you sensed the dog?"

He was whistling.
A rather portly and tanned elderly man carrying his bag and wearing the post office red uniform.
She waved Benji to sit down. "No worries, I think he must be holiday cover and had to bring his dog along as well."

Karen opened the door and greeted the postman.
He had a broad smile and a brown box shaped parcel in his hand.
He said loudly "Good morning. Karen Durgas?"
"Hello, yes that's me. Is our normal postie off sick, or maybe on holiday?"

Benji started to talk, "Karen, be careful, be…"
She waved him back, gesturing behind her for the robot to sit down.

Then she turned back to the smiling postman, noticing his dog was restless.
As Karen looked at the animal it seemed not quite in focus.
She frowned.
Her subconscious signalled danger.

The postman maintained his rigid smile and started to open the box.
He did not reply to her question.
In the same moment he quickly let go of the dog's lead.

Karen paused, her calmness evaporating and exclaimed "What are you doing?"

The animal snarled, moved like lightning, and leapt towards the front door.
Karen slumped against the door frame as the animal pushed hard past her.
She turned to see the dog had leapt onto Benji, the robot's head between its jaws.
The robot was squirming on the sofa with the dog on top of him.
A sort of crunching sound followed.

She cried "Oh God!"

"He won't help you I'm afraid."
She turned back to the postman.
The man had taken an object out of the box and placed it on his head, a Persian warrior's bronze helmet.

In his hand was a revolver.

Karen staggered backwards.
Inside the house the dog was snarling and growling. Benji's camera eyes had been punctured and smashed by the dog's teeth.

She stammered "What the hell do you want?.... oh my God the helmet! You're, you're ..."
He walked slowly towards her, his piercing eyes staring through the helmet slits.

"Yes I'm Irving Dekker, Miss Durgas and it is with the greatest of pleasure to meet you."

He raised the gun.
"Do not do anything hasty. Just go back into the house."

His voice sounded a little metallic, clicking.
Something very odd was circling the helmet.
She focused and refocused her eyes.
A sort of purple haze but with faint swirling bands of black mist.

A weak beam of something emanated towards her from it, rotating with misty tiny black hair like fingers.

Her thoughts screamed 'Deja vue, hell…my dream way back in January ! oh Mother…'

In the lounge the growling dog was sitting on a still Benji.
Karen cried out "Aah!"
She gripped her cross, it was leaden, it didn't move.
Her thoughts were screaming, 'This is it. He has the power, oh god what…what has happened to Benji? How could he have been disabled by a dog?'

Dekker gestured with the revolver.
"Firstly I want the cross you are wearing. Also I want the sword. I know it's here."
She cried out "no….NOooo!"
He aimed the revolver squarely at her head, point blank range.
"I will only ask you once Karen. Your life is of no consequence to me."
Suddenly a tremendous squeal erupted from the direction of the sofa.
The dog died as it was crushed by Benji's mechanical arms.
Dekker swore and fired at the robot, then turned and fired at Karen.
Karen screamed and staggered as the bullet hit the side of her head.
She felt a searing pain.

Then something extraordinary happened.

Dekker slumped and then collapsed onto the floor.

Behind him a tanned moustached man withdrew. He then dropped a bronze statue from both his hands.
A bust of her Grandad that had adorned the hall table.

As the helmet rolled off Dekker's head, blood pooled from a horrific and fatal neck wound. He lay quite still.
Benji retracted his machine pistol, unused.
The moustached man had beaten him to it with the heavy bronze statue.

"I am sorry, I had to …he…he tried to kill you."
Karen clutched her bleeding head and shouted, "Lord... you're Angelo!"
She just knew.
"Yes, and you are Karen, Karen Durgas?"
She nodded shakily, and then she flopped down into a nearby chair.

A grating voice behind her, "Karen, I had to wait before distracting that man. I have secondary vision but it is malfunctioning."
Benji was standing, his face somewhat torn, his mechanical eyes smashed. Behind him on the sofa was the motionless limp form of the dog.

Angelo examined Karen's head wound.
"A graze it seems. The bullet passed by. Have you first aid kit?"
"Yes on the shelf in the kitchen."
Angelo quickly returned, opening the kit.
She gripped his arm looking at him in earnest, "My brother."

He smiled applying a dressing and then winding a bandage around her head.
"Yes I am glad we meet now, I um….my English is poor….wish this not happen this way. Early this year I sent my man to hunt Dekker down, to kidnap and force him to help my Greek father Silenos."
Karen looked at him, "And what happened?"
"Irving Dekker killed him or one of his thugs did."
Angelo quickly glanced down at the prostrate form of Irving Dekker, then across at the damaged robot.
"That is not a man, is machine…"

At that moment, Karen broke down. She burst into tears.
Angelo took her close and held her as she sobbed in fits.

At length she cried, "It never stops… oh Jesus save us… one thing after another."

A little while later

The police had arrived in numbers, an ambulance too.
Before they came, she had taken and hidden the helmet.

Her thoughts rang distant alarm bells, 'possibly to try and save… mankind maybe?'

After what seemed forever, the police completed their work and despite Karen's vehement protests, Angelo was handcuffed and taken with them. They also took Dekker's body and the dead dog. Flashing her MOD ID she warded them off taking Benji as he was government property and they didn't have the authority to take him.

She said to Angelo as they took him out,
"Don't worry Angelo, my solicitor will get you out. Please just help the police."
She turned to the sergeant there, "He is innocent you know, I would have died if Angelo hadn't struck Dekker. It was self defence."
Maybe not quite but she couldn't think of the legal term. 'Maybe aggravated manslaughter or something?'
Angelo just gave a weak smile and nodded.
He said, "Thank you… sister."

Karen caught her breath, her hand to her mouth, "Oh Angelo… don't worry."

The paramedic said to Karen "You need to be checked out in hospital. That bullet graze is quite deep."

After initiating plans to bail Angelo, she called John.

From Houston in Texas a worried John exclaimed,
"Karen, I must come home now, I'll get the next flight out."
"No please don't. I'm ok, just shaken up a bit. Your work out there is so important."
"I love you girl and you need me there."

"Love you too. In fact I'm coming out to you now. Maybe they can find a spare spacesuit for me?"
He laughed. "Sounds great. I would gladly orbit the Earth with you Karen!"

She replied solemnly, "As soon as Sabrina's meeting is over, I will get the next flight out."

A day later at Sabrina's house.
Late afternoon.

It was a substantial gathering, maybe thirty people.

A hubbub of talk circulated around the huge high ceilinged lounge.
The tall windows were now hidden by long purple curtains that went from floor to ceiling. Subdued lighting was beautifully enhanced with many candles burning around the periphery.

Having just arrived with Bill Craswell and Jane Horsham, Karen surveyed the room. She sensed an immense calm, realising there were a lot of people there that she had never met.

Bill's invitation due to his contact with the white robed man from Omega Centauri.
Jane because of her experience with the alien encounter at the rest home and that she worked closely with Karen.
John too had an invite, but his training at NASA precluded his attendance.

A large circle of chairs dominated the room.
In the circle centre was spread a small blanket containing numerous sacred objects that represented a native medicine circle.
A sort of compass with as many as sixteen points.
East, west, north and south denoting the main spiritual gates.

Her friends Anne Whitfield and Christine Blackwood came up.
Anne cried, "Oh Karen, I hear you've been through the wars, again?"
She eyed Karen's head plaster covering the bullet graze.
"Sure have Anne. Seems I have a destiny with death."

She turned to introduce the others.
"Bill and Jane, please meet my very good friends Anne and Christine."
Bill frowned a little, "Christine Blackwood?"
"Yes" smiled a tall thin blonde woman with slightly old fashioned attire.
She wore a tweed suit over a white frilly chiffon blouse.
"You must be John Creeson's sister? Pleased to meet you."
She smiled again.
Bill continued, "Married to the famous scientologist Maxwell Blackwood? That guy on TV recently?"

He was stating what they knew already.
She took a breath then replying said, "Yes I am and yes he is on a mission. We are somewhat different in our chosen paths. But his heart is in the right place."
"Yes I see he has revealed the Omega Centauri civilisation to the world."
"It is their belief and it looks like they have been proved right. A very rare event in this world of many religions and cults."
Bill replied, "Absolutely. We live in incredible times."

Then Steven Crowley walked in with Lei.
Karen opened her mouth in amazement, and then exclaimed,

"Steven, Lei! So wonderful to see you." but she was initially puzzled as to why they were here.
Sabrina was close by, she took Karen's arm.

"Karen, Steven is part of the circle. Look on his arm; he has one of the sacred artefacts just like you, and Lei has done some unique work in discovering the moon machine."
Karen stared at the bronze bracelet with its dull lapis lazuli stone. She instantly went shivery, feeling something very strong inside her.
She was wearing her cross.
In her shoulder bag were the sword and helmet.
Now the bracelet had turned up.

She could feel the subtle energy. *The ancient circle was now complete.*

Steven took her arm gently and said "I heard about the attack on your life Karen. How are you?"
She looked at him and his blue piercing eyes. They held something more, a depth she couldn't fathom, yet there was a connection. Karen looked into his eyes for some seconds and she acknowledged a bond, something way, way back in time. Her perception tried to fathom further.

She said, "Steven, yes it was a very close shave. Irving Dekker tried to shoot me. He was possessed by a force I couldn't even begin to understand, but I'm ok, a bit shaken up and this."
She pointed to her head wound.
Steven cupped his hand to the side of her head.
He took a particular interest and replied, "You should rest you know."
Karen experienced a feeling of warmth, a gentle flow of kindness. She smiled "I think rest is a luxury at the moment."

Sabrina announced a beginning.

As a hush descended on the room, everybody took their seats, watching and listening.
She seemed even thinner than last time.
With her face a little pale and with serious eyes, Sabrina took her place just inside the circle of chairs, standing, raising one hand.

"Thank you all for being here this afternoon. As you know events around the world have become a serious cause for concern."
She paused looking around the circle.
"A special welcome to the Elders who have travelled long and far to be here today."

Sabrina broke into a lovely smile, she turned to the circle of people.

"I would like to welcome Nokomis, from the Cheyenne people. She brings much knowledge and wise judgement."
A small elderly woman simply but colourfully dressed, with dark wrinkled skin and tied back grey hair, nodded her approval.
"Next I welcome Gad, from the Navajo people. He brings to us strength and wisdom."
A tall warrior like man wearing a light brown suit stood and slightly bowed.
He had long dark hair, deep facial features on his tanned face and eyes like a hawk.

"Continuing… please welcome Maestra, from the Shipibo people of Peru.
She brings unique healing and guidance."
A deeply tanned, black haired lady, with tribal face tattoos and wearing a simple gown, smiled and turned nodding to the circle present.
"Our fourth elder has come from Isaan, Thailand.
Please welcome Chaow. He brings deep calm and foresight."
A thin dark skinned man in a grey suit briefly stood and bowed.
With the South American and Thai Elders had come their own people to translate the English dialogue.

Sabrina took a deep breath.
Then she spoke again. "Here we have gathered with a variety of experiences and skills that we must take forward in our fight. We represent one circle of dozens that are taking place around the world."
She paused, then said,
"This is the lead circle."

Karen thought, 'I've never heard Sabrina use the word *fight*?'

"For those that have not been briefed or not able to access what we know today, I will now describe our abilities."

Quiet, so quiet.
Not even a bluebottle fly would dare to come in and make a noise.

"We must thank Karen and also John who is unable to be here. Steve Crowley as well.
They bring us one means of repelling the alien threat.
I speak of the ancient objects that link to the sophisticated device in the moon."

A quiet murmur circled the room.

"Yes, indeed incredible, but devices constructed by our mentors from far away in our own galaxy.
An ancient race of mostly a physical dimension.
They have advanced technologically beyond our imaginations."
She stopped, ensuring her message was clear and everybody understood.

"However, even our mentors have physical limitations and do experience death after a considerably long life.
These beings too, like us, have links to and honour the spiritual kingdoms."

She turned to Karen and the others, "Thank you Karen, Bill, Steven and Lei for coming forward and bringing to light these objects and their power."

The guys acknowledged their acclamation.

A lull, some whispers.
Suddenly Sabrina spoke out loudly. It made many people look up quickly.

"BUT and you must know this, these devices cannot stem a larger tide that is coming. We pray and hope that they will slow it down. Hence our group is predominantly the shamanic cause and with our beliefs, strengths and joint efforts we must hold this tide."

Anne Whitfield was puzzled, she raised a question,
"Tide? Tide of what Sabrina?"

At that moment Sabrina, small as she was, seemed to grow in stature.
She stood with her hands in the air. "It is a tide of evil and of enormous power.
This tide comes from a very distant place and they represent a threat that can turn our home here on Earth and indeed our whole galaxy, into a macabre darkness that will be forever."

Low moans and gasps followed.

The elders already knew.
They also knew of the other threat, something horrifyingly final.

Steven Crowley said,"Surely the moon device implemented by these super beings from Omega Centauri and their powerful spacecraft will destroy this fleet?"
Sabrina replied "They will try but the omens are that they may fail."

He nodded, meekly acquiescing her statement.
Karen watched him curiously.

Bill Craswell couldn't contain himself anymore.
"Well, we will jolly well give them a fight. What with the moon device and the weapons being developed that I know of, we have a chance. I have seen the Omega Centauri spacecraft capability from a scientific viewpoint and they are damn impressive. We can do the same."

His ego was leaping ahead and starting to enter dreamland. The reality was, what indeed could mankind really hope to achieve.
It seemed that in order to survive the predicted onslaught, they would have to surpass even the Omega Centauri peoples' capabilities.

Sabrina smiled, she said, "I wish I could believe that Bill."
Anne suddenly interjected, "Sabrina, I feel an impending shadow, something that contains fear?"

At that moment they saw Sabrina purse her lips hard, trying and wishing that what she was about to say wasn't true.

A deadly hush surrounded them all, as they awaited the very sombre news about to be imparted.

Sabrina continued "From my dreaming and travels as far as I dare, I have established that the beings from Andromeda are predatory. They not only conquer and assimilate physical races on worlds they reach, but they also *assimilate those spiritual worlds* attached to the peoples concerned. How they do this we do not know. It is beyond our understanding even as Shamans, as to how they are able to encounter and desecrate our most sacred domains."

Karen gasped, uttering a little cry, "Oh Sabrina…"

Sabrina turned and faced Karen, "Yes I fought to deny this. I travelled mentally with full shields to the edge of their domain. Their arcane energies are very strange and I was almost overwhelmed. Only with all my strength and that of my guides, was I able to withdraw."

Shamanic dreaming.
The ability to use the subconscious to visit spiritual worlds and to travel huge physical distances.

The electric lights had been turned off.
Remaining illumination was provided by a mass of flickering candles casting long eerie shadows up the walls and across the room.
The circle was in semi-darkness, people sitting with their faces just visible.

Sabrina stopped, pausing for breath.
She motioned to the Cheyenne elder Nokomis, who stood and took the floor.

Nokomis closed her eyes and raised her hands to the ceiling.
She uttered a quiet chant, describing a motion with her hands.

Then continuing she shuddered, her voice raising an octave.
Her voice became a little shrill.
She opened her eyes and spoke in English to everybody.

"If they come here they will assimilate our spiritual worlds, our ancestors, our guides, all that have come before us. In other words as well as our physical world, *they will absorb and enslave Heaven as we know it.*
In my limited searches I have discovered that we would all be made to suffer, shackled and kept alive… perhaps for eternity.
So they can feed off our life energy."

She let the words sink in.
There were gasps of horror.

In the darkness outside, an owl hooted.
The moon high up in the inky black sky, gave a brilliant white crescent.
Clouds drifted by, quickly changing the ten acre garden from moonlight into shadow.

Facing outwards, surrounding the garden periphery, were a dozen armed Benji robots on full alert.

Courtesy of Colonel Arrack Mondone and the UK Ministry of Defence.
It had been a frenzy of work to get them completed and in place.
Despite the initial inertia of the British government, they had eventually given way to the robots' deployment.
In addition, a company of army soldiers, about one hundred and twenty men, were deployed further out.

Back inside the large lounge and *outside of the periphery of the main circle*, were placed four chairs.
Positioned at the main compass points, North, South, East and West.
There sat Karen, Bill, Jane and Steven.
Surrounding them were numerous candles in little ornate holders.
Held in their hands were the artefacts, Karen her cross, Bill the sword, Jane the helmet and Steven the bracelet.
Sabrina raised her hand and nodded towards them.

As the artefacts were brought to face each other in the four square base of a pyramid, multiple strong beams of blue light shot out from the artefact stones and locked the devices in place.
Then faintly, the pyramid sides appeared and a purple beam emitted from the top rising to and through the lounge ceiling.
Jane her eyes like saucers, just stared at Bill, meaning 'How incredible is this!'

He returned her look, totally mesmerised by events going on.

The pyramid of light enclosed the inner circle of Elders and the shamanic group.

A few aaahs rang out.

The drumming started, followed by the synchronism of rattling sounds from many shakers around the main shamanic circle. Sabrina was just inside, kneeling on her cushion and looking up, hands raised.

She started to chant and then in a low voice, croon.

Lei had joined the spiritual circle, sitting next to Gad the Elder.
Sabrina said out loud, "We must all be the hollow bone, just allow the energy to flow through you."
Lei watched mesmerised.
This was so out of her comfort zone, yet obligatory.
The old saying came to her mind, 'In for a penny, in for a pound.'

Suddenly a draught, no a wind… could be felt passing her body.
She thought 'This is so amazing, yet it is real. I can feel it.'

Energies offered by the spiritual domain that have been invoked by the human one.
The subtle power present was indisputable.

Sabrina had paused, her look was of fear. She started to shake.
All the Elders then moved and quickly drew close to her, each with a hand on her body.
They had their eyes closed, a union of deep concentration and focus.
Bill sweated profusely watching the proceedings, his forehead scar throbbing.
Karen quietly observed, with her own spirituality probing and engaging.

Jane looked painfully at Bill.
They were both felt very awkward, yet in awe.
A totally new experience.
He caught her tension and winked.
'God Bill, you are such a rock.' Her thoughts gave way to a smile.

Steven Crowley seemed insular, eyes closed, deep in whatever.
Lei just stared into the centre.

At that moment all the candles on the periphery of the lounge blew out in one big gust.
A gust of what?

Darkness descended on the room. Just the inner circle of candles flickered.

After what seemed an age, the Elders moved back, Sabrina stood up and motioned the drums to stop. Then she indicated for the artefacts to be moved so dissolving the pyramid beams.

She spoke, "Thank you. Blessings to all of you. We have shown that together we can connect not only to the protective moon device, but to our ancestors who are showing us how to prepare our kind in the physical world, for this ultimate threat."

Sabrina then looked right around the room.
Karen saw a flicker of despair in her face.

Outside in the dark, the Benjis remained motionless, each relaying their sensory data to the American and British technicians based at ESS in East Meon.

Colonel Mondone was also watching through his bank of monitors in JPL, California.
His thoughts were dark and brooding.

'Just where the hell are those alien bastards?'

Chapter 24

One lunchtime mid - June 2018
Challenger 7 Memorial Park
NASA, Houston, Texas

John had met the astronauts who would join him in space.
Daniel Ethen, a Space Shuttle veteran and Mark Vanderbrook, a RamJet test pilot.

There were to be two manned vehicles, the first a military mission and the other his, a scientific one.
Both launching late January 2019 when the Earth on its orbit around the sun, would come within reach of the portal Crackwell.

Sitting on a bench he looked across the calm lake in the park.
A special memorial area to the seven astronauts that perished during the launch and subsequent explosion of the space shuttle Challenger in 1986.

Quiet and peaceful with a breeze ruffling the lake waters now and again.
Some large birds swooped on something in the marshes.

He smiled reflecting on the past few weeks. Talk about going back to college.
Space flight systems, procedures, aeronautics, life support mechanisms, the list just went on. Not to mention his aggressive physical schedule.
Fitter than he had ever been.
He expected the medical tests, but nothing like this.
Every aspect of his physical and mental condition was being examined.

Failure was not an option.

Yesterday he had his first weightless experience in the modified Boeing airliner.
The plane entered a shallow dive from a very high altitude and with several other would-be astronauts he floated around the cabin for some minutes in near zero gravity.
He thought 'an extraordinary experience.'

John's mind wandered to his parents, his Mum Audrey pottering in her cottage garden. His Dad Reginald, who passed away four years ago.
Reginald Creeson, a wartime radar expert, had helped John down the engineering and physics paths.
Thanks Dad.

He wondered if his Mum had a little dementia.
On occasion, she did not recognise him straight away.
Forgetful and she tended to repeat things to him between visits.

A terrible disease, the person eventually stuck in a twilight world of their own, unresponsive to people around them.
Somebody you love, dying slowly before your eyes.

John pondered, 'Need to think sometime about a good retirement complex for her, somewhere with a reputation for care.'
He felt regret at his NASA training, in that his visits to Mum would be as and when he could get leave back to England.

Then his mind changed to Karen, he smiled.
Her flight was arriving later this afternoon, giving him reassuring warmth, anticipation, after so many weeks apart.

Arrivals
George Bush Intercontinental Airport

"John!"
Karen couldn't contain her glee, she leapt into his arms.

John whispered "Missed you so much girl."
They briefly kissed and then Karen turned to a man behind them.

She beamed, "John, meet Angelo my brother."

With his Mediterranean tan and bright smile Angelo shook hands, "It is good to meet you John. I heard a lot of you."
With both of his hands John gripped Angelo's and said "Thank you. Thank you Angelo, for saving my Karen's life."

Angelo struggled with his English, "Less ah no, least I do. If I had been earlier we might have Dekker alive. But he is evil man, he… how you say? Yes he double cross my Greek father Silenos. Has ruined him."

John replied, "Well I am very grateful and it is good to meet you at last. I hope your father can recover his businesses somehow. Karen says you will be taking a holiday here?"
Angelo paused, "Ah yes. Texas. Very interesting. The Space Centre. You know I am lorry driver but I dream about space travel. I plan see the museums."
He glanced at Karen and gave a great big smile.

Then John put his hand on her head near the faint scar, he said, "Seems to have healed quickly, was it bad?"
Karen replied "The bullet graze was deep but it has almost healed to a point where the scar is fast vanishing. I have never experienced healing this quick."
She frowned, her mind going over the last few days, trying to identify something she felt. A growing awareness.

She grabbed a man in each hand and they walked out of the airport to the hire car lot.
Dropping Angelo at his hotel, she shouted, “We’ll be in touch Angelo, probably in the next day or two. Bye!”
He waved back.
After clearing Karen through security, they drove to John’s onsite NASA apartment.
He made some tea.
Karen sighed happily “Ah English tea…mmm.”
John smiled “Yes, waste of time me bringing tea bags from home. The local Walmart has all the brands.”

So much to catch up on.

Sitting down to a candlelit dinner he had previously prepared, John raised a question, “So how are our two love birds?”
Karen smiled, “You mean Bill and Jane?”
He nodded.
She said “Despite the office gossip, they are still going strong. Could be love even!”
John’s face broke into wrinkles as he laughed, “Ha… really?”

Karen, “Thanks for booking Angelo into the Ramada Inn. That should be a great base to see the sights from.”
John had a little frown, “I know he is your ‘new’ brother, but apart from a holiday is there any other reason he is here?”
Karen quickly replied, “Yes I wanted him to come. He doesn’t know anybody in England and I think he can help us. Lord knows, we need help from any quarter these days.”

John “Oh?”
“Yes. Apparently he had been tracking Dekker for some time. Dekker has a network of contacts and as we know he is or was a member of Steven Crowley’s Druid circle.”
John took a gulp of red wine then said, “Go on.”

"Angelo said that Dekker has a house in Gibraltar. It's rather remote and built up against the island mountain wall, but only a short distance from the sea.
Anyway this house contains a large underground cellar. Angelo reconnoitred the empty place and said that the cellar is a vast cavern that goes into the mountain.
He managed to gain access, as apparently he became a bit of an expert at picking locks and disabling alarms when he worked for a security firm that looked after his Dad's manufacturing sites. That was before his current job, you know, lorry driving for his Dad's business."

"Fascinating" replied John chewing some succulent steak. It dripped with yellow mustard. He wondered about Crowley and what the hell was that man really up to.

Karen "What's more, part of the cavern goes underwater and Angelo reckons there is a large subterranean tunnel to the sea."
John stopped eating. "Really! Do you know what? It could be a hiding place for…"
Karen interjected, "Yes, the aliens and their demonic control of Irving Dekker.
Angelo had a walk around the cavern. He said that an awful stench hung around and some of the ledges along the water's edge were covered in a sort of shiny slime. But nothing like he had ever seen."
John chewed and swallowed quickly, "God, he took a hell of a risk going in there. This slime, did he get a sample for the authorities?"

Karen's face went very serious, "He said he thought about it but the slime seemed to be alive and observing him, so he got out fast. Creepy eh?"

John's eyes went wide; he exclaimed "Ok, I'll alert the British authorities on the island with a warning about this stuff."

Karen nodded, "Guess you're thinking about Steven's allegiances?"
John replied, "Funny you should mention that, yes I am. Why would he have the likes of Irving Dekker and July Craswell in his Druid circle? He is very astute and must have known about their assimilation by something awful."

She was doing her gazing out of the window again.
The evening was still light, long shadows from the low sun stretching across the green grassed area outside.
After a silent few minutes she said, "Steven knows what he is doing. I spoke to him at length during Sabrina's spiritual meeting. He said he wanted to keep these two under surveillance. Apparently the difficulty was preventing them from becoming suspicious."

"Ah I see…I think?"
Karen continued, "Steven has some sort of agenda that goes beyond his Druid circle.
Lei confided in me that she believes he may have healing powers."
"Good lord… you don't say." John stared at her, "So what do you think he is up to?"
"Hard to say John, he is very secretive, yet he fully participated in our artefact and spiritual session. I sensed only good in him."

"Hmmm, still… maybe we should watch him."

Karen's attention had wandered over to the wall which held a large picture of a Space Shuttle launching from Cape Kennedy spaceport.
She said, "On another subject, your NASA meeting tomorrow?"
John looked at her, "Yes?"
"Are you going to mention the armada of alien spaceships coming from the Andromeda Galaxy?"
John pulled a face.
He said "I think I must. Trouble is I have no evidence to support it, only our apparition the white robed man."

John's eyes probed Karen's for ideas.
She thought deeply. After a few silent minutes she replied.
"You said they have invited the astrophysicist Louis Redmond? Surely his observations of the cortex within that gas jet from their galaxy black hole, will lead you in?"
He replied "That would be a good starting point. If only our gravity arrays could measure that cortex and prove it is a tunnel right across space from them to us. No chance, not with the miniscule sensitivity the array would have at that range. "
Karen brightened up, "Ok. If… and they will scoff at your prediction but what if they choose to ignore you and you are proved right? Can they afford to do that? Maybe they can't. You just need to be sincere John, admit it is difficult to prove but you know this to be a fact and to ignore it may not be an option."
John "Yes you're right. I will have done my best to make them aware. After that the ball is in their court… if they choose to play. Hell the fate of the Earth is at stake."

Karen finished the last of her wine; she said "I know. It seems crazy that a year ago I was comfortably in teaching, with my biggest challenge being the marking of piles of children's homework over the weekend.
And you John, trundling along in ESS, fiddling with your gravity arrays.
Now we're like in the middle of espionage, alien attacks and God knows what!"

John nodded and said, "Yes a peaceful, no stress life seems a distant memory now."

He turned on the TV for the late news. The alien incident at Los Angeles was still the top story. Various photos, mostly long range from people on the beach, decorated the rear of the newsreader.
He continued, "*...and the latest we have is that the monster or whatever it was has disappeared. The US Navy have issued a statement on their nuclear attack out at sea.*

Quote 'It is with near certainty that the alien has been destroyed. Our fleet have been scouring the region and no sign of the adversary has been detected."

The backdrop changed to a tall thin mushroom cloud hanging over the ocean.

John shook his head, "Hell, deploying nuclear weapons is so crazy here on Earth. That explosion probably killed all marine life within a five mile radius. They did say it was a low radiation device and that the residue fallout is of little concern, but even still."
Karen "Serious stuff, do you think more nukes will be used?"
John grimaced, "Possibly."

They both watched the news bulletin change.

"A survey has shown that church congregations have significantly increased in the last few weeks. Possibly driven by this fear of the unknown, people are turning to find a faith. In another report, supermarkets are struggling to replenish their stocks after waves of buying. These are mostly essential items like toilet rolls, and long date food stocks. This is despite the ration controls brought in by the government."

They both continued to watch, then Karen sighed "Enough of this. It was a lovely meal John, but time for bed. I'm shattered after that flight."

Sleep came quickly for both of them.

In the morning they stayed in bed a little too long… enjoying a desperately missed lovemaking session. Of no matter to them, but the solid walls mostly contained their noisy passion.

Not surprisingly, John arrived late for his NASA training.

GU Room 2, Houston, Texas

Gail repeatedly crossed and uncrossed her legs.
She just couldn't quite sit still.

Arrack Mondone had been especially attentive last night in bed and she still had that lovely feeling.
She looked up at him as he stared at his laptop.
He sensed her and turned around.
"You ok Gail?" he felt a warmth, a knowing of their wonderful relationship.
She smiled her beautiful teeth, shiny red lip gloss contrasting the white.
Her outfit was deliberately conservative. A high neck navy blue blouse, adorned with a simple necklace and faint pin stripe black suit.
The forthcoming meeting would be tough and high powered.

Not like her garb last night.
Then she had worn very little, just some skimpy lace and heels.

Her jewelled eyes locked on his, as she leaned across and whispered, "Just fine Arrack, you naughty man."
He grinned, his eyebrows flicking up as he turned and glanced over to the other side of the room where Ming sat, still glued to her laptop.

Mondone gave Gail a wicked smile, winked and cleared his throat.

"Aarrh umm....Ming?"
"Yes Sir?"
"Have we any more from Trevor Chuan's rep on his no-show?"
"Not a whisper sir."
Gail returned to leafing through her folder notes.

Mondone replied "I know you did some investigation into his background which seemed all above board, but I'm very

suspicious of that character. Remember you mentioned way back about the RamJet fuel control modules manufactured by his corporation Arragon?"
"Yes, they still have the contract and we have received a new batch."
Mondone paused, his thoughts running through the scenarios.
"Can we alter the telemetry interface so that we have unique control of the modules?"
"I can investigate it Sir?"
"Ok do that. The last thing we want is sabotage. I will contact the Orion Project people and make them aware too."

Their planned trip to Amboise, France had been cancelled at the last minute.
It had been a chance to talk via Chuan to the Chinese, about their moon base knowledge and possibly getting some idea of their intentions concerning the latest outer space events.
In return, the dangling of British Gravity Array technology.
Not quite protocol but Mondone had been pressed to use this carrot by up on high.
If the Chinese could not obtain knowledge by foul play using their covert submarine, then perhaps by fairer means through negotiation.
He was rather relieved when Trevor Chuan's agent contacted them to say Chuan could not attend the meeting due to a sad death in his close family.
Bob Redford, CIA had discovered a brick wall Chinese reluctance to discuss anything about their base on the moon.
How useful family death's can be...

Mondone suspected they would have been offered disinformation and he would have given away some vital secrets for nothing. He hated the murky world of corrupt politics, two faced diplomacy and clever but empty words.

Ming said "Was a pity Sir. I so wanted to see the Leonardo da Vinci Museum there. Apparently it's based in his Chateau in the

town, where he lived the last few years of his life after being exiled from Italy."
"Is that so?"
"Yes, ostracised by the Papal decree rejecting his ideas and threatening his life."
Mondone smiled, "You are a mine of information Ming."
Ming grinned, "Hobby of mine Sir, history was one of my subjects at Uni.
Did you know that he was a confidant of the French King Francis I. Apparently there is even a secret tunnel from the King's Amboise chateau to Leonardo's.
Leonardo was able to sneak along the tunnel into the King's chateau undetected. How fascinating is that?"

Arrack Mondone chuckled, "Sure is Ming. Well, we should do the trip one day."
He turned right around so his back was to Ming and gave Gail a slow wink and pursed his lips.

Gail flushed a tiny bit, thinking, 'What is this man doing to me?'

Her leg movement continued.
At length she excused herself and went to the bathroom.

NASA Mission Briefing Room 3, Houston

Michael Swaine the New Projects Director, looked around the table.
He was in a bad mood.
His BMW Sedan had been stolen and he had taken a cab in.

Present:

Michael Swaine.

Colonel Arrack Mondone.
Mondone's Admin PA Gail Letchford.
Mondone's Technical PA Ming Zhao.

Air Force General Webern.
Vice President Enzo Fontana.
White House advisor: Cosmologist Heinreich Stuttland.

RamJet mission pilots: Daniel Ethen and Mark Vanderbrook.
UK Physicist & trainee astronaut engineer John Creeson.
Orion mission astronauts: Jack Wilson, Rickki Targalo and Ray Kingley.

Some NASA advisors and engineers.
French Cosmologist Louis Redmond.
CIA Director Bob Redford.

Most were already seated around a large black wooden table.
Ming stared momentarily across at her ex Rickki Targalo.
He briefly smiled. She didn't return it.

Swaine stood at his position and cleared his throat, looking at his wristwatch.
Everybody took their seats.
He introduced the new Vice President first then everybody else.

The Vice President, Enzo Fontana stood up, looking around the entire table.
He was in his sixties with a full head of silver hair, his Californian tan contrasted dark against the white shirt and light grey suit. His hands were joined and he flexed them slightly and deliberately outwards.
He had a voice like gravel.
Immediately some people thought about the alleged Mafia links he had.
None proven.

"Ladies and Gentlemen. Today, here at this meeting I welcome your views, your professional advice, debate and most of all, your complete commitment to this nation's cause. I have been tasked by the President to provide this nation's focus to… and…" he looked directly at John Creeson, "through the British Government their support, to make these NASA missions a success."

John felt a bead of sweat run down the back of his neck.

Enzo continued, "I cannot stress just how important all you guys are."
He paused, took a breath. A master speech maker.

"There are many possible outcomes as we have no idea what the other side are doing. Not that I mean our good friends the Russians or Chinese, but those out there."
He pointed out of the window and up at the pale blue sky.
"We have to be on our toes and able to change plans at the last minute. Mankind's future may depend on this very flexibility."

Silence engulfed the room.

"General Webern, please continue, thank you."

The Air Force General stood and motioned to the officer controlling the room's support equipment. The lights dimmed and the giant wall screen lit up.

"As you can see Ladies and Gentlemen, we are planning two missions next January.
One will be shall we say, quasi-scientific and the other military. These missions will require a total of four launches. It goes without question that this information is highly confidential and remains within these four walls and I don't have to remind you that the consequences of any leakage are extremely serious."
He stopped and sternly looked around the room.

John thought about Karen. 'Damn him, she will want to know. Anyway I'm a British citizen with rights.'
Then his mind drifted cynically. 'Rights. Yes, like *no rights…*'

Webern continued, "NASA will launch an Orion based vehicle containing a manned command module. A previously launched unmanned heavy lifter vehicle will deploy three weapons and the gravity cluster detonation modules.
Two of these weapons will be nuclear X-ray devices. The third is still under wraps.
From the command module you guys will control these devices, their final deployments and detonations."
He looked over at the Orion crew of Jack Wilson, Rickki Targalo and Ray Kingley.

"Another unmanned launch will deploy the US Space Based Gravity Array…and then a second manned vehicle will be launched. It will be based on RamJet atmospheric engines, then a Gravity engine to thrust it out of orbit. The men in the command module here will control final positioning and activation of this array.
Then the gravity cluster unit will deploy some of its gravity 'bombs'.

For the uninitiated, John Creeson can assist you here if necessary. These gravity bombs are tiny explosive devices scattered in deep space that when activated can generate micro gravity waves to enable the gravity array to 'see' what our extra-terrestrial folks are up to. Following this deployment, the array command module will remain on station and react, as and when the situation changes or deteriorates."
He looked over at John Creeson and Mark Vanderbrook.

John was perspiring even more. His whole shirt was now rather damp.
He thought 'God, wish I had the cool of these astronaut chaps. *Deteriorates... my foot, that's when the bloody aliens appear.*'

General Webern quickly moved on.
"The main objective is to use the Nuclear X-Ray detonations to close the portal as soon as it is within reach. If we succeed then any alien craft cannot exit it.
The AnGax as they have now been called, may exit at any time. However, the range of our vehicles prohibits an earlier launch so we must wait until the portal is closer.
The detonation also means that our and I shall say for now, our 'guardians', may not be able to exit either. The Nuclear X-Ray for those not familiar with this device is a weapon initially designed during the Ronald Reagan SDI era."
The old Strategic Defense Initiative to disable incoming Russian missiles from orbit with a powerful X-Ray beam.

He paused making sure all present had his attention.

"A substantial nuclear explosion is directed towards this grid array which transmutes the energy into highly focussed and extremely powerful X-Rays."

Louis Redmond looked hard at John.
A little previously, Karen had confided in Louis about the white robed man and his prophecy.

Webern "We know that the Russians and Chinese have not been sitting on their backsides. They too have offensive plans. The President has confided at the highest level to them that we intend to close the portal, solely and with no intervention invited."

Michael Swaine spoke up, "Can we assume that these countries will not intervene anyway?"
Webern grimaced "The understanding is that if we fail, then they will deploy against the portal or indeed at anything that threatens the Earth."

Heinreich Stuttland suddenly burst out, "Are we not totally reliant on these super beings and their spacecraft to protect us from an AnGax attack? What chances have we, against these awful beings with their advanced weapons?"

Mondone thought, 'Damn right, too feeble. Yet mankind will try every avenue if it's a fight to the death.'
Then he reflected on the massive manufacturing ramp up of Benji production.
A thousand robot soldiers a month at the moment, but not nearly enough.

Webern replied, "Then we must ensure we close the portal."

John Creeson nearly bit his tongue. He stood up and took the stage.
"May I interrupt?"
Webern stopped and waved John to speak.
John spoke loudly and solemnly "There is something I must convey to all of you now. It concerns this alien threat."

All eyes swivelled towards John.
"I cannot provide evidence of this but I know it to be true."
He paused, took a slow deep breath, then said, "Sometime during January next year, when the portal draws closer to the Earth, an armada of alien ships will exit this portal, or possibly nearby. I

am not totally convinced that they need the portal to arrive here."
Swaine piped up, "How do you know this? Have you seen them via your gravity array?"
"No Sir. It was through a manifestation of one of the, as you called them 'super beings' our guardians. He warned us of this and that they, these beings from the Omega Centauri system would attempt to thwart the alien armada. We must, I repeat MUST NOT attempt to close the portal, as I sincerely believe they are our only hope."

Swaine turned to the others around the table, "And has anybody else had this vision? Can we corroborate this information? And did we not see the black asteroid ship exit from this very portal?" he had a smirk on his face.

Louis Redmond interrupted. "I know for sure that an extremely long gas plasma jet originates from the centre of the Andromeda galaxy where these aliens are purported to come from. Using the Aurora probe we determined the existence of a stable cortex within the jet, potentially a corridor which comes right across the gulf between their galaxy and ours; and possibly, I say only possibly, connects into the portal corridor here."
He paused looking at Swaine for an ok to continue. Swaine nodded.

At this Louis, using the screen remote, brought up the Aurora satellite pictures.
He zoomed in on the plasma jet from the Andromeda Galaxy black hole. A jet over two million light years in length.
A monstrous distance.

Everybody at the table stared at the tiny worm like blue thread.
Then he enhanced the image to a small part of the plasma jet.
"You see a faint white line within? We believe that is a corridor and anything travelling along it will be able to travel many times faster than the speed of light."

General Webern interrupted, "How do you know this?"
Louis replied, "I worked with Karen Durgas, the English physicist. She proposed a huge distortion in space-time along the corridor. This is caused by the enormous energies emanating from that black hole."

Webern scoffed, "Proposed!"
Louis glared at him. "I tell you now, that you cannot afford to reject this and also that this corridor may not actually exit at the portal, but somewhere not far away from here."

John added, "I know it is a tall order for you people to believe this, but to ignore it is folly. From what I was told, the armada will be a large number of giant ships, perhaps as many as a hundred."
The Vice President kicked in, "We must have more than conjecture. The fact is our instruments showed the alien ship coming out of the portal. How about these guardians turn off their corridor and so deny the AnGax aliens access to us?"
He looked directly at Heinreich Stuttland.
Heinreich cleared his throat and said loudly in his strong accent "Mr Vice President, how do we know that the so called guardians have another agenda? Or indeed are somehow working with these AnGax aliens? Or incredibly they are one and the same, fooling us into submission?"

Arrack Mondone joined the fray, "I support John Creeson and that we must allow the portal to remain open. We cannot afford to ignore or cut off this help from afar."

General Webern retorted, "How the hell can you know this? Speaking to ghosts too perhaps? Well please reveal to us this 'super being' contact you have!"
Before John could reply, Mondone visibly angry, gripped the table edge and raised his voice, "Sir, we must consider this aspect and if we can prepare on an unprecedented scale to support the Omega Centauri defence when it arrives, then we have a chance, but to ignore this, puts humanity in great peril. I….."

His face froze with his mouth open. They hung on his words.

Mondone stopped speaking and clutched his chest.
He slid sideways and then down off his chair, crashing to the floor.
Gail screamed, pushing her chair back and falling to the floor to grab Arrack.
She cried "Arrack oh god no.........HE'S HAVING A HEART ATTACK!"

She rapidly loosened his shirt collar and propped him against the chair, taking his pulse. He groaned then fell unconscious. She shouted "Get the medics in... ...QUICKLY!"

Gail held him. He had gone very pale, his head lolled to one side.
Ming ran over. Together they removed his jacket. She tried again for a pulse.
Nothing.
The room was organised chaos, as people ran in various directions.
Shortly, two men in medical uniform ran in carrying their CPR kit.

Frantically they worked.
One muttered, "There's no pulse."
They started to massage his chest.
Gail clutched her hand to her mouth, tears filled her eyes, "Oh God, please no..."

"Stand back!"
They clamped the electrodes to him. "CLEAR!"
The electrical shock suddenly arched his body upwards.

Nothing.

"Again.....CLEAR!"

Mondone moved and then went limp.
No pulse.

The med shouted, “Adrenalin – one mill!”
It was one of those moments when things happen in slow motion.
People seem to be moving in a blur all around.
Yet you are frozen in time.
Gail clasped her hands tightly, she knew adrenalin might cause brain damage.
Tears streamed down her cheeks.
Ming could see more than anguish in Gail’s eyes.
She saw love.

People shouting, waving somewhere in the background.

Then silence.

“Again.....CLEAR!”

An agonising wait, more heart massage.

“There…a pulse…weak, but it’s holding.”

Gail gasped, “Oh Arrack… hold on baby.”
He remained unconscious.

After what seemed hours, but in fact only minutes, a portable bed was wheeled in and they gently lifted him onto it.

Outside Gail got in the back of the ambulance and it drove off, lights flashing.

Back Inside.

Michael Swaine spoke,
“Ming, I know you wanted to go with the Colonel, but you are needed here.”
She had a pained look, “Sure Sir.”
“He is in good hands and I know you prepped today with him, so I want you to take his seat.”

The meeting reconvened and Michael Swaine briefly uttered his concerns about Colonel Arrack Mondone and then they moved on swiftly.

The military missions would go ahead.
Closing the portal remained top priority.
General Webern then addressed John directly, "John, tell us about your ancient devices and how you believe them to operate."

John was aghast yet it was not unexpected.
The existence and power of their artefacts was known amongst high circles.
However, he was in no mood to be frittered with.
He slowly stood and looked first at the Vice Pres and then Michael Swaine, before addressing the table.
"Let me be very clear on this. I understand the importance of the space missions and my role. It is quite possible I may die up there."
He waited.
The room felt colder.
John continued "The artefacts are real and have an un-Earthly capability to link to a large device in the moon. This provides a screen of sorts and a defence against these aliens. The evidence is compelling as seen during the space conflict and twice more. Once in the UK against a rogue alien being and again on a Los Angeles beach."

Enzo Fontana spoke up, "Thank you for enlightening us. I understand this is not an easy issue to bring to this table."
John turned, "It is my conscience Mr Vice President. I will bring only the truth to this audience. I am not a guy to fabricate such stuff. My integrity as a scientist is at stake."

He looked directly at Bob Redford. The CIA man cocked his head with a slight chagrin, knowing his mission to unearth the artefact mysteries had stalled.

John continued "I know that the powers that be are very interested in these devices.
However, for now my friends and colleagues are determined that they remain within their possession. Yes, mankind does have the right for these to benefit everybody and that is currently what my friends are endeavouring to do."
General Webern exclaimed, "and what really gives you people the right? Surely they need to be part of a military force and under the necessary jurisdiction?"
"No sir, they cannot currently let that happen. In due course they may do this."

John was emphasising 'they' to distance himself and so not jeopardise the missions, but his allegiances were being tested. Trying to put the portal closure attempt to the back of his mind. Instead his control and focus of the space gravity array data back to Earth was his primary mission. His role was to support the space gravity array, in providing the utmost detail of alien threats in the hours of Earth's most worrying crisis ever.

He carried on "For now let me emphasise that any attempt to retrieve such devices from my friends will result in the devices' destruction. We have discovered a way for the artefacts to self destruct."

A lie.

With the most serious face he could muster he glanced right around the room and then sat down.

A sort of grunt came from the General.
Michael Swaine quickly intervened, "That may as be John Creeson and we need to talk this through off-line."
The Vice President in a commanding tone said, "Thank you John. Shall we say it would be prudent that we provide any help you need? And in return your cooperation is most welcome." His stern look said it all.

After the meeting Ming privately spoke to John and Louis.
"Well we tried. Guess it is out of our hands now.
I really have a bad feeling about you going up there in outer space John."

John suddenly felt enlightened, strong.
A resurgence of direction and hope.
He replied, "Don't worry. Whatever energy the Nuclear X-Ray devices can project at the portal, I doubt if they will close it. Imagine the colossal energies required to set this portal corridor in place, from twenty thousand light years away.
All I believe will happen, is that the portal mouth will reconstruct very quickly. Think of when you prune a rose back. You severely chop it, yet the roots are strong and push new growth back fast in the spring."

Louis smiled, "For sure. A strange but good analogy John."

Ming said, "I need to go to the hospital to see the Colonel. Just had a text from Gail."
John raised his eyebrows.

Ming sadly looked at him, "They're trying to save his life. He is in emergency surgery right now."

Chapter 25

A late Saturday afternoon – mid September 2018
The Ship Public House
Langstone Harbour, UK

Bill exclaimed "Where did the bloody summer go?"

He turned, looking at Jane.
She was dreaming, in a daze of sorts, looking across the sea water at the Royal Oak pub opposite. Next to it, the house with the black Windmill tower, rising from the shore on brick stilts. They were sitting outside the Ship on one of the benches under a marquee cover, near the sea wall.
It was warm, a gentle breeze coming from the west.
The Royal Oak was busy with people sitting outside in front of the white washed walls. Others were walking their dogs past the Oak and on behind the Windmill house following the coastal path.

Jane replied, "Yeah, think we've been spending too much time at work. Weekend overtime pay is welcome but it doesn't make up for precious spare time."
Bill said "I know. Our projects have been full on and I don't think we'll get a decent break until Christmas."

Their romance was now office knowledge.
Bill happy, despite being subtly being ribbed by his colleagues about his very young partner.
He didn't care a hoot. Jane was the woman who made him feel so good these days.
Bit of a handful at times and she was well able to give some stick.
A smouldering firebrand, but he loved it.

She asked a question, "What do you think will happen to us Bill?"
"Happen? Um …why what do you mean?"

"Our age difference must make you wonder? You know. I might have a roving eye for younger men."
She gave him a wicked look.
Bill took a gulp of his beer, slowly placed it on the table and took a deliberate slow breath, then said. "That's fine Jane. You wouldn't be human unless you did. But you know I am deeply fond of you and I treasure what we have right now. The future as we know is so uncertain."

He had an almost fatherly smile and squeezed her hand.
Jane leant across and kissed him, her hand on his stomach.
Bill was leaner and fitter.
The dusty mountain bike that July bought him months ago had been cleaned up and seen a lot of action lately.
His paunch was going and his waistline too.
He felt healthier than he had been for years.

She said, "Bill, it is only you I have eyes for. You have what it takes, a get up and go attitude. Sod them all sort of approach! You're the man. "
He laughed, "Thanks. You're lovely Jane. Trouble is my attitude has got me into some deep waters in the past."

Jane sipped her vodka and said, "You must meet my parents you know. It's been quite a while since they knew about us."
Bill's heart skipped a beat.
He thought 'how old might her Dad be?'
Replying "Yes definitely. Maybe have a little break in Scotland at the same time?
Just how old are your parents?"
She looked at him seriously.
"Well Dad is fifty eight and Mum a year younger."
Bill gave a little internal sigh of relief. His forty two years gave a bit of distance.

Abruptly they were distracted by the roar of a classic motorcycle as it entered the pub car park.

Bill exclaimed "Aha!" and waved.

The helmets came off and the leather clad couple sauntered up to their table.
Jane beamed, "Oh Karen, John… so lovely to see you guys."

John replied, "Likewise. You folks like a top-up?"

After John came back with a tray full of drinks, Bill said "John how long have you got before they whisk you back to the States?"
"Two weeks Bill."
He gulped the ale, smacking his lips. "mmm …I've missed this."
Karen her eyes twinkling replied, "And he is all mine. Sorry all holiday, we plan to be as far away from ESS as possible."
"Don't blame you." laughed Jane. "Ratcliffe is becoming impossible."
John frowned, "Is he still micro-managing? You know wanting to know everything that's going on? And when you do tell, his eyes just glaze over."

Karen laughed, "Well you do launch into the most technical stuff when he does ask."
Bill piped up, "Good that he fronts the politics and generally keeps that away from us. He has his uses and now he is distracted which is a good thing."
John "Distracted?"
Jane laughed "Yep. He has a young student woman doing his filing, admin… and little extras." her eyebrows rose.

They all chuckled.

Jane knocked her drink back, "Another I think. Note to self, drinking more alcohol."
They all were, except Karen.
Much welcome anaesthetic to numb the coming months.
"and where's Benji?"
Karen smiled.

"I left him cooking the dinner back at my place. I didn't want a bodyguard robot joining us today. Sometimes I wonder how much observation data is sent back.
Our privacy is so important especially these days."

Jane "Cooking, really? That sounds great, what a boon."
Karen replied, "Yes saves time although he's not a master chef by any means. Even with access to myriads of recipes on the web, he is rather clumsy."

"Like knocking things over or leaving the gas cooker unlit?"
"No, he is safe enough. The Colonel sent a housekeeping and cooking update to his software routines, prototype code he stressed."
Jane stared amazed; she said "Hey I want one of those."
Karen "You probably will get one sooner rather than later I reckon. I have him doing a beef and vegetable slow cook. Just cut it all up, a sachet of stock and a few herbs thrown in. Simple stuff really."

Then Karen burst out laughing.
"Only trouble is I had to put him right just before we left. You see he was peeling some parsnips and then was trying to peel a cork handle that was nearby! I had left it on the kitchen counter the other day as the bottle opener end had come off. What a laugh."

They all joined in, giggling and laughing.

At length Karen spoke, "I treasure these times. Good friends and all that. I try to be optimistic about the future but …I struggle…" she faltered and stopped talking.

Bill quipped, "have another Karen, you on the Chianti or is that Rosé?"
"No it's cranberry juice actually. I've not had any alcohol for a month. Juice would be good thank you."
Bill looked concerned, "You ok Karen?"

"Perfectly Bill. It's just that my spiritual side is much better off without it."
John exclaimed "Another ale for me, it actually helps my spiritualism!"
Karen poked him playfully in the ribs, "And you wanted to join me."

The afternoon wore on, John completely forgetting they had to ride the motorcycle home. Karen too. Their minds on many other things.

She started to think about Christmas.
'Would be a nervy one for us, knowing what is around the corner. Wonder if people generally have the same apprehension? Probably not… they don't know about the armada.'

Then across at the sea wall a guy's phone started to ring.
The ringtone was an old song, a Christmas song.
'There's a coincidence.'
Karen screwed her face up then remembered it, 'A Spaceman Came Travelling'.
She tried to remember the singer, 'Oh hell I know this…'

Then it came, 'yes… it was Chris De Burgh'
Quickly she searched for the lyrics on her smart phone and then quietly played the song,

A spaceman came travelling on his ship from afar,
'Twas light years of time since his mission did start,
And over a village he halted his craft,
And it hung in the sky like a star, just like a star...

He followed a light and came down to a shed,
Where a mother and child were lying there on a bed,
A bright light of silver shone round his head,
And he had the face of an angel, and they were afraid...

Then the stranger spoke, he said "Do not fear,
I come from a planet a long way from here,
And I bring a message for mankind to hear,"
And suddenly the sweetest music filled the air...

Chorus:
La LaLa ... La...
Peace and goodwill to all men, and love for the child...

Again deeply inside she felt something immense was going to happen.
Suddenly her thought trail was broken.

"Cracking ale mmm…tthis…is some mm brew.'
John was slurring his words. He had a silly grin on his face.
Karen sharply said, "Hey you're pissed. We can't go back on the motorbike with you like that?"
She softened, "You deserve a few ales John, I guess we must make the most of these 'happy' times."

Bill laughed saying, "Well my van is parked over there and I reckon we can get your bike inside and leave it there. Taxis back all round later?"
He continued, "How's the would-be astronaut?"
John smiled and took a deep breath, trying to clear his muzzy head, "Well mmm I've been through some amazing things. A little while ago they had me ah..space walk training."
Bill "In the tank?"
"Yes, you know, the huge water tank at Houston. It's probably the largest, deepest swimming pool in the world. They have a mock up of part of the International Space Station..nn..mm in it and the astronauts float about underwater practising stuff, you know."
Karen became serious, "They want you to space walk outside your command vehicle?"
"Well it is precaution…um precautionary. Need to be able to do repairs to any of the gravity array modules if they go down. That

sorr of thing. The spacesuit is quite cumbersome, takes a lot of gettin used to."
Bill said "How are you coping with the systems and procedures?"

John paused, he sharpened, yet all of a sudden he looked very tired.
"It's a gruelling schedule. There are times when I feel I just cannot cope with it all.
They have virtual reality simulations and take you through… um… no end of emergency situations. I ask myself if I'm really cut out for it, but the pressure from NASA and here gives me no option but to continue." Hic.
He yawned.
John's head was nodding.
The return to English ale had taken his body by surprise.
Jane chipped in, "Yes but you will be up there in deep space. Sounds amazing to me. When you get back you will be such a hero."
Bill thought, 'Wouldn't get me up there.'

The awkward silence was sudden.
Jane's words had hit a nerve.
'When you get back...'
What they were all thinking was '*If he got back...*'

Jane sensed the mood and quickly she changed the subject.
"Any more sightings of the white robed man?" she jested.
They all glanced at Bill.
He shrugged his shoulders, "No, not a thing. Could do with some more guidance now, like what are these beings up to?"
John yawned again and said, "It is strange that while they could still be around, they have not displayed any presence to the authorities. Like how about hunting down these wayward aliens? We need their technology now, not waiting until all hell is supposed to break loose next year."

Karen replied "Perhaps mankind has to learn to survive on its own. Only by our near destruction will we as a race come through stronger and wiser."
Jane "Wow... Karen, prophetic words I must say, but imagine the suffering."

A small fishing boat slowed in the channel to pick up its mooring. Men at the back were stacking their fishing rods against the railing.

Jane turned abruptly to a cacophony of bird noise.
A haphazard squadron of seagulls descended near the empty table at the end of the eating area. They flapped, squawking and cackling, walking rapidly to snatch potato chips that littered the ground. One seagull appeared to have blood on his white plumage.

Bill looked then swung back to the others, he asked "Colonel Mondone, how is he?"
John replied "As you know he had a partially blocked artery which gave him a heart attack back in June. They did an angio... mmm angioplasty on him and he is now back to work part time, but with warnings about overdoing it."
Bill briefly pulled the gargoyle face, "Bloody stress that is. That's the cause.
I hope to see him next month when I go out to commission the Gravity Engine in the RamJet vehicle, and do you know what?"
He let the question hang.

John looked at him.
"They're going to run it up to half thrust on the ground."
John exclaimed "Good Lord! What about the radiation?"
He sobered up a bit.
Bill smiled remembering his own miniature engine test, "They are going to fire it into a mountain cavern to contain the exhaust."
"Brave."

Karen was day-dreaming, well her mind was going over what Quentin Huxley had said about churches and temples. The Christmas song came back.
In her mind she contemplated the devices he said where in the walls.
'How to test this hypothesis?'

Jane's phone chimed.
She picked it up and read the text.

"Jane. Need to see you. Shane is dead. Murdered they reckon. Gavin x"

Jane gasped, "Oh my God…" she sent a reply.
Karen "What's up Jane?"
"Oh dear…well…um you know that terrible fight outside the pub with Roger's henchmen?"
"Yes I remember you telling us, awful."
"Well Shane saved us and now Gavin says he's been murdered."
Karen clasped her hand over her mouth…again.

Jane carried on, "Guess Roger is still alive…"
The men had overheard.
John said, "Where did he die and have they any idea who done it?"
Bill "I guess Gavin is in danger?"
Jane's phone chimed again.

She replied "Yes I think he must be. Says here Shane's body was found in an alley near the Denmead Queen pub in Waterlooville. He was knifed to death…."

Same day - Dusk at Dell Quay, near Chichester, UK

The large Westerly yacht Nemain chugged up the channel.
Darkness was beginning to descend and thick clouds were obscuring the moon.
A cool mist hung over the still channel waters.

"Can you see the mooring buoy?"
Lei Zhao was perched on the very front of the boat, leaning over the rail holding a long boat hook.
"No, not yet."

Steven Crowley was at the wheel.
He took a deep drag from his cigarette and then turned the forward spotlights on.
Enveloped in a blue smoke haze he shouted again, "See it now?"

"Ah yes, over there. Turn to Port a bit Steven."
He turned the yacht and throttled back.

Twenty minutes later they were moored, the boat gently bobbing up and down with the incoming tide.

They sat in the cockpit with a very welcome glass of wine.

"Let me have some."
She took the cigarette out of his mouth and drew on it.
Down below were sacks of Greek cigarettes, their latest smuggling run.
They had moored in Skiathos near Greece, and looked up their old friend Silenos Drivas.
The poor man had lost weight, the authorities bearing down on him with charges of illegal wreck salvaging.
Luckily the contraband cigarette business was still booming.
His wife Sarra, after her heart operation, was still weak and rather frail.

However, she had made efforts to be a wonderful hostess during their stay.

Steven looked at her, "Good run eh? Kind weather and no nosey customs."
Lei smiled, she replied, "Yes, not like poor Silenos. He seems in deep water."
Steven laughed quietly, "He's rich. Mayor of Skiathos does have its advantages.
He just needs to look after one or two officials, cross their palms you know.
It's rife out there."

Lei became serious, "I was thinking about the strain on his poor wife Sarra. Did you not say she wanted to leave him?"
"She did, they rowed and she had a heart attack. I think his total devotion to her afterwards, made her change her mind."
Lei "When we were alone with Sarra, wasn't it interesting what she said about Angelo? Karen never mentioned it; you know that he was her half brother."

Steven lit a second cigarette and drew hard on it.
Amidst a cloud of blue-white smoke, he said "Fancy that, old Edward Durgas all those years ago, fathering a Mediterranean son. The devil! And what's more Silenos has said nothing about that."
He stopped and glanced towards Lei. "But he is so glad Dekker is dead. Funny thing is he didn't question why Angelo was visiting Karen."
Lei "Maybe Silenos actually does know. Sometimes it's best not to rock the boat too much. Perhaps he's saving that little gem as ammunition if Sarra ever threatens to leave him again."
Steven frowned for a moment.
She continued, "Well if she tries to take his fortune, he could use adultery to eliminate her claim. If I remember right, Greek law is a bit funny there."
Steven stubbed his cigarette out.

"Lei?"
She turned back from the twinkling pub lights.
"Lei, there is something happening to my Druid group."
"Like people dying off?" she wasn't being flippant, just matter of fact.
"Yeah. Dekker gone and now Bruce Jones. These guys were straight, ok tough customers in their own world, but I trusted them."
Lei eyes wandered from his face to his arm where the bracelet was under his fleece.
Steven continued, "I believe, no. I know that evil influences have infiltrated some of my group. You know where from?"
"The beings from Andromeda?"
"Yes, but it is by my design."
"Design? Steven why?"

He rolled the lighter in his hand and after a while said, "There are things you are not aware of. Let's say I have protected you from great danger."
Her puzzlement grew.
Steven looked directly at her, his blue eyes quite mesmerising.
"I deliberately let these beings use their influence. I need to monitor them."
"Sounds like playing with fire to me."
Her face developed a frown, "Surely with their enormous powers, you don't stand a chance?"
"Oh, but I do." His eyes twinkled.
"What?...I'm not sure where this going Steven? What can you do?"
He just replied "Trust me Lei."
With that the conversation ended.

On the shore a burst of laughter came across from the pub patio area.

Lei took another drag on the cigarette and exhaling she exclaimed, "These will be the death of you…and me."

"Yeah probably… if something else doesn't take me first."

It was the way he said it.

Lei looked at him strangely. "and what do you mean by that?"

"I plan another stunt."
"Oh Jesus Steven. No more dangerous stuff eh? Like not underwater?"
He paused, reflecting and looking out at the remains of the red sunset.
Down below, a beef pot-roast dinner was cooking in the little gas oven.

Eventually he replied, "No not underwater. It has to be something very significant this time. I need to reach many more people."
Lei had that resigned look, "Ok, what are you thinking?"

"There are millions of people on this planet that don't have the faintest idea of what is going to happen. Especially those in the third world nations. I need to somehow reach and persuade them to join in the spiritual fight against evil."
"Sounds very grand."
"Don't patronise me Lei. This is my destiny."

"Sorry Steven, I DO believe in you and what you are trying to achieve.
But…but one man and well… some of your Druids and your congregation of what, a couple of dozen people? How can you achieve this?"

Steven Crowley was a man who contemplated his time.
Lei loved him.
She knew it even though she had denied the idea to her sister Ming.
There was something deeper about the man, something that drew her magnetically to him.

She added, “What about your high powered Druid members? Can they use their influence? The ones that you can trust of course.”

He spoke, “By using the internet and other media. I want to get some airtime on international TV and web sites like FaceBook, Twitter and then draw people into my message.
Snowball the process. There are apps that help you do this, reach the masses and yes my Druid friends are busy on several of these projects.”

Lei frowned, “Steven, where are you going with this really? What effect do you expect?”
He stopped and looked at her for a long time.
“Lei, I know you believe in me but I understand your frustration in not knowing exactly what my objective is.”
She watched the master play out his thoughts.

“I have a chance to reach out and convince people of the good in humanity.
With this threat from off world aliens, now is the time more than ever to focus the world’s people, whatever religion they are, Muslim, Christian, Buddhist, Hindu and the rest, to come together in harmony and peace. Stop all these crazy wars.”

She said, “I am with you all the way Steven. Whatever you want me to do, just say.”
Inwardly she thought ‘The man wants too much, how can one physical person influence millions of people, get their real attention?’

After a while Steven Crowley stood and looked up at the darkened sky, a silver moon catching his attention.
“The timing will be late January next year when the portal comes around. It has to be precise and just after what may be a colossal battle out there in space. I hope and pray that the evil armada will be destroyed. Yet I fear before that happens, it will wreak havoc

here on Earth. Their influence will be insidious and penetrate everywhere.
At that time Sabrina's spiritual circle will have its full compliment and engage together with many other circles around the globe, in an attempt to try and thwart this influence.
I must act at a precise moment. Even our networks may be unusable."

Lei still puzzled, perplexed. Something about her man. A deep conundrum.
He turned to her with a beautiful smile.

"Sabrina will be here in an hour, so let's eat, dinner must be ready."

Darkness was descending, making the inside of the Nemain all the more homely.
Lei's feminine touches added to the comfort. New curtains to the portholes, some colourful pictures of oriental temples hung on the walls and numerous aromatic candles flickered gently on shelves and the two small tables.

Later

Lei climbed back aboard the yacht after tying up the dinghy. Sabrina wrapped in a bright purple shawl, carefully followed her as they descended the steps down into the main cabin.

Steven stood and with a bold smile grabbed Sabrina's proffered hand with both of his.
"Welcome Sabrina. Tea or coffee?"
"Thank you Steven, fruit juice if you have it?"

Lei vanished into the galley area, clattering some cups and glasses.

Steven refrained from smoking.
"Well Sabrina, what would you like to talk about?"

Sabrina glanced towards the galley area and whispered, "I know who you are."
He didn't move a muscle, his face dead pan.
"Who?"

The Shamanic teacher smiled.
"Let us say you have been around a very long time. Much longer than your current Earthly years."

Steven smiled, nodded and turned to look out of a porthole. Not that one could see anything, it was quite dark outside.
"There's no fooling you Sabrina."

He glanced at the galley door.
"Let's wait for Lei to return. I think she needs to know now and I will require your help to convince her."
They waited.

Unexpectedly a crash was heard followed by a "Yeow! Ow, ow… ooh…"
Steven burst into the galley,
"You ok Lei….oh… you're hurt?"

Lei was holding her arm.
"The kettle fell off the stove and the lid came away, my arm is scolded from the boiling water…ooh…god it stings."

Quickly they ran cold water over her arm in the sink.
After carefully drying her arm, a deep red mark appeared about the size of orange.

Sabrina stood close by opening the first aid kit that Steven had given her.
Lei looked at her arm. The skin was starting to blister badly.
She painfully looked at Steven. "Do we need to go to A&E?"

Sabrina gave Steven a knowing look.
He took a deep breath and took Lei's arm in both his hands.
Glancing at Sabrina with a slightly resigned countenance he said, "No that won't be necessary. Sit over here."
Lei "But Steven, it's bad, the blisters are horrible."
Steven sat next to Lei saying, "Close your eyes Lei and trust me."
He very gently placed the palm of one hand over the blisters, and with his other hand held her arm underneath.

Sabrina wasn't missing a trick, her keen eyes watching everything.

After a few minutes, Steven removed his hand and said, "You can open your eyes now Lei."
Sabrina didn't blink.
Lei stared at her arm in amazement.
"Oh wow Steven, the blisters where are they? My arm is ok, um…how did you do that?"

The blisters had gone and only the faintest of red marks remained on her arm, disappearing as she watched them.
He smiled and replied. "Because I can."

Lei's eyes grew wide, "Oh my…you can heal. Oh… *Steven.*"
Her eyes watered in astonishment.
Steven Crowley looked at Sabrina and then back at Lei.

"It is time you knew. Sabrina is aware already."

Chapter 26

Friday 21st December - Christmas 2018
Sir George Ratcliffe's Office, ESS, East Meon, UK

"Crystal, can you get me the folder for Project Orange?
It's in the bookcase there, top shelf."

George watched the new girl wander over to the bookcase and reach up to retrieve the folder. Her skirt rose.
"There Sir George, anything else I can do?"

"Thank you, um no Crystal. Pop off now and have an early lunch."
"Oh thank you."
He watched his new assistant turn and disappear, closing the door behind her.

She was glad to be away from the old lecher.

He opened the folder, then looked at the spreadsheet on his computer display and started muttering.
"Damn it. We're still behind schedule."

A knock on the door.
He looked up irritated, "Come in!"

A smiling Bill Craswell walked in wearing a red Christmas hat with a white pompom.
Ratcliffe thought, 'Nobody is bloody serious around here. Damn Christmas lark, just gets in the way.'
He gave his best sickly smile. "Yes Bill?"

"George, we have an issue with the plasma weapon overheating again."
Ratcliffe pulled a face thinking Bill never addressed him as 'Sir'.
He said, "Yes, I have the Project folder open right here. So what is needed to resolve this?"

Bill replied, “The super cooling refrigerant system is not up to it. We need those top end pumps.”
“The damned expensive ones?”
“Yes.”
Bill just stared at Ratcliffe.
It was a ‘I told you so moment, but you didn’t listen then.’

“You know Bill we don’t have a limitless budget.”
Ratcliffe had been squirreling some of the funding away for his own purposes.

“Oh but I thought we did George. I remember Ranut saying money was no object in order to get this weapon out.”

Ranut Magrit – Home Office Minister

Ratcliffe huffed and pretended to leaf through the folder.
At length he replied, “Very well, order what you need. I notice that the schedule has slipped. God…and what with all these new engineers in your team. Why are we in this situation? The bloody Ministry keeps breathing down my neck for committed dates that I can’t see how we can meet.”

Bill paused then said, “That’s good George. I’m sure we can hit the schedule. I’ll call through the order right away and pick them up personally.”

Ratcliffe grimaced then said, “No dangerous short cuts old chap?”

“Absolutely George. We just need to push harder on the engineers getting up to speed on the gravity technology. Trouble is with John in the States, there’s only a few of us to do the training, although Jane is doing a sterling job on the logistics production of the materials for the fuel pellets.”
“Yes I understand, and Gustav?”

“No problem. He is a little shaken after the incident, but his knowledge of linear accelerators is getting us towards the muzzle velocity we need.”

Ratcliffe drummed his fingers on the table.
“I understand Bill, but we need to do the full test as soon as.”
Bill pulled a slight gargoyle face and replied, “Well I’m sure you don’t want anymore accidents Sir George?”

The debate was see-sawing.

George Ratcliffe looked at him. Thinking Bill was a fine one to talk after his Norfolk farm got its dose of radiation. He took a more condescending line.

“Absolutely. We will all be hung out to dry. Need to tread very carefully, especially after Gustav’s explosion. Ok, get those parts in pronto Bill. Let me know when we’re ready for the next test. Thank you.”

Bill closed the door and hurried down towards the lab. He wondered how they would ever make the thing safe to use.

The first test of the plasma weapon in their offsite bunker had been calamitous.
Luckily no one was injured, but the prototype gravity plasma weapon disintegrated inside the concrete bunker. Within it, the explosion had embedded bits of the weapon in the walls and spread some serious radioactivity everywhere.

Early evening - Sunday 23rd December
Scotland, near Loch Ness

Andrew Horsham turned from the pub window and looked across at Bill.
"Well you don't look as old as I imagined."

Jane "Dad! What sort of question is that?"

Bill Craswell raised his hand, "Well that's a relief Andrew. What's more I can attribute my new fitness and wellbeing to your daughter here."

Jane's mum Kay laughed and smiling she said, "You certainly look in good shape to me. Good work Jane."
She winked at her daughter.
Andrew pulled a face then smiled too, "Welcome to Scotland Bill, maybe we can do a wee spot of fishing in the morning?"
"Sounds great Andrew."
He winced inside thinking 'I'd rather be working on my Fountains of Paradise project.' Then he glanced out of the window across to an ivy covered brick built church. A chime from his distant past hit him.

Bill felt a little awkward, his eyes momentarily went out of focus. "Whooa" he whispered, quickly shifting his standing position, placing his free hand on a wall rail.
Jane glanced at him and frowned, "Bill?"

Then a memory flashed by of a tyrannical minister at the orphanage many years ago.
He said 'Look here sonny. God is watching you and I am the link between him and you. So you better obey me...'

A remote pain pinged at the back of his mind.

Covering with a smile he said, "Ah…um…yes. This local beer is strong stuff."
Back at the Horsham cottage yuletide lounge, a round of malt whiskies was in progress.
In one corner of the room, a real Christmas tree was overloaded with large gold and red baubles. The ancient tree lights were dimly trying to illuminate the myriad of ornaments on the fir tree.
A small row of cards hung along the wall.
At the side of the fireplace sat a large stuffed Father Christmas with a dodgy wispy white beard.
Nearly as dodgy as Andrew's.

Kay spoke, "Jane, Bill, thank the Lord you two were not badly hurt in Australia. We saw it on the news here."
Jane laughed, then went serious, "We were very lucky Mum. If Barry Westland hadn't shot the assassin, he would have surely finished us off."
She turned and looked painfully at Bill, "Poor Bill, God I was so distraught, I thought you were dying."
It was Bill's turn for humour, "Well my little physics book saved my skin."
He pulled out a plastic bag from his pocket and carefully withdrew the little shredded tome. "There, the police finally returned it. In a bit of a sad state now. I just carry it for good luck."
The book had a large hole in its front cover, bits of paper and debris dropped from it.
Andrew took it and exclaimed, "Ah, metal front and back. That is rare for a book?"
Bill smiled, "I had the covers fitted for a reason."

Jane burst out laughing, "Yeah… to protect him from Kryptonite rays."
Kay frowned and Andrew gave the strangest look.
Jane mentioned the missing piece of exotic rock.
Bill was squirming, his facial expressions pleading, please don't say anymore.

Jane said with a grin, "It's true, he is my Superman."

They all laughed and the glasses got refilled.
Eventually the evening came to an end with everybody retiring to bed.

"This is my room and ours for Christmas." Jane opened the door.
He said, "That's a small double."
Jane smiled and squeezed his arm. "Yes it's only four foot six wide. We'll just have to snuggle close together."
She had a mischievous grin.

Bill replied, "So nice Jane."
He opened the little wooden window and peered out. The odd murky star glimmered behind a haze of clouds. At length he said, "Glad I'm back in the UK. Those Americans can be so demanding and in your face."

He had spent three weeks during November at the Jet Propulsion Laboratory in California.
Mostly at their desert test complex.
Burning the gravity engine into a mountain cave.

"However, they were grateful and I must admit pretty awe struck when my engine howled its tune."
Bill had a great big smile on his face. Achievement was a marvellous feeling.

Jane looked at him, she said "I'm so proud of you Bill, you are such a successful man and even if they don't give you the deserved recognition soon, I'm sure you'll get it one day."
He moved close placing his hands behind her back and pressing her against him, he said, "Thank you Jane. I need you right here, you know. Glad you believe in me."

She kissed him softly on the lips and then reached down to take some pyjamas out of her case.

Their conversation had fallen to whispers. Next door was her mum and dad's bedroom.

Bill sat on the edge of the bed and exclaimed, "God…I'm tired. Guess I've been a bit on edge about how your Dad would be."
Jane feigned a frown and replied, "On edge?"
"Yes I was worried he might start accusing me of baby snatching his daughter."
"I don't think so. I am nearly twenty six and quite able to make my own decisions. Anyway Dad has warmed to you. I told him you were a world leading scientist with a pragmatic approach, making a difference while the theorists just talk."
Bill raised his eyebrows, "Oh and what did he say to that?"
Jane grinned "He was well impressed and he said 'Well chosen lassie. Make sure he spends a load of money on you and get married. With his track record he will blow himself up and you'll be a rich widow.' "

Bill jumped up "Bloody hell, he didn't?"
Jane had taken her top and skirt off. She pushed Bill onto his back. They both sprawled onto the bed.
With herself naked from the waist up, she undid his shirt while she sat on him.
Then she pulled his trousers off.
"Bill Craswell, you are a bit gullible at times." she laughed.
Before he could reply she leant over him, her legs straddling his waist, her hands pinning his arms and then she kissed him hard.

Coming up for air, Bill gasped and whispered, "Oh Jane… you are so wonderful…"
She had look of resignation, "Sorry Romeo we can't do anything. Not here in my parent's house."
He smiled craftily, "I knew already, we'll make up for it later."

Christmas Eve

Next morning at the crack of dawn, the four of them were down on the little beach.

Jane stared across Loch Ness with most of it enveloped in a thick damp, clinging mist.
Cold, very cold, the temperature was only a few degrees above freezing.
Although he was wearing his fur lined flying jacket, Bill still shivered.
He thought 'This fishing business is not for me. Rather be back in front of that log fire with hot porridge.'
They sat around a duel gas stove while Jane's Dad Andrew turned sizzling sausages and bacon in a frying pan.
Jane leaned over, 'Sure smells good Dad.'
In the other pot were tatties and neaps boiling away. Her Mum Kay passed around mugs of hot tea and coffee, the steam rising and flickering away in the chill breeze.
As the mist drifted away, dark patches of water started to appear along the Loch.

"No sunrise today." said Jane as she eyed the gathering dark grey clumps of clouds.

She smelt the damp air and looked around, "Better get a move on Dad, might be rain soon."
Andrew looked up and smiled, "Nearly ready, na bites though."
He glanced over the little shingle beach, to a clutch of fishing rods perched up in the air on their stays, by the water's edge, their lines stretching out over the calm waters.
No movement.
All quiet, the water gently lapping along the shoreline.
Bill said ,"So what fish can we catch here Andrew?"
"Well laddie, depends on the season but ye can catch salmon, trout, eels, sometimes the odd pike and on the rare occasion the big one…" he let the statement run.

Bill frowned, “Big one…um like what?”
At that moment a small fish jumped out of the water about thirty yards away.
Then at the same place a large V shaped current in the water appeared.
Something big was just under the surface.

Kay jested, “There see that? Might be the big one!”

Bill laughed, “Oh I get it, Nessie the Loch Ness monster?”
Andrew had a big grin and winked at Jane.

The sausages suddenly spat in the pan, distracting them.
Jane glanced around, the weather was deteriorating.

Kay still had her eyes glued to the large ripple in the water as it closed on them.
“Oh my, that is some fish…ooh look!”

Something rose and broke the surface of the water.
Andrew stared thinking, ‘That’s no fish I’ve ever seen.’
He was remembering what Jane had told them last time she was here.
About the alien beastie.
He had suspected bad dreams, but his gut was telling him something else.

He ran back to the pickup and grabbed his shotgun, quickly inserting two cartridges. Snapping the breech shut quickly, he grabbed a handful more.
“Dad!...Dad what is it?”
Jane’s face went pale, “Oh God…oh no not….. here…”

As the waters rinsed off the top of the object, a dark shiny mass could be seen.
Barnacles? Knots of seaweed?

The dual crash of two barrels in quick succession sounded right across Loch Ness.
Booming echoes reverberated down the lake valley.
Andrew was now at the water's edge methodically reloading. Debating in his mind whether at that long range the shotgun would be effective.
He keenly watched the rippling waters.

Then the rain came down in torrents.
Kay was holding her neck crucifix, with a look of anguish, water dripping off her hair and eyebrows.

Boom, boom again.
With a huge splash the object disappeared below a large surging fold of water.

They all stood motionless for some time.
Smoke curled from the shotgun barrels.
At length Jane stuttered, "I didn't really get a good look. Do you think it was the alien Dad?"
He turned towards her, "I cannie be sure lassie. Was not Nessie, that's definite."
Bill just muttered quietly, "Oh my gawd… oh my flippin gawd."
Then loudly, "Well whatever it was, it's gone now. Good shooting Andrew."

Andrew broke the gun and flipped out the spent cartridges. He inserted two more and closed the shotgun, his eyes never leaving the Loch.
He said "Well whatever it was, it didn't like the taste of lead shot."

Further out on the Loch a big splash made them look.
In the distance what looked like a great big tail rose and then disappeared below the waves.
Jane exclaimed, "Oh no… it looks like…like a whale. Oh Dad, you've shot a whale."
Her Dad was dead pan; he said "Well he seems unscathed."

They were all soaked; the heavy rain was coming down fast, with a wind whipping the water into little waves.
"Ok, let's go home." cried Andrew above the noise of the storm. He looked back over the waters, scanning left to right… nothing. They collected their stuff throwing it in the back of the pickup and the vehicle hurtled back up the muddy lane.

Later after drying off and changing, they all sat around to a second breakfast.
The first one lay abandoned down at the beach.

Kay was first to speak, "Well what do we make of that beastie?"
Andrew replied, "A right mystery. Jane, did it look like the thing you saw at the rest home?"
"Difficult to say Dad, I did feel very frightened just like the first time with Karen. Thing is, back at the rest home, her ancient cross invoked an energy to repel the monster. Here we didn't have it."
Kay spoke up, "Well I did grip my crucifix tightly. Maybe our dear Lord was watching from up there and saved us?"
Jane "Maybe. It could have been a whale? oh, I hope it's not injured."

Bill gave Jane a strange look and turned to her parents saying, "You did the right thing Andrew. Everybody needs to be on the offensive. In these times, mankind faces its biggest threat ever."

After breakfast, Jane helped her mother with the washing up.
Sitting in the little snug, Bill slurped his coffee, his eyes switching from the flickering flames of the log fire to Andrew sitting opposite.
The bearded man spoke.
"So Bill, our Jane has spoken much about space and what you are doing at your laboratory."
"Yes, she did mention taking you into our confidence. What we do is secret Government work." He reinforced the confidentiality.
"Ah yes, the Ministry who tell the people very little."

Bill smiled, "They do give that impression, but I can assure you we are working on stuff that is so important."
"Can ye disclose a bit? Like what is going on with these supposed rogue beasties?"
"I wish I knew Andrew. You see the authorities are keeping very quiet about them and that's despite photos and videos from the Los Angeles episode plastered all over the internet."
"Yes I have seen them."
Andrew nodded to the laptop on the little desk in the corner.
"I be a forester by trade but I do dabble from time to time on the computer, bit of email you know and checking on aerial photography of forests, that sort of thing."
Bill said "We must be vigilant and as Jane said; our friends are in possession of these ancient artefacts that appear to offer protection. Has she mentioned about next month and the portal?"
"Oh aye, something about aliens returning? Sounds the stuff of science fiction to me laddie. You see those Star Wars films?"
Bill smiled, "Yes I saw them a long time ago, but I'm afraid the baddies in those films pale into insignificance compared to these bastards. Sorry but I have to use that language."
Andrew stared at him.
Bill continued, "We must put our faith in the people from the Omega Centauri system, and that they will protect us. Also we are developing our own defensive weapons."
"Ah. Well I hope it's enough Bill."
With a huge sigh, Bill exclaimed, "It's all we have."

He then had a thought, 'If the extreme raging core of a nuclear explosion doesn't melt these aliens, what the hell can we hope to do with our plasma gun?'
His mind churned over the alien confrontations experienced by Karen and Steven using their artefacts.
A thought, 'Maybe…just maybe those devices confuse the bastards and weaken their defences?'

Andrew stood up, and looked out the window, "Rain is lightening up, some blue sky now."

Bill looked and nodded, but his mind was sorting through an idea.
"Andrew I need to make a phone call, sort of confidential?"
Andrew replied, "No problem, use the little den through that door."

In the den, well more of a tiny storage room full of cardboard boxes, old boots, a broom, and an old wicker basket, he called Karen.
"Hi Bill."
"Hello Karen, you ok?"
"Yes usual festive madness. You guys enjoying your break in Scotland?"
"Yes, it's so peaceful up here, well mostly, bit wet though." he recalled the Loch incident.
He continued, "Karen, are you home or at work? I need to run something by you."
"Sure Bill, quiet here in the lab, Christmas Eve and all that. Seems daft to just come in for this Monday and I think everybody will disappear down to the pub at midday. Ratcliffe is wandering around trying to galvanise people, talk about bah humbug."

She continued "What's on your mind?"
Bill, "Did the US Navy finally confirm the destruction of the alien with their nuclear strike?"
Karen became serious, "I talked to Lei and it appears that it was partially or completely destroyed. They showed some debris to the public, if you can call it that."
Bill, "Hmmm… don't know what to believe. They may have said that just to avoid public tension and possibly panic?"

Bill frowned, he gripped the phone tightly and pursed his lips, then said, "Can you see if there are any minute gravity distortions off the Californian seaboard close to the nuclear strike? Just prior to the explosion."

Karen realised what he was getting at.
Intense power distorting space and time, opening another dimension, a possible escape route.
Then she felt a distinct chill, but thinking, 'Very unlikely with the huge energies required to do that…'

"Um yes Bill. Yes I'll check the data. Call you back in a while. Take care."
"You too."
Click.

He screwed his face up, the gargoyle very evident.
Bill put his phone away and rejoined Andrew in the lounge.

Andrew looked up, "Come on let's go for a walk."
Jane came in "Walk? Tell you what? I need a run, how about we meet up at the old cabin Dad?"

With that and some cheese sandwiches that Kay made, they set off.
Jane's Mum stayed behind, walking in the wet and chilly forest was not her favourite pastime.

After strolling for a while Bill and Andrew entered a dense pine forest.
Bill, "So do you look after this Andrew?"
"Aye, all thousand acres of it. I manage it and produce a bit of charcoal too."
"Quite a job by the looks of it."
"Och, tis nothing. I have another ten thousand acres of woodland over the way that the Forestry Commission employ me for."
Bill looked around at the damp woodland and defrosting water dripping down through the tree branches. He pulled his jacket zip up as the chill wind hit them.

"What about this time of year, flippin cold and wet, can't be much to do?"

"Don't you believe it, there is always work. From clearing autumn leaf and debris that blocks streams and rivers, to early cutting and pruning ready for the spring growth."
"Ah ok."

They trudged on through mud and wet grass, reaching a small lake and disturbing some geese that screeched at them and then took to the air.
Bill glanced at Andrew and the split shotgun that he carried on his arm.
He thought 'Better than nothing, some reassurance I guess.'
Then it started to rain and he pulled his hood on.

In due course they came to a clearing and the log cabin.
The sides were horizontally clad in great big logs split in half.
A single large double glazed window divided the front wall.
On top a slanting roof made of overlapping hard wood shingles kept the rain out.
Wooden slates that can last hundreds of years.
The cabin stood on wooden piles about a foot above the leafy forest floor, with a single step onto a small covered veranda.
It was old, older than Jane.
Andrew had built it with his bare hands a long time ago.
Everything outside was damp. Rain trickled off the roof.
Thick green moss covered piles of logs near by.

Inside was another world.
At one end a small log stove with a stack of logs to the side.
In the middle a little table with three battered wooden chairs.
Some candles in holders decorated the top.
At the far end by the door, was a general dumping ground for muddy boots, tools, a petrol generator and shelving full of wooden boxes.
A door with the sign 'It's in here' led into a tiny corner room, the compost loo.

Bill broke into a cheery smile. "Ah this is more like it, a little haven."
Closing the door, Andrew took off his heavy waterproof Barbour coat and replied.
"Aye, it's a great escape from the weather. I read a bit in here too. Don't get much chance back home, Kay likes to chat ye know."
He winked at Bill.
Then he knelt and after making up the stove fire with paper and kindling, he lit it.

Concurrently

Jane ran quickly, her running shoes squelching in the soft wet ground.

Despite the thaw, ice from last night's frost remained along the edges of the track.
The forest was still, quiet, always there.

Clumps of stiff white blades of frosted grass, clustered along the hedgerow banks.
Trees devoid of their leaves stood like thin tall brushes, with the odd dark green fir interleaving the skeletal ones.

The bottom of tree trunks caught her eye, clad in bright green moss, others enwrapped in ivy.
Everything damp, with branches dripping ice water that twinkled in the sunlight.

The morning's scare was fading. Maybe it was just a whale.
She thought 'A whale in fresh water Loch Ness? Perhaps there are whales that don't mind.'

Jane felt safe here in Scotland, the place she grew up in and she knew all the forest tracks around her parent's home.
Her breath steamed out into the chill air as she pounded on.

Then as her eyes glanced left and right, she caught sight of a squirrel in the undergrowth, digging for nuts buried in the autumn. He suddenly froze, an eye watchful of her, a hazelnut between his paws.
Then in a flurried blur he ran straight up a craggy oak tree close by.

Jane smiled and pushed on down the muddy track, running even harder.
Luckily most of the icy places were in the shade on the edge of the track.

She paused to a trot as a haze of movement behind the bushes to the left caught her eye.

A crashing sound erupted.

Jane stopped breathless, arms in mid-air, her feet skidding to a halt, her legs poised to run. Then she held her breath, her heart pounding.

Just in front the side bushes erupted.

She jumped back as something like a dozen deer quickly broke through a gap in the hedgerow, leaping and running across the track and into the forest opposite.
A couple of calves clung close to their mothers.

They were all gone in seconds.

She smiled, her heart beat slowed.
Exhaling a great lung full of steaming air, she slowly broke into a run again, thinking,
'Life, the animals, the forest… all mine.'

Half an hour later, the track petered out and Jane turned into a dark cluster of pine fir trees.

Reaching a clearing she stopped to catch her breath and leaning on the half fallen tree trunk she glimpsed the small log cabin a couple of hundred yards away.
Blue smoke trickled from its chimney.

Her phoned binked a text.
Jane withdrew it and read,

'Look over to your right'
- Sender unknown.

She looked past the cabin and down the valley slope.
"Oh my Lord, oh…"

There some one hundred yards away stood a man shining in white. He gently waved.

Bing, another text.
She looked down again,

'Jane you have courage and tenacity. Help Bill as much as you can.'
- Sender unknown.

She quickly keyed a reply,

'Are you from Omega Centauri? Bill's confidante?'

- Unable to send message, unknown recipient.

Jane looked up, he was still there.
She shouted "What the?....who are you, what do you want?"
Bing, text in.

'Jane, protect Bill as much as you can, otherwise he will break. Trust in us, but know that we cannot interfere in Earth based affairs.

In the coming weeks all that happens is meant to be.'
- Sender unknown.

"He will break, oh poor Bill, I.......what are these riddles?"

She gasped and looking up she saw the man in white had gone.

Frantically she turned three hundred and sixty degrees looking for him.
She ran on, seeing nothing just trees, misty rain and the little log cabin.

A pale Jane opened the door and peered in to see her Dad and Bill drinking tea and munching cheese sandwiches at the table.
"Hello." She panted, her bosom heaving up and down.
Bill turned round, "Good run? Still raining? God you look as though you've seen a ghost Jane!"

"I think I just have, probably pictures in the mist I reckon."
She played it down a little.

Jane paused looking out the window expecting someone to look back in. "Yes brilliant run, the forest is wonderful, the air so fresh. Bit of drizzle, but the rain doesn't bother me." She managed to beam a smile.

Bill's heart glowed, he thought, 'That's my girlfriend, what a cracker.'
Andrew looked up, "Tea?"
"Great Dad and I'll have a sandwich if there's any left, I'm famished."
"Sure. Plenty here."

Outside the rain commenced to increase into a torrent, hammering down on the log cabin roof.
Then the forest slowly vanished in a fog of wet.

Andrew disappeared to the toilet.
Jane whispered to Bill about her seeing the man in white outside.
"There Jane, what did I tell you, he really exists…you ok?"
"Yes I am now, though I was bit shaken up before I came in."

Bill got up and went out.
Oblivious to the rain dripping off him, he stared all around.

This time, he Bill Craswell, went looking for the white robed man.

Chapter 27

Early morning - Christmas Day 2018
Old Winchester Hill – an ancient Iron Age Fort
Warnford, Hampshire, UK

The hill fort, or what was left of it, stood as a giant dry and grassy earth mound, surrounded by a huge ditch. The whole thing stood proud, prominently high, commanding a defensive position and a grand view over fields and woods as far as the eye could see.
The top was flat, nearly the size of two football pitches, and in its day a thriving village, surrounded by a high wooden barricade.

Not long after the invasion nearly two thousand years ago, instigated around 40 AD by the Roman Empire, the fort saw a ferocious battle and the defeat of the local peoples here.
The destruction of this Iron Age bastion, by the invading Roman horde.

At the top near one of the sacred burial mounds, Sabrina stopped, turned around and raised her right arm.
"Here will be fine."
She smiled, her teeth sparkling in the bright sunlight.
The glorious rising sun caught her flowing grey hair, it gave a sheen as she turned around.
A little warmth could be had.

Karen Durgas, Lei Zhao, Anne Whitfield and Christine Blackwood caught up with her and dropped their rucksacks.

They commenced the water ceremony.
A way of connecting with your inner self, your heart-mind, the eternal sun and all that is good, to far out there in the universe.
A circle was formed, each person holding a bottle of water.

Following Sabrina's spoken directions, they all did a little slow dance always facing the sun. At each point on the compass, they paused and stopped to drink sips of water, acknowledging the sacred chakra positions in the body.
Sun beams streaking and fragmenting through the crystal-like water bottles.

It was a cleansing and communicating the soul, to all that is.
Then finally they all gave some water to the Earth, our beautiful home.

Warm sunlight streamed into their bodies.
Five pairs of bare feet in a circle, pressed into the moist chilly grass.

A feeling so good that it cannot be explained.
It must be experienced.

After a few minutes stationary with their eyes closed, Sabrina spoke again,
"Wonderful. Ladies, now let's sit close."

Everybody had brought a fold up camp chair.
After towelling their cold feet, socks and boots were put back on.

Lei said, "Oh that was so good Sabrina. The chill air, the cool grass in your toes and that gorgeous sunshine filling my body, made me feel amazing, thank you."
Sabrina smiled, the sun catching her hair as it ruffled in the wind.
"Yes it is a marvellous feeling. Here we are on the day our dear Lord Jesus was born."

Karen looked out over the panoramic view of fields, patches of forest and a very misty horizon. .
Everything was becoming clearer.
She knew her inner self was slowly evolving her spiritual abilities and her physics skills into one fabric.

"Karen, Karen?"
She looked up at Sabrina calling her.
"Oh sorry, I was deep in thought Sabrina."
Sabrina grinned, "I know."

She said, looking at each person in turn, "Christianity has its roots in a divine being and an afterlife in Heaven. My interpretation is that it is another path to self awareness and eternal life; through selflessness, love and forgiveness in this life.
All the paths converge into one, to all that is."

The long grasses swayed as a soft breeze blew across the hill.
A cluster of tiny twittering birds flew up and around the bushes along the edges of the hill mound.

"Many of Earth's religions and beliefs converge at some distant point to a mutual position. Reality in the spiritual kingdoms."

Sabrina, her hair gently swaying in the wind, continued, "We have a chance in the coming weeks to make a difference. If our mentors from Omega Centauri can defeat the incoming armada, then our efforts will thankfully be much reduced."
Christine Blackwood raised her finger to speak.
Sabrina motioned with her hand, delaying the interruption.

Christine, sister to John Creeson, married to the famous Scientologist Maxell Blackwood.

Sabrina spoke again, "However, if our mentors fail in the hour of our need, then we are on our own."
They all shared the same thought that Mankind's specific fate was an unknown, but that evil would surely reign amidst huge suffering.

She continued, "When this hour comes, which may last hours, days or even weeks, we have to maintain our spiritual efforts."

She turned to Karen, "…and maintain the shield that your artefacts provide. Can this be done?"
Karen replied, "Yes I believe so Sabrina. I suspect that the moon device will continue to provide the defensive energy for a long time. We need to have shifts of people to maintain the artefacts alignment. You see they cannot be mounted in say jigs, they each need to be physically held by a person and probably someone who has some spiritual beliefs."

Sabrina, "In that case we must address the numbers and make sure we can hold out using shifts, for at least some days. If necessary for a week or more."

Anne Whitfield said, "Have other religions recognised the danger? If so are they willing to fight with us?"

Sabrina paused and spoke addressing all of them.
"Many religions believe in an afterlife. A spiritual existence. While the transitions across are very different and values change somewhat, I and the Elders are in contact with many Christian, Islamic, Hindu, Buddist, Taoist and other groups to try and be together and forge a common understanding.
So in answer to your question, yes I believe they are and they will be willing to fight in their own ways."

Christine keen to say her bit, interrupted. "Maxwell has asked me to mention that he has been in contact with our mentors."
She waited.
Sabrina looked at Lei then said, "Please tell us more Christine."
"From what he told me, they have communication devices, that is the Church have received a message from Omega Centauri."
Lei became intensely interested.

Christine continued, "Normally I am not involved with my husband's religious activities. However, in the last year I am, I guess… being slowly converted. Maxwell has asked me to convey to you the following message."

They all watched her and waited patiently.
Christine was uneasy but she continued, she read from a sheaf of paper.
"This is not easy for me, but this is what he said quote:

'Mankind stands on the brink of an evolutionary change. His spiritualism is gaining much ground and all religions will embrace this in their own way.
Our mentors in Omega Centauri have signalled that they are in decline. The reasons for this are unknown. They have been aware of this for several million years now. It is very subtle and they have tried for a very long time to reverse this deterioration.
We know that like us, they too have a spiritual kingdom where their souls return.'

Christine paused for a breath.
Sabrina had a puzzled look, she said, "So what are they trying to tell us?"
Christine responded, glancing at the paper,
"He says '*it is because the Andromeda galaxy harnesses an energy that we do not have in this galaxy of ours. A dark arcane force that cuts through the physical and ethereal domains. It is likely the culprit that is slowly undermining the people of Omega Centauri.*'"

Sabrina commented, "Please thank your husband. Our guides have indicated the same."
Karen interrupted, "I must investigate this, and I have the ability."

Sabrina placed her hand on Karen's arm, "It is too much for you. In any case this arcane force of energy appears to only exist in this far galaxy. At two million light years away, how on Earth can we analyse this let alone defeat it?"

Karen replied, "But there is an opportunity with the rogue aliens here on Earth. If we can trap or subdue one of these in some way, then maybe we have a chance to understand these awful monsters and their energies."

At that moment some noisy crows landed in one of the few trees on the hill top.
They squawked and jumped about.
Birds of prey, cannibals to their own kind.

The women were distracted.
They all looked up into the sky, blue and clear.
No snow this Christmas.

Sabrina spoke, "Thank you Christine. Karen, do what you can, your research is very important."

Then she said, "Let us meditate."

Lei reflected deeply.
The jigsaw was slowly coming together and she reflected back to her own healing.

A little while ago, the revelation on her lover's yacht was staggering.

Steven Crowley after healing her burnt arm had admitted to being more than human.
He said he was in a transitional stage and had connections with the people from Omega Centauri.
Then, Lei initially frowning before laughing had said "What the hell are you saying Steven? That you're an alien?"
"No, not exactly. I am as human as you are."

Suddenly a thump outside the boat hull made Steven disappear up the stairs to investigate.

Back then she had become even more perplexed, until Sabrina took her arm and said, "It's true Lei, he is special. He has, let us say 'enhancements' that give him this ability."
Lei, "No…ah yes… perhaps nano-machines, you know tiny, tiny devices that are programmed to repair cells in the body. Possibly from our mentors?"
Sabrina smiled, "You may not be far from the truth. A technology in its embryonic state here on Earth, but out there…" she looked up at the sky and continued,
"With such an advanced civilisation it would seem completely possible, but to us it is utterly miraculous."
Lei puzzled, "Then why cannot they reverse their own decline?"
Sabrina had then replied, "I suspect it is not organic, but more to do with the entire fabric of their existence. I must go now. I will wait for you up on deck Lei."
With that Sabrina went up top.

Steven came down again, "It was nothing. Just a floating piece of driftwood had bumped into Nemain."
Lei moved closer to him, her eyes glued to his. "Tell me more Steven."

Steven with huge wisdom in his face said, "In time all will become clear. But please don't press me for more explanations now Lei. Shall we say I have just *borrowed* this technology."
Lei remained speechless.

It was too much to take in.
'The man she loved and lived with for over two years was….. was…' she struggled to comprehend the situation, their future.
'What future? And what did he mean by… *all will become clear* ?'

Then she said, "Steven does this affect us? Our future? All of a sudden I feel very insecure right now."

He stooped a little and took her in his arms.

"It changes nothing my love. Just believe in me and in time all will be revealed, I promise."

Although he held her tight, she felt emptiness, a foreboding.

Noon – Xmas Day 2018
Horndean, UK

Karen glanced across the table towards the bookcase shelving. Whitfield family photographs were interspersed with Christmas cards.
Inside she was poignantly thinking of the Christmases at her parents' house and her absentee partner.

Anne Whitfield smiled and said, "I'm glad you've decided to come here for Christmas dinner and stay tonight. It would have been so lonely on your own."
Karen replied, "That's very kind of you Anne. Yes it would have. There's no real Christmas for John over in America. His NASA training schedule is full on."

She tried to cheer up, but a sad flicker was on her face.
Anne frowned, caught Karen's mood and said, "Karen? You seem sad?"

Karen looked at both Anne and Jim, she replied, "Although I am strong, a survivor. I have an uneasy feeling that just won't go away. It's the worrying about what's going to happen and John being up there in outer space, he will be so vulnerable."
Her eyes were moist.

Anne took her hand and said, "Our beliefs will give us strength."
Instantly Anne's husband Jim burst out, "Pa! I think we need more than airy fairy magic!"
Anne glared at Jim, "Jim! That's not fair, you have your beliefs and I have mine."

Karen was a little shocked, feeling in the middle. "I'm sorry I should not have spoken about this."

Jim stretched his arms and putting them behind his head, he snorted, "Beliefs! You know I don't believe in a god or any gods. I'm an atheist. There's nothing after this life, we all just turn to dust when we die."

The dinner was a quiet affair. Jim proceeded to drink copious amounts of wine.
Anne had a face like thunder.
As the afternoon wore on he became quite drunk, then slurred,"So willa, will we ..hic…be dancing round the cauldron at midnight?"
He drank the remainder of the wine in his glass, slightly missing his mouth.
Red wine dripped from his chin.
"Ah. Got a taste for this. Mmm…we got another bottle woman?"

"Fetch it yourself." Anne was adamant.

Karen remained wide eyed looking at Anne, not saying a word. Her quiet enlightened spiritual friend having to put up with this oaf.
Jim staggered to the kitchen to open another.
Anne turned to Karen, "Just ignore him. I'm so sorry Karen."

Ten minutes before the Queen's Christmas speech, Jim fell asleep on the small sofa in the corner. His snoring comparable to the sawing of rough wood.
Anne gave a little sigh, "He'll be out for some time now, dead to the world for a while, thank God."

They were both glued to the television.
Anne turned the sound up, and then the Queen appeared.
Although she was technically no longer Queen, with William on the throne as King for the last year now, she had insisted on a final speech to the people of the United Kingdom and the recipients

of the world broadcast. Countries like Australia, New Zealand, India, Canada, Kenya and many others that were once governed by little colonial England.

"Here on this Christmas Day 2018, I am emboldened by the peoples of the world.
As you can see I am in the great dining hall in Buckingham Palace, where we have received many heads of state.
It is a long time since I have broadcast from here. It is because in previous times, we have met our nation's and the Commonwealth's challenges."

The backdrop of the large, tall ceilinged dining room was stunning.
Gilt décor everywhere.
Huge ornate glittering chandeliers hung in a row down the room.
Across at the wall in a line, were small replicas of many, many nations' flags.
A long grand dining table was fully set in glistening crystal and twinkling silver.
Enough for fifty covers.

"This year has seen unique events and a glimpse of something un-Earthly. Yet it so very much affects humanity. It is with this monumental event and an unknown future that I want to convey mine and my family's heartfelt wish."

The Queen paused. In her ninety second year, she was frail but determined.

"Only by every nation, their peoples using all the strength they have, in love, kindness and kinship, can humanity survive and move forward into a new era. All persuations, of whatever faith must work together for a lasting peace."

The Queen abruptly stopped and she took off her glasses.
Her eyes were crystal clear and unblinking.

"Only by the cessation of wars and cruelty on this planet, that gives rise to suffering and death, can we as a species continue into the next phase of our evolution. I believe in our God and Lord Jesus to protect and guide us at this crucial time.
God bless you all."

The brief broadcast then finished.
Anne looked at Karen and said, "Well, I reckon that was the shortest Christmas message she has ever given! But wonderful."
Karen nodded, "She is well informed, naturally. That speech was concise yet has all we as humanity need. God and Jesus…" her voice tailed off.

Anne commented, "Yes God and Jesus. They seem so far away now. Memories of wisdom and guidance, mankind's saviors."

Next Day
10 am Boxing Day 2018
Dell Quay near Chichester, UK

Lei looked closely at her arm, where the burn had been.
Completely gone, healed.

She had called her sister Ming, exchanging Christmas best wishes across the Atlantic Ocean. They talked for a long time.
Lei felt lonely. She currently had the sole command of the yacht Nemain, as it gently rocked in the water on its mooring.

She was very worried for Steven. He had disappeared on a trip to Israel.
She thought 'He seems ill, very pale with a look in his eyes that was…absent?'

It was as though something was slowly draining the life out of him.

He said he would be back by New Year's Eve.
The only reason he gave was that he needed to investigate the origin of some artefacts.

She took another Greek cigarette from the pack and placed it in her mouth.
Picking up a lighter, she lit it and went up on deck, sliding onto the chair in the covered cockpit.

It was another bright sunny day with lots of people walking their dogs on the estuary path.
A gaggle of ducks were on the mottled green foreshore, waddling and picking their way through seaweed encrusted rock pools, pulling out wriggling shrimps.

One guy had a pair of binoculars and seemed interested in an old barge, rotting on the opposite shore.
Lei was sharp, her eyes roved around for anything unusual.
Slowly exhaling a puff of blue smoke, she watched him.

Then a cormorant took off from the barge and soared into the air.
The binoculars followed it.
Lei watched the guy take out a notebook and scribble something down, and then he looked through the binoculars at some birds in a nearby tree.

She smiled.
A passing yacht caught her attention. A small three person craft parted the waters, its mainsail filling with the stiff breeze.
"Good morning!" shouted Lei, "Lovely day for it."
Sitting at the back a man and woman both waved, their bright orange life jackets contrasting the white hull.
"Yes it is. We're making the most of the nice weather."

Smiling and drawing on her cigarette, she turned her gaze back to the binocular man.
He had gone.

She glanced up and down the shoreline and thought,
'How could he have disappeared in so short a space of time? there's no cover there.'
Then she laughed inwardly, 'God I am jumpy.'

Lei tapped a text and sent it.
'Steven, please, please take care. See a doctor there. I love you xxxxx'

A little later that week
Skiathos Airport, Greece

The old man quickly got up from the seat and walked to the new arrival.
"Hello Silenos my old friend, good to see you."
Steven Crowley the tall bearded man, wheeled his small case across.
He looked gaunt and a little thin as he shook hands with Silenos Drivas, still… Mayor of Skiathos.

Despite the smuggling accusations, Silenos had narrowly avoided prosecution.
Luckily for him, the wealthy Mayor had acquired a top lawyer.

"Steven, it's been a while. You look a little jaded, may I say?"
"Yes I am. On my way to Jerusalem to see a gifted physician."
"Ah."

Back at the Drivas residence, they all tucked into Keftedes.
Steven looked up forking some olives onto his plate.
"The meatballs are divine Sarra."
"Thank you Steven. How long are you staying?"
"Oh I shall be on my way to Jerusalem tomorrow, and Sarra how are you these days, after your operation?"
She paused, and then smiled, "God has been merciful. I can't believe after so much pain from the heart attack, I am still here. The doctors have given me a few more years."

Silenos moved his hand to his wife's shoulder. "Old as we are, I am so lucky to have such a beautiful wife."
"Oh Silenos…"
Angelo their son, looked up and quickly swallowed, he said "It was a worrying time, but Ma has pulled through well. We love you."

After lunch, Sarra disappeared into the kitchen to prepare coffee. Their maid was busy with the dishes.

Silenos was the first to speak.
"Now that our esteemed colleague Irving Dekker is dead, I guess you will need to deal solely with me?"
He nearly spat.
Steven nodded and replied, "Yes indeed. He met his end not before time."
He looked directly at Irving's killer…Angelo.
Angelo drew a long breath, eyeing the two men, "Yes and my sister Karen lives as a result."
He glanced at his Pa.
Silenos had guessed at Sarra's infidelity all those years ago and they had talked about it. The news had trickled back of the awful event at Karen's house, with Angelo bludgeoning Irving Dekker to death as he was shooting at Karen.

Silenos started to swear, "That bastard Dekker, he…."
Steven interrupted "Silenos, he is gone now and your business I hear is doing well again?"
"Yes, we have recovered. You know, Irving became a different man over the years. Don't get me wrong, he was always the shrewd entrepreneur and as we know a crook, but I liked him then."
Steven acknowledged, "I think an external influence maybe?"
Silenos coldly replied, "Maybe. You see in the beginning he was driven by money, but later he pursued odd quests you know. I think he was a member of a satanic cult. He was fascinated by

occult powers and achieving some sort of demonic existence beyond the grave."
Angelo was nodding, "That's why I pursued his trail to Gibraltar. He was muddled up with those aliens, I'm sure of it."

They retired to the balcony giving a panoramic view of old Skiathos Town and the bustling waterfront with a harbour full of tour boats and rows of white hulled yachts.

"Cigarette Silenos?"
"Of course, thank you."

Blue smoke surrounded the three men as they pondered the view.

A day later
The Old Quarter
Jerusalem, Israel

Steven Crowley was indeed not a well man, his complexion pallid, his blue eyes more of a grey now.
The little bulge on his belt contained the devices. Micro miniature semi-organic machines that could enter his bloodstream via his skin and so heal some conditions, but he knew that their capacity had been all but consumed.
They were failing him.

The ancient pain in his right torso just under his ribs, reminded him that time was not on his side.

He had walked through the narrow streets and noisy markets for some time.
Then he spotted it.
The little alleyway, so narrow.
Stuck in time, the same as when Edward Durgas stumbled upon it forty two years ago.

Only the odd washing line had changed. A new door or window here and there.
The alley and walls grey with grime.
The main difference today was the sheer volume of people traversing it.

Steven Crowley shaded his eyes and entered the alleyway, ducking under large swathes of washing hanging on lines across the path. At six and a half feet he had to stoop several times, then twisting and turning to avoid the crowd.
People coming every which way, both directions.

He coughed, climbed and stumbled up the winding rough stoned path.
It opened into a sort of courtyard with two more alleyways out of it.

Almost exhausted, he paused and then stopped. He was sure, yes there on the left, an old building with an ancient doorway. A man of about sixty wrapped in traditional garb was sitting on the doorstep smoking a cheroot.

Steven wandered over to him and said, "I am looking for relatives of Abdul-Muhsi."
He flourished a fifty dollar bill.
The man leaned forward to take it but Steven withdrew the note quickly.
"Not so fast old man, do you know where?"
All spoken in Arabic.

"Who asks?"
Steven pulled his shirt sleeve back to reveal the ancient bracelet on his arm.

The reaction was a blink, a rapid recognition, quickly followed by the blank face again.
"Who asks?" repeated.

"I do Steven Crowley! Holder of the sacred bracelet."

Instantly the Arab got to his feet and stared at the long haired, bearded man.
A moment passed, and then he said, "I am Abu Muhsi, son of Abdul-Muhsi."

Fifty dollars passed hands quickly.
Then he said, "Do you wish to speak with Abdul-Muhsi?"
Steven Crowley laughed out loud
"Well that would be good, but I imagine he is long dead! He met a colleague of mine Edward Durgas some forty odd years ago. Maybe you can help me?"

"But he is not dead…"

Steven froze, he said "Are you wasting my time?"
The banter was necessary and tokens were being exchanged.
Then knowingly, he said, "Well if he IS still alive, Yes, I would very much like to see him."
The Arab beckoned him inside.

They walked through a short darkened corridor and then into a large room illuminated by a cluster of candles at an old table.
In the grey gloom, one could just make out many dusty antiquities, piles of crockery, rolls of papyrus, stacks of old books, statues, faded carpets on the walls and an ornate light coloured wooden coffin standing against the far wall.
It momentarily caught Steven's eye.

Sitting there at the table was a shrunken bent over old man, holding a cane with one hand.
"Father, there is someone to see you, an Englishman, an acquaintance of Edward Durgas."
The old man looked up through his good eye.
A squeaky, rattling voice spoke in near perfect English,

"I have been waiting for you Steven Crowley."

He waved his son away.

Steven replied, "You're looking well for someone well over a hundred years old?"
Indeed the old man was beyond ancient, his head like a wrinkled walnut.
From a thin body wrapped in a coloured robe, a skinny brown arm was held out.
"And you are not looking well Steven. Please take a seat. COFFEE!"

The response was a rattling of crockery upstairs.
Steven replied, "I have been under duress. *They are continually seeking me.*"

The two men remained silent as a young woman in a dark burka carried a tray down the worn stone staircase.
Abdul nodded his thanks and she disappeared back upstairs.

"Abdul it is amazing, I thought you were long dead?"
"Don't play games with me Steven, you know who I am."

Steven Crowley smiled and said, "I feel strange at times and no doubt you do too."
The old man broke into a crinkled smile, "It is what we are."
Then Abdul-Muhsi took Steven's bracelet arm and with his own hand attached another bracelet next to it. This one was rather plain, with a few little scrolls along its edges.
Then he did something extremely unusual for a very old man in a backstreet museum shop in Jerusalem.
He rotated the dial on one of the ornate rings on his left hand, all the while staring intently at Steven with his good eye.

A tiny complex coloured pattern appeared on the second bracelet next to the ancient one on Steven's arm.

Steven cried out, holding the arms of the chair tightly.
He closed his eyes.
Within minutes his pallor started to improve. Then he opened his eyes which were returning to the blue fire they always had.
The pain in his side was diminishing.

"Ah that is so much better. I could not have waited much longer. Are we safe here?"

Abdul-Muhsi looked around slowly, then back at Steven.
"Yes, the building has protection like the churches.
However, in a few weeks we will be sorely tested."

"Yes."

"You are approaching a crucial time in your life Steven."
"I feel it."
"Are you afraid for this life?"

Steven took out his Greek cigarettes and proffered the packet to Abdul-Muhsi.
The old man cackled a croaky laugh and took one.
He smiled and said, "For old times."
They lit up using the candle flames and soon the room was full of blue swirling smoke.
Both the men racked a few coughs.
Steven exhaled slowly towards the dark musty ceiling.
A large plume of grey blue smoke drifted along it, the candle light accentuating the little wisps and curls of the nicotine cloud.

He said "Yes at times I have great fear. I have not always played the good person in this life.
My reasons are 'justified cover' and where lives have been taken, it was necessary for the greater good."

The good eye stayed on him, unblinking.

Steven continued, "It is the unknown you know, the direction of my mission is clear, however the detail evades me."

The old man watched him with a knowledge that stretched way back in time.
"It is good to have fear. It will steel you. Do not underestimate your strength Steven, but take courage that you have tremendous resources. You will meet your destiny."

Steven stared at him then slowly cast his eye around the cluttered room and said.
"As a brilliant sunny day follows a dark brooding night, I know that."

He shuddered slightly and said,
"It is the continual night I fear."

They drank coffee and discussed world events and other things too.

Steven was now well on the way to his old self.
After two hours, they said goodbye and embraced for some minutes.

Abdul-Muhsi gave Steven one of the rings on his finger.
The second bracelet remained reassuringly on Steven's arm.

As he left the candlelit room, Steven turned to wave farewell and just for a moment he smiled as he glimpsed a momentary change in the old man.

The robe had turned to pure white and a sort of white aura surrounded Abdul-Muhsi.

8 pm New Year's Eve 2018
The Old Custom House, Gunwharf, Portsmouth, UK

Upstairs in the large hall, a party was in full swing with a live band knocking out 'Sweet Alabama...'

It was the New Year's Eve Masked Ball, topped off with fancy dress to the theme 'Medieval Times'.

Jane couldn't stop laughing.
"Oh god Bill look at you, all those red frilly bits around your waist and nether regions, it so goes with the armour! Ha ha."

Bill grinned sitting there, wearing a suit of shiny silver overlapping plastic armour, sandwiched in between with red decorative frills around his neck, shoulders and waist.
His helmet had the front face plate open and swivelled up above his eye line.
Feet shoed in multiple steel like plates.
A little black mask covered his eyes.
He replied "Thank the Lord it's made of light weight plastic! But very realistic looking. How the hell am I supposed to dance in this though?"

Jane wore a King's daughter's one piece dress, a magnificient blue and white creation. A silver tiara held back her long red hair, with her pale blue mask completing the effect.
She carried on laughing and got up from their table, "I'll get another drink, same again?"
He nodded, grinning, trying to stop his loose helmet visor from flipping down.

The place was heaving with people.
Amazing outfits.
'El Cid' the Spanish hero walked past. He was wearing a white apron over chainmail
armour.

The bar was thick with knights, monks, damsels in long dresses, foot soldiers and a court jester dressed in bright orange and red. Plastic spears and swords stuck out everywhere.
Jane gently squeezed her way in.
As she approached the bar, Jane caught sight of tight grey weave 'chainmail' on a man's legs at the bar.
She thought, 'I know those legs anywhere.'
"Gavin!"

A worried bearded face with longish hair, wearing black spectacles over an eye mask, turned around to see who it was.
He was wearing an imitation chainmail waistcoat over a short brown robe.
Jane who had raised her mask exclaimed, "Oh sorry, I mistook you for someone else."
"Jane! No, no…it's me Gavin!"
"Good God Gavin, what's happened to you?"
Removing the mask and raising his voice above the noise, he replied, "Disguise you see, the beard and specs. Just plain glass in them. Quite good eh?"

Jane frowned, "Why Gavin, is it part of the fancy dress?"
Gavin moved close and with a serious face said in her ear, "No. I need to. Roger is still after me."
He grinned a little, "Good disguise eh? Reckon I could be a James Bond character, keep changing it and staying ahead of them."

Jane's eyes widened, she momentarily glanced around. "I thought he was dead?"
"Na. Crippled though. In a wheelchair now."
She said nothing, her mind was spinning that fact.

A slip of a girl in a milkmaid's outfit and white mask came up. Gavin quickly introduced her, "Ah…um Jane, please meet my partner Naomi."

Jane slightly taken aback, broke into a smile, "Nice to meet you."
Naomi just smiled a little sourly.
Jane took a breath, "Where's Roger now?"
"No idea. I hear he's pretty mad at us."
"Naturally."

Getting back to their table, Jane plonked the drinks down on it. Two blond beers.
"You'll never guess who is at the bar?"
Bill looked up, "Go on."
"Gavin, not only in fancy dress, but in disguise, real beard and specs."

Bill slightly suspicious replied "Really? What did he say?"
She told him about Roger and then Gavin's new girlfriend.

Bill instantly looked around at the sea of fancy dress and masks. Hard to tell if they were 'under surveillance'.

He couldn't see a wheel chair anywhere.

Chapter 28

Early morning - Wednesday 17th January
Cape Kennedy, Florida

Two launches had already happened.

The first was an unmanned US military heavy lifter rocket.
It took two nuclear X-Ray weapons and a still-under-the-wraps third weapon, up and into deep Earth orbit, in a vehicle called Horizon.

The second unmanned launch nicknamed Gray, had taken up the US Space Gravity Array. Which had now been deployed far beyond Earth's orbit.

Other nations had not stood still.
The Chinese had launched a huge vehicle on a rocket nobody thought they had.

Russia also had launched two rockets and deployed vehicles of unknown capability into orbit.

Now the US manned launches would follow…

Astronaut engineer John Creeson was really wishing he was wearing his brown corduroy trousers.
Metaphorically speaking of course, as wearing his spacesuit and helmet, he laid strapped into the cockpit of their spacecraft Rameses.

He forced a smile thinking of the email Bill Craswell had sent him.
It mentioned the trousers, wishing him well, a safe return and Godspeed to do whatever it took.

He turned his head and glanced through the faceplate at Daniel Ethen the pilot and then co-pilot Mark Vanderbrook.
In the back a Mark II Benji robot checked some instruments.
Most of these the robot could do via the Bluetooth radio links to the console, which meant the robot sat still apparently doing nothing.
From the cockpit came an occasional beep in between the voice comms.

Their vehicle, Rameses, was straddled across the top of a much modified Boeing 747 airliner, which was now flying at thirty thousand feet.

The Rameses Ramjet spacecraft was attached to the Boeing by release struts and looked every much the ugly bulbous duckling.
Back in the nineteen eighties, the first Space Shuttle had undergone the same to test its aerodynamic abilities, detaching and gliding back to the airstrip with no engines.

This was no test. They didn't have time in the schedule for it and worse there was no provision for re-entry or landing using Rameses.

Daniel winked at John.
Two days earlier Ming Zhao had been furiously working with a NASA software engineer.
They had uncovered rogue software in the fuel control suite for the Ramjet engines.

Sabotage software.

It had been hooked into the telemetry interface.
What that meant was that the software itself remained dormant until a certain unauthorised transmission was received. Then it could be commanded to do one of several things, including shutting the Ramjets' fuel off prematurely.
Resulting in a fatal nose dive to the ground.

Colonel Mondone could not praise them enough.
They didn't tell John Creeson or the rest of the crew. They had enough to worry about.

What nobody knew was that Steven Crowley had already ordered that no sabotage transmission was to be made. He knew the alien armada would exit its own portal and not use Crackwell and that the sabotage plan was only a ruse to satisfy *the enemy*.

As it happened, the Ramjet vehicle would not now be carrying the nuclear devices.
These were in the NASA heavy lifter rocket, and no access could be obtained to its control software.

Crowley had kept his intentions to himself, knowing that the no sabotage decision was always a given.

T-Minus Forty seconds

Daniel said "Here we go."
At that moment the Boeing airliner went full throttle and climbed fast.
John felt the perspiration running down the back of his space suit. With a finger from his gloved hand he touched the photo of him and Karen pinned to the control panel.

The Boeing pilot started a countdown, "Forty seconds to detach."

At thirty seconds, Daniel fired up the Ramjets in low thrust.
All green for go.

"Nineteen, eighteen..."

"This is it." thought John, "Outer space here I come."
He gritted his teeth.

"Ten, nine, eight..."

The ramjets started to roar.
All five of them burst into life in a large bulbous cluster circling the base of their rocket.

"Three, two, one…detach!"

A loud thump announced the explosive bolts releasing them from the airliner.
Daniel steadily increased the Ramjets thrust and turned Rameses slowly upwards.
He yelled to John "Here we go John! A white knuckle ride."
John's face had turned white, his gloved hands gripping the arms of his chair tightly.

Then the Ramjets opened up fully into a horrendous roar, air sucking into them and forced out at a blistering rate.
Rameses ascended steeply.

John was slammed back into the depths of his chair.
After three minutes of acceleration approaching three G, and their vehicle turning vertically, the Ramjets cut out.
Two seconds later the rocket booster flared into life and thrust the little ship hard out of Earth's atmosphere.
Through the window the deep blackness of space appeared over the blue Earth's curvature.
John bit his tongue, the acceleration was nothing like he expected, as he was pressed even harder into his chair.
A metal like taste of blood, entered his mouth.

His chest weighed tons, his breathing became laboured.
Speech was out of the question.
He couldn't even turn his head to see the others.

'Oh god.' he thought, 'and I believed all those extreme fun park rides were well behind me!'

The booster seemed to fire for ever.
Actually around four minutes.

Engine shutdown.
Then a crack and lurch as the bottom section of their vehicle was discarded.

Followed by nothing, utter silence.

Outside through the small windows, everything was inky black.
They had escaped Earth's orbit.
Both pilot and co-pilot were monitoring the screens and Benji-Ram as they had nicknamed him, was confirming systems integrity.

Mark Vanderbrook looked across at John and said, "Ok, ten seconds to firing your gravity engine."
John's pulse was hammering.
He thought, 'Ok Bill, I hope you've sorted everything out, because your engine is just twelve metres away from my backside.'
He knew that Bill and others on the ground were closely monitoring the telemetry from their craft.
"Nine, eight…"

They felt small vibrations as the gravity engine systems ramped up for three quarters thrust.

"Three, two, ignition…on…"

Mark never got to finish 'one'.
The colossal thrust instantly took the air out of his lungs as the three of them were crushed back in their seats.

A staccato of explosive charges and pellet detonations sounded like a giant nail gun hammering on the bulkhead behind them.
The little Rameses craft shot away from the Earth.
Two minutes later the gravity engine shut down.

Mark taking a lung full of air yelled out, “Beyond the moon here we come!”

After some minutes the two Americans unclipped themselves from their seats and floated out.
John with some trepidation waited. Floating in zero gravity would come in good time. Then a queasy tummy reminded him of the traumatic launch.
Instantly his stomach rejected its contents straight into the plastic bag he just managed to open from his side pocket.

The American astronauts smiled sympathetically.
The voicecom suddenly burst into life.
“John, Daniel, Mark. Bill Craswell here. Our stats showed perfect operation but how did the gravity engine feel?”

Daniel laughed, “Roger that Bill. The engine certainly did its stuff. Like a repeating punch in the back!”
A little chuckle came from the ground.

Four hours later.

John was still quite pale but now he had been working, doing something that put his dodgy stomach to the back of his mind.
He was communicating with the four US Gravity Array units. A distance of five thousand miles separated each module. The four modules formed a giant space based three sided pyramid, connected by infra red lasers to maintain position. Tiny thrusters micro managing the precise location of each. What couldn’t be seen without instruments, was the stream of tiny neutrinos travelling between the gravity modules.

He reminisced wondering what the inventor Conrad Thursule would think of this beastie in space. So sad that he died in that awful explosion back in ESS.
‘He would have been so proud. Such a genius, such a loss.’

News came of the Orion launch reaching deep Earth orbit.
In two hours, they would remotely manoeuvre the first Nuclear X-Ray device into position.
John focussed their telescope system on a point just ten million miles away.

There at that point sat Crackwell the conundrum, that non-physical *invisible* object.

A complex construction of pure energy projected from a source tens of thousands of light years away. It was mooted to be a portal created by the people from the dense globular cluster of stars in Omega Centauri.
A distance for man, that even with his fastest propulsion systems, would take millions of years of travel to get there.

John felt deeply disturbed by this attempt to close the portal.
He had tried in vain to persuade the Americans to reverse their decision.
However, his prime job was to monitor and tune the gravity arrays as events unfolded.
He turned to Daniel and said, "Are you ready to deploy a gravity bomb and test the arrays proper and highlight our friend Crackwell out there."

"Sure am. Say ten minutes?" Replied Daniel.
"Yes, Do your stuff."

Precisely ten minutes later a tiny gravity bomb was detonated far out in space.

They waited as the array processors gathered and processed the data.
Quickly it was transmitted to Houston, Texas.

Then their command vehicle felt a tiny thud on the outside of their craft, as the bomb shockwave hit them.

The large display screen in Rameses showed the space-time grid buckling around Crackwell.
Only slight but there it was the strange cone shape of the portal and the opening just a couple of hundred metres across.
After some minutes of analysis John spoke up, "Looks like the array is not balanced."
He keyed some numbers and then initiated a control transmission to the array modules in space.
"There all good now."

John was pensive, his face strained, thinking 'All quiet on the western front… so far.'

That same day…
ESS Systems
East Meon, UK

Bill Craswell was glued to the huge wall size display screens.

With him were Jane Horsham, Sir George Ratcliffe and Louis Redmond.
Karen had taken leave to be at Sabrina's circle, with Jane planning to sneak out later.

Jane had showed Crystal, Ratcliffe's new assistant, how to set up some online reports for him. Dynamic reports that were updated by real-time data streaming in.

Ratcliffe spoke, "Excellent performance from our gravity engine Bill."
Bill glowed with supreme elation, "Yes as I knew, it did the job admirably."
Ratcliffe turned to Jane.
"What's the response time like from the ground based American systems Jane?"

The US space based gravity array was controlled by the US gravity team, led by Brad Bannerman in Houston, Texas. Their computers had been configured to send a data feed to the ESS computer systems in the UK.

"Oh, about two minutes. It's a pity we don't have control of the viewpoint, we just get what they decide to send us. However, John can configure and focus data that we want to see."

Ratcliffe muttered, "Hmmm…yes I understand it is not the perfect situation. Can we not use our Gravity Array?"
Bill replied, "Ours is up and running, but it doesn't have a fraction of the resolution of the American system. There on the second screen is our array data."
"Ah…good."

Jane had been in discussion with Louis, she turned to Bill and George.
"Louis has just mentioned that he may have a handle on where the Andromeda armada could appear."
She motioned to Louis.
"Yes, I re-analysed the black hole cortex trail using a spectrographic approach and images from our X-Ray telescopes."
He paused.

Ratcliffe had an irritated look, "This so called armada. I am currently entertaining the idea, but until we have conclusive evidence, that's all I shall do, but Louis please explain."
Jane slightly scowled at Ratcliffe, and then looked knowingly at Bill, who displayed a slight touch of gargoyle.

Louis with his commanding French accent, didn't flinch but just piled in.
"It is possible that this cortex may exit somewhere in the vicinity of the planet Jupiter's orbit. We can narrow down the position as an intersection between this orbit and the direction of the plasma jet from that galaxy's black hole."

He brought up Andromeda on a new screen.
The cortex was still there. A snaking corridor in a jet of plasma, that stretched two million light years from our neighbouring galaxy Andromeda right the way over to ours, the Milky Way.
Ratcliffe acquiesced somewhat, reluctantly he said "Ok thanks Louis. Guess we should cover this eventuality."

He tapped his fingers on the table, his face going through the implications.
Then he muttered, "If you are right then we should not be caught with our trousers down….hmmm."

Crystal looked up from her display screen, with a slight scowl, thinking, 'Yes and you Sir George had better keep yours on…'

Then Sir George Ratcliffe spent some little time on the phone, requesting national and international astronomy and space centres, to monitor Jupiter's orbit.

Putting the phone down, he spoke to them all, "I have cancelled all holiday and as you know we are working through this weekend. Our alert levels must remain high and if necessary we work shifts through the night as and when."

Jane inwardly sighed.
Bill was desperate to leap to the rooftops and shout to the world, 'My engine worked up there. My bloody engine worked perfect. Eat that, all you disbelievers!'

He smiled, thinking of the accolades surely to come now.
Just briefly he had a very heartening feel good moment.

And then…the here and now hitting home with Armageddon probably just around the corner.

Late afternoon Wednesday 17th January
Sabrina Fay's house in Catherington, Hampshire, UK

The military presence onsite was not welcome.
Sabrina knew they had no choice.

The UK government was quite aware of Sabrina's shamanic circle and despite the intangible aspects, had gently intervened.

Ranul Magrit the Home Secretary had arrived and was making his way through a throng of people to Sabrina. He was followed by his Secret Service bodyguard.

The group had enlisted many people faithful to the cause. Sabrina was working with the Elders to plan the coming days and perhaps weeks.
A cyclic schedule of people had been arranged to maintain a powerful dreaming locked with the ancestors. In addition, she had worked hard to select people to maintain the purple shield provided by the artefacts.
Now just two, Karen with her cross and Bill, nominated to hold the helmet.
A frequent change of holders on the hour would happen.

Earlier Jane had been in discussion with Karen just after a news broadcast.
One item was that many mosques, temples, cathedrals and churches were seeing greatly enlarged congregations.
Some overflowing with converts.
Jane "Karen, remember what Quentin said about churches being a sort of sanctuary protected by those devices?"
Karen agreed, "Yes I do. People are finding their faith. It's incredible."

The third artefact, the sword was now in deep space with John Creeson.

The fourth, the bracelet, was with Steven Crowley, wherever he happened to be.
Nobody knew.

Lei had arrived not only to share the artefact schedule, but to help in any way she could.
Anything to take her mind off Steven's disappearance.
He had texted her briefly a week ago, saying everything was ok and he would be back soon.

Nothing since.
No replies to her phone texts or calls.

Karen briefly waved to her friend Anne Whitfield who was across at the other side of the room. Then she walked up to Lei and said "Any news of Steven?"
"No, nothing and Karen, I am afraid. He is up to something, no doubt preparing for another of his stunts. Although I sense he is doing something very important. Hopefully we shall see him soon."
Lei couldn't hide her face lined with worry.

They were distracted.
A loud whirring noise could be heard outside.
"Ah Sabrina Fay, an honour to meet you." Ranul Magrit proffered his hand.

"Mr Home Secretary, the honour is mine."
Her demeanour became cold, "What can I do for you?"

"Well I believe you are already doing all you can. I know this is a very, shall I say, private affair, but your influence in what may become, is valuable to our country and indeed the world."
"Thank you."
Ranul turned to an aid rapidly approaching.
He turned back to Sabrina and exclaimed, "and it is my pleasure to introduce you to the Prime Minister Samantha Yeareth."

At that moment the lounge inner doors opened and several black suited men arrived, wired earpieces prominent. They surrounded a tall grey haired elegant woman dressed in a dark blue suit. Bodyguards galore.

Sabrina walked to the Prime Minister and stopped.
"Sabrina Fay, please forgive our intrusion and the surprise of my visit."
"That's fine Prime Minister." replied Sabrina, but thinking 'We need to get on and dispense with these politicians.'
"I am here for a short time only and I needed to meet you personally and… ah yes this lady too."

Karen Durgas had walked over and they shook hands.
"It is a privilege to meet you Prime Minister."
"Likewise. The artefacts you have are of paramount interest. That is why I have ordered the presence of some of our most eminent engineers to witness and observe your operation."
Karen quickly replied, "I understand your motives Prime Minister, but we own these devices and they are tuned to say, our personalities. It is very likely that they would not function if put into other hands."
A little lie, but necessary.
She hoped the ministers would not twig about the planned schedule of artefact holders.

"That may as be, but you are taking on a huge responsibility by your reluctance to share this ability you have."
"Oh but I am sharing, to the whole world. If I fail then I foresee I may die."

Sam Yeareth stared hard at Karen, and then she came straight to the point.
"Karen, in the next few weeks the fate of mankind may be in the balance. We must engage every resource we have, no matter how unusual. This is why I am here, to provide any support that you and Sabrina require."

Sabrina gave her thanks and shook the Prime Minister's hand, as did Karen.
Their eyes locked in *mutual wariness*.
With that the head of the government left as quickly as she had arrived.
The helicopter took off from the lawn, shaking the house and trees as it left.
Several large candles were already burning in the lounge, flickering and casting odd shadows up the walls.
Karen looked at Sabrina, "Would you believe that?"
Sabrina, "I expected it actually. I had sensed she would come. Anyway we must get on. Karen we seem to be short of bottled water and long burning candles, are you free to get some."

Karen replied, "Sure. I'll go to the local supermarket."
"Ok, but please don't be too long, your cross is vital to operations here."

Anne Whitfield came across hurriedly, she said "I sense something very ominous."
Sabrina "Yes I do too…it is time."
"I'll be quick Sabrina."
"Thank you, take the utmost care."

Karen's Benji came from outside and accompanied her.

Anywhere other than here, Karen knew she would need her cross. She felt someone or something was not that far away.
"Hi Benji, come on. Please get in the car."
"Yes Karen."
Even the company of a robot was welcome, especially the protection of this military killing machine.

However, a creeping fear of the unknown didn't leave her.

Meanwhile.
In Deep Space, just beyond the moon.

In the Orion command module, three astronauts were preparing to deploy an ugly weapon.

Two million miles from them, the large unmanned silver pod manoeuvred under its own engine power, slowly towards Crackwell.
The Horizon module would release a fifty megaton nuclear missile, the warhead enclosed with an X-Ray grid constructed of the hardest compounds known to man.
A grid to withstand for a split second the ferocious energies of a nuclear explosion and by its design, focus huge X-Ray energies into a narrow beam.

Far away on the other side of the moon, John Creeson and his colleagues watched from their Rameses craft.

The distance slowly closed between Crackwell and its attacker the Horizon module.

Fifty miles.

A bright orange flame announced the launch of the nuclear X-Ray missile.
As it rapidly it approached Crackwell, Horizon retreated.

A mile.

Five hundred yards.

Two hundred……..

Automatically a gravity bomb some distance away was detonated to provide gravity waves as extra illumination.

John's mind didn't finish registering the heads-up numbers on the display showing the portal.
It was because they weren't there anymore.
An enormous flash had created whiteout on their monitors from the cameras.
In an instant the most devastating of mankind's weapons produced a hideous burning blast of nuclear fission.
The X-Ray grid vaporised in a split second.
But not before it did its stuff.

A massive beam of extremely high energy X-Rays hit Crackwell.

Then a second gravity bomb went off.

John instinctively turned away shielding his eyes.
Daniel Ethen the commander uttered, "Hell Almighty will you look at that!"
On the screen John saw something remarkable.
A blister of flashes and sparks erupted around Crackwell and then for the briefest of instants a tiny ghostly grey tunnel flashed visibly, disappearing back towards the centre of our galaxy.

Then nothing, inky black space returned to where Crackwell had been.
Invisible again.

Mark Vanderbrook was watching a coloured screen of graphs and numbers, he exclaimed, "Here it comes the blast wave. Come on you thrusters hold us fast!"
A shuddering bang on the outside shell announced the shock wave.
Simultaneously the small thrusters countered to maintain spacecraft position.

John paused, distracted, he glanced out of the porthole at the distant blue dot of Earth, so far away.
His mind shouted 'Karen!'

Frowning, his intuition said she was in trouble.

Twenty seconds later, with some super fast processing, up came the US gravity grid display.
John stopped the screen picture a millisecond after the hit and manipulated the data grid at that precise time.
He turned quite pale, then said quietly,
"Holy cow. Oh my… that is unbelievable."

Fanning out from where the X-Rays hit Crackwell were very tiny ripples in the gravity grid.
The other astronauts closely watched.
There it remained, Crackwell the energy portal, still intact.
John drew a massive breath trying to disguise his huge relief.

In addition, a rainbow of coloured energies starred out from the anomaly, but what really caught John's attention was away from Crackwell a sort of 3D mesh made up of faint light appeared.
He panned around the data grid until he was looking at the sun.
John blocked the sun's brightness using a software control and then gasped.
Daniel started to say, "What the hell…"

'Will you look at that…' thought John.
He said, "That's weird, could be a gas cloud?"
Mark replied, "Whatever it is, it's huge."

The gravity array showed something that stretched all the way to the sun.
A huge nebulous cloud of light that had layers of giant curves in it. He tried to measure the size, but it was enormous stretching far into the distance.

He instinctively looked out of the Rameses porthole, with its dark visor pulled into position filtering most of the sun's searing rays.
John squinted through the yellow glow.

Nothing, no faint clouds of light, no nebulous mass.
Just stars and our sun.

He knew.
Karen had discussed this stuff with him.
Some time back in the summer, after working a complex data restore they had managed to see again the thin spikes emanating from the Earth after the supernova gravity waves had hit, a year ago now.
What he saw on the gravity grid just held his mind in awe.
'Was it really what he thought it to be?'

Crackwell had automatically repelled the intense X-Rays with some of its as yet undiscovered energies. Energies that spread out rippling space and time.

John thought hard, 'A grey complex 'cloud of light' which could be… a spiritual dimension?'

The thought rocked him to the bone.

40 seconds before…

Earth
Morrisons Supermarket – Horndean, UK

In the almost deserted supermarket, Karen wandered down the aisle pushing a trolley.
It was piled with bottles of water.
She now headed for the household aisle hoping that there were some big candles left.
Trouble was, people had started buying candles in panic, afraid the electricity power stations might fail or be attacked.

She slowed down to pick a bottle of Elderflower cordial from the top shelf.

Then Karen stopped, she glanced through the skylight in the supermarket roof.
It was pitch black outside.
In outer space she knew they were going to use nuclear weapons on that tiny non-physical entity, the anomaly dubbed Crackwell.
Not good.

Then she saw it, a bright pin point flash, right out past that grey crescent moon.
Her heart fluttered, she grabbed the trolley handle tightly with her free hand.

Something weird was happening.
Goose bumps appeared immediately on her arms.
She felt cold and shivery despite the warmth of the supermarket.

Followed immediately by an extraordinary event...

Karen heard a familiar sigh.
She turned back and looked down the supermarket aisle.
Then she froze.

There was her Mum walking past the aisle at the end, carrying her Burberry handbag.
The Elderflower bottle fell out of Karen's hand and smashed on the floor.

Karen gasped, paled, then slid and half fell into the nearby shelf, spilling packets of food and tins from it. She grappled wildly at the shelves, spilling more items as she desperately felt for a handhold.
You see her dear Mum had passed away more than fifteen months ago.
...and then something even stranger occurred......
Her Dad followed her Mum.
He was dead too.

Karen scrambled to her feet, leaving the trolley and ran down to the end of the aisle, shouting "Mum, Dad!"

There they were deep in discussion looking at something on the shelves.
Her Mum Jenny then turned and seeing Karen she smiled.

A lovely, loving smile full of endearing goodness.
An eternal mother's smile.
Her Dad Edward, with his forever calm demeanour, grinned at Karen and held out his hands.

As she reached them, her Mum said "We wanted to say how proud we are of you my girl. You are doing all the right things."
Her Dad quipped, "Headstrong as ever my daughter and we love you for it."
He squeezed his daughter's hands with both of his.
Karen just melted with happiness.

Then her mother Jenny lifted Karen's cross with the chain until it was placed outside her blouse, and said, "Be one soul, trust only your friends and also those friends out there…this cross gives you protection."
Karen frowned but before she could speak, her Dad said, "You have the strength and you are on the brink of great discoveries. Use it all wisely."
She was on cloud nine, feeling happy and comforted beyond description.

A haze seemed to diminish the surroundings.
Her Mum and Dad were fading.

"no…NO! please stay…Mum, Dad...PLEASE DON'T GO!"

Waving and smiling, her Mum mouthed the words, 'I love you'.
Then they disappeared.

Karen moaned.

A voice, "Someone call an ambulance…she's coming round I think."

The male shop attendant gently eased Karen away from were she was lying, pushing away piles of tins and packets of food littered around her.
The trolley remained stationary a couple of yards away.
Spilt cordial and broken glass was strewn all around.
A shop girl helped Karen into a sitting position on the floor.

As Karen became more conscious, she exclaimed, "Where… where am I? where is Mum and Dad?... they've gone…oh."
"Easy, I think you fainted and had a bit of a fall."
The girl steadied Karen holding her arm.

Karen looked slowly around shaking her head slightly and stuttered, "Oh God…no can't be…I must have been dreaming?"

She reached inside for her cross.
Uncannily, it was on top of her blouse.

Late evening Wednesday 17th January

US Gravity Array Control Centre, Houston, Texas

Brad Bannerman had worked feverishly with his team after the first space nuclear detonation.

Masses of data to process and sort.

Colonel Arrack Mondone looked over his shoulder, "Well Brad, is Crackwell still there?"
Bannerman, "Yep, still there, see. Seems we just tickled it."

Mondone secretly sighed with relief.

He looked at General Rogers and said, "Well what's next General?"
Rogers had a look of thunder. "Indeed yes, what's next. I think we wait now."

To deploy the second nuclear X-Ray weapon against Crackwell and achieve the same negative result was not an option.
Rogers left the room to make a conference call with the Chiefs of Staff and then the President.

Mondone walked over to the NASA Control Centre building.
There Ming had been supporting the Ramjet operation, she turned as Mondone entered.
"Ming, how goes Rameses?"
"Pretty good Colonel. The Ramjets performed well, although the telemetry feed showed excessive vibration which was slowly increasing. I believe another minute and we may have seen a failure."
The Colonel's eyebrows raised. "Really? Ok, at least they got into orbit safely. I did have reservations about that damn gravity engine though."
Ming smiled, "I didn't."
Mondone had a puzzled look, he said "Why so sure?"

Ming laughed quietly and told Mondone about Bill Craswell's secret engine test in Norfolk and how it nearly ended in catastrophe.
Mondone exclaimed, "Hell, what a maverick. The British wouldn't let him test it on the ground because of the radiation safety issues. He would have been seen a long jail sentence here."
"Yes, but it enabled him to iron out the bugs in the engine Sir."
He grinned, "Yes, there is that and thank God he did."

Ming's expression became grave. She looked at the rows of monitors manned by many NASA engineers and scientists.
Mondone casually said, "Ming, you've put in some hours lately and I have welcomed that. You look a little tired?"

She turned back to Mondone and whispered, "Yes, I am Arrack. I know duty is paramount and what may happen in the next few days is anyone's guess, but…"
Ming didn't finish, she put her hand over her mouth.

Mondone said, "Come on let's grab a coffee in the cafeteria."

They sat down at the nearest table.
Most were empty, work demands had skyrocketed in the light of recent events.
She broke the enormous slice of chocolate cake in two and crammed some in her mouth.
Gesturing at the other piece she said, "Mmm… comfort food, very good. Want some?"
Mondone put down his cup and took the cake. In one fluid movement the whole piece disappeared into his mouth. Crumbs fell out.
Ming laughed a little, "Now I wouldn't have thought you would eat the whole thing in one go."
He chomped away, chocolate lacing his teeth, "Nor did I, but it is excellent cake."
She waited as if to say something, but thought better of it.
Mondone swallowed and frowned at her, "Ming tell me what's on your mind, besides the alien thing."

"Well um… Sir…I… "
She was alternating between his christian name and the correct military rank address.
"I desire to be with my boyfriend and family at these precarious times. You see if this so called armada arrives, surely we have no real defence? And… well I want to spend possibly my last hours with them."
Tears had formed in her eyes.

Mondone pondered a while, and then he looked at her in a fatherly way.

"Now that the Ramjet mission is well underway, I see no reason why you should not take a little leave. All I ask is that you remain in contact."
"Oh thank you Sir, Arrack, thank you."

He winked, wrote a duty relief slip, gave it to her and said, "Go." With that she left and booked the next flight to Hawaii.

Mondone walked back to the NASA Control centre.
Michael Swaine, his NASA boss, accosted him, "Colonel, good work on the Ramjet."
"Thanks Sir. We were up against the schedule as you know and to be honest I felt very uneasy about the curtailed testing we had to use."
Swaine looked him in a detached way, "Risks are what we have to take. Minimising them is our art."
Mondone thought 'Fancy words don't put spacecraft into orbit.'
"Absolutely Sir."
"How are you?" said Swaine nodding towards Mondone's chest.

Mondone pondered, took a long silent breath, "I'm ok, the doctors have given me the all clear, but to take things easy. No marathons yet."
Swaine gently patted his shoulder, "Good Colonel, I…"
A man quickly approached, "Director Sir, we have a situation with the ISS."
(International Space Station)
"Excuse me Colonel."
They both hurried to the ISS control area.
After five minutes the door swung open and Gail walked in.
All light blue today, jacket, short-ish skirt and blue heels.
White buttoned blouse.
Her blonde hair was pinned behind her head.
Light makeup and he thought 'and gorgeous lilac lipstick.'

Arrack Mondone nodded to her as walked across.

"Your reports Sir, on the search for the ground based intruders. Negative so far."
"Thanks Gail."
He grinned and dropping his voice to a whisper said, "You're looking good enough to eat."

She smiled and flushed slightly, that lovely feeling enveloping her again.

Back at the Array Control Centre

Brad Bannerman had asked one of his team to do some long range gravity data scans, particularly in the vicinity of Jupiter's orbit. Triggered by a recent call from a one Sir George Ratcliffe.

Nothing showed up.

He had also requested the James Webb telescope team look at the Jupiter area as well.
Swinging the orbital telescope around used more of its limited thruster fuel.
They were a little reluctant to respond, their main orders being to monitor closely the anomaly Crackwell and surrounding space.
Only a short period would be granted.

He scratched his chin watching the gravity screens.
The new space array was performing excellently, but its trigger systems remained quiet.

Thirty minutes later.

Brad's phone chimed.
Answering, "Bannerman…"
A rapid voice on the other end.

Bannerman's eyes went wide, he uttered, "Holy smoke, you sure? ..oh .hell."

His whole team watched him silently.

His face had quickly paled, solemnly he said "They are here… near Jupiter."

For once he couldn't think what to do next.

Fiction was becoming really scary reality.

Chapter 29

Dawn - Thursday 18th January
The hilltop at Kingley Vale, West Sussex, UK

Steven Crowley had been there all night.

His second vehicle a Land Rover, was opened up at the back.
On the rooftop a cluster of satellite dishes pointed in several different directions.
Whip aerials sprung from the side of the truck.

Inside the vehicle a stack of instruments glowed their electronic displays.
Cables snaked to an area a little distance away, where a single high backed chair stood perched on top of one of the ancient burial mounds.
It was surrounded by unlit projector lamps on stands.
Several cameras stood on tripod mounts in front of the chair, still dark in the early morning light.

A thick cold mist rolled along the top of the hill.
On a clear day to the south, one could see the spire of Chichester Cathedral rising above the surrounding murk. Far behind it the shining sea in the Solent channel.
To the north the view was a sprawling landscape of fields, hedgerows and clumps of woodland, going all the way to the town of Midhurst.
Today was just murk, low visibility.

A petrol generator quietly hummed to the side of the Land Rover.
He checked his watch, though there was no need to.
Steven knew the time.

He walked back to the cab and sat in the passenger seat.
Putting on a headset he keyed some commands into a laptop computer.

Tiny faint coloured lights dotted his second arm bracelet.

"Horst, are your networks switched in?"
The South African entrepreneur replied "Yes, we have the African and South American continents covered."
"Thank you. Wait for live broadcast at 9am. And as planned another at midday and the final one at 8pm this evening."

He then contacted Nadir Patel, the Indian plutocrat and repeated his request.
"Yes Steven. The Asian, the Far Eastern sub-continents and the Australasia countries will receive your transmission."
"Good, good."

Steven repeated the conversation with Nigel Humble the telecoms expert for Europe, Valentine Goryunov in Russia and Craig Akerman in the USA.
All those continents would receive the transmission.

A transmission that could override normal TV broadcasts.
It would be multi-lingual and tuned to dozens of different cultures.
He had the technology.

Another text message from Lei.
"Steven, please contact me. I love you and am worried sick."

He sighed and selected her number.
"Lei?"
"Oh God, where are you Steven?"
"I am not far away and am preparing a sermon for the world."

"How Steven? How are you doing this?"
"Lei, I can reveal where I am, but you mustn't attempt, nor anyone, to come and see me until tomorrow."
"Are you in danger?"

Steven paused, he drew a long and hard on his Greek cigarette.

Exhaling volumes of blue smoke, he replied, "No. No more than I have ever been in."
"What does that mean? If you love me please tell me where you are. It will remain just between the two of us."

"Ok…and I do love you."
He sighed heavily. She meant so much to him.

That was the danger.

"I'm at Kingley Vale, a nature reserve north of Chichester. I will be doing my broadcasts from the hill top."
Lei frowned, 'Why on earth was he there, why not somewhere with proper protection?'
"Steven do you know that the armada has arrived, the evil beings from Andromeda?
I am so scared."

"Yes I know they are coming, I feel their insidious probing already. Stay within Sabrina's circle, you will be safe there."

Then she remembered his ancient bracelet.
"Is your bracelet with you?"
"Yes."

Relief flooded her. That bracelet was a reassurance… at least.

Much Later

The 9am broadcast never happened.
Something had damaged part of his network.

The noon day one did happen.
Right across the world, TV and computer screens burst into a picture of a bearded white robed man, Steven Crowley.
He spoke in many different languages.

At 12.55 pm the transmissions abruptly stopped.
His Druid comrades around the world were unable to contact him to find out why.

It was because Steven lay bludgeoned unconscious in the grass, a few yards from his Land Rover.

2pm that same day
Rameses Command Module – 2 million miles out from the Earth

Despite the warm air provided by the life support systems, a distinct chill was felt inside the spacecraft.
Mark, "Jesus, they are damn invisible again!"

Daniel Ethen, Mark Vanderbrook and John Creeson were glued to the display screen.

Mark magnified the image.
It was coming almost live from the James Webb telescope which was in Earth orbit.
Their data stream had been received and pre-processed by NASA to remove distorted starlight and then enhanced to show what was really there.

Far out near the planet Jupiter, huge in itself, appeared a series of small dots.
Moving black dots.

They should have been impossible to see against the dark backdrop of space, clustered with millions of stars. However, even though the 'black dots' were invisible, the cloaking produced tiny distortions to the 'copied' light from those stars that were behind them.
NASA had applied some clever optical processing.

At full magnification they saw a stream of tiny black asteroid like shapes.

Mark was the first to speak. “How many do you reckon?”
Daniel grimaced and replied, “I count maybe twenty. The size, let me see…”

He used Jupiter and her moons as a datum, doing an approximate size comparison with their imaging applications.

“Hell, they are..um.. I’d say each one is perhaps six hundred miles wide.”

John fumbled in his pack bag and brought out the ancient sword. As he held it tight, a faint purple corona was apparent.

“What the devil! John you never told us you brought that along?” Mark frowned.
John replied, “It’s ok. I couldn’t tell you, I just used our personal belongings allocation to smuggle it aboard. It can give us some protection.”

Daniel moved closer and took the sword from John, examining it closely.
He said, “I’ve heard about these artefacts and the moon device.”
Mark chipped in, “You know with what is happening out there I sure feel a lot safer now that’s here. Good on you John.”

Daniel returned the sword, or rather the sword hilt. Only a few inches remained of the rusty blade itself.
He said, “Appreciate you bringing it aboard John. It’s the damnedest technology. NASA would love to look at this little gem.”
John smiled, “When we return, I’ll let them have a look.”

Mark continued to work the displayed image then panned to the right a little.

He did a quick visual count.
"There, see more have appeared. They must have a portal out there. I make it forty five now."

The voicecom broke in, "Rameses, this is Houston do you copy?"
"Yes, we copy."

"The objects in the vicinity of Jupiter are growing in number. In due course we need you to take an evasive line away from them. They are on an approach course for the Earth."

Daniel, "Roger that. Let us have the coordinates."

Then he thought about the military plans.
The Strategic Defense arm had feverishly reprogrammed a number of long range nuclear ballistic missiles. The old targets had been Russian cities and military bases. New targets to be assigned dynamically, as they reached medium Earth orbit.
Because of the limit of their range, the missiles would be striking close to our only home, mother Earth.
The Russian president had contacted world leaders to say that they were doing the same.

A common threat needs a unified defence.

On their other screen, was Crackwell, always invisible unless provoked by huge energies or gravity waves.

They only had ten gravity 'bombs' left.
Vital illumination, not to be wasted.

Rameses – an hour later

Daniel Ethen suddenly spoke, "Houston has just reported that it is indeed a huge number of invisible intelligent craft and they are travelling towards us at a phenomenal speed. They are now closer than Mars."

Mark who had been running sensor processing, said, "We are being flooded by radio energy and it's coming from them. I think our systems may become overloaded."
Daniel quickly replied, "Shut down all but essential comms. Switch in the Faraday shields."
The Faraday shields were a collection of steel mesh layers covering the outer hull.

He turned to Benji, "Benj-Ram, analyse the data broadcasts from the vicinity of the intruders and summarise."
"Yes Sir." rang a metallic voice.

Then it happened.
John was the first to feel it, a numbness in his mind, his thoughts slightly sluggish.

The robot turned and started to speak, "There are several very strong electromagnetic beams being directed towards us, the received energy is rapidly increasing. Measured frequencies span across the spectrum. Now in hundreds of watts on the outer hull. Calculating back to the source I estimate…ah zzz… energy levels there are in the thousands of gigawatts.. zzz kkk."
His artificial head jerked a little, reflecting and flickering the filtered sunlight coming through the glass porthole.
Fair hair, blue eyes, chisel jaw. He was one of the crew.

Daniel stammered, "Benji seems odd. We must be under attack. Mark prepare for engine firing. Those coordinates will take us behind the moon.
John take your launch couch."
Mark punched some console buttons, then started to pull down the metal window shutters to prevent the high power electromagnetic waves penetrating their cabin through the glass.

Daniel "Strap in guys. Benji-Ram report!"

The robot did not reply, he jerked a little as his metal hand reached for some instrument switches.
Mark shouted, "What the…"

Benji-Ram was dying. His eyes dulled.

He became motionless as his electronic circuits started to flood and burn out from powerful and unwanted alien energies.
Then a singing voice came out of his mouth.
It was Chris Rea.

'…this ain't no technological breakdown,
Oh no, this is the road to hell…ell..mm..zzz'
Rapidly a grim faced John said, "He has shut down. Been tampered with… by them."
Mark leaped across and pulled the window shutter down.

His face said it all, that's all they need, a singing dead robot.

With that Daniel fired the gravity engine.
As its huge thrust pushed the three astronauts back in their seats again, the little spacecraft hammered towards the moon.

Slightly later over in the Orion Command module

Jack Wilson, mission commander, had just received a priority order.
"Ok, we are to deploy the third weapon."

The second nuclear X-Ray device was being saved for later.

Rickki Targalo monitored the alien fleet approach using the NASA processed telescope data. He was inputting weapon target coordinates.
He said, "Target acquired and locked using gravity data from their propulsion systems. Sir, the enemy are very rapidly approaching."

Jack looked across at Ray Kingley, "Ready to deploy Ray?"
"Yup."

"Rickki, what is their range and speed now?"
Rickki was thinking long and hard, trying to concentrate.
He replied "I estimate thirty million miles and closing at, mmm… yes approximately one tenth of light speed."

Jack's craggy countenance became dark, he exclaimed, "Damn they're fast, lock the weapons computer to their track."
"Locked and tracking."

"Deploy."
"Missile away Sir."

Far out from them, the Horizon module launched a large missile. It was 'hardened' to withstand electronic warfare thrown against it.
Already it took a zigzag course, 'ducking and diving', to try and thwart the enemy.

One missile against dozens of gargantuan spacecraft.
The odds of success seemed worse than poor.

From within Orion, they watched trying to use visual and radar, but relying on the vital gravity data being fed to them by the US space array.

Suddenly the invisible fleet started to slowly split up. Red flashes could be seen.
Shortly their missile was within a million miles of the alien fleet, ejecting mini chaff rockets that burst into thousands of small metal pieces of foil.
Hoping to fool the enemy sensors.

The weapon wiggled and twitched as red beams flashed close by it.

Jack could still see its rocket flare, he said "Hell, they are travelling extremely fast. Prepare for the blasts."

Then their missile did its stuff.

Outer covers flew off and myriads of nuclear rockets shot out, spiralling in all directions into the alien fleet.
Cluster bombs, but now of a fearsome nuclear dimension.

Seconds later and the black sky towards Mars erupted in light.
Many, many searing flashes.
Yellow, white, red.
Multiple nuclear detonations dominated the alien fleet.

Rickki shook his fist at the porthole.
"Eat uranium you sons of bitches!"

Jack was watching the NASA scope screen.
Ray smiled at him and started to say, "That'll show them that we mean business."

Then he frowned at the display. "Godammit, they are still coming through…"

That was the last thing he said.

A fiery red ball of energy enveloped their Orion spacecraft.
It suddenly melted in a fierce explosion and vaporised in seconds.

Across at the edge of the moon, in Rameses, Daniel shouted, "They've got Orion…it's gone."
Mark, "My God!"

Daniel was wide-eyed watching the other screen.
Momentarily he saw more missiles heading for the alien fleet.

The Russians and Chinese had reacted.

More massive explosions dominated the alien ships… and still they came through.

Back in Rameses, John Creeson was shaking and holding the sword in front of him, his eyes screwed tightly shut.

NASA Control Centre, Houston

"Good God… Orion has been destroyed. Did their capsule escape?"
"Negative Sir."

Mondone looked across at the mission controller, "Rameses, where are they?"
"Behind the moon Sir."

Many pale and worried faces were now staring at the large display screen.
Over ninety colossal black asteroid spacecraft had been counted.

General Rogers came in and walked straight over to Colonel Mondone.
The Colonel turned to him, "Looks bad Sir."
Rogers muttered, "I'm afraid John Creeson was right and it seems they are unstoppable."
Mondone added, "I have seen reports from around the world. Their influence is causing terror in many places. Pilots losing control, several aircraft have crashed already. Ships being manoeuvred into danger. There are some major disruptions happening."

Rogers replied grimly, "They will reach Earth in minutes, our last ditch defence must be invoked." He then walked over to a couple of military controllers hunched over a battery of display screens and entered into a prolonged discussion with them.

Mondone strolled over to some chairs near the vending machines, punching a coffee out.

He needed to stay alert, and sitting down he wiped his brow. To use what little time they might have left, to take stock, to think what else could be done.

Gail pushed her laptop away and got up from a side table and walked across to him, gently placing her hand on his arm.
He looked up.
She whispered, "Arrack, you ok, you know?" her thoughts going back to the emergency operation he had been through last year, following his heart attack.
He smiled, "Yes I'm fine. Don't worry. I think everybody here is stressed."
Gail sat down on the next chair, she replied "Arrack, I'm scared." She glanced at the huge wall screens, a myriad of activities going on.
He took her hand and said, "Well we've tried to stop them. They have technologies beyond anything we have."

For once the normally upbeat Colonel seemed deflated.
Her eyes were wet, she said "I love you Arrack… I…I sense impending doom, am I right?...but…what is happening? Have we any chance? What do you think these beings want?"
Mondone smiled, he squeezed her hand. "I love you too girl and I want to marry you."
"Oh Arrack…"
He glanced back at the wall screens.
"We have no idea what they want. We tried all types of communication with them. Nothing back. Nothing at all."
It was clear that Rogers, the cool military man, was running out of toys.
Desperately he shouted to the controller, "That Crackwell portal, get Rameses to explode another gravity bomb. We need to see if the portal has widened as it did before."
"Yes Sir."

Thinking to himself, 'Maybe our saviours will return.'
Twenty minutes later and a negative came back.

On board Rameses

John Creeson worked at the screen analysing the gravity grid. The other two astronauts watched him manipulate the controls. On the magnified screen were the gravity propulsion trails left by the alien craft.

He said, "Look at that. The fleet has bypassed Earth and heading towards the sun. What the devil are they up to?"

Mark shouted, "Look, gees they are de-cloaking!"
Nearly a hundred gigantic alien spacecraft started to appear as rough black asteroids.

The James Webb telescope in orbit, had manoeuvred around to follow the alien fleet.
Daniel listened intently on his headset, then spoke "NASA control has just confirmed what the Aussies detected with their gravity array. They have identified one of those black asteroids as planet sized."
John gasped out loud, "That is unbelievable."

Going through their minds were shades of the old Star Wars films and a certain planet sized craft called the Death Star, *with a weapon capable of disintegrating whole worlds.*

Fiction then.

Nobody spoke.
To tempt fate with any utterance was not going to happen.
They watched for another hour.

Extraordinary events continued.

At five million miles from Earth the alien spacecrafts spread out into a shield like formation.

They blotted out the sun.

All of Earth plunged into darkness in a permanent eclipse.

Only moonlight remained.
Man and animals alike, started to panic.

7 pm Back on Earth
Sabrina Fay's House, Catherington, UK

The shamanic circle had been fully dreaming and locked with the ancestors, for some time. The continuous drumming was hypnotic, compelling everyone participating to focus with all their spiritual strength.

Recovering from her blackout in the supermarket, Karen had been quick to grasp the situation. Her parents had provided a veiled warning.
The threat was upon them.
Now was the time for strength, courage and love.

She sat holding her cross towards the helmet in Bill's hands.
A bright blue beam was locking the artefacts in place.
Above all of them a purple dome shimmered.

Surrounding the group were many people ready to take over as the shift patterns dictated.
Jane waited, ready for her slot.

Back at ESS in East Meon, some three miles away, Sir George Ratcliffe was ranting, 'Where had all his people disappeared to?'

Even Barry Westland was here in Sabrina's house as part of the British Secret Service coverage.

Lei watched somewhat helplessly.
She felt Steven was in trouble.

There had been no text replies from him for hours now.
With some of the networks down, mobile phones and access to the internet were intermittent at best.

Suddenly Anne Whitfield ran in from a side room.
She desperately looked around and seeing Lei grabbed her hand and pulled.
"Oh dear Lord, Lei you must see this."

Together they ran into the other lounge where a large TV screen was on.

Stopping abruptly in front, the two women became mesmerised by the broadcast.
It was a bit fuzzy and at times the transmission was blotted out, but the picture when it came was harrowing.

Lei cried and sunk to her knees, shouting "Oh sweet Jesus, Steven…oh no what has happened, STEVEN!"

There on the TV screen was the most gruelling of scenes.

Steven Crowley was talking and shouting at the cameras. He seemed incoherent, stopping and muttering, then bursting into speech again, but unintelligible.
You see his face was covered in blood and something like wire was wrapped around his forehead.
Large ropes bound him to the chair.

Curling around his feet was a long black tendril.

"Oh God, we have to rescue him. Who has done this?"
Anne shook her head. "All I've seen Lei, is Steven. It's so horrible."

Barry Westland walked in and saw the image, "Hells bells…what the…?"

Lei ran back into the main lounge just as Bill changed ‘artefact shift’.
She cried, stammering at Bill, “Steven is in great danger up at Kingley Vale, he is being tortured.”
Bill stared at her and gestured to Anne, “Can you take the helmet briefly?”
She took over, maintaining the blue beam lock.
Bill ran into the lounge and gawped at the TV, “Oh my gawd, the poor bugger!”
Running back he said to Karen “Steven has been kidnapped. Can you manage with just the cross?”
She paused, closed her eyes, took a long deep breath and then nodded.
Karen knew the urgency, “Go Bill. I can do this. He is in desperate trouble.”
The purple pyramid remained as strong as ever.

He took the helmet and with Jane, Lei and Barry they ran outside.

With that they took Bill’s Lexus SUV and hurtled out of the house grounds, flashing his ID at the guards on the gate.
Barry Westland looked at him and said “Thought you could do with some backup?”
Bill glanced at him, “Damn right Barry, thanks.”
They disappeared into a very black night.

He made a brief but fast detour to ESS.
“Wait here, I won’t be a moment.”
Jane, Lei and Barry remained in the car. Barry looked at them with a puzzled look.
Jane said, “It’s ok, he has to get his lucky charm.”
Barry pulled a face, “What?”

After an altercation with the security guard, and Bill stuffing his ID in the guys face, he was waved out.
He struggled, heaving and puffing back to the car carrying a very large heavy holdall on his shoulder.

Lei said, "What the hell is that Bill?"
Bill grimaced the gargoyle face and quipped, "Something that may be useful."

They took the side track as far as they could up towards the hill summit at Kingley Vale. A thicket of trees and undergrowth lay ahead, split by a twisting narrow path.

Getting out Jane said, "Bill let me help you with that, I know it's very heavy."
Bill, "Yeah about forty kilos." His forehead was wet with perspiration.
Barry Westland his automatic pistol drawn, was already gone.
He disappeared into the dark tree lined gloom, with a small pencil torch held low.
Some clouds hovered over the now gleaming moon, plunging the area into near darkness.
Jane followed Bill, pausing to pick up a broken off but solid piece of tree branch.
Again she thought in anguish about Bill and the white robed man's message.

'Protect Bill as much as you can, otherwise he will break.'

She doubly grasped the gnarled wooden branch trying its strength, her mind going through her Tae Kwando moves.

They made their way up the remaining hill track by intermittent moonlight.

Ahead was a scenario made in hell.

Back at ESS Systems – East Meon, UK

George Ratcliffe ran out the building into the dark.
He stopped at the guard sentry box.

"Who was that?" pointing down the road at the disappearing car lights.
"Bill Craswell, Sir."
"WHAT! Where the fuck is he going?"
"I don't know Sir. He had some equipment which I needed a pass for, but he overrode me."
"Equipment?" Ratcliffe frowned, "Was he alone?"
"No Sir, Jane Horsham and Barry Westland were in the car, plus a second woman of unknown identity."
"Thank you Corporal."

With that Ratcliffe stomped, fuming and cursing back into the main building.
Grabbing the phone he tried to call the Ministry in London.
Dead. No ring tone.
He thought 'What the f… hell, what is up with our damn systems?'

Back in his office Ratcliffe sat down with another coffee, quickly fetched by Crystal.
He watched her like some predatory animal and then gulped the steaming liquid, stretching his wrinkled face as he burnt his tongue.
She was fussing with some paperwork.

Crystal like most of the employees there, she had been asked, no… requested, to work long hours in this crucial period.
She was not happy.

Particularly by Sir George's insistence that she only wore skirts, not trousers, to keep in with Ministry standards…and all that boloney.

The old lecher had added that they must be knee length or shorter. The unwanted carrot was that he had given her an unexpected salary bonus and the promise of attending the Ministry's jamboree at the Cannes Film festival.

He reached for the phone again this time trying the internal network.
"Gustav? Yes, have you a minute? Ok, first check the plasma weapon rack in the blockhouse for any that are missing, then please come to my office."

The large framed blonde German walked in.
Crystal brightened up, said "Tea, coffee Gustav?"
With a great big smile he said "Thank you, tea, white no sugar."

She vanished through the door, Ratcliffe's eyes still glued to her.
He turned and addressed Gustav.
"Please take a seat. As you know things are happening at a pace now."
Gustav nodded, "Yes I have been watching the events in outer space, terrible.
Looks like there will be no sunrise tomorrow."

Ratcliffe shuddered strangely, then spoke, "The plasma weapons, any missing?"
Gustav guffawed a little, and then spoke, "No Sir George. Why?"
"Bill Craswell has just been in and out, he has taken something."
Gustav smiled cynically, "Sir George, to carry one of the plasma guns would take at least four strong men."

The plasma guns were large, designed to be mounted on a tank or a naval gun turret.
He added "Anyway they are still prototypes, we haven't been able to fix the overheating problem. They would be very dangerous to use."

Ratcliffe returned a puzzled expression, "Hmmm…I know."

Gustav had a very good idea what Bill had really taken, but he kept quiet.

Fifteen minutes later

The moon had come out, revealing the undulating hilltop.
To the south of it and far down below stretched the valley of Kingley Vale nature reserve.

They all crouched some hundred and fifty yards away behind a large clump of gorse.
Bright lights illuminated Steven. He appeared unconscious, bound and slumped in the chair on top of the mound.

A number of men could be seen moving around, automatic weapons slung over their shoulders.

Barry Westland was looking through a pair of miniature field glasses, he whispered, "There are too many. I count maybe ten men and there's a strange smell, can't place it."
Bill "Smells like rotting flesh to me. Look at the surrounding grass up there, looks sort of scorched or dead."
Jane "Oh Bill, god no…"
Lei stared wide eyed at stricken Steven, her face streaked with dried tears.

Then Bill undid the large black holdall and pulled out a number of bulky metal cylinders and then a long snout like barrel.

Lei "No wonder it was heavy, what on earth is that Bill?"
He grimaced, his face contorted in determination.
"It's a miniature plasma cannon. Gustav, Jane and I built it secretly."
Jane nodded.
Lei had a puzzled expression, "But what is it for? Oh hell….oh my god… is the alien here?"
"I reckon it is. Karen said we may be in trouble."

He quickly assembled the cannon, plugging in a heavy box underneath it.
The box was covered in ice.
Lei "Looks frozen?"
Bill replied, "It's the fuel or you could call it the ammunition container. In order for the cannon to consume quickly the uranium in the fuel pellets we took out some of the moderator."
Jane continued, "It makes the uranium unstable so we have to cool it right down AND use it up fairly quickly." She coldly said "It's unstable but maximises the plasma output. It may work against that damn alien if it appears."
She fearfully glanced all around.

Bill pulled the gargoyle face, "Tricky stuff…but cuts down the residue radiation as well."

He then took a bulky heavy backpack out of the end of the holdall. Looking up with perspiration running down his face, he put the backpack on and connected up some heavy cables to the cannon. "Pull the starter cord Jane."
On his back the petrol engine generator burst into life, humming quietly.
Bill switched on the controls, a panel was illuminated, sequencing up the weapon systems, and then several green indicators appeared.
"Flippin eck this bloody thing is heavy. Ah good. We're ready."

A spotlight lit the gorse bush, followed by a shout from one of the henchmen.

Barry "They've seen us! Let's split up and move to the sides of them. I'm going to try and take down as many as I can. Lei, can you handle this?"
He showed her a 9mm automatic which she took saying, "Yeah I've used one before."
Barry gave her a spare ammunition clip.

With consternation in her face Lei stammered, "Barry? shoot them?"
She glanced up and over to where the spotlights were on Steven's prone form.
Her pulse was thumping, her body keyed, it was an 'us or them' moment.
Resignedly she said, "I guess there is no other way?"

He paused and said coldly, "Look at Steven and over there on the ground if I'm not mistaken, is a body. See with a hood on? These men will not hesitate to kill."
"Oh god, yeah you're right."

"As you know steady it with both hands and aim for the upper body when you fire. They will not hesitate to kill you. Come with me."
He took out his own gun.
She was no stranger to firearms.

Proving Barry's statement, barely had they all dispersed, when automatic fire sprayed the very bush they had been hiding behind.
A gravelly command could be heard, "Remain here. If anything moves out there shoot it."
Jane thought 'I know that voice…'

Barry and Lei zigzagged through the cluster of bushes and small trees.
After fifty yards they crawled head first through brown bracken.
He whispered "Lei. See the men are in two groups the larger over there to the right. I'll take the larger group, you take the left." He glanced at his watch and synchronised with hers.
"At 7.45pm I will open fire on the right side group. At precisely that time you do the same on the other group. Use two shots per man. Stay very low."

Over the other side Bill lay flat in some long grass up at the hillside, closely watching

the shadowy forms of men.
Jane crouched right next to him.
"Strange, that they haven't come after us?"
Jane whispered, "Well I guess they can't see much in this light… oh…look what.. WHAT ARE THEY?"

They looked like dogs, but moved differently. Two large black beasts with red eyes straining on chain leashes held by a big man. *There was something sinister about these un-Earthly beasts... the product of ghastly nightmares...*
He let the snarling animals loose and they ran full pelt straight for Bill and Jane.
There was something really weird about the beasts, a sort of fuzziness, their shapes not quite defined. As the moonlight caught them, their legs pounded the ground furiously, a rapid thumping sound coming from the impact of their heavy bodies.
Blood curdling growls came from rabid mouths.

There is something very frightening about a large vicious mad animal tearing towards you.
Intent on ripping your throat out.

Quickly Bill put the helmet on.
A faint purple halo surrounded his head.

He staggered backwards with the heavy cannon trying to get his balance, the power pack surging as he hit the pre-charge.
"Ah shit…so bloody heavy this thing."

The animals snarled as they closed.
Jane paled, her heart was racing…
'Protect Bill...protect Bill!'

She took a deep breath and plunged in front, running to meet the threat.
Then raising her Tae Kwando stick ready to strike.

Bill exclaimed, “Jane! God! What are you doing? They’ll kill you!”

The beasts were almost upon them.
She jigged to the side and swinging her wood staff hard she hit one full across the face, then tried to sidestep but only managed to swipe the other animal across the legs.
She lost her balance as the first injured squealing animal ploughed into her.

Jane stumbled and fell.
The second snarling animal leapt in mid-air, mouth open showing rows of dripping razor teeth as it descended towards her.

Precisely 7.45pm

Across the other side of the clearing all hell broke loose.

The moon illuminated a running and ducking Barry Westland emptying his automatic pistol. Several men fell, blue flames ejecting from machine gun barrels as they tried to lock onto to him. At the same time as the others turned to join the fray, shot after shot came from Lei’s pistol. A good strategy, attack from different flanks.
They nearly all fell.

Thwack.
Hit from behind, Lei fell face forwards, the gun flying out of her hands.
Barry dived, rolled and knelt ejecting another spent clip and ramming home a fresh one into his pistol.
He nearly got to fire it.

A machine gun spewed flame.
Bravely, Barry Westland died as a hail of bullets entered his chest.
Coughing blood he fell flat on his face, still.

A powerful torch beam held a sitting dazed Lei in its light.

"Now my little pretty. You will pay dearly for this."

Roger rolled out into the open on a motorised wheelchair.
He held a gun in his hand.

Two men dragged her towards the demonic wheelchair man.

"YOU!" she exclaimed.

Fifty yards away

One beast was scampering and holding back. It growled, spluttered and then whined from a smashed nose. The other was in mid air over Jane, a split second from savaging her.
She screamed echoes down the valley.

Bill stood upright and took a monumental breath, yelling,
"OH MY GAWD!"

He quickly pulled the trigger.

Looking the Gladiator, with the shiny bronze helmet in place, he gripped the heavy weapon tightly at waist height. It erupted in flame, bucking and glinting in the moonlight.

A mind numbing rattling screech emitted from the cannon followed by an intense burst of extremely bright yellow liquid from its stubby mouth.
Plasma at six thousand degrees centigrade flashed across and ripped into the beast that was within inches of Jane.

It perished without a noise, falling on top of her.
He turned and fired another burst at the injured beast, the weapon recoil knocking him over on his back.
The animal howled then fell still.

Jane gurgled trying to get out from under the huge smouldering carcass, her hair singed from the plasma beam.
Bill staggered back up to see her push the animal off.

"Oh God Bill, it's horrible."
She grabbed her wood staff and ran forwards.
Bill tripped again sprawling over in the grass. The weapon was so heavy.

Jane ran on keeping to the shadows.

Lei was held with her arms tight behind her body.
She screamed at Roger, "You bastard! What have you done to Steven?"

Roger had a sickly smile and something faint like a black mist was circling his neck.
Lei continued, "My god, you are possessed by them!"
"Yes my pretty, and they are here. You will all be incarcerated. THEY want and need your life force."

"WHAT? What are you doing, why must we die?"
"BIND HER."

"HERE! We have another!" shouted a man as he leapt behind Jane just yards away.

He caught Jane a glancing blow as she stumbled into the clearing, losing her staff.
With his AK47 machine gun pressed hard into her back, he nudged her towards Roger who said,
"Ah, now we have both the trouble makers."

Lei gulped, "Oh Jane…"
Jane just stared at Roger, and then she said coldly, "I might have guessed it was you Roger. Pity Shane didn't kill you back then."

"Nah… he tried, but put me in this wheelchair instead. He has paid his dues."

Roger grunted a laugh then gestured at his henchman, "Mick, take them up to the chair and his royal highness."

Both women with their hands bound were led towards Steven.
Roger followed in his wheelchair.
Lei stared in desperation at her man on the hilltop. "Steven…. dear Steven…oh."

As they walked, they caught sight of the body in the grass, covered in a sack and hooded.
It was moving slightly and then the hood slid off.
Jane gasped, "GAVIN! Oh Lord..." she turned back to Roger, "What the hell is going on?"

Gavin's head was blood stained, his mouth gagged. Under the sack his hands and feet were tied.
He moaned a little.
"Yes he is still alive. Still to learn his lesson, but soon to meet his maker."

Roger burst into a hideous cackle.

As they approached the hilltop burial mound and Steven's chair, the bearded man strained on his ropes lurching his head back and opened his blue eyes. He struck a picture with his long hair wildly hanging down. Curled around his bloodstained head was a barbed wire crown.
The metal thorns penetrating his scalp.
Although his face was racked with pain he called out in a deep voice.

"IT IS TIME YOU HAD FAITH ROGER AND ALL MEN LIKE YOU!"

Then Steven looked at Lei and Jane.
"I'm sorry this was not meant to be. I…uh…I could not stop them."
He closed his eyes in pain.

Lei was crying. Forcing the tears back she said, "Oh Steven what have they done to you?"
As both women were forced to their knees, Lei gasped as she saw a knife buried to the hilt in the side of Steven's body, his white tunic stained red.

The artefact bracelets were no longer on his arm.

Overhead thick grey clouds had suddenly unmasked the moon and the hillside burst into light. A brisk wind had got up from nowhere.

An illuminated Steven glowed unnaturally on the stark hilltop.

At the same time brilliant forked lightning shot right across the sky, flashing through clumps of dark cloud. Seconds later the air erupted with sharp crackling thunder.

Roger still laughing said, "You die now… in front of your messiah!"
He burst into another cackle, pocketing the gun then raising his hand in the air ready to signal their execution.

One of the thugs was an Oriental.

He drew a long Samurai sword.

Chapter 30

8pm Thursday 18th January
Rameses Vehicle – Moon proximity

The three astronauts watched intensely as a small gravity bomb was detonated, generating gravity waves that surrounded the portal Crackwell.

"LOOK! Look… Crackwell has opened up!" John shouted with glee.

He looked at the measurements, "Wow, as before the diameter is now thousands of miles."

Mark, "There, look something has come out."

Sure enough a fuzzy grey craft was nearby, then after a while several others exited.
Daniel said, "Size, what size are they?"
Mark replied, "Around four hundred miles across, but they vary, some are smaller and there those two are perhaps eight hundred miles in diameter."
John just muttered, "It is truly astounding, ships that size."

Daniel, "Well the cavalry has arrived, let's see what happens now."
John frowned then exclaimed, "I don't see any small stars within their craft, like before? Just thousands of tiny black holes."

Red and orange flashing lights on the console distracted them.
Daniel interacted with the systems and said, "We have some systems failures. Minor at the moment. Backups have cut in. Life support ok. Mark, what is our communications status?"

Mark looked up from the telecoms console, "The networks are in a hell of mess. I keep losing Houston. The ether is full of powerful and strange transmissions. They are blocking out right across the frequency spectrum."

The massive shield of black alien space ships remained in place, blocking the sun.
Earth was the darkest since recorded history, temperatures were dropping.

It was like out of a science fiction horror film that gave you the creeps.
But this time you couldn't walk out the cinema or turn the player off.

This was reality.

An enormous red flash distracted them.
It came from the alien fleet, a red pulsing beam shooting across space to the anomaly area.

John instantly turned to the monitor showing where Crackwell was.
He gasped.
A pyrotechnic display of light erupted around the grey craft still pouring out of Crackwell. They all squinted as the screen flashed bright its message of doom.

Some of the grey craft disintegrated in balls of red fire.
Huge clouds of debris flew out from the explosions.

Daniel exclaimed, "Oh hell. They are being destroyed…"

Despite their distance and part protection from the moon, the little Rameses spacecraft was buffeted by blast waves.
"Strap in guys, we in for a rough ride." shouted Daniel.

WANG!
Something hit their vehicle.

A red light appeared on the console, followed by a klaxon sound.
Mark, "Hull penetration! We're losing atmosphere."
They frantically fought and scrabbled to get their helmets on.

Then Mark unstrapped and grabbed a small instrument, holding it in front of him as he moved around the interior. "There."
He pointed to a small jagged hole flapping with bits of wire and threadlike hull material.
They moved fast to plug it, but that wasn't the only problem.

Helmets came off and John sank back into his couch.
"Phew, hope no more of those."

A winking red icon on the screen caught his eye. John ran some diagnostics and muttered, "Damn, we have an arm of the space array down…looks like the master gate processor circuit board, possibly the chip itself. Probably hit by a fragment from the Crackwell explosions."

Daniel leaned over, "We've got spares here. Looks like a space walk John. That array has got to be back online pronto. Ok Mark, prepare to load coordinates and fire the gravity engine. Houston will be on us quickly….I think..."
Interrupting him, the speaker burst into life.

"Rameses, this is Houston, we detect an array failure up there. Do you have a plan? We cannot afford to be offline for long."
The astronauts stared at each other.
"Rameses we repeat, this is Houston. Do you have a plan?"
Daniel turned and looked at the Englishman.

John went cold inside.

The space walk simulator was one thing but now to go out into…. into nothing out there… was terrifying.
That test experience on Earth was like floating in a goldfish bowl, the giant 'swimming pool' back at Houston.

Now he was being asked to float in an infinitely large sea full of piranhas.

Daniel, “You ok with that John?”
“Oh yes,..um… no problem.”

Inside he was frantically thinking through the array system board design.
John said “There may be a way I can fix it from here. If so, it will be faster.”
Mark came over, “Sounds good John, you reckon you can?”
“I know Conrad designed these satellite boards with quite a bit of redundancy to cope with just this sort of failure.”
Daniel, “Yes but how do we know the damage is not extensive? Only a space walk would find out the detail?”
John, “Ok, let me have ten minutes. There is a backup board that just needs programming and then switching in.”
He pored through their software library.
“Yes, there it is. Right I will transmit a code update then a command script to do the live switchover.”
Daniel, “Ok, go do it John.”

John worked as fast as he had ever done.

“There final transmission.”

The red icon continued to blink.
Mark pulled a face, “Hmmm it’s not playing ball.”

After some seconds, gleefully they all yelled together, “Yea!”
The icon flickered on orange, then became green.
Green for go.

Mark slapped John on the back… again, “You’re the man!”

John Creeson returned a ragged smile.
He was relieved beyond measure.

8 pm that day
NASA Control Centre, Houston, Texas

Colonel Mondone watched the nightmare unfold, on six different giant wall screens.

Many people where behind consoles or coordinating pre-planned operations.
NASA the smooth well oiled organisation, thriving on adrenalin.
But options were running out.
His boss Michael Swaine, could be seen rapidly moving from one group to another.

The mission control teams were flat out desperately working on several space missions.

1. Protect Rameses and her crew.
   Maintain the space gravity array control and later design a safe return route to dock with the International Space Station.

2. Pick up the pieces of the Orion mission. No sign of the crew, but nobody is willing to accept yet, that they had all perished.

3. Monitoring and controlling the Horizon module which had one last weapon.

General Rogers walked in and over to Mondone.
"The International Space Station is in trouble. They suffered several shrapnel hits from the space conflict blast debris."

He continued, "Here on the ground as you know, a state of emergency had been declared. The army have mobilised to maintain order. There is much panic, particularly in the cities. If they come closer, NORAD is to initiate launch sequences for the ground based nukes. Colonel?"
Mondone raised his eyebrows, "Yes? Sir."

"The situation is looking bleak. If no more ships come through Crackwell then we are on our own. Maybe it was a decoy move?"
"Could be Sir, but they have sacrificed a number of large spaceships."
"Yes. Not good."

Mondone quickly continued, "The ISS is paramount to the Ramjet crew return home."

Rogers, "I know. We don't have a backup option. What I'm also concerned about is where the hell are those alien entities here on Earth?"

They both watched the live feeds to the wall screens.
One displaying telescope images from the alien sun blockade.
Another showing the mess around Crackwell.
A third focussed on the moon edge where Rameses orbited.

A loudspeaker burst into life.
It was Brad Bannerman from the Gravity Array building.
"SIR, LOOK. Look at Crackwell, more spacecraft are coming out."
The main screen showed the Crackwell area with many huge grey, super craft with revolving wheel like frames, pouring out. They glistened and spun, the sunlight catching their complex circular patterns.
Everybody held their breath, the room was bathed in silence.

It was broken by one of the engineers.
"I count forty have exited Crackwell and they are big, some over a thousand miles wide."

Somebody shouted.
A huge gasp was uttered by many.

On the second screen covering the alien sun blockade, it flared into many searing strings of gleaming red orbs of light coming from the alien asteroid spacecraft.
The beams hurtled towards the new entrants at Crackwell.

The screen showed Crackwell flaring brightly as a series of massive cataclysmic flashes and explosions erupted against a sort of giant invisible sphere around the Omega Centauri craft.
"My god they have huge shields and they're coming through, unscathed!"

Extraordinary events continued to occur.

Departing Crackwell at incredible speed the majority of the grey wheeled spacecraft shot past the Earth and towards the mass of alien spacecraft.

People just gasped and shouted as the situation rapidly changed. Others just stood in awe, hands over their mouths.

Then the grey craft carried on going, their outer peripheries flashing as they seemed to deflect the energies hurled at them by the black asteroids.
Taking a wide berth the Omega Centauri craft headed far away in the direction of our sun.

Mondone screwed his face up and said, "Where the hell are they going? Surely they're not leaving?"
Rogers his normally red face now quite pale, shouted at the controllers,
"Give me data on where they are heading!"
He started to talk rapidly into his headset mike.

A worried engineer from the ISS Space Station support group came up.
"Colonel, the ISS is badly damaged and the crew have entered the emergency escape capsule. The ISS is losing its orbit and fuel for

the position control thrusters is close to exhaustion. That's why it cannot maintain its position. We estimate it will break up in the atmosphere in ten hours."

Mondone replied, "Hell, that means the Rameses crew are stranded."
"Yes Sir… Sir?"
Mondone frowned at the man, "What?"
"There is a second escape capsule on the ISS that appears intact. Maybe they can make it back to using that one?"
Mondone scratched his chin and with a solemn faced replied, "From where they are round the other side of the moon, it would take a miracle to make it in time."

Rameses Craft, in moon orbit.

Daniel broke the news.
"Looks like we have a challenge getting home. The ISS is damaged and losing orbit.
It will start to burn up in the atmosphere in ten hours."

John knew that Rameses didn't have its own re-entry capsule. There wasn't time in the frantic build schedule to incorporate it. Instead the engineers decided on the alternative of docking with the International Space Station and using one of their re-entry capsules.

Mark said, "Our detour to the moon wasn't in the plan. We've used more fuel than expected."

John already pale, whitened a bit more, he said, "So THEY knew it may have been a one way trip?"
Mark looked at him, then glanced at a defunct slumped Benji robot.
He pulled a resigned face.

Daniel was scribbling some numbers on a pad, and then entering stuff into the computer.
He looked across at the other two.
"We have a chance. The gravity engine can get us back if we use full thrust and then reverse thrust somewhat and slip into the ISS orbit path. It means very heavy acceleration, some clever trajectory manoeuvring and cutting our timing very finely.
The fuel left is just enough."

Mark "How fine?"
"I would say if we docked first time, it gives us maybe forty five minutes to get inside the last capsule and detach, before the ISS starts to burn up during its re-entry into Earth's atmosphere."
Mark, "Sounds like a plan."
Daniel grimly smiled, "It's the only one we have and we need to leave in twenty minutes when Rameses enters the launch window as we come out of the moon's dark side."

A massive bang on the outside of the hull signalled another red light on the console.
Distracted into emergency procedures, the three astronauts worked to identify the latest problem.
The huge alien battle had just exponentially increased the amount of space debris flying around, some of it travelling at very high speeds.

NASA Mission Control Centre
Houston, Texas

Nobody left the centre but tiredness was wearing them down.
Desperation and possible salvation was on everybody's faces.

On invitation from Colonel Mondone, Louis Redmond the French cosmologist had arrived. Following his Jupiter portal revelation, his contribution was most welcome.

Mondone walked over, handing him a coffee.

"Good to see you Louis. As you can see things are becoming very warm."
"It is incredible Colonel. I am privileged to be here at the heart of NASA."

Mondone smiled, "NASA has many 'hearts' as you know. All our major centres are running operations to support us."

A shout from the tracking team distracted them.
All eyes swivelled to the Omega Centuari fleet on screen.

A swathe of grey spacecraft appeared as many shadow dots against our huge sun.

Louis exclaimed, "Mon Dieu! The temperature from the sun must be unbearable."
Mondone replied, "Maybe for us, but I'm sure their technology will shield them."

Louis nodded, "Of course. Look they are grouping, no reforming into....looks like a massive tube."

Mondone, "Hell, no surely not..."
Louis stammered, "Oh but yes they are...look at the focus and position."

And then something truly staggering happened.

The whole fleet of Omega ships had blurred, meta-morphing into a spiralling, rotating tube. Matter transformation and re-engineering on a gargantuan scale.
On the 'tube' outer, the gravity arrays showed millions of small black holes controlled by synthesised gravity.
Physical energy manipulation by enormous forces.

Then the scenario began a repeat of the staggering mechanisms deployed in the first conflict a year ago.

Hundreds of thousands of tiny black holes cycled extremely fast, along the inside of the 'tube' and on leaving the mouth, were whipped back along the outer edge towards the rear of the tube. A little way to the rear of the tube was a doughnut shaped ring, it itself rotating fast. A gravitonic vacuum cleaner.

Un-imaginable forces and power.

Technology of the gods.
More shouts from the floor.
"Good God!" spat General Rogers.
At first it was hardly visible. A pale thin yellow stream entered the doughnut ring and then the 'tube' of spaceships. It was liquid plasma at six thousand degrees centigrade, being sucked from our Sun.

YES, OUR SUN.
The provider of life on Earth.

In seconds the bright yellow stream had thickened and then it was ejected out of the front of the spacecraft tube of fiercely rotating black holes.
A narrow beam of white hot plasma stabbed out across the darkness.

It was of a speed and ferocity that could barely be described. Accelerating towards light speed, it flashed across to the formation of alien asteroid ships.

"Fuck, will you look at that!" shouted General Rogers completely forgetting himself.

One by one the asteroid craft disintegrated in a blistering mass of explosions.
They started to split up, trying to escape.

Again and again the plasma beam weaved into the alien fleet.

Michael Swaine came over to Mondone.
He was breathless, but stuttered, "Truly incredible. You would think our Sun was being depleted, but they are taking less than point oh one percent of its mass."

Mondone "It is stunning to watch."

Swaine replied, "If only we could learn and build that stuff…"

Mondone quietly said, "If only Sir. I think we are being given a lesson in humility."

45 minutes earlier
Kingley Vale hilltop, Sussex, UK

Bill hid in the gorse bushes lying on his stomach, watching in horror as the scene unfolded.
He had to make his move and very soon.

Now both Jane and Lei had been captured and as far as he could make out, Barry Westland was down, maybe dead.

He grabbed the plasma cannon, but knew he had to get closer to be sure of any half accurate strike. He crawled on his belly through the bracken and towards the girls, snaring his face on prickly bushes.
Bill looked up and stammered in horror. "Oh Lord…"

The raised samurai sword flashed in the moonlight.

With a hoarse cry, he got up and stumbled towards them swinging the plasma cannon into line.

He was too late.

Karen's Benji beat him to it.
She had dispatched the robot to sprint cross country, in the darkness.

CRACK, CRACK, CRACK!
The samurai sword fell backwards with the man as he stopped several bullets.
Again more shots rang out, taking down the second thug.

As the robot ran towards them, angrily Roger took out his pistol and started firing.
Then he turned and pointed it at Steven shouting, "You die now!"

Benji shuddered to a stop, something was wrong.

It was split seconds.

Jane somehow had loosened the rope tying her hands.
She staggered upright and sprinted the few yards before leaping and grabbing Roger's pistol hand as the gun went off. The bullet sailed over Steven's head.

With his free hand Roger whipped out a long bladed knife.
The ropes were still tangling her hands, she grabbed Roger's arm but could only deflect the knife plunge.
It sank into her thigh.
Jane shuddered and screamed out, punching Roger's face and then somehow the wheel chair toppled over, jamming his gun hand.
Forcing the ropes off and twisting his hand off the knife, she gripped the handle and pulled it out.
With blood spurting from her leg, she jabbed her free hand fingers hard into Rogers's eyes.
"Aarh…aaaarh !"
Screaming, she plunged the blade into Roger again and again.

Seconds passed.

Jane lay on the ground moaning, her hand over her leg wound trying to staunch the bleeding.

Bill staggered up breathing heavily, "Oh my gawd… Jane, JANE!"
The ancient helmet dangled on a cord around his neck.

He cut Lei's ropes and then went over to his wounded girlfriend.
Quickly he removed a med pack from the side pocket of his rucksack and proceeded to dress and bind Jane's leg.
Jane though in great pain, managed a little smile, "You think of everything Bill."
"Not quite. No pain killers I'm afraid."

He glanced at a motionless Roger, hanging out of the upturned wheelchair, quite dead.
"Bastard…"
Lei ran to Steven up on the burial mound.
Frantically untying the ropes around him, she cried "Steven, Steven…oh my God… hold on darling."

Benji stood still, an automatic gun protruding from his arm linkage.
He jerked up and started to move again, exclaiming,

"Warning there is extreme danger in the near vicinity!"

Bill turned and looked around. The black night failed to reveal anything.
He shouted "Where Benji? What is it?"

And then Bill reeled back almost falling over, he clutched his head.
Jane frowned hard, and despite her leg pain, something was trying to give her a massive headache.

Bill groaned, his mind churned.

"Ah…no……oh no….please…aaarh.."

Suddenly, there he could see the little boy in the orphanage crying and weeping, locked in the dormitory cupboard.

It was him.

Jane wide eyed, realised he was being distracted, used; something was making him lose his courage.
'Bill will break, don't let him break' Hammered in her mind.

Benji started to slur his words, “Warning…uurh”
Jane screamed, “Benji, identify the threat, USE YOUR WEAPONS!”
The robot quickly deployed his pulse laser weapon and fired up into mid air at the darkness.
A glob of searing white hot laser energy flashed into the black night.

It hit something invisible.
And then it wasn’t.

Jane yelled, “Oh Bill, Lei, God!... look it’s the bloody alien. BENJI DESTROY IT!”

A towering quivering opaque mass appeared lit up in the laser beam.
This time the innards showed a writhing mass of fungi like tentacles and grotesque weird faces.

Benji started to fire his rail gun, it screamed a torrent of lethal bullets into the beast.
His backpack power plant wailed full power and then his mini-chain gun screeched out a hail of lead.
The alien gave a ghastly noise, it was echoes of the dead it had consumed in the past.

AND THEN BENJI FROZE.
From his mouth came the words,

“……technological break…deern, ….road to hell.zz..sss.”

Jane got up wincing from her leg pain and hobbled over to a distraught Bill, she yelled, “Benji’s had it, Bill you’re our only hope!”

She grabbed the ancient helmet and managed to put it on his head, and then she fell to the ground with excruciating leg pain.

"KILL IT BILL!"

"Ah…ah god …what, where…oh Jane. Oh shit the monster!"

The beast loomed high over them.
A glowing red tendril shot out and melted Benji where he stood.
The robot half dissolved, smouldering and dripping metal, crashing to the ground.

With a monumental effort Bill got up, grabbing the plasma cannon in one movement.
The alien must have seen him and its whole bulk expanded and became partly visible in the moonlight. A grey streaked massive ball of unimaginable throbbing horror.
The multiple moving garish eyes were the worst.
Humanity's nightmares come true.

Jane could only watch helplessly as she lay on the ground.
Up on the mound a sobbing Lei was desperately trying to untie Steven's bonds.

And then a hoarse shout, "You are evil. Take some of this!"

With that a Gladiatorial Bill, his helmet glowing purple, held the cannon with all his strength and pulled the trigger.

The petrol engine generator on his backpack whined, the weapon demanding full power.
In the cannon, miniature explosions produced a deafening grating rattle and a sort of burping sound announcing the plasma beam ejection.
Bill buckled, trying to hold his ground as the weapon shuddered and recoiled.

The short burst of plasma hit the alien square in the middle.
Liquid death at the temperature of the Sun's surface.

A blood curdling noise came from the thing.
It had felt that. That is if it could feel pain.

Bill staggered but somehow kept his balance and stuck one leg solid behind him against the ground.

The beast seemed enraged, tentacles appeared all around it. The centre burst into a mass of cadaverous faces. They seemed locked in agonising horror.

A deep and ghostly, echoing groan emanated from within the alien, as it loomed closer.
Purple coronas burst around Bill's ancient helmet.

This time he kept his finger on the trigger.
The cannon screamed a deafening staccato, firing plasma continually into the alien.
He cried as his strength waned, "Take that…die …die."

Swathed in smoke and heat from the cannon, perspiration streamed down Bill's face. He was shaking to the weapon's bone grinding vibration.
Bill hung on desperately as the plasma cannon howled its death message.

Then the beast produced a deep bass noise and pyramid spoke shapes started to appear from the top of it. Through the dense haze, circling black tentacles appeared exiting from all around the alien.

It was a fight to the death.

He fought to maintain the weapon aim, as it kicked and vibrated spewing out its deafening screaming beam. His face white, his eye balls bulging behind the helmet slits.

Jane lay on the ground yards away, her eyes watering from her leg pain.
She was scared white, her eyes crying, "Oh Bill, do it, DO IT!… it's dying, keep on love…"

Great globs of white hot plasma thudded into the beast.

It started to screech a finale of weird gurgling sounds.

Then it did die, disintegrating into a jelly like foam and then vaporising into dense clouds of smoke and gas.
And something else, a gloopy matter flying out in all directions.
Seconds later it was gone with an awful acrid smell drifting across the hill.

Bill had emptied the fuel magazine.
Standing in almost shock he staggered haphazardly.
Suddenly he realised how hot his hands were.
Flinging the weapon away from his body, he collapsed down onto the smouldering grass, muttering "I got the bastard, I got it……"

Jane gasped, limped over and hugged him, "You did it my hero, the thing is dead….oh Bill."
Tears streamed down her face, she was crying and shaking with relief.

They sat for long seconds, in shock, dazed.

A shout from Lei made them look up.
"Steven's dying!"

In the light of the lamps, they had removed his bonds, but daren't remove the knife in his side. He would bleed to death even more quickly.
His face was white, his hair and beard matted with blood.

Lei was beside herself, she couldn't stop trembling.
They tried and failed to remove the barbed wire ring on his forehead, so tightly was it bound. Trickles of dried blood came from the imbedded metal thorns.

Then he spoke haltingly, "Please in my trouser belt…aah…um… on the inside is a pocket."
Lei quickly found it and pulled out a ring.
"Put it on my finger there." He raised his right hand. The other had been badly injured.
"aah…turn the top a quarter turn…quickly."
"But Steven we must get you to hospital."
Jane, "I've called an ambulance, they're on the way. Have to use the track we came up on."

Steven opened his eyes and looked to the sky, hoarsely shouting "FATHER GIVE ME STRENGTH…DO NOT FORSAKE ME!"

Lei stared at him strangely, then at Jane.
She rotated the ring top.

There across the other side of the clearing, the black stone in a mangled bracelet burst into colour. Instantly something switched on in the Land Rover.
Lei held Steven's body, she was puzzled. "Steven, the medics will be here soon. Hold on. Just what are you doing?"

Through his matted beard, his smile was just short of a grimace, "It is my broadcast to the world, it's pre-recorded. ….." he winced with pain, his head lolling back "ah…urh…..look at the moon."

They watched in awe as the full moon changed colour.
Bill gaped, "Oh my gawd, look at that."

It had become a giant display screen, with deep purple illustrations on its white surface.

A sequence commenced.
Pictures, smiling people holding one another, religious symbols. Each religion was depicted in pictures, cultural objects displayed in respect of each one. Then indigenous peoples were all honoured in the same way. Hundreds of cultures were being addressed. After each sequence, many hands wearing symbolic religious wrist bands, were shown clasping each other.

Lei watery eyed, dropped to her knees, "Oh Steven that is incredible, so beautiful."

He groaned.
Death hovered.

She grabbed him close, "Hold on my love…please. I love you so much."
Anxiously she turned to look down the way, searching for headlights.

Bill again searched vainly in his med pack for morphine.

Steven opened his eyes again and said, "I'm sorry Lei…. I have loved you too, but…"
He shuddered, "I must go now. I do not have a choice. Please forgive me."

His head dropped, he whispered, "It was all meant to be."

Lei "no….NOOOO!"

He raised his good hand as if to grab the sky, "FATHER! Do not forsake these people; I give them my life….."
He fell back in the chair and closed his eyes.

Steven Crowley, extraordinary preacher, died at that moment.

A massive bolt of lightning lit up the heavens and streaked down splitting the trunk of a large oak tree in a shower of sparks, just on the other side of the clearing.
Followed by deafening thunder.

"Oh Steven! .....oh god...No!"
Lei held him close, she burst into tears, sobbing.

Jane moved aside, dialling the emergency services again, shouted "We need an ambulance NOW! Where is it!"

Suddenly Lei got down on her knees, closed her eyes, held her hands together and began to pray.

Bill was still sitting, dazed.
Mesmerised he watched the moon shining out its messages.
He shuddered with a chill remembering where John Creeson was, up there somewhere in outer space, in all that bloody mess.

A muffled cry distracted him. It came from the prostrate form of Gavin on the ground.
"Oh my gawd!"
Bill ran over and sat Gavin upright, untying his bonds and removing the gag.
Gavin his face bloody, was wide eyed, he jerkily looked all around.
"Where's Roger?"
Bill motioned with his head, "Behind you Gavin, he's dead now. No more to worry about old son."
Gavin strained round and saw the toppled wheelchair with Roger sprawled stationary on the grass.

A surreal scene.

There in the moonlight they were all motionless.
Roger lay still, the wheelchair partly on top of him. The bodies of his thugs at strange angles, twisted on the ground. On the hill

illuminated by one arc lamp, the still form of Steven in the arms of Lei.
A frantic Jane, her face illuminated by her phone.

High up on the hill, a smoking metal stump was all that remained of a brave valiant robot.

All traces of the alien had vanished, evaporated.

Then flashing blue lights down the way announced the ambulance arrival.
Bill ran down to them.

Twenty minutes later

Lei, her face streaked with tears looked at the paramedic.
He said, "He died quickly my love. We tried all we could do, but he was already gone."
She broke down again, and then Jane held her.
Bill touched Lei's arm, he said, "Lei, he was a good man you know and look at that up there. Messages for all of humanity."

She looked up into the sky and then turned slowly to Bill.
"I know he was and let's hope they all look up and learn from this. He was more than a man you know, he was a healer. He is the….. the returning Messiah."
Bill said nothing, wanting desperately to believe Lei.
'And why not?' he thought. 'He was one of a kind… with a mission and I guess this was it.'

After checking for any life signs from Roger, his thugs and Barry Westland, the paramedics came over to Jane.
"Let's look at that leg love."
"Thanks, it's very painful. Is Barry Westland dead? That guy over there."
She pointed.

"I'm afraid so. He took several shots to the chest."
Jane felt tears bulging around her eyes.
"Oh god poor devil, he took out so many of those bastards. He saved mine and Bill's life in Australia too, you know."

She sat as the paramedics redressed her leg wound.
"Nasty one love, not that far from an artery. You need to come with us and get an X-Ray done."
"Ok. I must see my man first."

As the paramedics loaded Steven's body into the ambulance, Lei got in the back. Then more blue lights arrived.
Police and more ambulances.

Gavin having been treated for superficial injuries and a few bruises, was sitting on the grass gawping at the moon display, saying, "Oh man, look at that, so cool….it's magic."

Jane slowly limped over and put her arm around Bill's waist.
She winced at the pain, and then smiled tiredly at him, "Bill my hero. You got the damn thing you know. Your cannon did its stuff… I love you."
He looked at her, he seemed to have lost ten years in an hour.
"Love you too. Yes, I'm ecstatic. Now we have something we can fight them with. God Jane, I'm so exhausted."
He looked down at her thigh, "Hell… how's your leg?"
"Oh, bit sore, needs stitches and maybe an x-ray. They gave me a shot of morphine to kill the pain."
"Ok, we better get you on the ambulance. I'll follow in my car."

With the policemen coming up the hill, was a suited guy.
As the ambulance pulled away, he came over to Bill and said, "Bill Craswell?"
"Yes, that's me." sighed Bill.
"Ministry of Defence, you have been given temporary immunity from police questioning. We monitored your fight and how important your plasma cannon has become."

He gestured over the hill and down the valley.
There parked in the clearing just visible in the moonlight was an Apache attack helicopter.

Dozens of soldiers could be seen running across the valley and up to the hill.
Bill stared at the man, "Why didn't you attack the bloody thing and this bastard Roger with his henchmen here?"
"Because we only arrived as you engaged the alien."
Bill was knackered, he demanded, "Right, listen to me, I am following that ambulance. Inside is the person I love."
The man nodded, "Sir George Ratcliffe wants you to report back asap, but I understand if you must go after her now."
Several paramedics were carrying stretchers with the dead into the ambulances.

As Bill walked to the car, he turned to look back and there he was.

From the tree line the white robed man had watched the whole scenario.

Bill pulled the gargoyle face and muttered,
"I don't care even if you are God! There's people here I need to be with."

With that he got into the Lexus and gunned it down the road after the ambulance.

Chapter 31

9.15 pm
Rameses Spacecraft - Moon orbit

The astronauts had already donned their space helmets. This was to pre-empt any decompression loss in their spacecraft on their way back to Earth, from impacts suffered as a result of flying debris generated during the alien space conflicts.

Daniel glanced across at the other two, John and Mark.

"Ok, twenty seconds to Gravity engine firing. The course has been programmed and it's all automatic, including systems control of turning round and firing to decelerate to the Space Station."
He became more serious, "The G forces during acceleration are likely to render us unconscious. Personally I have set up a resuscitation module, but I hope to wake you guys more gently."
He grinned, "Eleven seconds…."

At zero the engine fired and went to full thrust within three minutes.
John gritted his teeth watching the G force meter.
The needle slowly moved up, 2.5, 3, 3.5, then 4G.
His body weighing four times more than normal.
The enormous acceleration made his body feel an inch thick, his face unrecognisably distorted.
Breathing was so painful, despite the pressure suit.

Before blacking out, his last thought was, "Karen my love, I'm coming home. These guys are made of the right stuff. Just hope… and pray... we can make it…."

2 hours later
NASA Control Centre
Houston, Texas

Colonel Mondone watched the console.
After the momentous events and the aliens' destruction, a massive euphoria had enveloped the building.

It would subside somewhat.
The devastating loss of Orion and her crew, Jack Wilson, Ray Kingley and Rickki Tagarlo, surrounded everybody.
Following close behind, the Rameses ground team were monitoring its rapid transit back to Earth and a perilous docking with the International Space Station.
Their only hope of returning to Earth.

The on board ISS crew themselves, had already escaped the dying space station using one of two re-entry Soyuz capsules.

Mondone's phone rang.
He saw it was Ming.
"Sir, I heard about the loss of the Orion."
"Yes, terrible."
She faltered then said, "You see Rickki was my ex. and oh god I can't believe it."
"I'm sorry Ming, but I don't think they suffered. Their ship was instantly destroyed."
She said quietly at the other end, "and Rameses, what are their chances?"
A worrying thought for her friends, Mark Vanderbrook and John Creeson.

"Not good. They have to get to the ISS which is in trouble and then use the Soyuz 2 escape capsule. What's more because of the erratic burn-up trajectory of the ISS and the moment of capsule detach, we have no real idea where they will land."

No reply.

“Ming?”
“MING!”
“Sorry Sir. I just hope and pray they make it back ok.”

A shout from the floor distracted him.
“So do I Ming, so do I…have to go.”
Click.

Rameses was already in trouble.

Telemetry to the ground had shown something had hit the space craft on its return path from the moon. It had caused the loss of the breathable atmosphere inside.

Nearly seven hours later at 5.30 am
Friday 19th January

Inside Rameses.
Deceleration completed – entering Earth orbit.

Utter chaos.
Stuff floating everywhere.

Mark unbuckled himself, he floated, turning to look at Daniel.
“Jesus…”

Daniel lay dead in his couch, his face contorted and white.
His helmet visor had a large puncture hole in it.
Mark looked up at the spacecraft hull directly above the commander.
A hole could be seen the size of a walnut.
It was crusted with ice from the escaping water vapour inside.

Then Mark looked through John Creeson’s helmet visor.

The monitor showed life signs, a heartbeat, and good blood pressure with his suit systems working ok, but he was still unconscious. Thankfully his spacesuit was intact.
Something made Mark look out of the window.
"Oh hell…"

The ISS could just be seen, but it was far away, probably three or four miles and slowly receding from them.
'Damn.' Thought Mark, 'That debris strike has knocked us off our target position.'
He checked engine fuel remaining and thrusters fuel.
Minimal.
Mark worked quickly at the console and Rameses lurched forward slowly.
After patching the hull puncture and restoring atmosphere he removed John's helmet and waved a revival pack under his nose.

Several times.

"Uuh…ah." John jerked his head back as the potent smell brought him round.
"Oh God….I…"
"Easy John, easy. Take your time."
"Hell…I thought I died. I feel absolutely awful. My chest is killing me."
"That's to be expected, the pain will reduce in a while."

After a few seconds, John turned to look at Mark then raised his head to stare at Daniel.
Mark grimaced, "Daniel is dead. A piece of shrapnel pierced the outer hull and didn't stop. He was a good man."
"Oh no…"
"John, we overshot our target position and now we are on course for the ISS. Trouble is that our escape window has been narrowed somewhat."
John eyes opened wide, his nauseous feeling increased; he tried to mouth some words.

"Instead of thirty minutes at the ISS to get into the capsule and detach, we have about fifteen."
John, "Is that enough, can we make it?"
"To be frank, the odds are not good John. Rameses will reach the ISS in about ten minutes. Only hope is to suit up now, let the automatic docking systems connect us. Then we equalise the pressures with whatever is on the other side in the ISS and move like hell to the escape capsule."

He continued, "Latest I have is that the ISS has sustained many hits from the space debris and it is descending out of control. The crew managed to escape some hours ago. We must hope the other escape capsule is undamaged. "

John, "Lord… bloody scary… Mark." He paused, "Gees it's freezing in here."
Mark, "A meteor strike knocked out our climate control systems during the flight from the moon."

The battered spacecraft closed on the stricken space station.
Mark looked out the porthole, "I can see wisps of smoke coming from the ISS."
John "Think it's on fire?"
Mark "Could be. I call ground see if they can still access the video systems on board."
He made the call.

Houston, "Sorry Mark, our comms with the ISS are in a mess. No video cameras are accessible. Some temperature sensors in the main section are elevated, between ten and thirty degrees centigrade."
"Thanks Houston."
"John, we have a link up with Karen Durgas, are you ready to accept?"
"Hell yes! That would be marvellous."
It could be the last time he spoke to her.
A rising queasy feeling engulfed him.

Karen appeared on the monitor, "Hi John, So glad you're safely in Earth orbit. I know you have a hell of a challenge ahead, but I just wanted to say good luck and Godspeed. Get home safely." She slightly bit her lip, her nervousness and tiredness apparent. Her eyes glistened with worry.
John smiled, he was pale, a little gaunt and he had lost weight, even in the short time in space.

"Thanks Karen." He winked.
She blew him a kiss and mouthed 'I love you…'
He felt warm and returned the kiss, her face a lovely smile.

Abruptly the monitor blacked out.

Mark said, "Buckle in John and put your helmet on, we're going in."

As they closed on the space station, John looked through one of the small windows and saw just how big the ISS was. An enormous assembly of cylinders, with more branching out at right angles along its length. The giant arms of dark orange coloured solar panels straddling right across the entire structure of the ISS. A damaged panel lurched at an odd angle.

The huge space station was already ploughing into the outer fringes of the Earth's atmosphere, its many edges pouring vapour trails. Tiny bits of debris flew in all directions.

CLUNK. Docking successful.

The indicator counted down until the air pressure equalised on both sides, avoiding a possible imbalance explosion when the hatch opened.
With their spacesuits and helmets on, the astronauts waited, a rope attached between them.
John's heart raced. Then a green equalisation light.

Holding the torch in front, Mark opened the hatch and drew a deep breath.

Instantly they were enveloped and buffeted in a cloud of dense smoke and floating debris from the ISS.
Mark checked the instrument panel.
"As I thought, there's very little breathable atmosphere in here. Too many hull punctures."

As fast as they could, they staggered in their bulky spacesuits down the ISS interior, ducking and avoiding floating objects of all descriptions. The escape capsule was about half way down and through a module to their right.
John kept drumming into himself, 'Stay calm, walk strongly, watch Mark. Capsule up and to the right.' He held the rope tightly, his literal lifeline.

The ISS lighting flickered haphazardly, with smoke drifting by in puffs and clouds.
A crash up front somewhere signalled a shudder through the entire space station.
Smoke curled in the beams from their helmet lights.

John's heart beat ramped up and his breathing became shallow and more frequent.
Mark shouted through the comset, "John, you ok?"
"Yep. Just ….I…uh am a bit …out of…breath."

They stumbled on and then gasped at the fierce fire up ahead.
Mark jerked to a stop, the rope was dead weight.
He turned back and scrambled the three metres or so.

John lay on his back hyperventilating.
He was gasping very short breaths.

Mark operated some controls on John's suit chest panel.

"John, JOHN! Listen…I'm enriching your air mixture. B R E A T H D E E P A N D S L O W L Y."
John reached for breath…wheezing, his eyeballs about to burst.
"SLOWLY… John, slow deep breaths."

After a few minutes they stumbled back on the trail, narrowly escaping the flames with Mark squirting an extinguisher as a shield.

Outside, the ISS had started to glow at the front.
The fierce heat of re-entry was upon them. Through out the space station came ominous shrieks and creaking noises.

With smoke billowing all around them, Mark dragged John into the escape capsule.
He shouted "IT'S STARTING TO BREAK UP. COME ON WE'VE GOT SECONDS!"

Quickly he looked around to try and see any visible damage to their only hope of getting back to Earth.

Only the capsule power up checks would be conclusive.
It takes a long three minutes to bring up the escape capsule computer systems.

Three minutes they didn't have.

Chapter 32

Three and a half hours earlier.
2am Friday 19th January

Sabrina Fay's house, Catherington, UK

The dreaming had stopped.
A quiet air of jubilation permeated the huge lounge.

After a prolonged connection with the spirits, which included very tired people in the circle being replaced at planned intervals, the atmosphere now was of quiet discussion.

Sabrina's kitchen was flat out providing refreshments.
Tea, coffee, soft drinks, sandwiches and various cakes.
A much required sugar hit and good comfort food.

Karen sat alone scrolling through her phone for any news, her thoughts dominated by John's dangerous mission in space.
She had a foreboding that he would not return alive.

Anne Whitfield came over and sat next to her saying, "Guess you're thinking about John? Any more news?"
"Yes I am. Cannot think of much else. So worried."

A strong voice distracted them.
"GE`!"
And then, "Please be quiet and listen."

It was Gad the Elder. The native American Indian from the Navajo tribe.
He stood tall, with a hawk-like tanned face and his long black hair cascading around his shoulders. Wearing a light fawn suit, he waited for everybody's attention.

"Thank you, all of you for your strength and perseverance. We have come through events that have resulted in the salvation of mankind."

He stopped and paused looking around, his knowing eyes piercing through you.
Raising his hand to the ceiling, he continued,
"The threat from Andromeda has been vanquished. Our counsel from Omega Centauri has protected us from an evil that is unimaginable. Yet today has been an enlightenment and a lesson for all.
We sincerely believe that our spiritual kingdoms have survived a most venomous threat. A species that has no conception of us other than to suck the life out of humanity and our eternal souls. "

The hush was cloying.

Karen put her hand over her mouth, it was something she had already sensed and now her psyche shivered inside.
Gad spoke again.

"Our spiritual kingdoms are safe and they have communicated so. They exist in another dimension of space and time. They convey gratitude and love at our successful efforts to ensure the continuance of humanity and the soul world.
This has been achieved through ours and many other peoples' efforts."

He paused again, and then spoke even more loudly,

"If the Omega Centauri salvation had failed, we would have eventually failed too. Both prongs of the spear were necessary.
The beings from Andromeda have been prevented from destroying and enslaving humanity here and also other species in our galaxy.
If they had succeeded in their depraved and evil way, with humanity as we know it gone, there would have been no possibility of seeding it again in this dark era.

This period of darkness could then have lasted for… possibly millions of years."

He bowed and sat down.
Sabrina stood clapping, "Thank you Gad, thank you."
Everybody joined in.

She turned looking around at everyone.
"For now the threat is gone. I'm sure you are all very tired. Please stay a little longer, maybe an hour, so that we can ascertain the intrusions have been completely vanquished.
Then go home and get some rest. Just stay contactable in case events change and we need you. Love and light to you all."
Sabrina then went over and conferred with the Elders and core members of her group.

Karen had disappeared into the small lounge, watching the news channels, all showing the same stark conflict in outer space.
She was on her phone.

Sabrina, "Ah, there you are."
Karen closed the call and looked up, she had one serious face.
Sabrina, "Karen?"
Slowly Karen replied, "Steven Crowley has died at Kingley Vale. Jane has sustained a nasty leg wound. Barry Westland has been shot dead."
Sabrina wide eyed exclaimed, "Oh dear Lord, what happened?"
Karen's eyes watered as she said, "I have just spoken to Jane. There was an almighty fight up on that hill. A local crook and his henchmen were torturing Steven, crucifying him it seems.
Barry Westland and Lei managed to shoot most of the thugs.
Then Bill destroyed the alien with a plasma gun.
Lei and Bill are unharmed. Poor Lei she is so grief stricken…. they are at the hospital."
Sabrina, "Oh dear God. The alien?"

Karen replied, "Yes, it was controlling the thugs and Bill fought it with a new weapon. Unbelievable."

Sabrina knew what was also troubling Karen, taking hold of her as she started to cry.
"You heard from John or NASA yet?"

"No, nothing. He is on route from the moon right now. God knows what they are experiencing, what with the destruction of the alien fleet and all that debris flying around. Also they might get taken out like the Orion spacecraft."

She shook uncontrollably.
Sabrina hugged her tight and said, "What will be is meant to be. Be strong."

Karen took a deep breath then said, "I will try. So much has happened… is still happening."

Some seconds went by, she seemed far away.

"Sabrina. In amongst all this, I have made a momentous physics discovery. I intend to publish a paper when I get straight."
Sabrina squeezed her arm, "Good for you Karen."

Karen paused then said, "I must go to the hospital now."

Sabrina, "Sure. Please give Lei my deepest sympathies and love."
Karen turned to go, "I will…."
"Karen?"
"Yes?"
"I wanted to thank you for your incredible contribution here, not only the protection that the ancient cross and helmet provided, but your spiritual support too. I felt you there, much stronger than before."

Sabrina broke into a beautiful smile.
Karen, "It is like someone is slowly pulling the curtains back on a brilliant sunrise.
I am starting to see so much."

Then she waved goodbye.

A shout from one of the outside doors.

"Sabrina, everybody! Come and see the moon. It is just amazing."

Much later
6:10 am GMT - The same day.
110 miles above the Earth

Grinding, tearing sounds announced the slow destruction of the International Space Station.
Once the pinnacle of man's achievements, the largest habitable environment in space ever created, was now doomed.
In the past, a significant portion of it, had been sent up as individual modules by the Space Shuttle over several years.

The core body of the dying ISS slowly twisted, the solar panels having been ripped away earlier.
Re-entering the Earth's atmosphere, it was burning, breaking up and melting.

A giant disintegrating meteor in the sky.

Barely a mile below it, was another burning craft.

The Soyuz capsule bucked and bounced in the hostile atmosphere.
It too was travelling at over thirty thousand miles an hour.
That is nearly ten miles every second.

With the capsule totally enveloped in flame, the automated system thrusters were battling to steady it.

The heat within the tiny craft was almost unbearable.
Both Mark and John lay strapped in their couches, perspiration streaming down their faces and the inside of their spacesuit helmets.
The searing, burning noise outside, dominating everything.

No radio contact possible.

John thoughts raced, 'How long would it take you to die, if the heat shield failed and the fierce flames of re-entry penetrated the capsule?'

Scared…he was beyond that.
His heart pounded, his bulging eyes staring through the little window at the bright flames.
If he lived he made a decision then and there, never to go up in space again.

Then he thought 'God, I need those brown corduroy trousers now. The ones that Bill joked about.'
He tried to laugh…

No one knew if the heat shield had been damaged from debris breaking off the space station when they frantically detached the capsule from it.

Minutes dragged. They seemed timeless.
Then after what felt like a lifetime, the orange glow outside disappeared.
The flames had gone and blue sky peered through the little portholes.
An explosive thud.

Ejecting the nose cone forced out a long thin parachute which in turn yanked out three huge parachutes.

WHAM.
As the capsule abruptly halted its downward flight, the jerk rammed the astronauts hard into their couches.

John nervously looked through his helmet visor across at Mark.
Behind his visor, the American had a big grin and he gave a thumbs up.
John breathed a massive sigh of relief, 'Thank God…thank God.'
Minutes passed…

Mark switched on the comms, "Houston, this is Soyuz 2. Parachutes deployed….repeat Houston, this is Soyuz 2, and we have deployed parachutes."

He repeated the message again.
Crackle…
"Soyuz 2, this is Houston. Congratulations team. Welcome home!"

Mark, "Houston, have you our position yet?"
Long seconds of silence.

"Soyuz 2, we estimate you are two hundred miles off Fiji in the Pacific Ocean."

Mark turned and gave John two thumbs up and then instinct made him check the altimeter.
"JOHN! Brace for impact!"

Seconds later… BOOOMFFF.
They hit the sea.
The little capsule tossed and bounced in a large swell.

Helmets came off quickly.
Mark grinned, "Welcome back to mother Earth!"
They shook gloves in a tight handshake.

John had a crinkly smile, ragged with tiredness and enormous relief.
Then a different motion started. It made his stomach uneasy… again.

Outside, wind and torrential rain battered the tiny capsule as it bobbed up and down between giant dark waves in a Pacific storm. Up above, huge streaks of garish lightning flashed across the black sky.
Far below, a miniscule and fragile dot of orange gyrated in the dark blue morass.

Only the bright orange flotation bags were keeping the tiny capsule from sinking to the distant seabed, a mile below them.

6:20 am GMT (The same day – Friday 19th January)
Pascal Laboratory
European Space Systems, East Meon, UK

It was still dark, with sunrise over an hour away.
A pile of mostly empty paper cups were spread out across the table.
All the plates had just crumbs left from an early and extremely welcome cooked breakfast, that the kitchen had rustled up for the teams.

With the exception of one plate, Karen's.
Scrambled eggs and toast, untouched.

Everybody was dog tired, having had no sleep the night before.
It had been pointless going to bed because nobody would or could sleep.

The past twenty four hours were ingrained in peoples' faces.
Going back to ESS seemed a good idea, with its hook ups world wide to other nations' communication systems.
Scientists and engineers alike, ragged yet alert for any more information.

Lei Zhao had returned to the yacht Nemain.
She needed to be back at Steven's and her home, to be alone with her grief.
Despite the others who had begged her to stay with them.

There was a lot of crying to do and then always some.

Sir George Ratcliffe stood watching his teams.
He looked about a hundred years old but with a beaming smile on his craggy face, his eyes flicked around.
Inwardly he was a little shaky and his cheek bore a large reddish-pink mark.

Jane Horsham had sat down looking at him, her crutches from the hospital beside her.
Pain killers had helped the ache of the stitched knife wound in her leg.
She smirked at his glowing cheek.
Quickly glancing around she looked for his girl assistant Crystal, …..no sign of her.

Come uppance, as they say.

Bill leant slightly against Jane's chair, his arm on her shoulder.
If you could have framed Bill's subtle smile, it said everything.

Love, happiness, and achievements beyond what even he dared to think possible.
Yet he, like all the others was desperate for news of the space capsule that John might have got to in time.

Gustav Huck sat with a non-descript face on the other side of the room.
Inside, he too felt a wonderful elation with their work on the plasma cannon.

Karen Durgas, pale and drawn, her eyes wet with worry, sat scrolling through the news broadcasts and a NASA live feed.
On one screen a video appeared showing the ISS re-entry high up in Earth's atmosphere.
The destroyed space station, now a multitude of streaming meteor-like fireballs.

Her hand on her mouth, thinking, 'John could be in that…oh my dear God.'
She was desperate for that Houston call, one way… or the other.

Bill, "Karen… anything yet?"
"No."

Ratcliffe spoke, "Bill you are damned secretive you know. I would have authorised the mini-plasma gun anyway."
The gargoyle in Bill's face appeared showing an enormous satisfaction that everything he had done had been successful. Well nearly everything.

He replied, "I was going to George, but the risks of the thing exploding were high.
The cooling problem meant we had to freeze the pellet fuel, the ammunition if you like. Otherwise the tiny amounts of uranium in them would have gone into thermal runaway, nuclear meltdown. As it happens I used all the fuel in destroying the alien, so quite lucky really."
Ratcliffe murmured, "Yes you have a point…"
Bill quickly interjected, "And you wouldn't want to have been associated with a disaster like nuclear meltdown."
"Hmm …very true Bill." replied Ratcliffe quickly.

Jane quick fire as usual, "Sir George. We need more of these weapons and quickly. The alien Bill tangled with may have been all three combined, after all it was huge.
Or the other two are still loose on this planet."

"Hurrmmm…quite right. I have already issued a directive with the Ministry to acquire the necessary logistical approval and developm….."
He was loudly interrupted by a newsreader, then Karen's shout.

"The intrepid astronauts return to Earth, they…"

"LOOK! Look! …they're safe….oh John… and Mark…there!"

On the NASA live feed was an aerial video of the capsule descending on three huge red and white striped parachutes.
Then the feed switched in the radio conversation with the capsule.
"Houston, this is Soyuz 2. Parachutes deployed…. Repeat Houston, this is Soyuz 2, we have deployed parachutes."

Crackle…
"Soyuz 2, this is Houston. Congratulations team. Welcome home!"

"Houston, this is John Creeson, just to say thanks guys for getting us back."

Karen closed her eyes and sank to her knees, her hands clasped tightly together.
"Thank you Lord…oh John."

TWO DAYS LATER.
Early, 7am Sunday – 21st January
Onboard the yacht Nemain in Dell Quay harbour.

Lei Zhao was expecting guests for a late lunch today.
She was ready now with grateful anticipation to see her friends again.
This was despite the awful grief tearing through her soul.

Yesterday Jane and Karen had come over to see her, trying to help and give comfort.
Followed by a very long private video call with her sister Ming.

Two days of desperate sorrow and tears.

The boat gently rocked in the waves of the incoming tide.

She turned in the bed, looking at the empty space on Steven's side and breathed out a long sigh. Lei reached and hugged his pillow, his scent still faintly there.
Speaking quietly she said "Oh Steven, I miss you so much. Why… oh why…"
She cast her eyes over to the photo of the two of them laughing in Skiathos, Greece.
Her mind wandered back to their smuggling holidays in the Mediterranean.
Pools of water formed in her eyes.

Something out in the small lounge caught her attention.
The portholes still had their blinds drawn, but a light flickered in there.
Probably a candle still going from the night before, forgotten after that now empty bottle of wine.
It was a bit unlike her safety conscious self, with naked flames and all that.
Especially after that nasty burn in the galley.
She glanced at her arm, healed completely, no tell tale marks.

Lei smiled in thought 'My Steven, a wonderful healer.'

She got out of bed in her pyjamas and walked over to a small chest of drawers, and opening the middle one she took out two mangled bracelets and a ring.
Lei had managed to retrieve these precious artefacts before the authorities had arrived there on Kingley Vale hilltop.
Rubbing gently the intact Lapiz Lazuli stone, she felt a little uneasy.
Returning them and closing the drawer she turned, feeling quite chilly.

Lei slowly walked to the door which adjoined their bedroom with the boat passageway.
Then she pulled back a porthole curtain and saw a faint moon in the dawning sky, still sequencing its purple images.

She almost crept the few steps into the lounge, apprehension riding high in her thoughts, 'a draft down here?... no something uncanny.'
The hairs on her neck sprang out and her arms prickled.

Then she gasped out loud, grabbing the door frame to steady herself.

There across the lounge sitting in his chair was Steven Crowley, wrapped in a white cloth down to his knees. His long hair had been combed, his beard tidy.
His face was a little pale and he seemed to have the slightest white glow, no, it was more of an aura surrounding him.

"Oh Steven…oh…you… you are ALIVE!....my love."

"Yes, but not here."

A single candle burned in the holder on the table.

She walked slowly across to touch him, to see if he was really real or just a dream.
He smiled in that hypnotic way of his, the blue eyes radiant.
Lei almost flinched as she hesitantly took his hand and knelt before him.

His hand felt and was solid.

"You are truly the Messiah. I love you so much."

"Lei, so much good has happened. I know I have let you down. This is why I was hesitant to declare my love for you. Not wanting to hurt you so."
She watched him, her watery eyes wide open, and then kissed his hand.

He spoke softly "I do love you with a light that outshines the stars. Come close."

Steven placed his hand on her stomach and looked at her with what seemed ten thousand years of knowledge.
He said, "You know?"

"Yes I do, it is our unborn child."

"I will never be far. I have to go soon… back to my kingdom. Tell our message to all you trust and for the little one, pass on all our wisdom."
With his other hand he reached into a fold in his cloth robe and produced a flower.

It was the most beautiful and delicate purple flower. Tiny long petals that had a brightness as though in direct sunlight. A green stem with vivid patterned leaves.
The base showed a bit of root wrapped in damp moss.

Steven gave it to her and said, “For you and me, forever.”
She quickly moved and kissed him.
Slow, sweet and real.

He smiled gloriously.

Lei’s face said it all, supreme elation. “So beautiful, I must put this in a little water.”
She went out to the galley and filled a small crystal vase with water to place the flower in.
Then a frown puckered her face, ‘…..but not here…?’

Quickly walking back to the lounge, Lei said, “It is so beautiful Steven, …….what ? …..STEVEN!”

He had gone, completely.

She quickly checked the rest of the boat and then ran up the short stairs to the deck. She stared all around the yacht.
No sign of her Messiah.

The breeze ruffled her long dark hair, tears streamed down her face.
She fell to her knees and cried.
“Oh Steven, where are you?”

Lei knew he would go.
‘Was it a dream?’

Wiping her eyes, she looked at the flower in her hand.
Placing her other hand on her tummy, she looked up at the cool blue sky as if to transmit her thoughts to the distant stars.

She whispered, “Steven, wherever you are, I will always love you. Come see us sometime.”

Six hours later
On deck – the Yacht Nemain

For late January the weather was surprisingly mild, just jumpers or fleeces sufficient to keep the cold out.
On deck a leisurely lunch was being consumed.
No deadlines, meetings or other stuff to curtail their reunion.

Despite her grief, Lei had insisted it went ahead.
She needed to be busy and preparing the lunch was fine.
Her early morning experience would remain secret for now.

As they all came aboard, she was hugged individually by everyone.
So sorry's, deep condolences how are you? …sympathy poured out.
More tears, they shared her sorrow.

After lunch Anne Whitfield raised her glass.
"A toast I think, to many things."

They all sat squeezed around the fold out picnic table.
A gentle chilly breeze rattled the mast lines and fluttered the little flag on the stern. Streaks of sun peaked out like wheel spokes from a bunch of cumulus.

Anne with her glass of grapefruit juice.
Sabrina Fay smiling raised her glass of water.
Karen Durgas, a glass of orange juice.
John Creeson, his glass of ale.
Bill Craswell with a large scotch whisky.
Then Jane Horsham with a glass of ale too.
Finally Lei Zhao with a glass of elderflower cordial.

Anne, "First to the intrepid hero returning from his awesome adventure in outer space and his safe return."
"Here, here!"

They drank to John.
He smiled. It felt so good, to be safe back home.
"Thank you, yes, so glad to be back, but we lost Daniel, our commander."
John looked so sad, he continued, "A man of such calibre and such a good friend, such a loss."

Karen spoke, "He, you and Mark coordinated the space gravity array so the Earth could mount some sort of defence. I'm sure a defence that distracted the beings from Andromeda, enough for our salvation. It is a sad but proud moment."

John raised his glass solemnly, "To Daniel and the Orion crew that I got to know so well."

Then Anne said, "To Sabrina and Karen for coordinating our spiritual and technological defences against the tide of evil."
Glasses clinked again.

Karen looked across at Sabrina and said, "What a surprise with the Home Secretary and the Prime Minister dropping in on us? Spiritualism has never had so much visibility."
Sabrina the oracle smiled, she replied, "I would love to believe that Karen, but to politicians our dreaming circles have little tangibility and perhaps it is better that way. I'm sure the Prime Minister Samantha Yeareth was much more interested in your ancient artefacts, Karen."
"Yes, I guess you're right and already both John and I have been asked to relinquish them for investigations by the Ministry."

Sabrina replied, "Maybe offer to help in the investigations and so keep tabs on your cross, sword and helmet. Your talents are almost certainly a factor to their operation."
"Yes, that sounds a good idea."

Anne turned to Lei and said, "and for Steven. We owe him so much. Lei please accept our most heartfelt feelings. Anytime just

say and we'll be there."
They all murmured the same.
Jane placed her hand over Lei's.
Lei a little weepy said, "Thank you, thank you Anne, Jane…all of you. It is very hard for me at the moment. I just can't accept Steven is gone. In my heart I know he is out there somewhere, maybe in another time or space."

She said nothing about the seven week old baby she was carrying, nor Steven's visit that morning.
The time for announcement will come, but not now.

Lei raised her hand and everybody waited.
"There is something I know that Steven was involved with. He never mentioned it directly but I am convinced that he and his kind were somehow responsible for the devices we believe are in the churches and temples."

Karen and Jane instantly thought about Quentin's revelations in the rest home.

Lei became intensely profound and said slowly, "We have seen in the last few days and particularly this morning, a massive increase in religious congregations for many, many of the world's churches, mosques, temples and other sacred buildings."

"Hear, hear."
She continued, "I propose a toast for mankind, for all peoples of whatever religious or other persuasion, to live together in peace, forever."

A unison of shouts and glasses clinking, "For peace!"

Bill spoke up, "and now I would like to toast a young lady who has changed me in a wonderful way and she happens to be a brilliant scientist too. Also she saved my life up on that hill."

Karen glanced and smiled at Jane.
Bill continued, "Jane bravely took on those awful dog beasts. Also that bloody alien had entered my head and it was tearing my mind apart….and…and…"
He caught himself and overcome with emotion, he clammed up.

Jane quickly grabbed his arm, "Bill, it's ok now, you were fantastic."

Wiping an eye he managed to speak, "I was finished you know… until Jane put that helmet on me. It…it generated a calm, a confidence, a strength that made me battle on. Also her brilliance in the plasma cannon development. Thank you. I give you Jane!"

More alcohol flowed.
Some seagulls screeched overhead.

John Creeson tapped his glass with a spoon.
"That leads me straight into the next toast and not least of all it is to say a special thank you to someone. Someone with the guts to follow through when everything is against them."

They all knew.

"I give you Bill Craswell, our mad and gifted scientist who has achieved so much."

"BILL, BILL CRASWELL!" they all shouted in unison.

He blushed red.
Jane glowed with pride and admiration for a man she was slowly coming to adore.
He waited for the acclamations to die down and then said, "Thank you so much. Now I think Karen has a little announcement to make."
He looked at her smiling broadly.

"I…oh… I don't know..um."
Bill said, "Karen, go on and tell them, you clever clogs."

Karen paused, she looked at them all staring at her open eyed, to possibly another major revelation.
"Well I have made a discovery. I took the time to check and recheck my equations and thanks to John and Bill's gravity array, I was able to formulate my theory."
They waited with baited breath.
Even Sabrina was unsure as to what Karen had uncovered.

"You see I believe I have discovered the origin to the universe."

The silence was total for a few seconds.

Then some geese waddled down to the foreshore, cackling and honking.
Mum at the front, followed by a straddle of little ones jumping, running and pushing.
At the back came Dad goose, the rear guard.

Nature always cautious, and yet a new world all around for these unusually early toddlers.
Eyes swivelled back to Karen.

"Where to begin?"

Anne laughed, said, "Don't go too deep Karen, you'll lose me."
Karen smiled, "Ok. It started with the first clash in space. Using our gravity array data I could see and measure tiny streams of plasma escaping into some of the black holes that the Omega Centuri spacecraft were controlling."

John gulped his ale, wonderful stuff.
He already knew of Karen's revelations.
His insistent and rapid return late Saturday after some intensive

NASA medical checks, nearly cost him his temper with their authorities.

Plucked from a turgid restless Pacific sea with sharks circling the Soyuz capsule, he and Mark were winched up into a US Navy helicopter.
Hot, sweaty and damn hungry, after switching from the other freezing extreme in their damaged craft Rameses.
The terrible shrieking noise of the disintegrating space station, as they jerked loose in the escape capsule, had stayed in his head. It was still there. All he wanted to do was get home.

Karen continued, "To keep a long story short." She grinned. "I realised the enormous gravity of a black hole pulls material towards it so fast that it reaches close to the speed of light near the event horizon. That is the edge of the black hole.
The edge of darkness."

She paused.

"When broken up material from stars, planets and other debris enters the black hole, as the colossal gravity pulls it in, this stuff accelerates to a fraction past the speed of light. At that point a lot of the material is sucked into the centre of the black hole and where that goes is still an unknown. What I have discovered is that the other superfast fragmented material misses the centre and plummets onwards between the event horizon and the black hole mass. It is no longer in the time domain of the black hole."

She had told Bill some of it, but now he had the oddest expression on his face.
His mind was already there, it just needed Karen to confirm it.

"This rock, debris, whatever used to be stars and planets, as it surpasses the speed of light due to an almost infinitely strong gravity pull, *is sent back in time.*

Einstein's Theory of Relativity demands it."

Lei silently gasped. An unconscious distraction from her grief.

"It is a new past, not ours, but a past somewhere else in space and time.
From our present, what we see is a guaranteed future being created. The passage of matter from our time is sucked beyond the black hole and into a new past, the debris creating fresh hot gases and eventually new stars and planets."

Sabrina "That is amazing Karen, a truly creative cycle."
"Yes it is and on a huge scale as all the galactic black holes must have this matter leakage. It is also possible that the central black hole mass does the same thing."

Bill quietly said, "My gawd…you are a flippin genius."

Karen concluded, *"It means the universe is able to renew itself forever."*

Lei said "Wow Karen, that is so profound. So what will happen now?"

"I am going to publish a physics paper. It will create an enormous controversy you know, with all those established 'other' theories."

A seagull briefly landed on the edge of the table and stole a piece of cake.
He flapped away with a squawk.
Bill shouted, "Look at him, matter escaping from our own cake-holes!"
They all burst out laughing.

Time had marched on.

As Karen washed the dishes in the galley, she noticed the little purple flower in the glass vase and suddenly exclaimed,
"Oh Lei, that is such a pretty flower! ...and I have never seen one like it? "
Lei had just come down the steps, "Yes it is and yes it is very unusual. I like to think it is unique."
She smiled and looked at Karen in a sapient way.
Karen slightly shook her face, as if to say '...and you mean... what?'

Suddenly Lei glanced at her watch, it showed 4:30pm and then she said, "Ok. Let's hook up with my sister. It's the crack of dawn for them and I guess they might be a bit sleepy. Come on!"
She jogged up the steps to the deck and set up her tablet with its camera so they could all see and then she hit the call button.
The screen burst into a Hawaiian sunrise with two grinning faces, Ming and Akoni.
"Hiya all!"
Lei smiled and said to her sister, "Hi Ming, Akoni so good to see you! What a glorious view you have."

Ming smiled, "Likewise. Ok, you lot of under achievers! what's new?"
From the deck of the Nemain, came a chorus of laughter.
Then Lekika, Akoni's Ma looked in, "Well done I must say, you are all heroes."

Ming's phone panned around showing a couple of new builds next to Akoni's mum's Hawaiian house.
They were sitting in Lekika's newly landscaped back garden.
Lekika continued, "Look at my lovely garden and I have new neighbours, see those fang-dangled houses. They come ready to assemble, went up in no time."

Slowly the ruin caused by the Hawaiian tsunami a year ago, was being reversed.

Off camera came a 'meow'.
Ming picked up Jimmy cat with a "Oh your are a lump." and placed him on her lap and into camera.

Lei, "Ooh, lovely puss…hello Jimmy!"
He was having none of this limelight and quickly jumped off with another plaintive meow.
Ming laughed, "He wants his breakfast… and nothing will distract him."
She became serious and looked closely at the camera.
"Lei, please come out soon. Be with us for as long as you want. Love you Sis."
"Love you Ming. Thanks, maybe in a few weeks I will. Just can't get my mind around anything at the moment."
Ming smiled as though she was there, "Your sorrow is our sorrow. Call anytime."

The yacht rocked from the swell of a passing motor boat.
Long gone was the sun, now hiding behind grey clouds.

Karen brightly said "I fancy some Hawaiian weather. Swap for some of our dismal January." she waited, still with half an eye on Lei.
Akoni replied, "Come out anytime, surf in the warm sea."
Ming looked in, "Say, we have some visitors here."
She panned her phone around.

There sitting opposite was Arrack Mondone and Gail, smiling and tanned in the streaming dawn light.
Wearing colourful bright Hawaiian garb, they both waved at the camera.

Arrack spoke, "Hi folks, good to see everyone! How're you doing?"
In unison, "Good!"

Arrack quickly replied, "Lei, please accept our deepest condolences. Steven was a fine man and he achieved wondrous things for mankind. Anytime you're over LA way, please drop in and see us for as long as you want."
"I will, thank you."

He continued, "John, are you missing something?"
John had a puzzled look, "Um…I don't think so, why?"

Arrack Mondone pulled out a battered, but polished sword hilt, with short rusty bits of blade protruding above it.
"Oh hell, I must have left it in my spacesuit leg pocket in my hurry to get home."
"John, I'm keeping it safe until I can return it."
"No worries Arrack, no rush. Might come in useful…"

He instantly wished he hadn't said that, saying, "But holy cow I hope you don't have to."
Arrack smiled, "A little insurance is not a bad thing."

He moved off camera, and suddenly the screen went into deep shadow.
Karen stared and frowned at the tablet display.
Then a glint as something flashed in the sunshine.

Lei, "What's that sparkle Gail, on your hand?"

Gail held her hand to camera to show a substantial diamond rock on a silver ring.
Then the phone drew back to show the smiling couple.
Gail beautifully grinned, "Arrack has asked me to marry him."
The sunlight glinted in her blond hair, her teeth making little stars in the bright dawn light.

Arrack quipped, "I had to make sure it was large enough!"

Gail momentarily glanced at Arrack Mondone's trousers, then quickly looked at her ring diamond and with a cheeky smile said, "Yes it's so lovely."

She caught Arrack winking at her, making her blush and crossing her legs….again.
"Arrack…" she murmured, and then a thought 'you gorgeous naughty man…'

A round of thunderous applause came from the deck of the Nemain.

Epilogue

6 Months later – early July 2019

Just about nobody really knew who Steven Crowley was or where he came from.
There were lots of theories.

Some believed he was a being from the Omega Centauri star system with god-like technologies.
Others thought he was just a crackpot who managed to get on TV.
The world's governments and major institutions had reserved judgement.
Despite the undeniable fact of the moon display and the power of the device in the moon itself, no authority was willing to convey any prestige to Steven Crowley.

However, Lei Zhao had no doubt he was the returning Messiah.
To her, the correlation with the first one, Jesus Christ, was more than uncanny.

With Karen's help they had talked through the possibilities of reincarnation and the likelihood…

That Steven was a super-being with extraordinary powers and that he had lived and died through both of those Earthly lives as human incarnations.
What strengthened this postulation was during the early hours of that Sunday morning, Steven's body had mysteriously vanished from the locked morgue in the hospital.

Lei had made up her mind.
She felt good and smiled, for a marvellous event was to happen soon.
She placed her hand on her tummy as the baby kicked.

For the man on the street, the native in the jungle, or the farmer on his land, their lives had changed. Impinged on their minds was the clash of titans in outer space and then the moon messages.

The first world wide interruption of TV broadcasts with Steven's initial message of peace had achieved a brief impact on the peoples of our planet.
After that the moon display sequence continued for forty days and nights, showing recognisable pictures that represented the symbols and the important values for all of the world's religions. It also included clever pictures for non-believers, atheists and many other non-conformists.
The repeated showing of all these religions and cultures living in peace via clasped hands was having a strong effect, maybe even lasting.
Churches, mosques, temples and other sacred buildings were seeing record attendances.

A new world wide, super group was set up with representatives from every culture and religion. Strangely enough it was called The United Peoples Commission or UPC.
Its prime role was always to promote peace and help resolve conflicts peaceably.

We shall see.
After the destruction of the Andromeda black spaceships, the Omega Centauri fleet had moved to Jupiter's orbit. They then proceeded to dispatch thousands of small black holes into the Andromeda Galaxy exit portal, together with a few large ones.
These messengers of death would absorb and disrupt the cortex and plasma jet, as they hurtled towards that Galaxy centre.
In doing so, any menacing Andromeda spacecraft travelling up the cortex would also be obliterated.

On reaching the huge black hole at the centre of the Andromeda Galaxy, the collisions with these travelling black holes would result in cataclysmic events.

Effectively rippling massive energy blasts throughout the Andromeda Galaxy.
With this portal destroyed, it would take millions of years for any evil craft to travel the normal distance and emerge again from that Galaxy and into ours.

Time to prepare.

However, during the giant space conflict, two errant black asteroid craft had escaped towards the centre of our own galaxy.
The Omega Centauri beings had dispatched spaceships to hunt them down.
As for the Crackwell portal, when the rest of the Omega Centauri fleet finally left, they closed it behind them.
Bill Craswell had felt a slight pang of disappointment, for he believed it was his baby in the beginning but, with things tidied up so to speak, he was content that the anomaly, the portal had finally disappeared.

The question was, why didn't these beings show themselves to the world?
Instead, only to a few brave souls.

Regarding the cross, sword and helmet, they knew the Defence Ministry would not wait any longer, with the threat of forced sequestration imminent.
Quickly with the help of her lawyer, Karen had drawn up a legal lease contract with the artefacts on loan as her property.
A fixed term loan of the ancient artefacts was offered and accepted by the Ministry scientists, together with Karen and John's full cooperation.
Smart girl.

John raised the matter of his sighting of the nebulous white mass towards the sun which he saw from Rameses, using the space gravity arrays.
Sabrina, Karen and Anne listened with fascination.

Also they shared the discovery of the hair like spikes surrounding our planet.
All of this only visible via the tiny gravity distortions, showing something that was in another space and time.

After a while Sabrina said, "I believe we have been deliberately enlightened. To be given a new view of the spirit domain is important, but as a species, humanity is far from a level of maturity that would allow us to know more."

At the time Karen felt some disappointment. She had been intensely interested in further investigation on both a scientific and spiritual basis. Yet Sabrina was indirectly telling her to put the brakes on for now.
It was for Karen's own protection against a vast 'known' and an infinitely huge unknown spiritual universe. Out there were areas of extreme danger for the un-initiated.

Conversely, the publishing of Karen's paper on the origin of the universe caused the predicted mayhem in the physics world. Attempts to extinguish her appearance as amateur, together with closed-mind intolerance of this upstart in the physics world, fell by the wayside. No flaws could be found with her equations and proofs.

Her life would never be the same again.

St James Church, Clanfield, UK
8.15 am One very wet Sunday morning in late July 2019

Karen and John sat in pews about half way down towards the altar.

Above them a wood roof was held in place by huge dark wooden beams.
The morning sun streamed through the window, strengthening the deep colours of the stained glass panels.

Outside a glorious rainbow arced across the patchy blue sky

The east windows were plain frames, but Karen could picture much more.
To one side she envisaged a design depicting the Madonna holding the Christ child. With the other side dominated by a proud crusader knight kneeling in his armour, his apron coat of arms evident across his chest, and helmet held in the crook of his arm.
A mismatch in time, but a bond across centuries.
Karen's mind floated with brilliant colours.

Briefly the cannon walked over to the table near the altar, placing some booklets on it. She turned in her long robes and with a smile said, "Welcome."
They nodded their thanks. "Good morning."

Karen looked ahead at the simple cross, high above the altar.
"John, this is so special. The atmosphere here is of serene peace."
"Yes. I feel it so much more now."

He paused then said, "You know, my Mum stayed in Clanfield with her family during the Second World War. They evacuated from Portsmouth as it was being bombed and the first night they all slept in the pews here in this very church."
Karen, "Really? When you think of people's lives during those awful times.
Not knowing the future and being bombed as they went about their daily lives.
Or worse, asleep in their beds at night, bombed after failing to hear the air raid sirens."

Both of them, the earliest of the congregation, sat for quite a while in silence.
The cool air and stone smell of the church drifted around them.
Fresh flowers coloured the grey walls and blossomed around the central aisle steps.

Peace, reassurance, comfort and faith.
Some voices at the entrance.

Another couple quietly walked in and joined Karen and John.
"Good morning Jane, Bill. Lovely to see you."

Bill grinned, his short hair dotted with little drops of rain. He kissed Karen on the cheek and shook John's hand. Jane quickly did the same saying, "Bit wet outside, but I love the smell of damp grass."
Karen whispered, "So nice. Let's see if the weather keeps the congregation away."
She had a knowing smile.

Then Jane's face burst into a grin, "Guess you've seen the papers this morning? Although you might already know?"
John smiled and replied, "I think I know what you are about to say."
Jane, "I'm so excited, they say, quote 'For outstanding scientific discoveries, Bill Craswell and Karen Durgas are jointly nominated for the Nobel Physics Award.'
How marvellous is that?"

Karen winked, "Yes it's a proud time for all of us…and Bill I think you have another achievement too?"

Bill felt warm and very proud. He knew the accolades were coming but felt now that he just wanted to get on with life. Actually he wouldn't mind keeping out of the limelight……just for a while.

Jane quietly interrupted, "Yes Bill and I am so proud of you."

Bill looked at them all and whispered,
"Thank you, thank you all. You have been my crutch, my support in tough times and my confidants. As you jolly well know, Jane and I managed to finally isolate a new element that could be used to reinforce graphene. Using this, we believe a long ultra thin,

extremely strong cable can be constructed. To give inertia to my sky elevator project."

The sky elevator that in theory could winch equipment to a geo-stationary orbital platform right out in space from the Earth's surface. In production it would be at a fraction of the cost of the alternative of getting materials and structures up there via rocket launches. Potentially making the construction of a newer, larger space station much less costly.

He continued, "Jane suggested a name for this element, and to my surprise, the scientific society responsible have accepted it."
He gestured with his eyes at Jane.
She grinned and said "The new element will be called Craswellium."
John patted Bill on the shoulder, "Well done old mate, you thoroughly deserve it."
Bill with a massive grin said, "Well Arthur C. Clarke should get some credit, so I'm thinking of calling it the Clarke-Craswell Gateway."
He beamed.

Unspoken was a big thanks to that man in the white robe.

Bill then whispered, "And you our hero astronaut, being awarded the American Presidential Medal of Freedom."
John smiled with sadness, "Yes and Daniel our commander, together with the Orion crew have been awarded Medals of Honor posthumously. Mark Vanderbrook also received one."
He paused and smiled, "First and last time for me…. crazy. You know when I looked out of our tiny capsule bobbing in that Pacific storm and getting soaked, I thought I would never be so glad as to see rain again."

Bill, "Brave men all of you."

Jane quickly replied, "You're brave too Bill tackling that awful alien."
He smiled, the hint of the gargoyle, "I did what had to be done and thank god the plasma gun worked."

Then Karen looked strangely at Bill and Jane, "You two? Is there something up?"
Jane said, "Tell them Bill."
He paused then with watery eyes he said, "Jane is with child and we know it will be a little boy."

"Oh congratulations!"

He was bursting with pride.
Then with a warm glow inside, he made himself a promise,
'This lad will get the most loving mum and dad.'

Fleetingly John Creeson had a reservation, thinking just for a moment…
'OH NO! …not more Craswells!'

Within an hour the church became three quarters full with more people arriving.
Drifting through the cool interior, were the tunes of a quiet organ piece, 'The Silent Organist'.

Naomi followed her man in.

Gavin looked up in awe at the church stone walls, the dark roof and then the central platform and the altar. Finally his eyes rested on the Crucifix at the end of the aisle and then a bright beam of sunlight from the window illuminated his face.
He turned and looked at the congregation and said, "There, there's Bill and Jane…and oh look, their friends Karen and John too."
Naomi quickly took his hand and walked them up the aisle.

Reaching the four she said, "Bill, Jane hello. Please forgive me for my awkwardness on New Year's Eve. I just want to thank you so much for rescuing and saving Gavin up on Kingley Vale hill. Thank you."
Bill smiled, "It was nothing really."

Jane took Naomi's outstretched hand and reflected on Bill's flippant comment.
Then she said "That's ok. It was them or us in the end. Gavin? How are you these days?"

To say that Gavin had the look of a converted man, would have been an understatement.
He replied, "I have seen the light. This is the way now.
Truly, I am a better person for it."

He turned to Naomi and she smiled giving his arm a big squeeze.

Lei Zhao would have been there too, but she was on a mission.

She was making a pilgrimage to Jerusalem.

The End

Acknowledgements

To Beverley my partner, for her patience and undying support during the time I have been writing these books.

My first novel 'The Skiathos Scandals' was a huge learning experience and a joy to write. This sequel, 'Beyond Skiathos' gave me different challenges plus enormous satisfaction at achieving closure to the main story lines.
The words just flowed.

The key being a notebook Beverley had given me as a Christmas present, with the name 'Hot Off The Press' on the front cover.

Inside went ideas, thoughts, summaries of future chapters and many other jottings.
Even questions concerning my progress, the book's directions and difficulties in expanding the many scenarios. This notebook was invaluable as I revisited it time and again, changing and improving the many aspects of the novel.

To Lesley thank you, for reviewing my final draft and giving me much needed feedback.

General Acknowledgements

With the greatest respect to the following,

The kind permission from NASA to use the photograph of the real M87 Galaxy and its black hole streaming out a vastly long jet of sub-atomic particles.
I have used this image for the front cover.

The novel 'Fountains of Paradise' by Arthur C. Clarke

Harry's Café de Wheels in Sydney, Australia

The song 'Road to Hell' by Chris Rhea
The song 'A Spaceman Came Travelling' by Chris De Burgh
The music 'The Silent Organist' by Lone Frederisen

Cheyenne and Navajo Tribes of North America
Shipibo people of Peru
The Isaan shamanic region in Thailand

The book 'Journey of Souls' by Michael Newton

The Church of Scientology